SURPRISED

— *by* —

LOVE

THE HEART OF
SAN FRANCISCO
· 3 ·

SURPRISED
— *by* —
LOVE

A NOVEL

Julie Lessman

Revell

a division of Baker Publishing Group
Grand Rapids, Michigan

© 2014 by Julie Lessman

Published by Revell
a division of Baker Publishing Group
P.O. Box 6287, Grand Rapids, MI 49516-6287
www.revellbooks.com

Printed in the United States of America

Library of Congress Cataloging-in-Publication Data
Lessman, Julie, 1950–
    Surprised by love : a novel / Julie Lessman.
        pages cm. —(The heart of San Francisco ; Book 3)
    ISBN 978-0-8007-2165-7 (pbk.)
    1. Single women—California—San Francisco—Fiction. 2. San Francisco
(Calif.)—History—20th century—Fiction. 3. Christian fiction. 4. Love stories.
I. Title.
PS3612.E8189S87 2014
813'.54—dc23   2014021051

Most Scripture used in this book, whether quoted or paraphrased by the characters, is taken from the King James Version of the Bible.

Scripture quotation on page 222 is from the Holy Bible, New International Version®. NIV®. Copyright © 1973, 1978, 1984, 2011 by Biblica, Inc.™ Used by permission of Zondervan. All rights reserved worldwide. www.zondervan.com

Scripture quotations marked Message are from *The Message* by Eugene H. Peterson, copyright © 1993, 1994, 1995, 2000, 2001, 2002. Used by permission of NavPress Publishing Group. All rights reserved.

14 15 16 17 18 19 20   7 6 5 4 3 2 1

To my precious reader friends—
whose relentless support and encouragement
have kept me going through two fictional
families and eleven books—
when I count my blessings in writing for Him,
YOU are at the very top of the list.
I love and appreciate you more than I can say,
and we all know from the length of my books . . .
that's A LOT!

Surprise us with love at daybreak;
   then we'll skip and dance all the day long. . . .
And let the loveliness of our Lord, our God, rest on us,
   confirming the work that we do.

—Psalm 90:14–17 Message
(emphasis added)

1

I hope you're hungry, Mr. Caldwell, because I'm serving up crow. The very thought steamed eighteen-year-old Megan McClare's cheeks as scarlet as her sister Alli's dress while the two stood before the gilded vanity mirror of Meg's bedroom. She chewed on the edge of her lip, mortified such a brazen thought had popped in her head. Even if Devin Caldwell—the most popular boy in school, who'd once called her "four eyes" and "fatso"—*did* deserve it, she thought with a sigh.

"Now, there's a thought that's up to no good," her sister said with a mischievous grin. Alli's green eyes twinkled while she looped an arm to Meg's tiny waist. "Are you wondering what Bram's going to say when he sees you," she said with a chuckle, "or just afraid he'll faint dead out?"

More color toasted Meg's cheeks at the mention of the best friend who'd been there for her through thick and thin. She released a wispy sigh. *Thick before Paris, thin after.* Palms damp, she reflected on her senior year in Paris with the Rousseaus, never dreaming one year would change her so much. She smoothed the gold silk waist of her Paul Poiret evening gown—a goodbye gift from Mrs. Rousseau, who just *happened* to be dear friends with the up-and-coming Paris designer that took Meg under his wing.

She swallowed hard, pulse picking up at the thought of seeing Bram again—the one man who didn't scare her silly and the only male she trusted outside her family. "Bram, yes," she said with a timid look, peeking up at her sister with a shy smile, "but the one I'd really like to see faint dead out is Devin Caldwell." She nibbled on her pinkie, almost ashamed to put voice to her feelings. "Flat on his handsome face, maybe with a crow feather in his teeth?" She slapped a hand to her mouth, green eyes expanding wide and no longer obscured by glasses. "Oh, Al—am I awful?" she whispered.

"Yes," Alli said with a thrust of her chin, dispensing a tight hug. Her low laughter tickled Meg's ear. "*Awfully* gorgeous! Can't wait to hear about that little brat's reaction after all the years he's picked on you." Her sister wiggled her brows in the mirror. "A little salt with that crow, Mr. Caldwell?"

Heart racing, Megan pressed a shaky hand to her stomach, wondering if it was even possible the boy who'd hated and humiliated her since the first grade would actually think she was pretty now. Boys in Paris certainly had, if the last six months were any indication—although she hadn't put much stock in their compliments.

Devin Caldwell cured me of that.

Singlehandedly, the boy on whom she'd once had a crush taught her the danger of trusting in a handsome face and a teasing smile. Not unless it belonged to Abraham Joseph Hughes, the one man who'd made a shy and awkward little girl feel beautiful despite baby fat and glasses. She drew in a deep breath while her pulse slowed to a peaceful rhythm, relishing the calming effect Bram always had on her life. Without question, he was her champion, her defender, her very best friend.

And maybe the one beau I can trust with my heart?

Her cheeks flashed hot again, clashing with the color of her upswept hair—now the same deep russet as her mother's rather than her own mousy carrot red, compliments of henna. Brooking no arguments, Mr. Poiret insisted on "setting her hair aflame" with the gentle hair dye that gave her rich color and shine. Leaning in, she studied white, perfectly straight teeth, void of the revolutionary braces applied over three years ago by Uncle Logan's dentist friend. *And* thanks to Mr. Poiret, those unsightly freckles were nowhere to be seen, hidden beneath rice powder dusted with just a hint of rouge on her cheeks and lips.

"Goodness, you look absolutely breathtaking, Megs! How do your eyes feel?" Alli asked, as thrilled as Meg that the unsightly glasses were no longer part of her wardrobe except for reading in bed at night. Megan had been shocked when Mrs. Rousseau sent her to Germany to be fitted with a new invention called *contacts*. Apparently the inventor, ophthalmologist Adolf Gaston Fick, was an old medical school chum of her husband's. Although Meg couldn't wear them longer than several hours at a time, she adapted quickly to the frequent "eye rest" periods, reveling in the freedom from eyeglasses most of the day.

"Oh, I love them," she whispered, once again amazed at the striking hue of her aquamarine eyes, something she'd never really noticed before. With a nervous grate of her lip, she blinked several times, in awe of the sweep of dark lashes Mr. Poiret had deemed "ridiculously long." No longer an invisible pale blond, they were now lush and dark with an application of the Rimmel mascara French women loved. But despite Alli's claim that she was "breathtaking"—a statement that stole Meg's breath more than anyone's—sometimes she still felt like that same chubby little girl inside, playing dress-up. She offered her sister a tremulous smile, feeling a bit awkward that the girl in the mirror didn't match the shy wallflower in her mind. "Mrs. Rousseau claims men will get lost in my eyes," she said with a fresh dusting of rose that had nothing to do with her rouge, "but I don't know . . ."

Alli pinched her waist. "Well, I do, and I say she's right. And let's hope Devin Caldwell is the very first one—to 'get lost,' that is—once and for all."

Meg actually smiled, thoughts of Devin Caldwell no longer the primary focus of her daydreams anymore. Not after assisting Dr. Rousseau with his charitable work among prostitutes in the Pigalle district. Now the only daydreams Meg entertained were those about a future of service to the less fortunate. A future in which she, too, could better the plight of young women and girls ensnared in the brothels and cow-yards of the Barbary Coast. Like her mother, who dreamed of teaching disadvantaged young girls through their Hand of Hope School, Meg had had a dream of her own before going to Paris—to become a lawyer who fought for the rights of those very women and girls. To stand up for those who'd been ostracized and beat down—like her family and Bram had done for her. To help free them from their prisons of demoralization, be they physical places such as the Barbary Coast . . . *or* in the dark recesses of their minds like her, paralyzed by ridicule.

But since working with Dr. Rousseau, her dreams had changed. *She* had changed. Drawing in a deep breath, she smoothed her beaded bodice with trembling fingers, well aware she had a decision to make regarding her future. Yes, she still longed to reach out to disadvantaged women, but how? Through medicine or law? God had given her a thirst for learning and a passion for the poor, and like her mother, sister, and cousin, she hoped to extend God's grace to those in need. No longer that shy, mousy girl afraid of her own shadow, she was now a young woman whose confidence was slowly changing from being anchored by others' approval to the approval of the only One who mattered. Under the tutelage of Mrs. Rousseau—Mother's dearest friend from college—Meg had literally been transformed both inside and out, just as Mother had hoped. Giselle Rousseau had undergirded the lesson that Mother had begun—that true confidence blooms in the soil of a relationship with God, following His path rather than one's own, pursuing His truth rather than the world's.

Tears of gratitude sparked Meg's eyes as she studied the slim, lithe body she saw in the mirror, hidden for years by layers of baby fat and self-loathing. Following a bout with the flu that had stolen her appetite, Mrs. Rousseau's eagle-eye diet and endless trekking about the city had accomplished the rest, melting pounds off Meg's chubby body. Worrying the edge of her rose-colored lips, she tugged at the modest bodice of her dress—which seemed anything but modest on her—certain she'd lost weight everywhere but there.

"Oh, leave it be, Meggie," Alli said with a wink, "you have a beautiful figure now, so just take a deep breath and enjoy being a woman." Her sister pressed a kiss to her cheek. "Ready to head down?"

Ready? To face Bram Hughes once again? Megan froze, stomach swooping over the very thought of her brother's friend who was ten years her senior. As far back as she could remember, Bram had always been part of their family, a second older brother who'd made her feel pretty and special while other boys called her names. But what if he didn't feel close to her anymore? What if he thought she'd changed too much? She tried to swallow past the runaway emotions that formed a knot in her throat. "Al?"

Alli glanced in the mirror, her smile dimming when she saw the furrows in Meg's face. "Yes, sweetheart?"

"What if . . ." Meg stared at the girl in the glass, the daughter who now looked like her beautiful mother and sister for the first time in her life. "What if . . . Bram doesn't like the new me?" she whispered. "What if . . ." Her voice trailed off. ". . . he doesn't feel comfortable with me anymore?"

"Aw, Megs . . ." Al turned to face her, cupping her jaw. "Bram loves you, honey, always has, and whether you're a little kid with braces or a grown woman who turns a man's head—he is your friend for life. Although . . ." She tucked a stray curl behind Megan's ear. "I'm not sure he'll recognize you right off. Mother, Cass, and I sure didn't when you stepped off that train."

Megan's lips edged into a sheepish smile. "I know—Mrs. Rousseau wanted to surprise you."

"Ha! 'Surprise' is an understatement." Alli squeezed Meg's waist as she grinned in the mirror. "So brace yourself for several dropped jaws tonight, sis, including Uncle Logan's."

Megan whirled to face her sister. "Oh, that reminds me! What did you mean in your last letter that things have gotten edgy between Uncle Logan and Mother? They seemed fine at Christmas."

Alli sighed. "Yes, they were—at Christmas. But ever since the new year, it seems Mr. Turner has taken a shine to Mother, pushing her to go out with him every chance he gets, and you know how Uncle Logan feels about Andrew Turner."

A silent groan wedged in Meg's throat. Yes, she knew. The district attorney with whom she'd hoped to acquire a position after law school was, unfortunately, the one man her uncle despised more than any other. Her uncle's former best friend from youth through law school, Andrew Turner butted heads with Uncle Logan in the courtroom and out. Especially now, apparently, with

Mr. Turner indicating interest in Mother—the very woman with whom Uncle Logan was in love. A reedy sigh drifted from Meg's lips, brows tented as she studied her sister. "Mother and Uncle Logan haven't reverted to that awful stiffness like that time in Napa, have they?"

Alli expelled a heavy breath and plopped on the edge of Meg's bed, her shoulders slumping as much as Meg's from the discord over Andrew Turner. "No, nothing that stilted or cool, but Uncle Logan is definitely more on edge, like a caged animal whenever Mr. Turner happens to show up." She bit on a thumbnail, the edge of her lip curling in a half smile. "Rather like Nick on a good day."

Meg's smile was tender. "Come on, Al, Nick seemed perfectly wonderful when I met him at Christmas, and Mother wrote she's never seen you happier."

Alli caressed her engagement ring, eyes trailing into a dreamy stare before she glanced back up. "He is, Meg—I'm crazy about him, but as happy as I am, it doesn't stop me from worrying about Mother and Uncle Logan." She spit out a sliver of nail. "Everybody can see they're a perfect match, and they clearly care about each other deeply, but Mother refuses to allow anything more than friendship. And now with Andrew Turner in the mix, I worry he may cause a bigger rift between the two people we love most. Or worse yet—steal Mother away from Uncle Logan altogether."

Meg gasped, fingers fluttering to her throat. "No, Al, it's not that serious between Mr. Turner and Mother, is it?"

"Not yet, I don't think. Mother claims she and Andrew are only friends, but he's got that smitten twinkle in his eye, Meg, whenever he looks at her, just like Uncle Logan does, and frankly, I'm worried. We all know Mr. Turner is nothing if not tenacious, and his exemplary record as district attorney is certainly proof of that. He and Uncle Logan are clearly the two best lawyers in the city, but as a district attorney who seldom loses?" Alli shuddered. "Andrew Turner usually gets his man . . . or in this case, maybe his woman."

Stunned by Alli's revelation, Meg slowly sank down beside her sister, eyes lapsing into a vacant stare. "I don't understand it," she whispered. "Uncle Logan's the most eligible bachelor in the city, but Mother refuses to see it and I have no idea why."

"Me either, but I've been praying for God to open her eyes, and for a while last summer, after you left for Paris? The two of them seemed to be getting closer all the time, almost flirtatious, I'd say. And then, *poof*! Right before Jamie and Cassie's wedding, that romantic mood I'd sensed was suddenly gone, and now they're back to being friends again—as comfortable as a pair of old slippers."

A sad smile tipped Meg's mouth. *Yes . . . like Bram and me.*

Alli jumped up, giving her sister's hand a quick squeeze. "Enough with the gloomy talk—it's time to put our smiles on, Megs, and turn a few heads."

"Or 'roll heads,' as Lily would say," Meg said with a giggle, suddenly missing the Rousseaus' daughter, a dear friend who had a knack for butchering English idioms. "*Especially* if it belongs to a certain—and I quote—'Devin *Cad*-well.'"

"*Oui*," Alli said with a chuckle as they made their way down the hall. "And 'heads will roll,' indeed. I believe Mother received a call just last week from one of your classmates, issuing an invitation to a graduation party."

Megan's body turned to stone on the top step of the rose-carpeted staircase, her limbs as wooden as the mahogany balustrade beneath her bloodless hold. "Wh-what?" Her breathing accelerated as she stared at Alli with wide eyes.

Alli smoothed a stray wisp of hair from Megan's Gibson Girl

pompadour before ushering her down to the three-story marble foyer where paintings graced satin-papered walls. "You don't have to face your old group of friends until you're ready, Megs, really, so just send your regrets."

Sucking in a deep breath, Megan nodded, barely aware she'd halted on the last step until Alli coaxed with a gentle hand from behind. "Ready, sweetheart?" she whispered in her ear.

Was she? Ready to face the family who loved her, the new life that awaited her, and the best friend who held her heart in the palm of his hand? A warmth unlike any she'd ever known emanated through her chest along with the keen thrill of adventure. *Oh, yes!*

Suddenly Devin Caldwell's handsome face popped in her mind, and she swallowed a lump in her throat. But ready to face her academic nemesis who'd belittled and beleaguered her until her confidence was nil? A shiver rattled her shoulders as Alli led her into the parlour.

"Never" might well be too soon.

2

"Checkmate." Grinning, Bram Hughes glanced up at his best friend Jamie MacKenna in the McClares' Victorian parlour. The familiar clang of the cable car off Powell, the summer scent of eucalyptus from Mrs. McClare's garden, and Meg's homecoming made the win all the sweeter. The McClares' three-story mansion on Nob Hill had been his second home for as long as he could remember, a teenage respite from the guilt he felt over the hurt he'd caused the parents he loved.

"I swear, Hughes, you are one lucky stiff," Jamie groused, leaning back in his chair with a fold of his arms. "But put a cue in my hand, buddy boy, and you're dead meat."

"Luck doesn't have a whole lot to do with it, Mac," Bram said with a smile, lounging back in his chair with hands propped behind his neck. "Chess is a game of intellect, my friend."

"Which leaves you out in the cold, MacKenna," Blake McClare quipped with a broad grin. His gray eyes twinkled with affection for the best friend who'd just married his cousin. Casting a quick glance at the far side of the room where his mother played cribbage with his uncle while his cousin Cassie—now Jamie's wife—played fish with his seven-year-old sister Maddie,

Blake lowered his voice. "How 'bout a quick game of poker to even the score?"

"Awk, ante up . . . ante up . . ." A screech echoed in the parlour as the family parrot, Miss Behave, cocked her head at the trigger word "poker," tutored by Uncle Logan long ago.

Blake's mother glanced over her shoulder with a faint frown, the auburn hair piled high on her head a stunning contrast to her emerald gown. "Blake Henry McClare—I do not approve of gambling in this house, and well you know it."

"Snitch." Blake shot a mock glare in the direction of Miss B., who only unleashed more squawks while she danced back and forth on her perch with pinwheel eyes.

Bram laughed. "I'll tell you what, my friend," he said, resetting the chessboard, "I'll let you try and redeem Mac's pride as long as you promise not to . . ." He paused to give Jamie a grin while he raised his voice in volume. "Cheat."

"Awk, Blake cheats . . . Blake cheats . . ." A grin stretched wide across Bram's face while Jamie chuckled over the insult Alli had taught Miss B. a few years back when her brother had whipped her soundly in chess.

Despite the grin on Blake's face, a ruddy flush crept up his neck when his mother glanced his way again. He tapped Jamie on the shoulder so he could take his chair. "Move, Mac—apparently I have a lesson to teach this smart mouth."

"Awk, put your money where your mouth is . . . put your money where your mouth is . . ."

Chuckling, Bram lined his chess pieces up. "There may be some question as to who's the 'smart mouth' here, old buddy, because you gotta admit—that is one smart bird."

"Okay, Padre," Blake said, employing the nickname he'd given Bram in college because of his deep faith and preference for ginger ale over alcohol. "You best say your prayers." His gray eyes gleamed like the newly minted half dollar he slid onto the table, gaze darting to his mother and back as his voice dropped to a near whisper. "Challenge accepted, but expect to empty your pockets."

Shaking his head, Bram couldn't help but smile over the sweet justice of Blake—a certifiable rogue like his Uncle Logan used to be—living in the same house with his widowed mother. As a devout teetotaler and staunch opponent of gambling, Caitlyn McClare was president of the city's Vigilance Committee, spearheading the reformation of the Barbary Coast. *And* a gentle beauty who, like President Roosevelt, spoke softly and carried a big stick. Bram's smile broadened into a grin. Not only with her wayward son, but with her wayward brother-in-law too. His gaze flicked from Blake to his uncle, then to Mrs. McClare.

Her green-eyed gaze homed in on her brother-in-law with the barest trace of a smile. "You know, Logan, if you were a better influence on my children, I might be inclined to defend you when Rosie goes on the attack."

Logan grunted, his smile taking a slant. "A muzzle's the only thing that can defend me from that pit bull housekeeper of yours, Cait, so don't make promises you can't keep." Blake's uncle shuffled the cards with a casual and confident air befitting his status as one of the city's top attorneys, in whose firm Bram, Blake, and Jamie each practiced law. At forty-six years of age, he seemed to have forsaken his prior reputation as a rogue to spend more time with his sister-in-law and nieces and nephews—a welcome change Bram had noticed over the last few years. Despite butting heads over politics, religion, and influences over her son, Caitlyn and Logan seemed to have formed a cohesive bond that made this unconventional household feel like the most close-knit of families.

Gratitude swelled in Bram's chest while Jamie and Blake bantered back and forth, and as always, he silently thanked God for the McClares in his life. As the only child of elderly parents, Bram thrived on the male camaraderie and close friendship between Logan, Jamie, Blake, and him, as well as the deep faith and gentleness of the McClare women. Alli and Cassie were fun-loving tomboys that always made him laugh, and Caitlyn and Megan McClare were mother-daughter depictions of everything a lady should be—kind, soft-spoken, and gracious.

Thoughts of sweet little Meg warmed him inside with both affection and pride for the one McClare daughter who had long ago nabbed a piece of his heart. From the start she had elicited a protectiveness in him he hadn't experienced since his own little sister Ruthy died at the age of six, a tragedy that sent Bram's life spiraling into a black hole of bitterness. But with her gentle heart and battered self-esteem, Meg had offered redemption through a friendship that brought out the best in him at a time when there was little "best" to be had.

"Ahem—may I have your attention, please?"

Bram glanced up at the sound of Alli's voice at the door, her arm hooked around the waist of one of the prettiest girls he had ever seen. "I'd like to introduce you to our guest from France."

Bumping the table, Bram shot to his feet while Blake did the same, causing Jamie to chuckle when the table swayed in place. Rising with Logan at a considerably more leisurely pace, Jamie leaned close to Bram's ear, his voice low and heavy with tease. "Settle down, Hughes. I expect The Rake to respond to pretty women like this," he said, referring to their nickname for the womanizing Blake McClare, "but you're supposed to be the steady one, so don't fail me now."

But he was barely listening, gaze glued to the striking girl with the deep auburn hair.

"Gentlemen—allow me to introduce the Mademoiselle Megan McClare from Paris, France."

Thud! Bram's stomach dropped along with his jaw, his gaze expanding as he stared at the pretty redhead being swarmed by Cassie, Maddie, and Mrs. McClare, each doling out giggles and hugs. Swallowing hard, his breathing was as erratic as his pulse. "B-bug?"

"Hello, Bram," she whispered in that shy way he'd grown to love, and all he could do was blink, his renegade eyes scanning head to toe.

"Holy thunder, Hughes," Jamie whispered in his ear, "not too sure your nickname fits anymore, because our Megs is well beyond 'cute as a bug's ear.'"

Bram cleared his throat, unable to speak or breathe, his gaze locked on Meg's face, her eyes . . . that mouth.

"Move over, Hughes." Jamie butted between a slack-jawed Blake and Bram, scooping Megan up in his arms before Bram could catch his breath. "If all you're going to do is gape, I'm going to welcome the lady home good and proper. We sure missed you, Megs, but it appears that Paris has made a new woman of you. You look beautiful."

"Thanks, Jamie," she whispered over his shoulder, and Bram gulped, those sinfully long lashes making her seem almost seductive rather than shy.

"Meg?" Crossing the room, Uncle Logan barged in to take Meg's hands in his, stepping back to study her with a slow smile of awe. "Sweet thunderation, sweetheart, you are simply stunning—a beautiful woman just like your mother and Alli."

"And me too, Uncle Logan?" Maddie peeked up beneath a riot of auburn curls, clinging to his leg with concern in her green eyes.

"Of course you too," he said with a swoop of his niece in the air, never taking his eyes from Meg. "But blue thunder, there are beautiful women in this family . . ." Hooking an arm to Meg's shoulders, he pulled her into a one-handed hug, kissing the top of her head. "You look like your mother when I first met her years ago," he whispered, his gaze flicking to where Caitlyn stood off to the side with a proud glow. "And a higher compliment I couldn't pay you, darling."

"Thank you, Uncle Logan."

"Okay, out of the way—I need a hug now that I know who you are, kiddo." Blake hauled Meg into his arms and whirled her around, making her giggle like the Meggie of old. "I'm not sure what you did to yourself over in France, but I heartily approve."

"So, Bram . . ." Jamie strolled over to cup an arm to Cassie's waist, giving his best friend a sly grin. "You planning on giving Megs a hug anytime soon? Because I'm hungry and would like to move this homecoming into the dining room if we could."

Cassie elbowed him. "Jamie MacKenna, Hadley hasn't even announced dinner yet."

"Ahem." The McClares' elderly butler stood in the doorway as if on cue, impeccable as always in black tails and tie. "Dinner is served, ladies and gentlemen . . . in honor of Miss Megan McClare."

A soft giggle bubbled from the lush lips of the very stranger who'd just stolen Bram's tongue, her laughter the only thing he recognized from the Bug he used to know.

Logan slapped Bram on the back, jolting him out of his shock over Meg all grown up. "Bram, I assume you'll escort the lady of the hour into dinner while I escort her mother?"

"Yes, sir," he said in his most efficient manner despite the dampness of his palms. He proffered his arm to Meg with a smile while Logan ushered Caitlyn from the room. "Shall we, Miss McClare?"

Meg giggled and slipped her arm through Bram's, and for a moment, she almost seemed like the old Meg once again.

Looping her arm through Jamie's, Cassie paused to squint over at Alli. "Wait, Al—where's Nick? And don't tell me that fiancé of yours has to work tonight."

Alli's lavender ruffled bodice fluttered with a heavy sigh. "'Fraid so. Surveillance duty on that suspicious death at a brothel on the Coast."

Cassie shook her head and hooked her free arm through Alli's with a sympathetic smile. "I thought when Nick was promoted to chief of detectives, he'd have more say over his hours."

"He does, but you know what a workhorse he is, Cass, and it doesn't help that it's a high-profile case Captain Peel personally asked him to handle."

"Excuse me, ladies," Jamie interrupted, "but can we continue this discussion in the dining room before we have another suspicious death right here—Frisco lawyer found belly-up from starvation?"

Bram laughed, anxious to deflect his nervousness by joining in on Jamie's conversation. "I doubt it'd be suspicious in this household, Mac, not the way you gloat after pinochle or pool."

"Bram?" Meg's voice was as soft as he remembered, but the firm pull of her arm surprised him when she tugged him to a stop. "Could I . . . speak to you privately before we go in?"

Jamie winked at Bram while he ushered Cass and Alli from the room. "It's been six months, Hughes, so I'd say our girl deserves that hug. We'll tell the others you'll be in shortly."

"Thanks, Jamie," Bram said with a nod before turning to face the new Meg—who shouldn't be making his heart race this way. Drawing in a quiet breath, he took her hands in his while he stepped back to assess. "I'll tell you what, Bug—I sure didn't recognize you."

"So, what do you think?" she asked, twirling before him like she used to in her best dresses, eager for his approval. Only this time there were curves in the dress that made him downright uncomfortable, while some heavenly scent wafted into the room that triggered his pulse.

What do I think? His throat was so dry, the words adhered to his tongue like glue. He tried to remind himself that the vision before him was merely his sweet little Meg, more like a sister. Heat crawled up the back of his neck when his eyes swept from delicate wisps of auburn hair framing a peaches-and-cream complexion, down a body that took his breath away, along with every coherent thought in his head.

"You're staring," she said with that self-conscious giggle that always plucked at his heart, and suddenly she was his "little bug" again. An endearment that no longer fit, he realized—she was drop-dead beautiful. "You look . . . uh . . . different," he said, squinting hard to see the lost little wallflower that cried in his arms whenever Devin Caldwell stomped on her feelings.

"I know!" she squealed with a little dip of her knees, and then promptly took his breath away when she launched into his arms. His eyelids slipped closed while memories played in his mind of a younger Meg bouncing on his shoulders during games of piggyback badminton or Marco Polo at Sutro Baths. Stepping on his toes while dancing at family functions or giggling when she'd finally beaten him at chess. Expelling a silent sigh, he tucked his head to hers and gathered her up in his arms like he used to, trying to conjure up that plump little girl who'd become the little sister he'd lost.

She pulled away with a teasing twinkle that seemed so much older now, more playful, and almost flirtatious. "But you do like the new me, right?" she asked with anxious eyes—a striking aquamarine like her mother's—fixed on his while she chewed on her lip.

The expectant glow in her face carried him back to games of fish and carrot-colored braids, and all at once, melancholy ached in his chest. Releasing a slow breath, he nodded, gently cradling her face in his hands. "I miss my little buddy, Meg, I won't lie, but you've grown into a beautiful woman over the last year, a perfect match for the beautiful person inside."

His heart clutched when water welled in her eyes and without warning, she thrust herself into his arms again and clung as if he were a lifeline. But then he supposed he had been over the years, a role that had been both an honor and a great joy. He bent his head to hers, and the fresh scent of violets—light, sweet, with a hint of raspberry—calmed the turmoil inside just like the old Meg used to do. "Oh, Bram, I'm so grateful for your friendship, and I missed you so."

He pressed a gentle kiss to her hair and gave her a tight squeeze, his smile light, but his heart heavy. "I missed you too, Bug, more than I can say," he whispered.

And right this very moment? He ushered her from the room with a stiff smile and a firm hold.

More than ever.

3

Aujourd'hui . . . je recommencer.

Today . . . I begin anew. Meg closed her eyes to savor the velvety taste of chocolate cream pie on her tongue. The contentment of being home again was as sweet and thick as the whipped cream she licked from her lips. The heady scent of her mother's blush-tinted cottage roses filled the air along with the tinkle of china, silverware, and the laughter of family. She was finally home again with the people she loved, poised on the threshold of her dreams. Finally unshackled from an image that kept people from seeing her for who she really was, the woman she aspired to be, and a person who longed to bring kindness into the world.

She opened her eyes, and her heart warmed when her gaze settled on Bram across the way, candlelight flickering across his handsome features. Gaze glued to Alli, he seemed completely captivated by her vivacious rendition of one of the adventures Meg had shared with her sister in the sanctuary of her bedroom. Alli's colorful commentary made Meg laugh, along with everyone else, the topic being the day a duck followed Meg around the streets of Paris.

"But that's our Megs," Alli said with a wink in Meg's direction, "a heart so big, she draws both friend and fowl." Chuckles circled the table, coaxing Alli into more wonderful memories that Meg relished from her year in Paris. And yet—tonight—she relished something else even more. Family. Friends.

Bram.

She hadn't seen him since Christmas, but it seemed a lifetime, and she was perfectly content for Alli to steal the show while Meg stole glimpses of the hero who'd owned her heart from the age of seven. He seemed older somehow, and maybe that was because she herself felt so much older too, so much surer of what she wanted. The sandy blond hair she loved that lightened to corn silk in the summer was neatly trimmed as always, stylish and not a strand out of place—so like the man. Blue eyes that could read her very soul always sparkled with humor and kindness and affection, keeping her afloat through all the emotional storms of her life. His laughter was always rich and warm and low—like now when his dimples deepened in a flash of white over something Alli said. Meg couldn't help it—her chest rose and fell with pride that Bram Hughes was her best friend.

"No, she didn't actually ride on the thing, did she?" Blake asked, and Meg blinked, painfully aware all eyes were now focused on her, *especially* those of one Abraham Joseph Hughes, whose open-mouthed expression registered both humor and surprise.

"Good heavens, Meg," her mother said with a note of alarm, "please tell me you did *not* get on a motorbike . . ."

Heat braised Meg's cheeks as she blinked again, unable to derail the dare of a smile that inched across her lips. Adrenaline coursed even now at the shocking memory of flying through the streets of Paris on the back of Pierre's motorbike, her hair tearing free from her pins while she clung on for dear life. She'd discovered a piece of herself she hadn't known existed that day—as wild and free as Cassie on her father's Texas ranch or as adventurous and high-spirited as Alli in her treks about the city. *Fearless.* Her smile blossomed into a grin. Not an easy feat for a shy wallflower who feared the disdain of others.

"Oh, my goodness! Megan Maureen McClare—you did, didn't you?" Her mother's jaw fell.

"Uh-oh." Alli's voice squeaked with a nervous giggle, fingertips pressed to her lips as if to restrain further damage. She peeked at Meg out of the corner of her eyes, brows puckered in repentance. "Was I supposed to keep that a secret?"

Meg laughed and hugged her tightly. "Not really, Al, so don't worry. Not only will *I* have to adjust to this new me, but everyone else will too." She glanced up at her mother with her usual sweet smile, although she was certain it lacked the timidity to which everyone was accustomed. "Please forgive me, Mother. I know a lady hopping aboard a motorbike with a near stranger is not the most dignified of scenarios. But Paris does something to you—it dares you, entices you, liberates you in ways I never expected."

"Sweet thunderation, Megs, you really and truly got on a motorbike with a complete stranger?" Cassie's sagging jaw matched Meg's mother's.

"Not exactly a stranger," Alli piped up, eager to redeem herself, "a friend of the Rousseaus named Pierre." She glanced at Meg with a sudden gleam of mischief in her eyes. "Apparently he was one of several smitten young men who asked Megs to marry him."

"What?" Uncle Logan was on his feet in a heartbeat, face ruddy with shock. "Megan Maureen, you best tell me there is nothing going on here, young lady—"

"*Nothing* is going on, Uncle Logan, truly." Meg offered a conciliatory smile, her gaze darting to where Bram was actually frowning—a most infrequent occurrence—before she returned to her uncle. "Pierre is Dr. Rousseau's colleague's son, and a dear friend of the Rousseaus, but I assure you, he and I are only friends."

"So, tell us, Bug," Bram said, hunkering down on the table with a fold of arms, the lazy bent of his smile at odds with the slight narrowing of his eyes. "Exactly how many hearts *did* you break in Paris?"

"More than I ever have, I can tell you that," Alli said with a wink, shimmying in to prop her chin in her hand. "So tell us about riding the motorbike, Megs—was it exciting?"

Meg's gaze flitted to Alli with a mischievous grin that made her feel alive, as if she were coming out of the shadows for the very first time. "Oh, yes, very much so! The wind in your face while your hair whips behind you, free and unfettered." She stole a glance at Bram, wishing his disapproval didn't bother her so. "And I didn't 'break' any hearts," she said softly, "just the mold of who the old Meg used to be." She scanned the table from her mother at one end to Uncle Logan at the other. "Please don't worry—I did nothing you wouldn't expect Alli to do, I promise. It's just that I'm Meg, the shy and withdrawn bookworm, so it comes as more of a shock, I suppose." She settled on Bram with a tender look she hoped conveyed how deeply his opinion mattered. "I'm still me inside," she said quietly, "only a little braver, a little happier, and a little more excited about life than ever before."

For several beats of her heart, he just stared, and then his chest rose and fell while the planes of his angular face softened into the same warm affection that had always been oxygen to her soul. The blue eyes held a hint of a sparkle while the almost imperceptible curve of his lips told her he cared—had always cared—as a friend, a mentor, a brother. Her own mouth tipped in shy response, gratitude welling that she was still the only woman in her best friend's life. She knew from her brother's letters that he saw other women from time to time and one in particular of late, the daughter of a friend of the family. And yet, at the ripe age of twenty-eight, his heart belonged to no one, for which Meg felt both relieved and a wee bit guilty. Quickly reaching to sip her water, she shifted her gaze to Alli. "So, yes, Alli, the motorbike was quite exciting, although it scared the wits out of me, I must admit. But you would absolutely love it."

"Don't give her any ideas," Uncle Logan groused. "We have enough trouble reining her in as it is. And speaking of reining her in . . ." He peered up at Alli. "Where's Nick?"

"Surveillance duty," everybody at the table said in unison.

Uncle Logan's mouth compressed along with his eyes. "Why is it that I'm the last one to know anything in this family?"

"What's surveillance duty?" Maddie asked.

"It means Mr. Crankypants has to work tonight." A sigh drifted from Alli's lips. "Which bodes a lot better for us than it does for the crooks he's after, I suppose."

"Oh . . . he has to shoot people," Maddie said casually, as if shooting people were an everyday occurrence. She dove into the remains of her pie.

"Madeline Marie McClare, Nick does not go around shooting people, for goodness' sake." Her mother's stern tone was offset by a squirm of a smile. "He's the chief of detectives for the Barbary Coast and merely carries a gun for self-defense, to ward off anyone who might be a threat."

"Like Alli." Jamie shoveled in his last bite of pie, shooting Alli a wink.

Ignoring the chuckles that ensued, Caitlyn took a sip of her coffee, gaze sweeping the table. "Would anyone like more dessert?"

As if reading Caitlyn McClare's mind, their spunky, sixty-seven-year-old housekeeper Rosie barreled through the swinging door with a tray of additional desserts while Hadley followed on her heels with a fresh pot of coffee. A study in contrasts that afforded no end to the humor found in the McClare household, Mrs. Rosie O'Brien was as devoted to Caitlyn McClare as she was annoyed by Uncle Logan, a disdain she had once also attached to Hadley, Uncle Logan's butler from youth. A tiny woman with dark chignon heavily sifted with silver posed a stark contradiction to Hadley's tall and dignified demeanor, his regal bearing crowned with a glorious head of white most likely earned from working with Rosie. Where Rosie's steel-blue eyes and sharp tongue could whittle Uncle Logan down to size, Hadley's ever-calm expression and patient manner offered a tranquil buffer when needed. Like now, when the lovably deaf and near-blind manservant proceeded to Uncle Logan's end of the table to pour coffee.

"Hadley!" Rosie paused the butler mid-tilt, her scowl softening into a smile while she addressed him in a loud voice. "I said to serve Miss Cait *first*," she enunciated sweetly, eyes narrowing in Uncle Logan's direction. Her voice lowered to a mumble. "Not the *worst*."

"Very good, miss." Hadley tipped the pot upright and moved to the other end.

"Really, Cait?" Lips flat, Uncle Logan arched a brow, ignoring the titters that circled the table.

"Now, Rosie . . . ," Caitlyn said softly, her affectionate tone hardly an admonishment to the former nanny who was like a second mother after Caitlyn's own had passed away. She offered Uncle Logan a smile of apology. "I don't care for any more dessert, but I believe Mr. McClare might. Would you like more pie, Logan?"

"Does it matter?" he grumbled, glaring at Rosie as she plopped a second piece of pie on Caitlyn's plate.

"Chocolate cream is one of your favorites, Miss Cait," the housekeeper groused, "and heaven knows you could use a little meat on your bones." Rosie divvied out the rest of the pie till it was all gone, then paused on her way to the door, giving Logan a smirk. "Uh-oh, fresh out, but I'll fetch you some five-day-old pound cake if you want. It's passable if you cut off the mold."

"No, thank you," Uncle Logan said in a clipped tone that mellowed when Hadley poured him a fresh cup of coffee. "Thank you, Hadley."

"My pleasure, sir." One eye on the swinging door through which Rosie had just departed, the butler produced a generous piece of pie from behind his back, setting it before Logan. "Compliments of Miss Cait, sir," he said with a faint smile.

Logan glanced up, meeting Cait's tender look from across the linen-clad table. "Thank you, Cait. I suppose this is the next best thing if you won't rein your attack dog in."

"You're welcome, Logan," she said with a gentle smile before clinking a spoon against her water glass to draw everybody's attention. "All right, everyone—I have good news to share."

"Rosie's retiring?" Logan muttered.

Ting. Ting. Ting. Caitlyn tapped her water goblet again, excitement fairly shimmering in her eyes as she smiled at Meg. "In addition to the good news of having Meg back home, I also have some very good news for Meg."

Meg blinked. "For me? What kind of good news, Mother?"

"Well . . ." Caitlyn paused, cheeks flushed with excitement. Her eyes darted to Uncle Logan in a hesitant smile before returning to Meg with a raise of her glass. "I'd like to propose a toast to Megan McClare—our prospective lawyer who has been awarded the honor of a brand-new internship this summer in the district attorney's office."

Cheers and applause broke out as Meg stared at her mother, hardly daring to believe what she'd just heard. "M-mother, are you s-serious?" she stuttered, hand to her chest. "The district attorney's office?"

Caitlyn nodded, her smile blooming into a grin. "I'd mentioned to Andrew your aspirations to become a lawyer, and would you believe he told me he'd been considering an internship program for some time now? Said he figured the district attorney's office was the perfect opportunity for aspiring young lawyers such as yourself. And the best part? It's a scholarship internship, Meg, awarded to the candidate with the highest grades, so when he heard you were valedictorian of your class, that cinched it. Congratulations, darling."

"Yeah, Meggie, great job!" Blake raised his glass in a toast. "I knew being the smartest one in the family would pay off someday."

Stock still, Meg finally grinned, a tiny squeal slipping through the fingers pressed to her mouth. "Oh my goodness! When do I start?"

"June 20th, darling." Her mother paused. "Of course, you do understand it's not a paid internship—the district attorney's budget can't afford that."

"Oh, Mother, I don't care!" *The district attorney's office?* The dream of every lawyer longing to make a difference? Her heart thudded in her chest. *And I start in almost three weeks?* She clasped hands to her chest, pulse taking off in a sprint. "I am beyond thrilled!"

Uncle Logan grunted as he downed the rest of his water. "If it's an internship you want, sweetheart, why didn't you talk to me?" He slammed his glass down a little too loudly, lips in a scowl. "I'd rather have you in our firm than working for the DA. And *I'll* pay you."

Meg's heart skipped a beat, not wanting to hurt her uncle's

feelings, but not wanting to miss this golden opportunity either. "Oh, Uncle Logan, thank you so much, but Mother knows I've had my heart set on the district attorney's office for a while now—hopefully to work there after I graduate law school." Her eyes beseeched his. "You see, I hope to provide legal assistance to the residents of the Barbary Coast, especially the women and girls trapped in the cycle of poverty." She worked her lip. "Goodness, I can't do that in a prestigious law firm like yours."

"You sure, Megs?" Jamie latched an arm over Bram's shoulder. "Blake, Bram, and I can teach you an awful lot. Especially Bram—he's the firm's golden boy."

Heat crawled up Megan's neck, braising her cheeks as she avoided Bram's eyes. "I'm sure you can, Jamie, and thank you, Uncle Logan—*so much*, but I need to start from the ground up, and the DA's office sounds like the perfect place." Noting her uncle's scowl, she rose with a cheery smile, hoping to change the subject. "But what I *would* love to do is challenge you counselors to a card game my friend Lily taught me in Paris, with tricks just like whist. Any takers?"

Blake rose and tossed his napkin on the table, shooting a smirk at Bram. "Count me in—I'm all for tricks, especially if I can play 'em on the Padre here after the beating he gave me in chess."

"Yeah, what's this game called, anyway?" Jamie asked. He extended a hand to help Cassie up. "I'm always looking for new ways to humiliate Blake and Bram as well."

Meg smiled. "Tours Royales, which means Royal Tricks, and there's a card known as *the fool*, which turns out to be a good thing rather than bad."

"What's a fool?" Maddie asked with a blink of blue eyes.

"Someone who acts like your brother," Jamie said with a grin, slapping Blake's shoulder.

Bram stood and upended his water before nudging his chair in with a chuckle. "The boy does seem to have a talent for it, so it's good there are games in which he can excel."

Blake sauntered to the door with a devil-may-care grin. "Hey, Hughes, I've taken you down in your own game of chess once or twice, so we'll just see who makes a fool of himself, shall we?"

"Lead away." Bram scooped Maddie up on his shoulders, then made his way around the table to offer Meg his arm with a crooked smile. "And let the games begin, right, Bug?"

"Right," Meg agreed, heart racing as she, Maddie, and Bram followed the others from the room, leaving Mother and Uncle Logan to finish their coffee. She released a languid sigh, her smile pure contentment.

And my new life as well . . .

4

A satisfied sigh slipped from Caitlyn's lips as she cradled her cup in her hands, the warmth of her coffee seeping into her fingers like peace had seeped in her soul the moment Megan stepped off the train. *Her daughter, home! Oh Lord, thank you—my family together again.* Savoring her coffee, she couldn't help but smile while Logan silently polished off her piece of pie, his gaze focused on the dessert before him with the same intensity with which he did everything—whether acting as the consummate lawyer, the doting uncle, or the brother-in-law who took great pleasure in annihilating her at cribbage.

And the man who can buckle my knees with the touch of his lips?

Heat flashed at the unbidden thought, the memory of how close she'd come to courtship with Logan McClare last year—for a second time—stealing the shine from her good mood. Oh, how she had longed to be his wife—*badly*—but the issue of trust still stood in the way. It had taken years to get over his betrayal from their first courtship at the age of seventeen, a heartbreak so devastating, it sent her sobbing into the arms of his older brother. Dear Liam had been a loving friend who provided comfort and then marriage, leaving her bereft when she'd become a widow four years past. Since then, Logan had won her over, slowly restoring her confidence until she'd been ready to finally trust him with her heart once again. Her hands shook as she sipped her coffee, the taste suddenly as bitter as the memory of six months ago when she'd learned the brother-in-law with whom she was in love had lied to her once again.

Pushing the painful memories aside, Caitlyn was grateful they'd been able to resume their close friendship despite Logan's initial anger over her refusal of courtship. She slowly placed her cup in the saucer before patting her lips with her napkin. Although marriage with Logan was never to be, having him in her life as her dearest friend provided the strength and solace she needed, and for that she would always be grateful. Heart full once again, she offered him a teasing smile. "So, Mr. McClare . . . are you ready to finish me off in our game of cribbage?"

He peered up, and instantly her stomach tightened at the cool look in his eyes. Pushing his plate away, he rose, lips compressed while he adjusted the sleeves of his jacket—a habit indicating he was peeved—and one with which she was more than familiar. "Sorry, Cait—not in the mood. I have a big case to prepare for this week, so I think I'll just head on home." He shoved the chair in hard enough to shiver the table before turning to go. "Thanks for dinner."

"Logan—wait!" She jumped up and followed him to the door, restraining him with an urgent touch of his arm. "You seem angry—why?"

He turned, his jaw like rock. "I have to spell it out?"

A lump ducked in her throat as she stared, absently rubbing her arms from the chill of his tone. "Honestly, Logan, if you're upset about Rosie—"

His gray eyes glinted like the silver vase in the flickering candle-light. "Blast it, Cait—this has nothing to do with your pit bull.

That woman has chewed on me for years now, thanks to your indifference, but have you once ever seen me react like this?"

She picked at her nails, peering up beneath sloped brows as she attempted a sheepish smile, hoping to tease him out of his poor mood. "Well, actually, Logan, I seem to recall a wide range of responses, from boyish pouts to withering scowls." She gently grazed his sleeve. "I just assumed Rosie triggered that Irish temper you're so good at keeping under wraps."

"This isn't funny, Cait," he hissed, flicking her hand away. "I'm going home." He stormed from the room, his back rigid as he strode into the foyer.

"Logan, stop—please!" Her voice rose several octaves as she ran after him, halting him with a clasp of his arm. "I've obviously angered you in some way, but I honestly don't know how." She darted a nervous gaze into the parlour where laughter and good-natured teasing could be heard before her eyes sought his again, begging him to stay. "Can't we discuss this—please? In privacy, out on the study veranda?" He paused, and her fingers captured his in a gentle squeeze. "It breaks my heart thinking I may have hurt you. You're my dearest friend, Logan, you know that."

A muscle twitched in his cheek, every inch of his six-foot-two height shimmering with a silent fury she seldom saw in a man who'd learned long ago to contain his emotions. His powerful shoulders rose and fell as he gouged the bridge of his nose. Without a word, he stalked into her library, leaving her to follow as he jerked the French doors open to step outside.

She sucked in a deep draw of cool air, the summer night filling her senses with the scent of the sea and the trill of tree frogs. Desperate for privacy, she clicked the doors closed behind her as a salty breeze wisped tendrils of her hair. The groan of foghorns blended with the clang of cable car bells while the faint music of steam pianos could be heard from dance halls in the Barbary Coast. A knot ducked in her throat as she stared at Logan's back, his suit coat straining over broad shoulders while he leaned on the marble balustrade, palms flat on either side. Moving to stand beside him, she placed a tentative hand on his arm. "I ache inside, Logan, that I've hurt you in some way. Please," she whispered, voice hoarse with regret, "tell me what I've done?"

A nerve pulsed in the granite line of his jaw as he stared out into the night, his chiseled profile strong and taut. "Megan is *my* niece, Cait," he bit out, "*my* blood, and yet you chose to seek Turner's help over mine." He angled to face her, intimidating her with his height while he loomed over her like a shadow, fist clenched on the marble wall.

She blinked, her jaw slack as she took a step back, hand to her chest. "I . . . don't understand. We discussed this weeks ago, you and I, after Andrew made the offer, and you never voiced any objection, so I just thought—"

"Trust me, Cait," he ground out, gray eyes as black as night, "if you'd mentioned Turner, I would have remembered. You know how I despise him and yet you go behind my back—"

"No!" Her chin lashed up. "I would have never agreed to Andrew's offer without consulting you first, you know that!"

"No, Cait, I *don't*. I knew *nothing* about Turner's offer until your announcement tonight, when you soundly humiliated me in front of my family."

She shook her head, hand to her temple as she tried to remember, desperate to recall the night she'd told Logan over their game of cribbage. It had been the one night she'd had a rare win, unleashing his competitive nature, that insatiable need for control. She peered up, fingers kneading the onset of a headache. "But I told you that Meg was questioning her calling to law, I know I did. That working with Dr. Rousseau over the last year had sparked her interest in medicine as well. You don't remember that?"

"Of course I remember that!" he snapped. "Meg's my niece—I remember everything about everyone I love, but you did *not* mention Turner, of that I am certain."

Panic stabbed when she realized Logan must have misunderstood somehow, so absorbed in his game, perhaps, he obviously hadn't fully comprehended her meaning. Her stomach cramped at the thought, and she laid a shaky hand to her throat. "Oh, Logan," she whispered, her hand clutching his as it lay tense on the wall, "I always avoid mentioning Andrew's name directly because I know he upsets you so, but when I mentioned an internship at the district attorney's office, I just assumed you understood Andrew was involved. I will admit, I was surprised you took it so well, but I honestly thought you were in agreement because you never objected. You even said an internship was a wonderful idea, giving Meg the option both at Cooper Medical and the DA's office to help her decide which direction to take, did you not?"

He slipped his hand from hers to fold his arms, his posture stiff despite the barest softening of his tone. "Of course I did, and I even offered assistance in procuring both, if you recall, but for the love of family, Cait, I thought you meant *after* Meg pursued college, not now, at which point I hoped Turner would be long ousted from the DA's office."

"Oh my," she whispered, heart aching over the hurt she'd caused this dearest of friends. Eyes misting, she cradled his face with her hand, voice reedy with regret. "Please forgive me, Logan—I truly thought you understood." She tipped her head, intent on assuaging his wound. "You must know I care about you deeply and would never, *ever* deliberately hurt you like this."

Chest expanding in a heavy exhale, he covered her hand with

his own, the spark of anger she'd seen earlier tapering into that slow smoldering heat with which she was all too familiar. "Do you, Cait?" he said quietly. "Love me deeply?" The warmth of his palm shimmered through her as his thumb slowly skimmed the sides of her fingers. His voice turned husky while his eyes lowered to her lips for the briefest of moments, but it was more than enough. Heat curled in her belly so strong, her body convulsed in a silent gasp.

No! Her rib cage tightened at the tenuous danger she faced. Her refusal of courtship six months ago had almost severed their friendship—a friendship as critical to her as the very breath in her lungs. Yes, she was in love with Logan McClare, but she couldn't trust him as a man any more than she could do without him as a friend. Unwilling to risk either, she flung herself into his arms, gripping so tightly, she could feel his heart pound with hers she lay her head on his chest. "Oh, Logan, I do." Her eyelids drifted closed at the haunting scent of lime shaving cream and the starch of his crisp white shirt, well aware her next words could resurrect his wrath. "You are the dearest friend I've ever had," she whispered, clutching all the more when the mention of friendship stiffened his body. "And I would be lost without you, truly. But please," she whispered, her voice no more than a rasp. "Be my friend and only my friend."

She may as well doused him with ice water—all desire coursing Logan's veins froze at the sound of her plea, reminding him once again that putting a gold band on Caitlyn McClare's hand would be no easy task. *Bide your time*, the thought came, and he issued a silent grunt, wondering just how long a man like him could wait for the only woman he'd ever wanted to love. A man used to squiring women and breaking hearts. Only this time, it was his heart that had been broken by a widowed sister-in-law who refused to marry a man she was always meant to love. It was almost two years since that fateful stolen kiss in Napa, when he'd nearly ruined any chance he'd ever had to make Caitlyn his wife. Since then he'd vowed to win her heart through friendship—giving up other women to focus only on her—a plan that had succeeded well, culminating in Cait's consent to allow him to court her. His eyelids weighted closed. Until she'd discovered a secret he'd kept for over twenty-six years. A secret he'd had every intention of telling her at the right time. Only the right time never came, thanks to the man who had foiled his chances with Cait not once, but twice. Acid churned in his gut as his jaw calcified to rock. *District Attorney Andrew Turner.*

"Am I forgiven?" Her whisper was soft, muffled against his chest as she held fast, the twist of his heart and the warmth of her body a painful reminder of just what was at stake.

Drawing in a calming breath, he carefully released it and laid his head against hers, the tension in his muscles relaxing enough for his arms to slip into a tender embrace. "I'm in love with you, Cait," he said, punctuating it with a noisy sigh of surrender, "what choice do I have?"

She squeezed him so fiercely, it prompted a reluctant chuckle from his lips. "Oh, Logan, I don't deserve you, but I thank God every day for you in our lives."

He pressed a kiss to her hair, his smile slanting at the irony of the very God to whom she'd reintroduced him taking His sweet time to answer Logan's prayers. *Come on, God, I'm only human,* he countered, wondering just how long the Almighty—and Caitlyn—would make him wait. Holding her in his arms like this, he could feel the race of his pulse and the throb of blood in his veins, blatant proof of all he'd given up for this woman.

He closed his eyes and breathed in the intoxicating scent of lavender and clove, well aware few women could reform a rogue like him and turn him to God. A high price to pay for a notorious womanizer. The faintest of smiles edged his lips as he bundled her close, knowing two things for dead sure.

One—Caitlyn McClare was definitely among the few.

And two—she was worth any price he had to pay.

5

*P*lodding into the McClares' conservatory, Bram glanced at his pocket watch and sighed, dropping into the plush floral pillows of the wicker love seat. He rested his head on the back cushion while he stared at the steamy panes of glass over-head where a haloed moon glowed, as hazy as his mind at the moment. The calming scent of mulch and loam and flora did nothing to soothe the knot in his stomach—an absolute first in the McClare household.

He sucked in a deep breath of clean air, barely seeing the bright splash of bougainvillea that meandered up the sides of the greenhouse, perfectly at home in a lush jungle of ferns, ficus, palms, and orchids. He was almost grateful for the headache that throbbed, which allowed him to duck out of Meg's game of Tours Royales without question. He and Meg had partnered on the last few rounds and had lost miserably. He expelled another heavy sigh. Primarily due to his discomfort around a little girl he'd once nurtured and adored, now a woman who provoked unsettling feelings.

"I don't think I've ever seen you so off your game before, Hughes," Jamie had ribbed, giving Meg a wink that had sent a hot burn clear up Bram's neck. "Even Megs can't save you."

"Sorry, Bug," he'd said with a tight smile, well aware everyone knew the loss was all his. A child prodigy of genius proportions, Meg could handily win any game she wanted, although she seldom did, opting to spare the feelings of those she loved. He glanced at Alli as he rose. "Mind taking over while I scrounge up some aspirin powder? I feel a headache coming on." *By the name of Megan McClare.*

Grunting, Bram settled into the chaise and kneaded the bridge of his nose, his discomfort around Meg making him feel downright silly. What was wrong with him, anyway? This was Meg, his little shadow since she was seven, and he didn't like having this uneasy feeling around her—like she wasn't Meg at all. He huffed out a noisy blast of air and propped his feet on the wicker coffee table, glancing at his watch again before he closed his eyes. Eight o'clock. Too early to go home.

Memories of the shy little bookworm Meg used to be invaded his mind, and a sad smile lined his lips. She'd been the perfect replacement for the little sister he'd lost when he was eleven, someone to protect and care for like he used to take care of Ruthy. Gentle and sweet like Meg—except with a hint of the dickens—Ruthy had brought so much joy to Bram's family, the warmth of the sun to elderly parents who all but idolized her. It had crushed them all when God had taken her away, destroying Bram's faith and leaving a silent tomb of a home he longed to escape.

And escape he did—straight into the arms of rebellion—thwarting God and his parents at every turn. Shame shivered through him. Until he'd destroyed their trust, their hope, and their dreams . . . along with so much more. His eyes snapped open to ward off the guilt, his breathing shallow and raspy from memories he wanted to forget. Memories that Caitlyn McClare and her daughters had helped to put behind him with their deep faith in

God. And healing memories when Logan, Blake, and Jamie had given their invaluable friendship and support. The McClares had shared with him a close bond of love like he'd once shared with Ruthy and his parents, and Bram had thrived in their midst, their family restoring both his faith in life and in God.

Especially Bug . . . the little girl who'd healed his heart over the loss of a dear sister, making him feel like the doting big brother he wanted to be. Bram's throat went dry when the face of a beautiful stranger intruded into his mind. Stifling a low groan, he hunched over and mauled his face with his hands, alarmed and dismayed at the attraction he felt for a woman who was only a friend and little sister. *Until tonight.* The realization caused his headache to pulse even more, and he gouged the socket of his eye to help relieve the pain. *God, please—restore what we had before . . .*

"I hope you don't mind," a soft voice said from the doorway, causing Bram to jolt straight up on the chaise before he jumped to his feet. His throat convulsed as Meg—or the beauty who used to be Meg—moved into the conservatory like an apparition, her manner timid like the Megan he used to know. Head slightly bowed, she glanced up beneath heavily fringed lashes, fingers fiddling with a pleated ruffle on her shapely gold dress. "As we both know, Alli's a little too competitive to suit, so I thought I'd see how you're feeling instead." She peered up, a pucker of worry above a perfectly shaped nose that once sported a riot of freckles. "Did Rosie give you the aspirin powder?"

He expelled a breath and managed a half smile while he kneaded his temple. "Yes, she did, so hopefully this headache will be gone soon."

Her beautiful smile caused a lump in his throat, doing absolutely nothing for his blasted headache. She offered a jerky gesture toward the chaise. "May I join you?"

"Of course," he said with a rapid step back, intent upon sitting in the separate wicker armchair rather than on the chaise with her. He waited for her to sit before he settled on the edge of his chair, striving for a casual air with a relaxed fold of hands.

"Bram?"

He managed a smile. "Yes, Bug?"

Her gaze skittered to the empty cushion beside her before she peeked up, teeth tugging at impossibly full lips he'd never even noticed before. "Other than Christmas, I haven't really spent time with you for almost a year. It'd be so much easier to talk if you could sit here." She patted the seat beside her with a gentle smile. "Do you mind?"

Completely. "Of course not," he said quickly, claiming the other half of the settee. Butting up to the far side, he angled to face her, arm draped over the back in a comfortable pose he hoped would mask his unease. "So, tell me, Bug—what was your very favorite thing about Paris?"

Her face lit up, and glimpses of the old Meg shined through, twisting his heart. "Oh, Bram, without question my favorite part was accompanying Dr. Rousseau on his rounds at the various clinics he attended. I always hoped to be a lawyer like my father and Uncle Logan, and you, Blake, and Jamie, of course—to defend those with no funds to defend themselves. But when I saw those poor souls Dr. Rousseau treated in the Pigalle district—mere girls and young women forced into prostitution, bodies ravaged by disease . . ." Meg pressed a shaky hand to her chest, her features pinched with pain as water welled in her eyes. "I just knew I had to do something to help those in the Barbary Coast who are afflicted in the same way."

Bram's heart softened at the compassion he saw in her face, a compassion birthed long ago in a little girl who'd been hurt by the taunts of others. A glimmer of the easy rapport they'd once shared eased the tension at the back of his neck, and he couldn't resist giving her hand a light squeeze. "I always knew God had big plans for you, Meg. He gives tender hearts to those He's called to serve, and never have I met anyone with a more giving, loving nature than you." He sat back and folded his arms, studying her with the same fascination he had when she was a child, wondering just where her keen mind and boundless compassion would lead her. Certainly the sky was the limit for someone with her remarkable intellect. "So it's a battle between medicine and law, eh?"

She nodded with enthusiasm, drawing his gaze when a wispy strand of auburn hair bounced against the creamy skin of a perfectly chiseled collarbone. "Which is why the internship in the district attorney's office this summer is such a blessing. I've been so confused as to the direction I should take, so internships in both fields seem like the ideal solution." Her eyes sparkled with an excitement and passion Bram had seldom seen in the little girl he'd known. "And Uncle Logan has assured me he can procure an internship at Cooper Medical next summer as well, so I'm excited to see which path God wants me to take."

Both relief and a sense of pride purled through Bram's chest at Meg's mention of God, grateful her newfound physical beauty hadn't altered the beauty he'd always seen inside. Never once in their countless spiritual discussions about life's cruelties and pain had he ever known Meg to be anything but beautiful—gracious and kind, never holding a grudge. "That sounds like a perfect solution, Bug," he said with a warm smile. He paused, anxious to pursue a conversation more familiar to their prior relationship, where deep conversations and intense games of chess were the norm. "So what was your least favorite part of Paris?"

In a blink of green eyes, she tilted her head, brows sloping with a hint of sadness he'd seen far too many times. Her voice lowered to a whisper. "Missing you."

In the past, that statement would have warmed his heart instead of his neck. But now, uttered from lush lips that only distracted, the effect was akin to a face on fire from a day of sailing too long in the sun. He cleared a frog from his throat and managed a smile as stiff as his body in a chaise suddenly *way* too small. "I missed you too . . . Meg." For a man notoriously easygoing and relaxed, his words came off annoyingly stilted and for one selfish moment, he wished the old Meg were back, sweet and stout and scattered with freckles.

And so very easy to love and hold.

"You know it's odd, Bram," she said quietly. "I missed our friendship more than anything and yet . . ." The faintest of shivers traveled her body, shimmying the silk of her dress. Traces of the hurt little girl shadowed her eyes. "Right now—this very minute—never have I missed it more."

Her words paralyzed him for the briefest of moments before his heart cramped. Suddenly he was painfully aware that despite ready smiles and surface banter, he had distanced himself from a young girl who all but idolized him, wounding her as thoroughly as anyone in her past.

"Aw, Bug . . ." Ignoring the race of his pulse, he swallowed her up in his arms, eyes shut to picture the little girl who'd been so needy for his love. "Forgive me," he whispered, his voice gruff against the soft scent of her hair. "I'm an idiot, and you and I both know I've never been too fond of change."

Her sweet chuckle made him smile before she pulled away. "I suppose I should be grateful it only took you hours to come to your senses tonight instead of the months you refused to play chess when I first obliterated you."

He laughed, the sound all but chasing his tension away. "Obliterated?" he said with a jag of his brow. "Hardly, Miss McClare. I was as close to a win as the former freckles on your nose, young lady, and if I hadn't been deluded into thinking a twelve-year-old couldn't master her teacher, it would have been checkmate."

Her head tipped in an impish tease she'd obviously learned in Paris. "It took you three months to forgive me, you know, and finally start playing with me again." She scrunched her nose in a mischievous manner far more reminiscent of Alli than her. "Which kind of makes Alli and Jamie look like the good losers in this family, wouldn't you say?"

"I do believe you've picked up some sassy tendencies," he said with another fierce hug, ignoring the scent of violets to focus on the sweet satisfaction of hugging his "Bug" once again. "And if you let that information slip to anyone, our friendship is over."

"Never!" She clutched all the tighter, and Bram marveled at how delicate she felt in his arms, the feel of a woman instead of a little girl. Releasing her hold, she kicked her shoes off and snuggled like she used to, tucking her legs beneath her skirt while she rested against his side. Out of sheer habit, he drew her close with an arm scooped to her waist, remembering all the times he'd held and comforted her during all the tragedies of her life. Contentment swirled through him when she emitted a wispy sigh. "Although I must admit I worried I'd already jeopardized our friendship by the shock in your eyes tonight."

He inhaled slowly, considering his response before he expelled a quiet sigh. "Like I said, Meg, I'm an idiot, and one not prone to rapid change. Although it's taken almost a year for you to blossom into a woman, for me it was in a blink of an eye, and I'm a man who needs time to adjust." He tucked a finger under her chin. "In my mind's eye, you left in pigtails and braces." He swallowed hard, mesmerized by the silky sweep of dark lashes, the lush curve of lips that triggered far too dangerous a response. "Now you're a woman who obviously turns heads and races a man's pulse, and that takes some getting used to."

She peeked up with surprise in her eyes while a soft haze of color dusted her cheeks. "Is that what happened then? Tonight when you saw me? I . . ." Her blush deepened. "Raced your . . . pulse?"

The heat in her cheeks had nothing on him—blood gorged his face. He shifted away, removing his arm from her waist to drape it over the settee, then cleared his throat. "I guarantee you, Meg, you raced everybody's pulse in that room tonight from sheer shock over one of the most remarkable transformations any of us have ever seen."

A perfectly adorable grin skimmed her lips. "So I *did* race your pulse."

His palms began to sweat as he slipped her a smile, wishing he could just lie. "Blue blazes, Bug, I didn't even know it was you at first, so yes, of course you raced my pulse—you're a beautiful wo—" He swallowed hard, his prior awkwardness returning in force. "Young lady."

Never had he seen Megan McClare preen before, but the little brat was definitely gloating, head cocked and lips pursed in a satisfied smile. "And you called me a beautiful woman, Bram Hughes, so you might as well admit it—our friendship has progressed beyond pigtails and piggyback rides to an adult friendship between a man and a woman."

Bram shook his head, unable to stifle a grin despite his discomfort over her reference to "a man and a woman." Giving his watch a quick glance, he rose to his feet and tugged her along. "Yes, you are a beautiful woman, Miss McClare," he said with a tweak of her earlobe, a habit of his over the years, "but I prefer posturing our 'new' friendship as an adult relationship between a brother and a sister, if you don't mind." He hooked an arm around her shoulders as if she were still that shy little girl in need of approval, steering her to the door with a teasing clear of his throat. "Trust me—it will be a lot less awkward that way."

She peered up with a Mona Lisa smile. "And what if I don't want to?" she said, the mischief in her tone definitely belonging to the old Meg, but the subject matter? Obviously left over from Paris.

He paused. "Don't want to trust me?" He stalled, brows dipped in humor to mask prickles of alarm.

Her chin notched up, almost a dare in the tilt of her head that was as foreign to the Megan he knew as that confounded city that put all sorts of crazy notions in her head. "No—what if I don't want to 'posture our friendship' as between a brother and a sister?"

He ground to a halt at the door, turning to brace his hands on her shoulders like he'd done dozens of times when Devin Caldwell had made her cry. His smile was gentle, but firm. "Doesn't matter, Bug. I'm ten years your senior, a fourth cousin, and an unofficial brother since you've been seven. I see you as family, and the fact you've evolved into a stunningly beautiful woman doesn't change that in the least." His eyes narrowed to squints while his smile slanted toward dry. "What kind of batty ideas did those Parisians put in your head anyway?"

He blinked when her chin notched even higher, as if he were arguing with Cassie or Alli instead of the sweet and soft-spoken McClare. His jaw dropped when she fluttered those ridiculous lashes till he swore he could feel a breeze. "It's the City of Love, Bram," she said with her sweet giggle. "What kind of ideas do you *think* Paris put in my head?"

Heat stung his collar as he hooked her arm, all but dragging her down the hall while he peered at her out of the corner of his eye. "Well, get 'em out, Bug, because there's no room in our friend-ship for that." He ushered her into the parlour, all awkwardness replaced by resolve.

Or in my heart.

6

"Come on, Meg—exactly how many marriage proposals *did* you get in Paris?"

Meg paused, a handful of popcorn poised at her lips as she sat against her polished cherrywood headboard between her sister Alli and cousin Cass, a bowl of popcorn in her lap. She was grateful she hadn't yet put it in her mouth lest she choke on Alli's question. "Goodness, Al," she said when she'd caught her breath again, "I don't know—two or three, maybe?"

"Two or three?" Alli said with a gasp, jolting straight up as she gaped at her sister. "You received *three* proposals of marriage?"

Meg sighed, nose wrinkling to deflect the embarrassment she felt over the lavish attention she'd received from boys, something she *still* wasn't used to. "From *French* boys, Al, which are never serious proposals." She squinted as she tossed some popcorn in her mouth, a "Lily memory" easing her lips into a smile. "Although Lily claimed I 'cracked' Pierre's heart, but I'm pretty sure it was his pride instead."

Alli gaped. "Good night, Meg, did you kiss all these boys too?"

Heat pulsed in Meg's cheeks. "Good heavens—no! I would never do that." Meg battled a shiver, the subject of kisses far too painful since the time a boy had cornered her at a classmate's party last year. Goose bumps pebbled her skin at the awful memory, the boy's garlic kiss making her nauseous even now. Mortified, she had warded him off in a knee-jerk defense, accidentally flipping his glasses over the stone wall into the bushes below. She'd felt sorry for him at the time, apologizing profusely when he stormed away. *Until* he'd told Devin Caldwell and the other boys he'd kissed her. "Like kissing a greased pig all trussed up in steel," Devin had repeated in front of everyone at the party, the lie drawing raucous laughter. "Smells like pork and tastes like tin." Meg's eyelids drifted closed, the very thought of kissing a boy so steeped in hurt, she felt sick to her stomach.

"Good girl." Alli gently tucked Meg's hair behind her ear. "If I'd been more particular about who I kissed, I mightn't have had my heart broken three times."

"Agreed," Cassie said with a launch of the lariat she'd slept with since the age of five. She roped one of Meg's stuffed bears, yanking it onto the bed with a grunt. "Kissing boys just makes a girl more susceptible to hurt." She tossed the bear back across the room, landing it on its head. "Or at least it did with me and Jamie. Nope, Megs, take my word for it—being particular about who you kiss and waiting awhile is never a bad thing."

Meg offered her Texas cousin a tremulous smile. "Thanks, Cassie."

Alli bent to peer into her sister's eyes. "Goodness, Meg, I can hardly believe how much your life has changed in the last year. I know you've come back from Paris as a woman, but I can't help but see you as my shy little sis, so it'll take time for me to adjust."

"Me too, Al," Meg whispered, expelling a sigh while Alli pulled her into a tight hug. Eyes closed, Meg squeezed right back, grateful Cassie and Jamie were spending the night. There was nothing she needed more than to chat and giggle with her sister and cousin while the boys engaged in a game of late-night pool.

Alli shook her head and settled back against the headboard, reaching for more popcorn. "But merciful Providence, Megs, I still can't believe you received three proposals without a single kiss!"

Meg laughed. "Must I remind you we aren't talking bona fide proposals of marriage here? This is Paris, Al, where men propose on a daily basis. And trust me, Mrs. Rousseau stuck to Lily and me like glue, so we couldn't give gentlemen callers *anything*, much less a kiss." She giggled so much over Alli's feigned expression of shock, she began to choke on a kernel of popcorn.

Alli slapped her on the back, waiting until Meg started laughing again before she grabbed her by the shoulders and gave her a shake. "Sweet thunderation, Megan McClare—three proposals and a saucy comment. Now aren't you the little minx!"

Cassie chuckled while she roped another bear. "Says the woman who's been engaged four times." The bear sailed onto the bed.

Alli's jaw dropped as she aimed a kernel at Cassie's head. "I'll have you know four times in five years is a far cry from three times in six months, Cassidy MacKenna."

Cassie ducked, rubbing the smooth hemp between her forefinger and thumb while her eyes narrowed in mock threat. "You are either awfully brave or awfully stupid, Cuz, pelting popcorn at me when I have a lariat in my hand."

"For mercy's sake, Cass, I can't believe you *still* sleep with that stinky rope now that you're married." Alli tossed a piece of popcorn in her mouth, then snatched more from Meg's bowl before she leaned back with a waggle of brows. "Unless it's to hog-tie Jamie when he gets out of line."

"You have no idea how tempted I am when that pretty boy gets my dander up, trust me." Cassie rose up to swing the lariat in a circle overhead, launching it at one of Meg's rag dolls perched on a small velvet settee. She jerked hard, and the doll landed in her lap with a plop, delighting Meg to no end. Gently fingering the hemp, Cassie breathed in its scent with a soft smile. "To be honest, I don't think I could sleep without it—it's my lifeline to my parents, Texas, and home." A glint of trouble suddenly sparkled in her eyes. "Not to mention the perfect threat a time or two before Jamie and I were married last year."

Alli bumped shoulders with Meg. "Knowing Jamie like we do, I can certainly believe that, but when it comes to Nick?" She flipped a piece of popcorn in the air and snapped it with her teeth, holding her hand up to admire her own diamond ring. "I prefer the stick method, thank you, which has proven most effective in taming Mr. Crankypants."

Cassie cocked her head as she recoiled her rope. "Exactly how many times did you whack poor Nick with that stick anyway?"

Meg's mouth fell open. "You whacked Nick with a stick?"

"Trust me, he deserved it," Alli said with a dignified lift of her chin, promptly chomping several pieces of corn. "Each of the five times he tried to bully me around, not to mention breaking both my pointer *and* my ruler."

Meg gasped, almost inhaling a piece of popcorn. "Good heavens, Al, what on earth did the poor man do?" She giggled, memories of Lily surfacing once again. "Did he get a little 'fris-kee,' as Lily would say?"

"No, not as 'fris-kee' as Jamie did with Cass, but if he had, I assure you that a stick works as nicely as a lariat in keeping a suitor in line. But just for future reference, Megs, if a so-called gentleman makes advances or tries to kiss you against your will, the palm of a lady's hand also works quite nicely when needed."

Avoiding her sister's eyes, Megan tucked her knees to her chest, cheeks warming at the question tiptoeing in her mind. "So noted. But . . . what if . . ." She gulped down several pieces of popcorn, the flush in her cheeks traveling all the way to her toes. "A girl would *like* a certain boy to kiss her? Is there . . . you know . . . any particular way to do that?"

Alli and Cassie exchanged looks. "Sweet th-thunderation, Megs, do you have your eye on someone?" Alli stuttered, the shock in her voice a perfect match for the stunned look on Cassie's face.

"Uh . . . I don't know . . . m-maybe . . . ," she whispered, wildfire blazing in her cheeks. She slid a timid glance at her sister and cousin. "I suppose there could be someone I *may* have daydreamed about once or twice in the past and *maybe* even mentioned to Lily a few times." She sighed, the action depleting her lungs as much as her hope. "But I've always known it was nothing more than a daydream, so I didn't want anybody to know."

Alli's jaw dropped. "*Please* tell me it's not Devin Caldwell," she said, the whites of her eyes expanded in shock.

Meg averted her gaze, her finger slowly tracing the edge of the popcorn bowl. "No . . . not Devin . . ." Sucking in a stabilizing breath, she swallowed the knot of jitters impeding her words. "I know this will sound a little bit crazy, but it's . . ." She closed her eyes to brace herself for their shock, her voice tapering off to a whisper. "B-Bram."

Silence ensued, prompting Meg to chance a peek. Alli and Cassie looked like a matched set—blank stares and mouths gaping.

"See, I told you it was crazy," Meg said with a sad smile. "But that's okay because it doesn't matter anyway—Bram made it pretty clear tonight he only sees me as a little sister."

Both Alli and Cassie's jaws dropped a full inch. "You actually talked to Bram about this?" Alli squeaked.

Meg bobbed her head, expression somber. "He'd been acting so strange since he first saw me tonight—distant, stiff, so unlike himself—that I decided to confront him."

"He did seem out of sorts," Cassie confirmed.

"Goodness, Megs," Alli said, voice bordering on shrill, "how on earth did you do it?"

Meg shrugged her shoulders. "I just told him I missed his friendship tonight, and he finally apologized for being so distant."

"Did he say why?" Cassie asked, grabbing Meg's arm to get her attention.

Meg sighed. "I think it makes him uncomfortable I'm no longer the pudgy little wallflower he's used to." A knot ducked in her throat as warmth fanned in her cheeks. "He said I've turned into a woman who obviously turns heads and races a man's pulse."

Alli shook Meg's arm, reclaiming her attention. "Including his?" she shrieked.

"I think so," Meg said softly, a furrow of confusion ridging her brow. "But he said it was only because he didn't know who I was at first. Claims he's ten years my senior, a fourth cousin, and an unofficial brother since I've been seven. Says the fact that I have 'evolved into a stunningly beautiful woman' doesn't alter the brother-sister friendship we have one bit."

"*Stunningly beautiful woman?*" Cassie said, her voice rising to Alli's level.

Meg nodded, shoulders drooping as much as her spirits. "That's what he said."

Cassie and Alli traded grins. "Who would have thought our sweet and straitlaced Padre Hughes would admit to being attracted to little Meg!" Alli clasped her hands in delight. "This is wonderful!"

"Not if he only sees me as a little sister," Meg said with a sad shake of her head.

"But that's just it, Megs." Alli had a dangerous gleam in her eye. "He *doesn't* see you as a little sister—he sees you as a 'stunningly beautiful woman.'"

"Even so," Meg said with a rare show of pluck, "Blake mentioned in one of his letters that Bram was seeing someone, so I've made up my mind that if I can't have a man like Bram Hughes, I will devote myself to a career in law or medicine instead." She slumped against the headboard with a sigh. "Besides, I don't want anything to jeopardize our friendship."

Cassie gnawed on the edge of her lip, clearly immersed in thought. "Mmm . . . Jamie did mention Bram escorted Amelia Darlington to several functions, but he never brings her around, so we just assumed it wasn't serious."

Alli grunted. "Knowing Bram, it's more likely because of his allegiance to his father rather than any interest in Amelia. Rumor has it that Mr. Hughes and Henry Darlington have been planning a merger for a while now . . . in more ways than one, apparently."

Meg set the bowl aside, no longer interested in nibbling. The thought of her best friend courting another woman left her unsettled and more than a little blue. Scooting against the headboard with shoulders square, she shook the melancholy off, determined to focus on her dreams of service to others instead. "Well, it doesn't matter anyway," she said quietly. "With the internship in the district attorney's office followed by the one at Cooper Medical, and then my schooling, I'll be too busy for a romantic relationship anyway."

"You're right," Cassie said with a toss of Meg's bear, twirling her lasso to retrieve it once more. "There's nothing wrong with focusing on your dreams instead—both Alli and I did that before we met Jamie and Nick. But the truth is, the main reason was because we'd been hurt and wanted to make sure it didn't happen again." She parked the teddy bear in Meg's lap. "And fear is never the right motivation, Megs, so, yes, focus on your dreams. But you're a beautiful girl on the threshold of womanhood, so don't be surprised if God throws a monkey wrench in your plans."

"As long as the 'wrench' has nothing to do with a 'monkey' named Devin Caldwell," Alli said with a scrunch of her nose.

Meg grinned. "No, Al, monkeys are cute," she said with a tilt of her head, employing a trace of French spunk along with the sass. She gave her sister a wink. "Our Mr. Caldwell is more of a baboon."

7

$\mathcal{S}$o . . . what's the excuse tonight?"

Bram glanced up to see Jamie in his office door, arms folded and hip butted to the frame, and instantly the headache he'd been battling notched up several degrees. Giving Jamie a tired smile, he glanced over his shoulder at the clock on the credenza and winced. Six-forty-five—time for Jamie to be long gone to the McClares'. His gaze automatically trailed past a picture of Blake, Jamie, and him at graduation to stare out at the overcast bay, where the roiling whitecaps appeared as restless as he. *And churning way less than my stomach.* Venting with a weary sigh, he tossed his pen on his desk and leaned back in his chair, closing his eyes to knead his temple. "Come on, Jamie, have a heart—I've been chained to this desk for weeks now, you know that."

"Ah, yes—the McCarron case," Jamie said, ambling in with hands in his pockets, his overly casual tone not boding well for Bram's peace of mind. "I remember it well. The case Logan turned over to you since he needed a cool and steady hand." He plopped into the chair in front of Bram's desk, hazel eyes locked on his best friend with a faint smile.

Bram expelled another heavy breath and hiked his shoes up on his desk. "Only because the case was too personal for you and

61

you know it. It would be difficult for anybody to calmly defend a sleazy bigwig accused of murdering a Barbary Coast dance-hall girl, much less a man whose own mother was forced at the age of fifteen to work in one."

"Difficult, yes, but not for you." Jamie's half smile faded into admiration and respect, laced with more than a little affection. "Everybody knows that other than the partners, you're the best lawyer in this firm."

"Second best, my friend," Bram said with matched loyalty, his friendship with Jamie MacKenna one of the few things that kept him sane of late. Lunches in Jamie's office or his when they were too busy to go out. Workouts at the Oly Club gym where Jamie always bested him in boxing. The occasional evenings out with both Jamie and Blake. *Or dinners and pool tournaments at the McClares'?* Bram ignored the niggle in his gut. *Yes, except for lately . . .* Shaking the thought off, he folded his arms and studied his best friend. "You're the one who's tallied more wins than me, Mac, even as a newlywed with other things on his mind."

Jamie grinned outright. "Good point, but you're the one who's snagged some pretty high-profile wins lately, along with some very impressive headlines."

"Which apparently go hand-in-hand with late hours and no social life." Bram rested his head on the back of his chair, the fatigue of the last few weeks causing his facial muscles to sag along with his smile. "It's almost seven—what are you still doing here anyway? Cassie finally wise up and throw you out?"

The grin was back. "Nope, that cowgirl is hog wild about me, Padre, no question." He winked. "Can't keep her hands off me, which makes for a *very* happy home." He laid his head back like Bram while the humor dimmed in his eyes. "Unlike the McClare household at the moment."

Bram's stomach clenched. *Here it comes.* Striving for a casual pose, he braced hands behind his neck, tone suddenly as serious as Jamie's. "Why? What's going on?"

"Well, as you know, it's no secret there was a hint of tension between Logan and Cait last time you came to dinner, when she announced Meg won that internship in the DA's office."

The bridge of Bram's nose puckered. "Yeah, but they seemed fine later in the evening while they were playing cribbage," he reasoned, grateful the subject steered clear of Meg.

"Yes, well, you weren't there for the next dinner, I might remind you, when Andrew Turner showed up unannounced. Trust me—the tension was high." Jamie paused, eyeing Bram through pensive eyes. "Then of course, there's the upset over you avoiding Meg."

A groan escaped Bram's lips as his eyelids weighted closed, hand splayed over his eyes to massage temples with forefinger and thumb. "I am *not* avoiding Meg, for pity's sake." The lie slipped out before he could stop it, and he groaned again, finally huffing out a sigh as he faced Jamie head-on. "Okay, maybe I am somewhat, but the *main* reason I couldn't go last week nor this week is because I'm swamped and you know it."

Jamie pierced him with a painfully honest stare, the kind that had marked many a discussion over the years when Bram would try to talk to his best friend about God. "I know that, Bram," he said quietly, "but I also know you haven't been the same since Meg came home, and to be honest, it worries me—for both you and for Meg." He hesitated, as if he knew what he was about to say would not be easy for Bram to hear. "Alli told Cassie she found Meg crying in her room after dinner last week when you didn't show."

Bram's heart cramped as his eyelids lumbered closed. *Aw, Meg, no . . .*

"Excused herself after dinner, a headache, she said, but when Alli went up to check on her, the poor kid was sobbing her heart out, convinced your friendship with her was over."

The moan that left his lips was painful, causing a physical ache that matched the one in his gut. He mauled his face with his hands. "Heaven help me, I'm an idiot."

"Actually you're not," Jamie said softly, the depth of feeling in his voice assuring him that he understood. "You're just a very good friend who's confused over something he never expected—attraction to a little girl you nurtured and loved as a sister. Am I right?"

Bram's answer stuck in his throat, cracking his voice when it scraped past dry lips. "Yes," he whispered. He sucked in a deep breath and raised his gaze to Jamie's. "Is it that obvious?"

Jamie's smile was edged with sympathy. "Only the coat-hanger smile and mime mode when Meg's in the room, but don't worry—I covered for you when you left to nurse your headache, telling everyone you're under the gun on a big case."

"I am *such* an idiot," he repeated, shaking his head while his eyes lapsed into a dazed stare. "She must hate me."

"Nope, she loves you, Bram—always has. You've been her guardian angel since she bloodied her knee at the age of seven on the terrace of Logan's Napa estate. You swooped her up so fast and carried her around the rest of the night, forging a bond unlike any she's ever had."

A soft smile shadowed Bram's lips. "Yeah, I know," he said, his voice thick with emotion. He fought the moisture that threatened his eyes. "She reminded me so much of Ruthy, Mac, I couldn't help but love her."

"She needed you, Bram—everybody knew it. Alli's the fun and dramatic older sister and Maddie took over as the baby of the house. That left Meg in the middle as the awkwardly shy and very insecure sister who would have faded into the woodwork except for you."

Bram nodded slowly, his thoughts straying to the painfully shy little girl who'd been so in need of a champion, someone to shield her from the blows of the world like God had done for him. "She did need me," he said softly, "and I sensed it so strong back then, like God whispering in my ear."

"She still needs you, you know." Jamie perched on the edge of his chair, eyes locked with Bram's. "Maybe now more than ever."

A muscle jerked in Bram's throat and he looked away. "Maybe, but I'll be honest, Jamie—I'm having trouble with it, with my physical attraction to a girl I've seen as a sister all these years." He glanced up, his body weary from the stress of it. "I'm not sure I'm comfortable with a close friendship with this new Meg."

Jamie studied him with that unblinking confidence that won many a jury's vote. "I've never known Bram Hughes to put comfort before friendship," he said quietly.

A grunt rolled from Bram's lips. "Yeah, well, you've never known me to be this conflicted before either. I'm the calm, steady one who never gets ruffled, remember? Only this time, I'm in over my head, Mac, I can sense it. It's bad enough I have to fight my own feelings of attraction for an innocent young girl I have no business thinking of that way, but now there's a complication. I have the will and stamina to be her friend and stay removed from anything more, but Meg is a naïve young girl who alluded to similar feelings that night, and to be honest, that scares the daylights out of me."

"Why?" Jamie cocked his head, a hint of challenge in his tone.

"Why?" Bram stared, the hinges of his jaw giving way. "Because Meg is vulnerable right now with this possible infatuation she may have with me, and I can't allow that. For pity's sake, MacKenna, she's like a little sister, not to mention I'm ten years older than her."

Jamie squinted. "Neither of which would hold up in a court of law, counselor. In case it's slipped your mind, Meg is *not* your sister and to be honest, the way you're acting right now—like a tongue-tied adolescent? I'd say she's way older than you."

Bram's legs flew off the desk, hitting the floor with a thump while he grabbed a pen and paper, dismissing Jamie with a rare show of temper. "I don't have time for this right now, MacKenna," he growled, jerking several briefs forward, "so why don't you just mosey on out and give them my regrets."

"Now there's an appropriate word." Jamie stared him down, never budging an inch. He hesitated, and the worry that threaded his tone made Bram feel like dirt. "What's going on, Bram? I've never seen you this irrational before, so out of sorts, reclusive."

The pen dropped from Bram's hand with a clunk as he rubbed his face, "regrets" mounting by the moment. "I'm sorry, Mac," he whispered, expelling a shaky rush of air. "These awkward feelings I'm having toward Meg just came at a bad time, that's all."

Jamie squinted. "Because you're swamped at work?"

He shook his head, too tired to be angry, too resigned to debate. "No, because I have no right to have these feelings toward her, much less act on them."

"Why? Because you think she's too young or you see her as a sister even though she's not?" Jamie leaned forward, hands clutching Bram's desk with the same intensity that shimmered in his eyes. "Did it ever occur to you that loving Meg as a woman might be the very progression God intended all along?"

Bram's heart thudded in his chest. "No." His Adam's apple dipped. "At least not until the other night when I saw her again.

Suddenly she was no longer my little Bug, but this woman who triggered my pulse, and frankly, Mac, I just didn't know how to deal with that."

"So you ran." A trace of a smile shadowed Jamie's lips. "I've never seen you run from a situation in your life, so you must really be scared."

"You're bloomin' right I'm scared." He gouged fingers through his hair, indifferent to the neat and clean-cut style he so meticulously maintained. "Between my feelings and Meg's, this is a vulnerable situation where I could end up hurting her even more, and I refuse to do that."

"I don't get it, Hughes—Meg's one of the most important people in your life and you already love her, for pity's sake. Now it seems you're both attracted to each other and for the umpteenth time, the woman is *not* your sister. So how on earth would you end up hurting her?"

Bram peered up, throat convulsing several times while sweat beaded at the back of his neck. He supposed now was as good a time as any to reveal the secret that had been eating a hole in his gut for the last six months. He expelled a weighty sigh. "By marrying another woman," he whispered, the very words jolting him as they left his lips.

"What?" Jamie's dark brows cinched in a frown. "What the devil are you talking about? We're as close as brothers, Bram, and the most serious I've seen you with a woman is when you flirt with Stella, the seventy-five-year-old waitress at the diner we go to for lunch."

Bram actually smiled, the thought of the spry little grandma who gave him extra portions lightening his mood. He drew in a cleansing breath and blew it out, sobriety settling in once again. "I wish it were as innocent as flirting with sweet little Stella, but

I'm afraid it's more serious than that. I'm committed to Amelia Darlington."

Jamie squinted. "I knew your parents strong-armed you into occasionally escorting her to high-profile fund-raisers, but you barely know the woman."

"That's because up to now, it's only been as a courtesy to my parents since they and the Darlingtons have become good friends." Exhaling loudly, he cuffed the back of his neck. "Unfortunately, both my father and Amelia's have developed the gleam of merger in their eyes, both with their companies *and* their children."

"So, don't do it," Jamie said, a pinch of annoyance between his brows. "This is the twentieth century, Bram, not the Old World where marriages were arranged."

"It's not that easy," he said quietly. "My mother accidentally let it slip that this merger is important to my father. Since then, I've discovered through a friend at his bank that Pop's company is on the verge of bankruptcy, so he needs Darlington's money. And Darlington apparently needs Father's stateside connections, international expertise, and his once-lucrative contracts overseas. Not to mention our bloodline, Mother suspects, since Darlington is, and I quote, 'nouveau riche' and snubbed by the old money in society. To make matters worse, Darlington is dead set against Amelia marrying some duke she took a shine to on her Grand Tour, who apparently has turned out to be a penniless fraud." Bram rubbed his jaw with the side of his hand, the sandpaper feel of his late-day beard as abrasive as his mood. "So Darlington is making the merger contingent upon our marriage, which sews it up rather neatly that I can't risk Meg developing deeper feelings for me."

"Why?" Jamie demanded, the same steely glint in his eye as when he took on an opponent in a boxing bet at the Blue Moon.

"Why?" Bram reached into his bottom drawer for the aspirin powder his doctor prescribed for the onslaught of headaches over the last six months. "I just told you why."

Jamie stood and slanted forward, palms flat on Bram's desk. "No, *why* do *you* have to sell your soul and future to the devil for the sake of a business merger that will probably happen anyway without your blood sacrifice?"

Blood sacrifice. Bram froze, memories of the day he almost lost his father crashing into his mind, when he'd found him bleeding on the floor of his study, face down in a pool of blood.

"Bram!"

He sucked in a sharp breath as Jamie blurred back into focus, then swallowed hard, his voice hoarse with regret. "Because I owe him, Jamie," he whispered. "It's as simple as that."

Jamie paused, his jaw shifting almost imperceptibly, clear evidence he was grinding his teeth to contain his anger. "So . . . have you prayed about it?"

Bram blinked. "What?"

"This laying waste of your life for the sake of money or guilt or whatever else is putting this gun to your head—have you asked God what He wants?" Jamie folded his arms, mouth flat as he seared Bram with a challenging glare. "That's the nail you'd always pound in my coffin whenever I was pinned to the wall about something. So tell me, Bram—was that just rote advice you give to your friends or is it something that applies to you too?"

Heat singed Bram's collar along with a touch of anger. "I already know what God wants, Jamie—honor your father and your mother, remember?"

Jamie leaned on the desk again. "I've never met a man who honors his parents more than you, but you do *not* owe them your life—"

Bram shot to his feet, a nerve flickering in his jaw as he thrust a thumb to his chest. "That's where you're wrong, MacKenna. Because of me and my rebellion, my father almost lost his life thirteen years ago, so yes, I *do* owe him my life, as a matter of fact, and nobody's going to change my mind on that, counselor, so case closed."

The tick of the clock on the credenza seemed deafening as Jamie rose to his full height. "All right, Bram, I'll leave it be— for now. But that won't stop me from praying that you come to your senses before you make the biggest mistake of your life." He turned to go.

Bram slashed his fingers through his hair, feeling like he'd just gone several rounds with Jamie in the ring. "Mac, look—I'm sorry, but don't worry about me, please. I'm fine with this."

"Sure, Bram, but let me ask you a question." Jamie paused at the door, eyes narrowed in a contest of wills. "How fine would you be if it was me in your shoes instead of you?"

Blood drained from Bram's face, the truth hitting dead center. If it were Jamie, he'd hound him until he saw the folly of his ways, insisting on praying whether Jamie wanted to or not. If? Dash it—he'd done just that when Jamie was bent on marrying another woman despite loving Cassie.

"I thought as much." Jamie shook his head, lips leveled in a grim smile. "You know, Padre, other than Logan, there isn't a man alive I respect more than you. I've always admired your careful deliberation, your cool head, and your solid faith." His dry smile was a half grunt. "But I guess nobody's perfect." He gave a casual salute. "Which means after all these years of you bailing me out with the Almighty, the shoe's finally on the other foot. Because as sure as McCarron is guilty, you can bet I'll be praying you come to your senses."

A soft chuckle broke from Bram's lips. "About time, MacKenna—I'm tired of carrying you. It's your turn to carry me."

"Don't think I won't." He cocked his head, his smile tempered by unspoken warning. "All the way to the McClares' for dinner next week, if I have to."

Exhaling slowly, Bram nodded. "I'll be there."

"Good." Jamie glanced at his watch. "I'll cover for you this week, but after that, you'll have to deal with Meg on your own, telling her the truth so you can get your friendship back on solid ground. She deserves that if nothing else, agreed?"

Bram nodded. "Agreed." He watched Jamie leave, the sound of his footsteps echoing down the hall while his words echoed in his brain.

Friendship, yes. A knot of regret jerked in his throat.

But that and nothing more . . .

8

Swoosh! A mushball flew by Meg's face while Bram stood on the pitcher's mound in the McClares' backyard, grinning a little too broadly.

Male cheers erupted into a brilliantly blue sky while Meg blinked, the cool breeze from the sixteen-inch softball doing nothing for the heat in her cheeks.

"Strike one!" Smug confidence fairly rang in Bram's tone as he stood, hip cocked and a gleam of challenge in his blue eyes. The sweet scent of fresh-mown grass and Mother's cottage roses permeated the June air, merging with the sounds of catcalls and laughter to remind Meg of joyful summers of the past. Summers spent matching wits in tournaments of mushball or croquet with her family, where she and Bram were always a team. She blew a stray hair out of her face, gripping the bat all the tighter. *Now* they were on opposing sides . . . in more ways than one.

The sleeves of Bram's normally pristine shirt were tightly rolled to reveal muscular arms tan from his love of sailing while he bent to retrieve a second ball at his feet. He tossed it from hand to hand with a lazy flash of white teeth while little Maddie returned the other ball, red curls bouncing from excitement at being able to play mushball with the grown-ups. Vest shed and draped over the wrought-iron settee on the patio where Mother and Uncle Logan watched the game, Bram seemed far more relaxed than he had at her homecoming dinner over two weeks ago. His suspenders and loosened tie lent an almost reckless air while the sea breeze toyed with loose strands of his wheat-colored hair. Although he hadn't spoken directly to her yet other than pleasantries over a picnic lunch Rosie provided on the patio, he seemed more like himself today, boding well for the private discussion she hoped to have with him later.

"Two more outs and the men reign supreme," Blake called from first base while Jamie and Nick covered second and third. "Send her packing, Bram!"

A wispy sigh parted from Meg's lips as she raised her bat high. "He already did," she muttered, her feelings still hurt over Bram's sudden disappearance since she'd come home from Paris. Over two weeks without a word, note, or phone call—nothing to indicate their prior close friendship was still intact. Not after her bumbling attempt to flirt and catch his eye as a woman instead of a little girl. Heat braised her cheeks at the memory of his outright rejection when she'd boldly implied she no longer wanted a friendship between a brother and a sister.

"It's the City of Love, Bram, what kind of ideas do you think Paris put in my head?"

"Well, get 'em out, Bug, because there's no room in our friendship for that."

The sting of his words stiffened her jaw, as hard as the bat she held in her hands, shocking her with a sudden desire to aim straight at his head. She hunkered down, knees bent beneath the cream gabardine skirt she'd rolled several times beneath her wide black belt for ease of running, offering a peek of her stockinged ankles.

"Hit it out of the park, Megs," Alli called from third base, hands cupped to her mouth and one knee bent to race for home. "Make 'em suffer!"

Nick chuckled behind her, tugging on a loose curl from Alli's chignon. "You'll have plenty of time for that after we embarrass you in mushball, Princess."

"Ha! When buffaloes fly!" Cassie bellowed from second base, crouched at the bag with skirt hiked to her ankles while Jamie grinned behind.

Cassie's sass coaxed a grin to Meg's lips, taking the edge off her nerves as she eyed Bram with a steely-smiled squint. *Just one good whack, Mr. Hughes, to redeem my pride . . .*

Hunching his shoulders to apparently work out the kinks in his muscles, Bram fired the ball in an underhand windmill motion, his athletic ability evident in the fluid movement of his body. Holding her breath, Meg eased the bat back, unleashing a hard swing that connected with the ball in a surprising pop, sending it sailing over Blake's head.

Groans and squeals filled the backyard as Meg flew the bases, running so hard, several hairpins came loose, tumbling heavy curls down her back.

"Bring it home, Megs—you can make it!" Cassie shouted, she and Alli leaping into the air with whoops and cheers while little Maddie danced in circles on the sidelines.

Meg glanced over her shoulder as she rounded third base, stomach lurching when Blake scooped the ball up at the back of the yard. Lips pressed tight, she barreled forward, inwardly groaning at the sight of Bram hovering over home plate, body poised to field Blake's throw.

Chest pumping, she gave it her all. Each and every sound faded away except for the pounding of her heart as her gaze fixed on that ragged square of old carpet that served as home base. And then in slow motion, Bram stepped in front of the base with arms in the air and eye on the catch while she continued to charge, tucking her head low with a grit of her teeth.

Boom!

The wind left Meg's lungs as she plowed into something solid. A shocked cry wrenched from her lips when she tumbled to the ground, landing on top of Bram with a thud. Too stunned to move, she was barely aware of female shrieks as the ball she'd knocked from Bram's hand slowly rolled to a stop, ensuring the girls' win. As if bonded by glue, all she could do was stare at him with saucer eyes while she lay on his chest, the familiar scent of Bay Rum making her dizzy. With their parted lips mere inches apart, ragged air passed between them as neither moved a muscle, fire scorching her cheeks at the warmth of his body beneath hers.

It seemed like eons, but it was only seconds before he cleared his throat with a hoarse laugh. Gingerly lifting her off with hands at her waist, he carefully set her beside him before jumping up. A ruddy shade of red crept up his neck as he offered his hand, popping her up so quickly, she felt dizzy all over again. "Are you okay?" he asked, a note of concern in his voice as he avoided her eyes, surveying her skirt for grass and dirt stains.

"Holy thunder, Megs," Jamie said with a wink. "Haven't seen a tackle like that since college football. Hate to be a spoilsport, but that looked like interference to me, what you do you think, Blake?"

"Positively blatant." Blake hooked an arm over Meg's shoulder. "Sorry, kiddo, it's textbook interference—you're out, and the men win."

"Oh no you don't." Alli barged in between Jamie and Blake, hands on her hips. "Bram was blocking the plate before he even touched the ball, so Meg is allowed the run, right, Nick?"

All eyes turned to Alli's fiancé, who was tickling Maddie over his shoulder. He paused, gray-green eyes in a squint while Maddie's stubby legs kicked in the air. "Well . . . the obstruction rule states a defensive person cannot hinder or impede the progress of a runner without possession of the ball."

The girls launched in the air with a chorus of cheers while Alli gave Nick a kiss on the cheek. "And that, Nick Burke, is only one of the many reasons I love you," she said, unleashing giggles from Maddie when she tickled the little girl's tummy.

"But . . ." Nick hooked an arm to Alli's waist, a lazy grin tipping the side of his mouth. "That said, there is one rule that will trump the obstruction rule, but I want the bat safely removed before I tell you what it is." He set Maddie down and tweaked the little girl's neck. "Can you take the bat to your mother for me, sweetheart, before your sister gets feisty?"

"Sure, Nick!" Maddie swooped up the bat and ran to her mother.

Alli spun around, arms folded while she tapped her toe. "If this other rule is going to rob us of a win, Detective Burke, you haven't *seen* 'feisty.'"

"Break it to 'em gently, Nick," Bram said with a lazy smile. "We don't want them too riled when we challenge them in charades."

"Spit it out, Nick." Cassie stepped forward, Alli's competitive nature obviously catching. She stared him down, blue eyes narrowed in threat. "But first let me get my cattle prod . . ."

"Ah-ah-ah . . ." Jamie looped his arms around Cassie's waist from behind. "No idle threats, Mrs. MacKenna. Let the man speak."

Nick's grin was sheepish. "At the risk of stirring a hornet's nest, ladies, the rules state that when a defensive player has the ball"—he nodded to Bram—"such as Mr. Hughes obviously had . . ."

"Hear, hear!" Blake shouted.

"And the runner crashes into him, then . . ." He took a casual step back, obviously distancing himself from the wrath of Alli. "The runner is out." Hostile groans rose as Nick held his hands up. "Hey, don't shoot the messenger, ladies."

"No firearms, Mr. Spoilsport, but how 'bout a whack with a stick?" Alli's smile was thin.

"Okay, ladies, what's next—charades or croquet?" Blake ambled to the patio with the others, tossing a mushball in the air while Jamie did the same with the other. "We'll give you a chance to redeem your pride."

"Ha! Best not to be too cocky, Cuz." Cassie slid him a narrow gaze. "Keep in mind that pride goeth before the fall, especially if a cattle prod is involved."

"Or a stick," Alli confirmed. She plucked a croquet mallet off the table and waggled her brows. "Croquet, anyone?"

"You're on," Jamie said with a flap of his rolled shirt, perspiration beading his brow. "But first, I need something to cool off."

"Great idea." Bram unrolled his sleeves. "Who's in the mood for ice cream?"

Maddie shot into the air, arms flailing. "Me, me, me!"

"Well, that's a definite yes." Uncle Logan scooped the little tyke from Caitlyn's lap to his, making her giggle with a noisy gobble-kiss. He glanced at Bram. "What did you have in mind?"

Bram grabbed his jacket off the chair and put it on, his gaze veering to Meg. "I thought Meg and I could head over to Carter's Confectionary and buy ice cream sandwiches for everybody before we tackle croquet. What do you say, Bug?"

"Sure, Bram," she whispered, fanning her face to cool the heat in her cheeks. "I'm about to melt here, and ice cream sounds wonderful!"

"Yes, well, that's what happens when you run people down at home plate, Miss McClare." He latched a hand to her neck like he used to do when she was younger, steering her toward the door while he chatted about how busy he'd been at work. Ushering her through the house, he patiently waited as she pinned on her hat at the door, then held it open for her.

They stepped outside and despite the glorious blue of the sky and the teasing scent of summer from Mother's eucalyptus, a shadow settled over Meg's mood, piquing her ire. An ire she never knew she had, truth be told, until Paris had set the woman inside of her free to be all she had longed to be—the *real* Megan McClare. No longer cowering beneath people's disapproval or silent beneath their scorn, but free to think, live, and be all God intended. Somewhere amid Bram's casual banter, the joy of children's giggles drifted in the air, and at the sound, a firm resolve straightened her shoulders. With God's help, she would be that woman with or without the love of any man, even Bram Hughes, to whom she'd given her heart so many years ago. His friendship had sustained her for most of her life, and if that's all God intended, then by His grace, it would sustain her for all of the rest. Because life was a gift from the Creator, meant to be savored and enjoyed, not spent pining over things that could never be.

"Hungry?" Bram asked as he led her down the brick steps to where his cherry-red Stanley Steamer waited at the curb, pausing to dodge a sunken step that always teetered Meg's gait.

She breathed in the fresh smell of hope and promise and dreams along with the scent of the sea, her acceptance of Bram's friendship suddenly setting her free. For the first time, she felt as if she could see beyond all the hurts and daydreams of the past to a future as bright as a sunny summer day. "Hungry?" she repeated, her cheeks warm with excitement as her smile eased into a grin. "Oh, yes . . ."

For a future full of promise and more . . .

9

Sweat layered Bram's collar, a condition due, he suspected, as much from his need to clear the air with Meg as from the unseasonably warm day. Never had he felt this unsettled around her before—except for the night of her homecoming, of course—yammering nonstop as if he were Jamie after a pot of espresso. Smiling that secret smile that unnerved him, she'd let him simply ramble on as he'd lifted her at the waist into the seat of his car, releasing her so quickly, she'd actually bounced on the tufted leather seat.

Neck blazing, he'd rounded the vehicle in record time and hopped into his car, his jabbering unceasing as he pumped the throttle until the pungent scent of kerosene floated in the air. Opening the drip valve briefly, he maneuvered the tiller, easing the vehicle into the street while a breeze from the bay cooled the sweat on his brow. Quiet for once, he chanced a glimpse at Meg out of the corner of his eye and marveled for the hundredth time how much she had changed in a single year. Stray wisps of auburn curls fluttered about her face and neck as she lifted her face to the sky. He took advantage of the moment to study her pose—hands folded serenely in the lap of her cream skirt, back straight and head high. Gone was the timid little girl who used to slouch as if she wanted to curl up and disappear, replaced by a woman who now took his breath away.

Jaw tight, he returned his gaze to the road, grateful for the chug of the steam engine that dispelled any awkwardness from his sudden silence. A silence that needed to be broken regarding the direction of their relationship in the future.

And soon.

Bram pushed the hook-up pedal to the floorboard and opened the drip valve, releasing the brake to coast down Powell to Market. With a quick glance behind, he veered toward the curb in front of Carter's Confectionary, finally bringing the car to a stop with a hiss of steam. Two freckled boys in dirty knickers glanced up from where they knelt on the cracked sidewalk playing marbles, ogling Bram's car with mouths agape. He closed the drip valve and applied the brake while a group of little girls playing hopscotch paused to stare. One of the girls in a frayed pinafore giggled when Bram gave her a wink before he turned to smile at Meg. "You know, Bug, I'm totally prepared to make up for ignoring you these last few weeks." He cocked a brow. "Say, a bag of jelly beans?"

Meg laughed, flashing dimples Bram had never really paid much attention to before. But now no gold braces barred her teeth nor thick eyeglasses goggled her gaze, causing the muscles in his throat to duck like he'd swallowed a fistful of those blasted jelly beans she so adored. She tipped her head in a playful pose, and a wisp of titian hair caressed the softest, creamiest cheek he'd ever seen. He fought the rise of a gulp. *How on earth have I never noticed before?*

The softest of smiles played at the edge of her lips. "Really, counselor—bribery?" Those remarkable green eyes twinkled. "I would have thought better of the noble Bram Hughes."

His smile faded as he shifted to face her, her words pricking his conscience. He strove for a casual air with one arm over the back of the seat while the other absently fiddled with the leather head of the tiller. "Yes, well maybe you shouldn't, Bug, because it wasn't very 'noble' of me to avoid you for over two weeks, which is why I wanted you to come with me to get ice cream—so I could apologize and explain why."

She picked at a seam in her skirt as she avoided his eyes, a hint of rose stealing into her cheeks. "I already know why," she said softly, "and the truth is it's I who owes you an apology."

"No, Meg, you're wrong—"

"Am I?" A sweep of dark lashes lifted to reveal a gaze riddled with regret. "You're my best friend in the whole world, Bram, and I made you feel uncomfortable with my—" a nervous lick of her lips told him this was not easy for her—"brazen overtures," she whispered.

He tipped his head, gaze softening while a crooked grin skimmed across his lips. "Come on, Bug—brazen?" He nudged her chin up, coaxing her eyes to meet his. "There's not a brazen bone in your body, Megan McClare, and an apology is hardly necessary." Boosting his courage with a fortifying breath, he leaned back against the door with a fold of arms, his smile sloping off center. "Trust me—you had every reason to assume that mindset the way I gawked at you all night like a starry-eyed adolescent." Sobriety stole into his manner, dimming his smile. "You've grown into a beauty, Meg, and some lucky guy will be blessed beyond his wildest dreams with a woman who is bright, gentle, and beautiful—the perfect girl, really." His chest rose and fell with a heavy sigh. "It just can't be me, Bug," he said quietly, his gaze locked with hers.

"I know," she whispered, and his chest constricted at the sudden sheen of moisture in her eyes. "It was childish of me, Bram, to think you could ever be attracted to me that way."

Heart thudding, he grasped her hand, swallowing it in a firm grip. "No, you *don't* know, Meg—at least not the reason why. And trust me, there is nothing childish about you at all, so don't say that." His fingers strayed to gently stroke the curve of her jaw, eyes intense. "You're wrong, you know," he said quietly. "Any man could fall in love with you, including me, Miss McClare, so don't sell yourself short." He released her hand with a heavy exhale. "Attraction is not the problem—it's simply a matter of what's meant to be and what's not."

She studied him with a gentle bent of her head, a flicker of hope in her eyes. "But how do you know it's not meant to be? Sometimes friendships can grow into something deeper."

Nodding, he refolded his arms, determined to speak his mind and get their relationship on safer ground. "True, but as two people of deep faith, we both know God's will always prevails, and the truth is He ordained our friendship years ago as more of a fraternal friendship."

"Platonic," she uttered, that sweet smile thinning the slightest bit.

"Exactly," Bram stated, relieved she understood the situation without further explanation.

The lashes fluttered several times, as if in confusion, before she peeked up with a shy grate of her lip. "You mean just like Cassie and Jamie used to be . . ."

"Yes—I mean *no!*" Bram squinted at the little minx, well aware she'd always been a genius in a little girl's body, challenging him in everything from cribbage to chess. She stared at him now through wide eyes, an innocent who knew exactly what she was saying despite the naïve look on her face. "Jamie was attracted to Cassie from the outset, Bug, not her big brother for over ten years like us. Besides, there's only a three-year age difference between Cass and Jamie, not ten years like you and me."

Childlike eyes blinked at him from a woman's face. "But my father was ten years older than my mother . . ." Her voice was soft, but its impact hardened his jaw.

"Meg," he said, his tone gentle yet firm, "listen to me, please—there can be nothing but friendship between us because I'm committed to someone else." The words came out harsher than he intended, and he felt like dirt when she sucked in a sharp breath, the flare of her eyes registering a hurt he had never meant to cause.

"Aw, Bug." Expelling a weary sigh, he pulled her into his arms, tucking his head to hers. "I meant to tell you in my letters, but I couldn't bring myself to put it in writing, hoping it wouldn't come to pass. Pop has hoped and prayed for an alliance between me and the daughter of a dear friend for years now, but I've conveniently ignored it." His eyes weighted closed at the prospect of his father in financial ruin. "Until now."

He felt her tremble when she clutched him tentatively like the little girl she used to be, her voice a fragile whisper. "So it's true then—you've been courting Amelia Darlington?"

The very name jolted him all over again, reminding him his life was no longer his own, but a gift of restitution to the father he'd wronged. "Not courting exactly, Bug, at least not yet, but a commitment all the same that prevents me from following my heart in any other direction." He pulled back, his heart bleeding at the sadness in her eyes. "Do you . . . understand?"

She nodded with a soft sniff, and the little girl he'd fallen in love with claimed his heart all over again.

"Oh, Meg." He swallowed her up in another hug, pressing his lips to the silky touch of her hair. The clean scent of violets and Pear's soap took him back to when their relationship was wholesome and safe and a refuge for them both. He kneaded the nape of her neck like the big brother he needed to be, desperate to protect a friendship threatened by feelings he had no business entertaining.

Ever.

"I miss our friendship, Bug," he said quietly, "and I want it back."

"Me too," she whispered, the gentle pat of her fingers on his back easing the ache in his soul. She pulled away with a tremulous smile, eyes glossy with resignation that both soothed and saddened. "So it would appear, Mr. Hughes, that both of us have some adapting to do."

He managed a smile. "Agreed, Miss McClare, and since you have proven to possess great intellect and insight over the years through umpteen victories at chess and cribbage, perhaps you can enlighten me as to how we should navigate this new friendship between two adults."

Dispensing a final pat, she sat back against the seat with a pert lift of her chin. "Quite simply, Mr. Hughes. Now that we've established that friendship is to be our happy fate, you will continue to be my hero and champion as big brother and friend, and I will continue to fine-tune your humility with impossible bouts of chess."

Bram laughed, unable to resist a tug of her ear. "And what makes you think I won't be fine-tuning *your* humility, young lady?"

Meg scrunched her nose in a sassy manner that both surprised him and made him grin. "Because you, Abraham Joseph Hughes, are a sheer marshmallow when it comes to the feelings of others, so I suspect lessons of humility are something you go to great lengths *not* to impart.

He arched a brow. "Are you saying I let you win in chess all these years, Miss McClare?"

"As a matter of fact I am, mostly," she said, the sparkle in her eyes matching the gleam of a perfect smile. "But that's about to change because I've been tutored for the last year by none other than Dr. Harold Rousseau, chess expert extraordinaire."

The sound of his deep laughter caused the boys to look up from their game of marbles as Bram hopped to the sidewalk with a grin. Shaking his head, he rounded the vehicle to assist Meg from the car. "Ah-hah—this new phase of our friendship promises challenge at last."

"You haven't *seen* challenge," she quipped, rising to allow Bram to help her down from her seat.

His husky chuckle filled the air, buoying his spirits. *Challenge, oh yes.* Hands to her waist, he whisked her to the street, her slim body a mere wisp of a feather despite ample curves.

She peered up with a disarming smile, convincing him that her statement bore more truth than he liked—his challenge was, indeed, just beginning. With a sassy tilt of her head, she gave him a look that was pure imp. "So if I were you, my friend, I'd prepare to surrender."

Prepare to surrender? Smiling, he offered his arm to escort her to the door, his manner light but his resolve as heavy as the guilt that weighted his shoulders.

Not in a million years.

10

*H*adley eased the Packard up to the curb in front of the Hall of Justice on Kearney Street, and Meg prayed her breakfast would stay put. Her eyes scanned up the imposing pink clock tower soaring high above the elaborate brick-and-terracotta building that held court over Portsmouth Square. Just like the district attorney's office held court over the crime in the city. A knot jogged in her throat as she stared at her future, the bleating of autos and sounds of children's laughter in Portsmouth Square barely audible over the pulse pounding in her ears.

As if sensing her trepidation, her mother reached to squeeze Meg's hand. "The district attorney's office is going to love you, darling, I promise."

"And you already know Mr. Turner, Megs, so it's not like everyone will be total strangers." Alli patted her knee.

Hadley opened the door and stepped aside, waiting to help Meg alight.

She gulped, suddenly not all that sure. "But there's so little I know about law, Mother—what if I'm a hindrance instead of a help?"

"Oh, boo," Alli said with a thrust of her chin. "You have a brilliant mind, Megs, so hold your head high and teach them a thing or two."

Her mother stretched across Alli to press a kiss to Megan's cheek, her voice soft and low. "You're going to shine, Megs, you mark my words. Just remember our prayer this morning, darling, that the Lord goeth before thee and will be with thee. He will not fail thee nor forsake thee, so fear not and neither be dismayed."

At her mother's words, Megan closed her eyes. The tension in her stomach slowly uncoiled as she breathed in deeply, filling her lungs and her mind with the calming peace that only came from a rock-solid faith. Lashes lifting, she expelled all anxiety with a slow exhale, the smile on her face brimming with a quiet confidence and hope. "Thank you, Mother." She stroked her mother's cheek, eyes misting at the love she saw in her eyes and Alli's. "I love you both so very much, and I'll be praying we all have a wonderful day."

She blew a kiss to each of them, then took Hadley's proffered hand to step down from the car, excitement replacing her fear. "Thank you, Hadley," she said with a light squeeze of his gloved hand. "Wish me luck."

The barest of smiles shadowed his lips as he closed the car door behind her, turning to offer a slight bow of his silver head. "Pardon me if you will, young miss, but luck is not paramount for one who possesses such intelligence and faith."

"Oh, Hadley!" Meg lifted on tiptoe to kiss his weathered cheek, his kindness bringing a sheen of tears to her eyes. "You are such a blessing to us all, you dear man."

"As are you, young miss." He nodded toward the steps that led to an arched doorway. "And in there as well. Godspeed, Miss Megan." With another short bow, he rounded the vehicle and started the car, allowing her one final wave before the Packard chugged away.

Spinning on her heel, Meg adjusted the wide lapels of her navy linen walking suit, its Eton jacket open at the bodice to reveal a silk pleated shirtwaist with high-neck collar. The crisp white blouse was a perfect complement to the white piping on her floor-length hem and slim cuffs. She brushed her damp palms down the smooth lines of her gored skirt, still not used to the soft swell of slim hips that gently curved beneath her tiny waist. Inhaling deeply, she drew in air laced with the sweet scent of gardenias from a row of bushes lining the walk. "Okay," she whispered, releasing a wavering breath as she scaled the steps, "ready or not, here I come."

The marble lobby pulsed with activity like Meg's body pulsed with anticipation. The notion she'd be working shoulder-to-shoulder with the district attorney and his team raced her heart more than her sprint up the stairs, her drawstring reticule bouncing as much as she. Two flights up, she stopped short at the sight of a bubbled glass door emblazoned with the circular Seal of the City and County of San Francisco. A rich and glorious emblem, the seal boasted a miner and a sailor on either side of a steamer entering the Golden Gate while a Phoenix proudly perched above in a bed of flames. Pride swelled in her chest over the rich heritage of her city, a formidable city, Uncle Logan always said, built on commerce, agriculture, and mining.

Her gaze trailed to the gold letters that thickened her throat. *District Attorney Offices of San Francisco.*

Her eyes flickered closed. *Fear not and neither be dismayed. The Lord goeth before me and will be with me . . .*

The door flew open and Megan jumped with a little squeak as a tall man barreled out, sending her hand flying to her chest along with her reticule.

"Oh, pardon me." Andrew Turner stood in the doorway with an attaché in one hand, as startled as she. His clean-cut Nordic hair boasted a hint of silver at the temples, providing a distinguished frame for light-blue eyes and a chiseled jaw. "May I help you, miss?"

Megan's pulse stuttered when she realized Mr. Turner didn't recognize her. "Good morning, Mr. Turner—I'm Megan McClare, and I can't thank you enough for this incredible opportunity to work in your office this summer."

"Meg?" A slow smile worked its way across his handsome face as he surveyed her head to toe, mouth dangling open in a smile. "Well, I'll be. Cait told me Paris was good for you, but I had no idea just how good." He pulled a pocket watch from his gray pinstriped waistcoat and grinned. "And thirty minutes early? I like that in an intern."

Hooking her arm, he ushered her into a large but stark reception area with scuffed hardwood floors and wooden chairs, its dirty white walls sporting faded photos of the city. The room seemed oppressive despite the glare of an overhead light and large window, where a yellowed shade completely blocked out the sun. Laughter drifted from somewhere down a wide hall that opened in the center of the room, spilling sunlight from a row of offices on both sides.

Mr. Turner angled to face a shy, bookish girl hunched over an antiquated desk, her stooped shoulders and awkward manner instantly striking a chord. About Alli's age, the young woman wore a severe and tightly pulled bun at the nape of her neck and horn-rimmed glasses that greatly magnified eyes the color of fresh caramel. The owlish effect lent a studious air to a skinny frame that appeared quite tall. Her lenses were even thicker than Meg's own, which prompted an immediate kinship. Somehow Meg suspected she, too, had been the object of ridicule among her peers, much like Meg herself.

Bracing a hand to Megan's back, Andrew offered his reception-ist a smile that prompted a blush, highlighting beautiful cheek-bones Meg hadn't noticed before. "Bonnie, I'd like to introduce you to Miss Megan McClare, who is interning with us this summer." He turned to slip Megan a wink. "Megan, this is my right hand, Miss Bonnie Roof, whose talent for organization and stenogra-phy is second to none." Andrew leaned close, his whisper loud enough to elicit a shy smile from the blushing girl on the other side of the desk. "Bonnie is my secretary and the most important person in this office who all but carries me, but don't spread that around." He winked at Meg. "I need this job."

Bonnie rose and extended a hand to Meg, her lanky frame rising to a height that surpassed Meg's five foot three by a head. "It's a pleasure to meet you, Miss McClare—Mr. Turner has spoken highly of you."

"Thank you, Miss Roof," Meg said, shaking the girl's hand. "And, please—my friends call me Meg, so I hope you will too, since I'm sure we'll be good friends."

Surprise flared in Bonnie's eyes before a genuine grin slid across her face, revealing a lovely smile with perfectly white teeth. "Thank you Miss Mc—" She nodded. "I mean, Meg."

"Bonnie, will you call Howard and tell him I'll be up shortly for our meeting—I want to introduce Meg to the rest of the team before I go."

"Yes, sir." Bonnie reached for the receiver of a candlestick phone, offering Meg a final smile. "Welcome, Meg—I'm glad you're here."

Laugher and male voices rose in volume as Mr. Turner led Meg down the hall, identifying his own spacious office overlooking Portsmouth Square before he stopped in front of a much smaller office just beyond. At his presence, all chatter ceased while three pairs of legs tumbled to the floor from where they'd been perched on a disheveled desk, clunking so loudly Meg had to stifle a smile.

"Ah, your taxes hard at work, Miss McClare," Mr. Turner said with a jovial tone that indicated he was anything but a hard taskmaster. "Allow me to introduce my very capable staff—*when* they're working, that is." He extended a hand toward a towering young man behind the desk whom he introduced as George Crane. Meg couldn't thwart a grin over the suitability of Mr. Crane's name. He was a scholarly looking man who resembled one of her favorite literary characters—Ichabod Crane from *The Legend of Sleepy Hollow*. A ruddy shade of red crept up his pleasant face, causing a very pronounced Adam's apple to bob furiously in his throat.

"George is my executive assistant district attorney or second-in-command, overseeing daily activities, supervision of specialized divisions, hiring staff, and prosecuting some of the larger crimes within our jurisdiction." Mr. Turner nodded to Meg, eyes scanning the other two gentlemen who stood stiff as soldiers on either side of Mr. Crane's desk. "Gentlemen, this is Miss Megan McClare, valedictorian of St. Vincent's and our intern for the summer as well as future lawyer in this office, I hope." He hooked a protective arm over Meg's shoulder. "Not only is Megan like family to me, but her mother is president of the Vigilance Committee, which is also an important part of my life, so I'm hoping you'll provide any assistance she may need."

"Absolutely," all three men agreed, their voices cracking in unison.

Mr. Turner cleared his throat in what appeared to be an attempt to suppress a grin, turning his attention to the two men who stood on either side of Mr. Crane. "Mr. Theodore Burkle is my senior assistant attorney," he said, extending a hand at a rather rotund young man with carrot red hair the same color as Meg's before she applied the darker henna rinse. "Which only means he's been here longer than the next guy in line." The buttons on Theodore's silk vest seemed ready to pop, the blush on his plump cheeks barely obscured a sea of freckles across a kindly face with gentle brown eyes. "We call him Teddy, not in honor of the president, mind you," he said with a twinkle in a gaze warm with affection, "but because he's so gentle and large, he reminds us of the president's namesake—the teddy bear."

"Aw, boss . . ." All freckles disappeared with a gorge of blood to the poor man's cheeks, tingeing his ears pink.

"Sorry, Teddy, but Megan needs to know who she can go to if our junior assistant district attorney there gives her any problems." He nodded at the other man who was standing beside George's desk with hip slacked and hands in his pockets. Easily the most attractive of the three, he delivered a slow smile that transferred some of the heat from Teddy's cheeks to Meg's. "Meet Conor O'Neil, junior assistant district attorney and office rogue, so stay away from him or your mother will have my head."

Conor gave her an easy nod, his thick dark hair the exact shade of shuttered ebony eyes that pierced hers in spite of a lazy smile. "Definitely my pleasure, Miss McClare."

Meg offered a weak smile, averting her gaze to George and Teddy. "I'm looking forward to assisting in any way I can and please—call me Meg."

"Then I'd say work just got a great deal more appealing, 'Meg,'" Conor said with a wink.

"See what I mean?" Mr. Turner nabbed her arm with a low chuckle, steering her back into the hall. "Conor's a bit of a ladies' man, so just ignore him and he'll be fine, all right?"

Meg nodded, fighting a gulp while Mr. Turner tugged her to

a larger cubbyhole area right off the conference room. More of a galley kitchen than an office, the room featured a sink, a small icebox, and a coffee percolator. A pretty brunette sat typing at a compact desk in the corner, fingers flying in front of built-in shelves that boasted neatly stacked supplies. The moment Andrew moved into the cozy space, heavy lashes lifted to reveal hazel eyes caught by surprise while a smile curved on full lips. "Good morning, Mr. Turner—I didn't expect to see you till this afternoon due to your meeting." She patted the back of her perfectly coifed pompadour, offering a coy tip of her head.

Andrew glanced at his watch, brow furrowing in a wince. "Good morning, Linda Marie, and yes, I have a meeting this morning with Mr. Tepper, but I wanted to introduce our new intern for the summer before I left." He cupped the back of Meg's neck, making her feel like a little girl in front of a sophisticated woman whose smile seemed to fade a tad when her eyes lighted on Meg. "I'd like to introduce Miss Megan McClare, who will be interning with us this summer." He tweaked Megan's neck before resting his hand on her shoulder, a subtle implication of a casual relationship that thinned Linda Marie's smile considerably. "Megan, Linda Marie Finn is our all-around secretary—research, typing, proofing, ordering supplies, and filling in for Bonnie when she needs it." He gave Linda Marie a wink. "And she makes the best coffee I've ever tasted, bar none."

Eyes narrowing a degree, Linda Marie offered a smile Meg's way that seemed as stiff as her starched white shirtwaist, its snug fit accenting an ample bodice. "What exactly will Miss McClare's duties be, Mr. Turner?" she asked sweetly, the steel edge of her tone not lost on Meg.

"Meg has aspirations to work in this very office as a lawyer someday, so her experience here will be to that end. Which means she'll work closely with George and his team in any legal capacity they need, including maintaining and organizing briefs, conducting legal research, and drafting documents." He braced her arm, giving it a paternal pat. "Megan is a lawyer in the making, Linda Marie, not a secretary, and it's my hope this internship will give her a leg up. I'll need you to help her get settled if you don't mind—personal paperwork, directions to the restrooms, general introductions to departments in the building, especially Mrs. Beata Andrianova in the district court clerk's office. Then that will get Meg off to a good start, all right?"

"Yes, sir." It was hard to miss the cool tenor of Linda Marie's tone, although Andrew didn't seem to notice.

"We'll let you get back to work then," he said with a smile.

"It's nice to meet you, Linda Marie," Megan said with a soft duck of her head, praying the woman's dour welcome was not an indication of the type of relationship they would have.

With two friendly taps on her arm to signal their departure, Andrew guided her out and into a conference room that surely spanned the entire length of the hallway, boasting a beautifully crafted cherrywood table with burlwood insets along an oval edge. Sunlight streamed through a bank of tall windows along the outside wall, giving the room a warm, welcoming feeling despite its large size. "This is where you'll spend a lot of your time, Meg—observing depositions, plea-bargain negotiations, client meetings, staff meetings, research, what have you." He indicated the far side of the room where an entire wall offered a floor-to-ceiling library. "The bright lighting and extensive law library makes this the ideal spot for research since you can spread papers and books to your heart's content. And, of course," he said with a wink, waving toward cherry-paneled walls resplendent with gilded-framed artwork, "it's relaxing in here with high-class decor that helps intimidate the defense attorneys when needed."

He steered her back into the hall and then into an office across from Linda Marie's, nudging her with a palm to the small of her back. "This is the spare room we use for interns, specialty attorneys, or extra help when needed, so for now, this will be your office."

My office! Meg's pulse sped up, the good-size room lending a cozy air with two desks and a wall of file cabinets along one side. Brass lamps and framed maps and pictures of the city graced the walls, evoking a comfortable, businesslike feel. The entire wall behind the side-by-side desks was filled with volume after volume of rich leather books, infusing the cozy room with the sacred scent of a fine library. "It's perfect," she whispered, breathing in the wonderful smell of leather and lemon oil while she skimmed her fingers across a freshly polished desk.

He chuckled. "Yes, well we can't have our visitors and interns working out of a storeroom, now can we?"

She whirled around, a sheen of gratitude blurring her eyes. "Oh, Mr. Turner, I am so very grateful, sir, and will do everything in my power to be a credit to your fine department."

"I have no doubt, young lady," Andrew said with a kind smile. "You possess the same quiet strength and intelligence I see in your mother, Megan, two attributes that will serve you well, both in your chosen career and in this office." His smile eased into a sheepish grin as he scratched the back of his neck. "Of course, it's no secret I'd do anything for her or her children."

No, none at all . . . Meg smiled. "I assure you, Mr. Turner, her gratitude is as boundless as mine, and I honestly don't know how I can ever thank you for this incredible opportunity."

He checked his timepiece again and then snapped it shut with a teasing wink. "Well, you could always throw in a good word for me with your mother." His offhanded tease warmed her cheeks, Andrew Turner's interest in her mother an uncomfortable subject. "I'm gone for most of the day, but get acclimated to your new surroundings, Meg, then Linda Marie will run you through the paces with general office orientation before George assigns your first task, all right?"

"Yes, sir."

He gave her a quick salute before leaving her alone to ponder her fate.

Linda Marie will run you through the paces.

Meg gulped, the sharp tap-tap-tap of a typewriter all too loud from across the hall. "Yes," she whispered, placing her reticule on the desk with shaky fingers. She sucked in a deep breath. "I'm quite sure."

11

"Thank you, Lord, for this food and the hands that prepared it . . ." Caitlyn's tone was reverent as she said grace, offering a peek of a smile at Rosie and Hadley while they stood at the kitchen door, hands clasped at their waists. Her gaze strayed to Logan at the other end of the table, head bent and eyes closed like the rest of her family, and her pulse skipped a beat. "And please, Lord, bless our evening with laughter and fun, peace, and harmony . . ."

Especially harmony, she thought with a tiny tumble of her stomach, well aware Logan's last two dinners with the family had been marred by impromptu visits from Andrew. Once for Vigilance Committee business and a second time to discuss his desire to throw Meg a homecoming/internship celebration at the brand-new St. Francis Hotel. It was bad enough Meg was interning for Andrew instead of Logan, but she was certain that Logan would see the dinner at The St. Francis as just another of Andrew's ploys to upstage Logan with his family.

The Palace Hotel—where Logan lived in a penthouse suite— had been the crème de la crème of San Francisco society since 1875, but by seven o'clock on the evening of March 21st, 1904, that all changed when The St. Francis opened its doors, boasting a line of carriages and automobiles that stretched three blocks.

The new darling of high society, The St. Francis was now *the* place for Nob Hill nobility to see and be seen, and Caitlyn suspected Andrew was anxious to show off his new apartment suite. Which would drive Logan crazy when she finally got the nerve to tell him. *But not tonight—the week of his birthday.* She was determined to soothe Logan's ruffled feathers with a wonderful evening with family where she doted on him and praised his sure win at cribbage. Picking at her nails beneath the linen tablecloth, she silently beseeched God to quell this growing unease Andrew seemed to be causing between Logan and her. With a silent sigh, she finished saying grace and looked up with a smile. "Amen."

At her nod, Rosie and Hadley disappeared into the kitchen while Caitlyn placed her napkin in her lap, sending a bright smile to where Meg sat mid-table, chatting with Bram on her left. "So, Meg darling, I for one am most anxious to hear about your first day of internship," she said, wanting to get the subject out and over with so the family could ask their questions and move on. *Before* Logan's mood soured.

Meg glanced up, the twinkle in her eyes a key indicator it had been a very good day. "Oh, Mother, it was absolutely more than I ever dreamed," she gushed, cheeks abloom with excitement—a response that Caitlyn noticed put a crimp between Logan's thick dark brows. "Mr. Turner absolutely couldn't have been nicer, and his assistant district attorneys either. Oh, and I feel like the head secretary, Bonnie, and I really hit it off." She expelled a sigh as contented as the smile on her face. "I just know we're going to be good friends, which is just icing on the cake."

"Mmm . . . ," Alli said with a grin. "Any 'delicious' prospects as far as the male variety on this so-called cake?"

Meg laughed, diving into her salad with gusto. "Actually, yes, because they are all very 'sweet,' as a matter of fact, especially Mr.

Turner's chief assistant George Crane, who, I might add, is a dead ringer for Ichabod Crane."

Cassie elbowed Alli's arm with a chuckle. "Not so good, I don't think, especially if he's holding a pumpkin."

Chuckles echoed around the table as Meg continued, ignoring the quirk of Bram's brow when she exchanged her darker roll for his lighter one. "Goodness, George spent the entire afternoon explaining procedures, legal terminology, what have you. He's extremely knowledgeable."

"All right, all right," Alli said with a wild wave of her knife, "let's move on from Mr. Pumpkinhead, shall we? Any other handsome prospects?"

Meg ducked to avoid the knife, consequently bumping Bram's arm. He blinked when the tomato on his fork plopped into his water goblet with a splash, tugging a smile to Caitlyn's lips.

"Uh-oh." Meg giggled while Bram fished the tomato from his glass with a spoon. "Sorry, Bram," she said, hiding her grin with a hand to her lips, "but Alli made me do it."

He popped the tomato in his mouth, eyeing Meg and Alli through narrow eyes. "You ladies are a liability at the dinner table, but all is forgiven if you keep your mitts off my food."

"Hear, hear," Jamie said with a grunt, slapping Cassie's hand away when she tried to filch an olive from his salad.

"Anyway, to answer your question, Al . . ." Meg paused, a blush tingeing her cheeks as she peeked at her brother with a sheepish smile. "Yes, one of the three assistants is particularly handsome, but he reminds me of Blake in that he's a bit of a flirt."

"Hey, that doesn't have to be a bad thing," Blake muttered, dousing his salad with pepper.

Bram chuckled while he buttered his roll. "Only if your nickname is Rake."

"Anyway," Meg continued, "he's actually very nice although he does like to play the devil's advocate with poor Theodore Burkle, a dear young man everyone calls Teddy. And the name certainly fits because he's as sweet and cuddly as a teddy bear and just as softhearted."

"The 'devil's' advocate, you say?" Jamie slapped Blake on the back. "Hey, Rake, he's sounding more like you all the time."

Caitlyn bit back a grin, hoping to steer the conversation into safer waters. "Any other females in this male bastion of law?"

Meg sighed. "Only another secretary," she said with a scrunch of brows. "She's very pretty and about Alli's age, but she doesn't seem to like me."

"Nonsense, sweetheart." Uncle Logan nodded his thanks when Hadley offered iced tea. "Who could possibly not like a sweet, bright, beautiful girl like you?"

"Mmm, maybe a jealous female?" Alli ventured, offering Meg a conciliatory smile.

Meg absently grated her lip. "Maybe. It's possible she resented Mr. Turner's fawning over me like he did because after he left, she wasn't a bit nice. And the way she looked at him, it almost seemed like she had a crush on him."

"I wouldn't be surprised," Cassie said with a roll of her eyes. "Mr. Turner is certainly handsome."

Logan scowled.

"So, do you think you'll enjoy the job, darling?" Caitlyn said quickly. Anything to steer the conversation away from Andrew.

Meg pursed her lips, as if considering all facets of the job. "I really do, Mother. Mr. Turner couldn't have been nicer, but it's really his staff that gives his office a warm, cozy feel, as if they're a tight-knit team, so I'm anxious to become a part of it."

Rosie and Hadley arrived with the main course, and Caitlyn

expelled a silent sigh of relief, grateful when Jamie and Bram embarked on a ribbing campaign regarding one of Blake's latest cases. When dessert had been delivered and devoured—apple pie, one of Logan's favorites, no less—Caitlyn thanked Rosie and Hadley for a wonderful meal and rose. Easing her chair in, she smiled at Logan as he leaned back with a satisfied look, deftly unbuttoning his silk vest. "Don't get too comfortable, Mr. McClare," she said with a hint of jest, "you still have to battle me in a game of cribbage, you know."

Her stomach fluttered when he peered up beneath a shuttered gaze, wine glass in hand and head resting on the back of his chair. "Comfort isn't even an option, Cait, when I'm matching wits with you," he drawled, obviously relaxed from the rare glass of wine she'd allowed in honor of his birthday.

"Pity," she said with a secret smile as she rounded the table, ruffling Blake's hair. "I do so want you to be comfortable and unaware when I put you in your place."

He rose and tossed his napkin down while he eyed her with a faint smile, pushing his chair in before offering his arm. "Where's that, Mrs. McClare—the winner's column, as usual?"

"Oooo, sounds like a challenge to me," Blake quipped, patting his hair back down.

"And you should know." Jamie rose and pulled out Cassie's chair. "Because everything's a challenge to you." Both he and Cassie tousled Blake's hair as they passed.

"Hey, what's with the hair tonight?" Blake groused, smoothing it back as he rose from his seat. "Just for that, MacKenna, I challenge you to a card game of your choice—*if* you're brave enough." He sent Caitlyn a smirk. "And Mother—for starting trouble? I hope you lose."

Caitlyn shot Blake a serene smile as Logan ushered her from

the room. "Of course I'll lose, son, it's your uncle's birthday—it's part of my gift."

"Ha!" Blake and Logan said in unison.

"Oh, and Blake," Caitlyn said over her shoulder, "comb your hair, darling—it's a mess."

"My, my . . ." Logan slid her a crooked grin. "Aren't we feeling our oats tonight."

She tipped her head to give him a playful smile. "As well we should, Mr. McClare—this is a very special and remarkable birthday week in this household."

His eyes softened. "Thanks, Cait," he whispered, then tossed Megan a wink. "But I'd say 'special and remarkable' in this household is when you beat me at cribbage."

"Goodness, Uncle Logan," Meg said, the tease in her tone matching the twinkle in her eyes, "don't you know 'pride goeth before the fall'? Just ask Bram."

"I beg your pardon." Bram tweaked Meg's neck on their way to the parlour, the rest of the crew following with banter and chatter that warmed Caitlyn's heart. Releasing a contented sigh, she smiled up at Logan as he seated her at the cribbage table while Bram and Meg settled in for a game of chess. Maddie's giggles rose when Blake tossed her over his shoulder to follow Cassie, Alli, and Jamie to the card table Logan had given them for Christmas. Although the parlour was a good size, Caitlyn had argued that two game tables—one for chess and one for cribbage—were more than enough, but Logan had insisted on yet another. Extravagantly carved with wooden claw feet and plush leather chairs, the circular table boasted a green felt top with burlwood edging and looked suspiciously like a poker table. Of course, Logan quickly informed her that felt topping merely aided in the shuffling of cards for games of a more innocent

102

Julie Lessman

nature, so she'd finally consented. And now she had to admit she was grateful for a cozy room in which everyone could enjoy their game of choice.

Settling into her padded needlepoint chair next to the hearth, she leaned in with arms folded on the table, watching Logan while he commenced to shuffling the cards. "You *did* reserve Saturday night for your birthday dinner, I hope? The children begged to celebrate at the Cliff House, so I thought a family dinner would be lovely in one of their private parlours after browsing the art and photo museums."

The cards fanned together in a perfect whoosh before he slapped the deck in the center of the table with a grin. "Sure—I can always use a little culture. Never have seen the displays."

Caitlyn's jaw dropped into an open-mouthed smile. "Logan McClare, are you telling me with all the Cliff House functions you've attended over the last eight years that you have *never* once stepped foot into Adolph Sutro's fabulous galleries? Have you no culture?"

"If not, it's your fault," he said with an off-center grin, his nod at the deck of cards indicating she should take the first cut to determine the deal. "How many times have I asked you to accompany me to the opera or poetry readings at Montgomery Block, only to be turned down cold?" His lip quirked. "At the Block's Adolph Sutro library, no less?"

Her cheeks warmed as she focused on cutting the cards, avoiding his eyes. "You know very well I make it a rule to never go out without my children."

"Yes, I do, Cait, better than anyone. And if you recall, I invited the children on each and every occasion, but they were less than enthused about a wonderful evening with either Puccini's *Madame Butterfly* or essay readings by Mark Twain."

103

A smile twitched at the edge of her lips despite the discomfort of the conversation as she remembered with perfect clarity her children's moaning and groaning when Logan had invited them along. Almost as much as she'd moaned silently over missing two productions she had very much wanted to see. But an evening alone with Logan that might be misconstrued as a date by either her family or high society had not been her idea of a "wonderful evening."

He won the cut and proceeded to shuffle the deck again. "And I know for a fact that both Puccini and Twain are strong favorites of yours, Mrs. McClare, which means it's unequivocally your fault if I lack in culture."

She peeked up beneath a veil of lashes, cheeks still hot. "I'm not the only woman in San Francisco, Logan—I'm certain the list is quite long of those who'd be delighted for an evening of culture with one of the city's most eligible bachelors."

His gaze never strayed from her face as he laid the deck down for another cut, his faint smile at deadly odds with the sobriety in those piercing gray eyes. "I already told you once, Cait, that I haven't been with another woman since Napa, and as far as you not being the only woman in San Francisco, I beg to differ." She made the cut and he dealt six cards face down to each of them, his penetrating stare all but searing her face. "You are for me."

"Awk, awk, ace in the hole, ace in the hole . . ."

Never had Caitlyn appreciated Miss B.'s poker squawks more than at that exact moment, and she took full advantage, head jerking to glance at the game table where Blake was dealing a deck of cards. She hefted her chin in a show of mock displeasure. "Are you instigating a poker game, Blake McClare, because so help me if you are . . ."

Laughter circled the card table where Blake rallied with a good-natured scowl. "We're playing pinochle, Mother, and Cassie was taunting about having an ace in the hole as a figure of speech. But I'd like to know why you always assume *I'm* the one to blame?"

"Because you and your uncle are the only two troublemakers in this family, young man, when it comes to the corruption of poker and games of chance."

"Hey, that's not true," Blake argued, scrubbing Jamie's black curls till they stood up on end. "Cassie took a chance on this joker here, and if that's not a gamble, I don't know what is."

Cassie chuckled while she arranged her cards. "He does have a point."

Jamie slapped Blake's hand away with a scowl. "You're just jealous because now *I'm* the good son in this family." His gaze shifted to his wife with a dangerous smile. "And any more snide remarks from you, Mrs. MacKenna, and I'll be showing you 'trouble' at home."

Alli bumped shoulders with Cassie. "Not if she hog-ties you with her stinky rope, eh?"

Caitlyn shook her head and grinned, turning her attention back to the man whose narrow gaze was as thin as his smile. He arched a brow. "Troublemaker, Cait, really?"

She scraped her lip with her teeth, hoping a change of subject would sidetrack him from an awkward conversation. Picking up her six cards with an attempt at a casual air, she discarded two before gliding them to the crib hand at the side of the table. Logan followed suit at the exact same moment, and she caught her breath when a jolt of static electricity sparked at the touch of their fingers. Her breathing suddenly shallow, she quickly jerked away to cut the center cards once more per cribbage rules, then fixed her eyes on the deck while Logan turned the starter card up. "So, Logan," she said in a rush, "the children and I would like to get you something special for your birthday—what do you suggest?"

His pause drew her gaze. "You know what I want, Cait," he said quietly, the stark look of love in his eyes belying the half smile on his lips.

Heat swirled in her belly before it shot to her cheeks. Yes, she knew what he wanted, but he hadn't been so bold as to express it since she'd denied his request for courtship over eight months ago. The night she'd learned she couldn't trust him for a second time in her life.

As if sensing her sudden malaise, he gently grazed her arm, a hint of a jest in his tone. "But . . . since we both know I can't have *that*, then I suppose there *is* something else I'd like . . ."

The breath she'd been holding slowly seeped through her lips, which now curved in a grateful smile. "Anything, Logan, as long as it has nothing to do with poker or courtship."

He leaned in, dark eyes locked on hers. "Go to the Barrister Ball with me, Cait. With our boys attending this year, I want to be there too, and I've missed the last few because of you."

"B-because of me?" she repeated lamely, desperate to stall. Her hands were shaking so hard, she lowered them to the table, cribbage cards face down.

His fingers slowly brushed the tips of hers before sliding beneath to capture her hand, his thumb grazing her wrist as if to gauge her pulse. "I only want to go with you, Cait," he said softly, "no other woman but you, so show a little mercy to your brother-in-law, Mrs. McClare, and give me a birthday present I'll never forget . . ."

Oh, Logan, how I wish that I could . . . She gently eased her hand from his, adjusting her cards before she lifted her gaze. "You and I both know that the Barrister Ball is one of the social highlights of the season over which the society pages drool ad nauseum." Her stomach cramped at his look of disappointment, and with a ragged breath, she dropped her cards to the table and grasped his hand in hers. The intensity of her gaze, her hold, begged him to understand. "The last thing either of us needs are rumors running rampant that you and I are romantically linked."

"We're seen together all the time Cait—at church, at The Palace for brunch or dinner."

"But that's different, Logan, and you know it. My children are always with me, and you are their uncle after all, so it's nothing more than a family gathering."

A nerve twittered in his jaw. "Nothing more than a family gathering? Seriously? Is that all it is to you because that's not all it is to me."

Her cheeks flamed hot. "No, of course, Logan—I treasure your friendship, and I care about you a great deal, you know that. But the Barrister Ball is seen as a . . ." She swallowed hard. "Romantic event, if you will, for couples, be they married or—"

"Lovers?" he finished quietly, jaw tight. "And we're certainly not that, are we, Cait? Nor ever will be, will we?"

Tears stung at just how much his betrayal had stolen from them both. "Oh, Logan," she whispered, "I have no way of knowing the future. All I do know is that I'm not ready now."

He nodded, slipping his hand from hers to pick up his cards. "All right, Cait," he said with a heavy exhale of air. "At least you left me with a glimmer of hope, no matter how faint."

Her rib cage contracted with relief. "But you need to attend the ball, Logan," she said in a rush, desperate to coax him in that direction. "Truly there must be someone you can take."

His lips went flat. "There are dozens of women I could take, but I'm only in love with one. No, thanks, Cait—I'll pass." He reached for the walnut cribbage board and notched his peg two points. "Two for his heels," he said with a mock scowl, "so at least my luck is holding in cribbage if not love."

"Logan, I'm so sorry . . . ," she whispered.

His smile took a slant. "True, but not as sorry as you're going to be, Mrs. McClare, after I crush you in cribbage." He assessed his hand for several moments before his eyelids lifted halfway. "And trust me, Cait, it's going to hurt."

A muscle convulsed in her throat. "It already does," she said quietly. Before she could stop it, tears welled in her eyes. "I do love you, Logan—more than I can say."

He paused, studying her with an intensity that thickened her throat. "I know, Cait. And more than you can do, apparently."

"Pardon me, Miss Cait," Hadley said at the door, "Mr. Andrew Turner to see you."

A low growl rumbled from Logan's throat, which neatly matched the silent groan in her own. "Blast it, Cait—what's he doing here again?"

She glanced over her shoulder with a stiff smile. "Thank you, Hadley—I'd appreciate it if you would show him to the study for me."

"And I'd appreciate it if you'd show him to the street," Logan mumbled, slapping his cards on the table with no little force.

"Yes, miss, and scones with that tea?" Chin high, Hadley awaited her response.

"No, Hadley, *no* scones and *no* tea, please," she said too loudly, her tone so sharp that all chatter ceased with curious stares. "Mr. Turner won't be staying, so no refreshments are needed." She shot to her feet, heat climbing her neck as she attempted to placate Logan with a gentle smile. "Don't move a muscle—I will dispense of him posthaste."

Logan grunted. "I'd rather you let me dispense of him." He rose to rid himself of his coat. "And the devil with 'posthaste,'" he muttered, "I'll take postmortem."

Shaking her head, Cait hurried from the room, burying a smile beneath lips pinched tight. *Postmortem, indeed.* She sighed. *Right after I wring Andrew's neck . . .*

12

*S*houlders square, Caitlyn marched from the room with steel in her spine and temper in a flare, determined to give Andrew Turner a stern talking to as far as his habit of dropping in unannounced. *Especially* on nights when Logan was here. She had enough trouble containing Logan's temper where Andrew was concerned—she didn't need any more thorns in Logan's side.

Andrew was staring out the French doors when she entered the study, his charcoal suit coat straining broad shoulders with hands clasped to his back, fedora dangling from his thumb. She paused to study the man Logan McClare hated and completely understood why. Andrew Turner challenged Logan in every way—in the courtroom, in politics, in social circles, in wealth, in his appeal to women and, she thought with a quiet exhale, in his attention to her. Like Logan, Andrew had his choice of women to court and yet Cait couldn't help but wonder if part of Andrew's attraction to her stemmed from his rivalry with the man who'd once been his best friend. A competition, if you will, like the night she'd first met them both at The Palace so many years ago, when he and Logan had vied for her attention and Logan had won. A wispy sigh escaped her lips. *While both Andrew and I had lost . . . .*

Arming herself with a deep breath, she pushed the door half closed with a faint squeal. He spun around, a broad smile spanning his face that might have tripped her pulse if Logan were not so firmly entrenched in her life. *And* in her heart.

"Cait!" He crossed the room in three powerful strides, taking her hands in his. "You look beautiful this evening, Mrs. McClare, as always."

Some of her anger thawed as she gently tugged her hands free, gliding past him to seat herself at her desk, determined to put some distance between them. Back straight and hands folded on her leather blotter, she hitched her chin into business mode, offering a smile she hoped was both warm and distant at the same time. "Thank you, Andrew, you're very kind. To what do I owe this honor, your visit at this late hour of the evening?"

A sheepish smile shadowed his lips as he slowly moved forward, fiddling with the hat in his hands like a little boy who'd been caught pilfering from a cookie jar. He promptly disarmed her with a mischievous smile, rendering an apology that held not a hint of regret. "Forgive me, Cait, I know I shouldn't just barge in whenever I feel like it, but honestly, if you had any idea how often I feel like it, you would have great admiration for my restraint."

Exhaling, she shook her head, unable to thwart the smile that tugged at her lips. "Andrew, Andrew—what am I going to do with you?" she said softly.

Laying his hat on her desk, he promptly perched on the corner with a casual fold of arms. His blue eyes glimmered like his wheat-blond hair in the light of the crystal chandelier. "Oh, I don't know—court me, I hope?"

She pursed her lips, fighting the smile that itched to break free. "*Why* are you here, Mr. Turner?" she repeated with another heft of her chin.

"Okay, Cait, I can see I interrupted your evening and I regret that, really I do—"

"Now why do I have trouble believing that?" she said with a tilt of her head, brow arched like a schoolmarm addressing a wayward student.

He hopped up to loom over her desk, palms flat and eyes twinkling like that wayward student he so reminded her of. "Why? Probably because I've been hounding you for months to go out with me. And no doubt you suspect tonight is more of the same with the added incentive of riling Logan so much, you'll say yes just to make me stop. Which," he said with a devilish smile, "would be very close to the truth if I didn't have a better reason."

She folded her arms to ward off succumbing to his little-boy charm, allowing him a patient smile. "And that would be . . . ?"

Slipping his hands in his pockets, he stood straight up, rocking back on his heels with a proud grin. "We did it, Cait—the Vigilance Committee now has the force of Terrible Terry behind it. Father Caraher has agreed to a much closer, more focused association."

With a catch of her breath, her lips parted in a breathless smile as she shot to her feet. "Oh, Andrew, seriously?" Her hand flew to her mouth, the news causing her heart to thud. Not only did the Vigilance Committee have the powerful support of the district attorney's office, but now the most prolific and vocal advocate for morality in San Francisco! Father Terence Caraher, pastor of St. Francis of Assisi Catholic Church, was chairman of the Committee on Morals of the North Beach Promotion Association. It had been Father Caraher's relentless crusade against the vile Nymphia brothel that finally forced it to close last year. *And soon*, Caitlyn thought with a skip of her pulse, *the same would happen for the Marsicania and the Municipal Crib—the two biggest prostitution blights in the Barbary Coast.*

A sense of giddiness bubbled up and Caitlyn laughed, rushing around the desk to squeeze Andrew's hand, quite certain her face had to be glowing. "Oh, Andrew, just imagine—joining forces to shut down both the Marsicania and the Municipal Crib! It's almost too good to be true."

He took both of her hands in his, his tone as soft as his eyes. "Now, Cait, I don't want you to be disappointed, but you and I both know this will be one step at a time—first the Marsicania, then we set our sights on the Municipal Crib."

Some of her euphoria faded. "But why? Wouldn't now be the best time to go after the Municipal Crib, with it barely open a month? Heaven knows the momentum is on our side with all the free press Fremont Older has given us in the *Evening Bulletin*."

"Yes, and Fremont is laying the groundwork for us to tackle the Municipal Crib down the road, but right now, we need to focus our efforts on the Marsicania, and Father Caraher agrees. Believe me, Cait, what we're doing here will trigger a domino effect this city has never seen, sweeping depravity out of the Barbary Coast and into the sea." He ducked to stare into her eyes, his gaze tender. "Remember the homily this week? 'Be not therefore anxious for the morrow: for the morrow will be anxious for itself. Sufficient unto the day is the evil thereof.'" His voice lowered to a whisper. "Which means, we need to take this one day at a time, step-by-step."

She took a deep breath and allowed it to escape in a shaky exhale, disappointed at the slow pace they needed to keep. "All right, Andrew—as district attorney, you certainly have your finger on the pulse of what we need to do more than I, so I respect your leadership in this."

"Thank you," he said softly, unsettling her further when his thumb slowly circled the palm of her hand. "You have no idea how much that means to me, Cait."

She attempted to pull away, but he held on, halting her retreat with a gentle grip. "There's just one more thing I need to tell you, but you're not going to like it. Or at least, Logan won't like it."

A cold chill slithered across her skin, countering the warmth Andrew's touch had created. She swallowed hard, not anxious to hear anything that would disrupt her peace with Logan any more than Andrew already had. "What?" she said, her voice a near rasp.

He studied her for several moments, brows pinched as if deciding how to impart news he needed to share. "Father Caraher's main hesitation in joining forces with the Vigilance Committee thus far has been his objection to lengthy time parameters outlined in your original proposal to the Board of Supervisors. So . . . his partnership is contingent upon implementing parts of phase two sooner than we planned." He paused, weighting his words with a probing stare. "Which means going after the dance and gambling halls now rather than later."

She blinked, the magnitude of what he was proposing tumbling her stomach. *Gambling halls.* Including several of Logan's business holdings in the Barbary Coast, like the Blue Moon, where Jamie used to work and his mother still did. Her eyelids weighted closed, remembering with perfect clarity her insistence to Logan that phase two would not be overnight, and likely not for another three years at least.

"Cait, I know you proposed a slower timetable of up to five years, but we lose ground if we don't tackle some of the smaller stuff along with the Marsicania." He lifted her chin, prompting her to open her eyes. The regret she saw there convinced her that Andrew's motives had nothing to do with Logan and everything to do with his own dream—and hers—to free their city from the depravity of the Barbary Coast. "Logan will understand, Cait, and ultimately it's for his good and that of any respectable business owners on the Coast."

A sigh quivered from her lips as she nodded, and Andrew drew her close as he'd done in the past when Vigilance Committee business had dragged her down. "The lives of hundreds of women and children are at stake, Cait," he whispered.

"How soon?"

He paused. "Six months."

Her head jerked up. "Oh, Andrew, no . . ."

His gaze was somber. "You or I can't let our feelings or those of the people we love sway us from the ultimate good, Cait, you know that."

Yes, I know that . . . The sting of her regret caused her to sink into his comforting hold once again, the clean smell of soap and musk shaving cream reminding her just what a wholesome and godly man Andrew Turner was. A man whose heart beat for the same causes as hers. She closed her eyes to soak up the solace of his embrace. *And* to delay the inevitable. Her eyelids shuttered closed. *Informing Logan of the new timeline for phase two.*

The squeal of the door interrupted them, along with a steely tone. "I'm going to head out, Cait—you obviously have things to attend to." Hand fisted on the knob, Logan loomed in the doorway with a stone face except for the flicker of a nerve in his jaw.

She spun around, heat swarming her cheeks as she quickly distanced herself from Andrew. Her fingers trembled while she absently hooked a strand of hair over her ear. "Oh, Logan—no, please!" Heart pounding, she hurried to where he stood as cold and unmovable as the marble statue that graced her foyer. "Mr. Turner was just leaving," she said, whirling to face Andrew with a plea in her eyes. "Thank you for the critical update, Andrew.

I'm most anxious to discuss it further at our committee meeting Monday evening."

Andrew's gaze flicked from Logan to her, softening considerably as he gave her a tender smile. "My pleasure, Cait. May I offer you a ride to the meeting?"

"N-no," she said too quickly, Logan's tension so palpable, she stuttered her words. "Thank you, but I don't want to trouble you. Hadley will drive me."

Head bowed, he fiddled with the fedora in his hand, peering up with a half-lidded look that held way too much affection. "It's no trouble, Cait," he said quietly, "truly."

"That's very kind of you, Andrew, really, but Hadley will drive me, thank you."

He nodded and moved toward the door, jaw compressed despite the smile on his face. "Good to see you, Logan. My apologies for interrupting your evening."

Logan didn't respond, his rigid body a granite barrier. He made Andrew wait several seconds before he moved to let him pass.

"Good night, Cait." Andrew strode into the foyer.

"Turner." Logan's voice was harsh.

Andrew rotated, hand on the knob of the glass front door.

"If you persist in bothering Cait at home, I strongly advise you to avoid the nights that I spend time with *my* family." Cait didn't miss the tight clench of Logan's fists at his sides, as rock hard as his tone. "In other words, Turner, if my vehicle is out front—*stay away.*"

"Logan, really . . ." Cait laid a gentle arm on his sleeve.

Andrew offered a calm smile. "No, Cait, he has a point. In the future, I'll confine my visits to evenings we can spend more time together." With a short nod, he placed his fedora on his head and opened the door. "Till Monday evening, Mrs. McClare."

The door clicked behind him, and Caitlyn released a fractured breath. "Logan—"

He turned his wrath on her, a rare flash of temper in gray eyes that gleamed like ice crystals. "*That* was your idea of 'dispensing posthaste'? Wrapped in his arms like the blasted prey of a python?"

She exhaled slowly and took his hand in hers, no energy left for another tussle with the man who already held too much sway over her heart and her life. "Please, Logan," she said quietly, eyes flicking to the parlour and back. "May we discuss this in private?"

He didn't answer, his hand as stiff as his stance before he pulled it from her hers.

"Please?" Ignoring his obvious ill humor, she moved into the study and waited.

A near growl rumbled from his chest as he charged into the room, wheeling on his heels with fire in his eyes. "Blast it, Cait—Turner's after you, and I don't like it."

Her heart squeezed at the scowl on his face—a little-boy scowl that reminded her just how very much she cared for Logan Mc-Clare. And how much he cared for her, given the possessive look in his eyes. With a gentle dip of her head, she peeked up beneath a sweep of lashes, lips curved in a soft smile. "Yes, Andrew has made it abundantly clear he would like more than friendship, but you need to know that I've *also* made it clear that I would not." She took his arm and led him to the love seat where she nudged him to sit before she eased down beside him. "Logan," she said softly. "You have nothing to worry about."

"Don't I, Cait?" His Adam's apple jerked while his hands swallowed hers in a warm grip. "He ruined what we had before, and he has every intention of doing so again."

Her chest rose with a heavy inhale before she released it again, her gaze tinged as always with that hint of regret both of them had lived with for over 27 years. "No, Logan," she said quietly, unwilling to allow him to blame Andrew for his own sins, "he simply told the truth." She steeled herself with a deep breath. "Just like I'm about to do right now." Uncomfortable with the warm shivers his touch produced, she carefully eased her hands from his, locking him with a potent gaze. "I am *not* interested in courting anyone for the foreseeable future, but let me put your mind at rest." She grazed his jaw with her fingers, the rough texture of his late-day beard raspy beneath her touch. "If I were," she said with a rush of love, "it would be you."

He didn't blink for several seconds, and then with a low groan, he swallowed her up in a crushing embrace, unleashing a warmth that stuttered her pulse. "So help me, Cait, I love you more than anything in this world, and I would do anything for you, you have to know that."

She squeezed her eyes shut, and a single tear trailed her cheek. "I know," she whispered, the heady scent of lime and Logan taunting her with what might have been while her stomach skittered over what might be. *But will you support me on phase two?*

With a kiss to her hair, he pulled away, holding her at arm's length. "I'll wait for you, Cait," he whispered, voice gruff, "as long as it takes." The corners of his mouth quirked. "But I won't wait any longer to take you in cribbage." He patted her arms and rose, extending his hand to help her up. "Prepare for the onslaught, Mrs. McClare."

"Logan?"

"Yes?" He sat back down and she avoided his eyes, focusing on the beds of her nails at which she nervously picked.

"I . . . have something I need to tell you," she said quietly, finally meeting his gaze. "About news Andrew had to share regarding the Vigilance Committee."

"Yes . . . ?" He grabbed her hands to still her picking, those gray eyes boring into hers. "You're nervous, Cait—what is it?"

She swallowed hard. "Father Terence Caraher has agreed that a three-prong thrust—his organization, the Vigilance Committee, and the district attorney's office—is in the best interests of our goal to clean up the Coast, so he's driving the effort to close down the Marsicania."

Logan arched a brow. "That sounds like a good thing."

"Oh, it is," she said quickly, giving him a shaky smile. "It's just that . . ." She gulped, refocusing on the scarlet-and-gold Oriental rug beneath the claw-foot coffee table. "Father Caraher also wants to implement parts of phase two sooner than we anticipat—"

"Which parts?" His voice carried an edge.

She sucked in a calming breath and closed her eyes. "The gambling and dance halls," she whispered, waiting for his explosive response.

Silence.

Holding her breath, she peeked up and stifled a groan. The tic in his cheek had returned. "How soon?" he snapped.

"Six months," she said quietly, knowing full well Logan would see this change of plans as a betrayal of sorts, almost a broken promise . . .

"Your proposal cited up to five years, Cait." His tone was curt, a total departure from his declaration of love mere minutes ago.

"Two to five years," she corrected softly.

Those broad shoulders straightened while the cleft in his chin deepened enough to show he was transitioning to lawyer mode, setting her up. Her heart skipped a beat. *Going in for the kill.* "Which is fine for the dance halls, Mrs. McClare—everyone knows they're little more than brothels in disguise. But *you* led me to believe you wouldn't touch the gambling halls for five years, did you not?"

"I ... I b-believe my proposal to the Board of Supervisors stipulated two to five years." Her voice trailed off and she sucked in a harsh breath at a sudden sting of pain, vaguely aware she'd picked one of her nails clean off, too close to the nub.

He rose slowly, an imposing tower of intimidation with smoldering gray eyes and a jaw sculpted in steel. His words were clipped and cool, like the night he'd opposed her in the Board of Supervisors meeting two years ago. "Yes, but you assured *me* personally, Mrs. McClare, that the timeline would be closer to five, which is what I assured the board when the final vote was deliberated." Body taut, he loomed over her with fists tight at his sides, his cool anger fairly shimmering off his body. "Board members who like myself, Madame President, not only have business interests on the Coast, but hundreds of employees dependent upon them for their livelihood."

She wobbled to her feet, legs so weak she had to steady herself with a hand to the carved wooden arm of the love seat. "Logan, I know this is a shock—"

"Shock?" One thick brow jagged high. "No, Cait, I think this qualifies somewhere between sleight of hand and fraud, and I assure you any shock to be had will belong to the Vigilance Committee when the Board of Supervisors revisits phase two for a second vote."

She felt the blood drain from her face. "They ... w-wouldn't," she whispered, never dreaming Father Caraher's push on phase two might jeopardize the Vigilance Committee's plan.

A glimmer of compassion dimmed the fire in his eyes as he huffed out a noisy exhale, hip slacked while he mauled the back of his neck. "Blast it, Cait, I know this isn't your fault—it has Turner written all over it, but I'll be dashed if he thinks he can railroad the Board of Supervisors like he's railroading you."

His comment prickled, squaring her shoulders. "No one is 'railroading' me, Logan, unless it's you with your bullying and temper."

He paused, gaze wary before he finally shook his head, a smile skimming his lips. "And *this* from the woman who bullies me into friendship rather than courtship, then uses her influence with her brother-in-law on issues before the Board."

Face on fire, she thrust her chin up in self-defense. "Oh, now *there's* the pot calling the kettle black."

A chuckle parted from his lips, dispelling the tension between them. "Come on 'kettle,'" he said with a hook of her arm, tugging her back onto the love seat, "we need to scour the soot before we both get burned."

Shifting to face him, she clutched his hands. "Oh, Logan, I never meant for this to happen, truly. In my heart of hearts, I feel the Vigilance Committee needs to focus on shutting down the major brothels like the Marsicania and the Municipal Crib first, which would have ensured the timeline I originally proposed. But now with Father Caraher involved, insisting on putting all of our efforts into the Marsicania alone and leaving the Municipal Crib for phase three, I'm afraid to rock the boat."

Eyes suddenly tender, he slowly grazed his thumb along the edge of her jaw, sending an unexpected tingle through her body. "Trust your heart, Cait, not your fear. Isn't that what Liam always tried to drum into our brains, no matter the situation?"

She nodded, suddenly missing her husband so much, she wanted to break down and cry. Instead she sniffed and rallied with a square of her shoulders while contrition burned soft in her eyes. "I'm so very sorry, Logan—please forgive me."

Exhaling a weary sigh, he took her hand and squeezed it. "I know, Cait, and I'm sorry for losing my temper too, but this puts both of us in a very awkward situation, you know."

"I know," she whispered. A tiny smile tickled her mouth. "And it's not as if you actually lost your temper, I suppose . . ." She nibbled the edge of her lip, eyes warm with tease. "More like testy and tyrannical, I think."

He grinned. "Yes, well I'll show you testy and tyrannical in a few minutes, Mrs. McClare, when we return to the game, but for now—we need to address the issue at hand." He rubbed her hands between his, eyes intense. "What do you think the chances are of slowing Turner and Caraher down on phase two?"

Her nibbling turned into a full-fledged grate as she peered up beneath lowered lashes. "Not particularly high, I don't think. Andrew said Father Caraher's partnership was contingent upon implementing parts of phase two sooner than we'd planned."

He muttered something under his breath that sounded like "contingent, my backside," then gouged his temple with the ball of his hand. "Well, I'll certainly expend my influence, Cait, but I can't guarantee this won't provoke a revote, and I sure can't guarantee approval if it does."

Her heart sputtered in her chest, equal parts of fear and gratitude colliding within. "Oh, Logan, you mean you'll support us in our efforts to expedite phase two?"

His lips took a slant. "I mean I'll support *you*, Cait, in your efforts to expedite phase two, not Caraher and certainly not Turner."

She couldn't help it—she lunged into his arms, evoking a husky chuckle that tumbled her stomach. "Oh, Logan, you are absolutely one of the greatest joys of my life."

The warmth of his breath against her neck heated both her skin and her blood. "Then I'm on the right track, Mrs. McClare," he whispered, his words caressing her ear and braising her cheeks. "Because joy is only the first of many things I hope to give you someday."

A lump bobbed in her throat. *Oh, Logan, if only . . .*

He caressed her back for a moment, and her eyelids fluttered closed. His touch filled her with both longing and distress, an unsettling reminder that trust in a marriage was as important as love, at least to her. As if sensing her disquiet, he gently patted her back before he rose to his feet and extended a hand. "Of course, at the moment, there are other things I intend to give . . ." Covering the hand she placed on his arm, he slid her a dangerous smile that put a spike in her pulse. "Such as a sound defeat, which will put you at my mercy."

His mercy? Caitlyn swallowed hard as he escorted her from the room, painfully aware that when it came to Logan and his effect on her?

There was no such thing.

13

Pure sludge. Megan peered inside the cup of coffee she'd just poured and scrunched her nose when its dark contents coated the side of the white ceramic mug like tar. Shaking her head, she actually missed Linda Marie today, wishing she were here instead of home with stomach problems. Meg's lips quirked as she tossed the contents of her cup into the sink, certain that her fate would be the same if she actually drank the coffee Conor had made.

A smile tipped the corners of her mouth as she thought about Conor and the others with whom she was privileged to work five days a week. Definitely low man on the totem pole, Conor had been delegated by George to make coffee on the days Linda Marie was absent, which—praise be to God—wasn't all that often. Ribbed as a womanizer by everyone from Andrew to Linda Marie, Conor had actually turned out to be a pretty sweet guy with an honest-to-goodness appreciation for the opposite sex. It didn't matter what they looked like—shy and willowy like Bonnie at the front desk, perky and petite like Jennifer Fuchikami, who manned the lunch cart in the lobby, or even sweet Wanda Barefoot, the night cleaning lady who was a grandmother of six. Flirt or no, Conor had a knack for making a woman feel beautiful, and it was his God-given ability to do that for Bonnie that had completely won Megan's heart.

Bonnie. Affection surged in Meg's chest over the new friend who, if possible, was even more painfully shy than Megan had been before Paris. A friend with whom she had so instantly connected, that they now met early on workdays in the conference room to chat and pray before the office was open—their secret. A smile flitted across Meg's lips. Their secret, yes, but the best-kept secret in the district attorney's office was the fact that Bonnie Roof was a beauty in disguise who, unfortunately, carried herself like the frumpy, stoop-shouldered wallflower she believed herself to be. As a "wallflower" from way back, Meg had a keen sense of seeing the beauty in people no matter their outward appearance, something she'd learned the hard way at the cruel hand of ridicule. *And* something she learned to counter most effectively in Paris, teaching her that although the naked eye admires outward appearance, it's in the mind's eye where true beauty and confidence begins.

Scouring the pot until the sludge was gone, Meg hoped to do the very same thing for Bonnie—scour the sludge of insecurity from her self-perception so she could blossom into the woman that Meg knew she could be. Just like Mrs. Rousseau had done for Meg, both spiritually and physically. Excitement flooded within like the clean water flooded into the coffeepot, filling Meg with anticipation for this shy new friend she'd gotten to know so well over the last two weeks.

When Meg had arrived two hours early the second day of her internship, she had hoped for some quiet time alone to pray and prepare for the day. But to her surprise, she'd discovered it was Bonnie's habit to do the same, spending devotional time in the comfortable conference room with a fresh-brewed cup of coffee.

Now she and Bonnie began every workday chatting and praying before the others arrived, forging a friendship made all the stronger through prayer. It had been in one of these intimate sessions that Meg had mentioned a subject near and dear to her heart, and what Dr. Rousseau had cheerfully referred to as "soul surgery."

"Feed a mouth, feed a faith," he used to say when they distributed bread to prostitutes and tended to their maladies. "Heal a body, heal a soul." And Meg had seen it firsthand in the polluted streets and sewers of the Pigalle district, where her heart had been slashed to ribbons over the plight of sore-infested women inflamed with disease and shame. Few could escape their fate in the brothels, it would seem, and yet Dr. Rousseau had labored on, performing "soul surgery" in the name of Christ. He'd rescued hundreds over the years, be they mere babes in a brothel or on the deathbed of disease, ready to meet their Maker. Tears pricked Meg's eyes as she set the coffeepot to boil. No matter their situation or scourge, Christ within infused them with hope, faith, and an inner beauty that all but glowed from pocked faces or ravaged bodies.

Down the hall, the crisp tap-tap-tap of Bonnie's Remington could be heard, and anticipation simmered in Meg over some soul surgery of her own. Not life and death in the Pigalle district, certainly, but a surgery of light where the dark was pushed away—be it a gloomy reception area badly in need of a boost or the poor self-esteem of a dear friend, badly in need of confidence. She slipped back into the conference room to work on research while the coffee brewed, jumping up moments later when the rich aroma wafted in the air. Pouring a steaming cup, she added cream and sugar the way Bonnie liked before carrying it down the hall to where her friend typed.

When Meg poked her head around the corner, she couldn't

126

help but grin at the transformation Andrew had allowed her to effect in Bonnie's waiting room. Her heart swelled with pride over the hazy shafts of sunlight spilling into an office area that now sported rolled-up blinds, clean windows, and a fresh coat of paint—not stark white as before, but a warm maple color that lent a cozy feel. Shoulders straighter than usual, Bonnie worked at a gleaming desk graced with a simple crystal vase of fresh flowers. The scent of jasmine happily mingled with lemon oil from furniture polish and lilacs from the French perfume Meg had given her.

Yes, Andrew had quirked a brow when Meg asked if she could spruce up Bonnie's area, but he'd grinned when he saw the Monet-style oil paintings of San Francisco Bay, Sausalito, and Cliff House hung on the walls. Paintings from her junior year art class, their deep mahogany frames and wide molding showcased the beauty of San Francisco in pastel hues that gave the space a light and airy feel. By the time she'd added a Tabriz carpet in soft hues of brown and gold she'd found in Mother's attic, he'd laughed outright, never blinking when an old brass floor lamp appeared, which she'd polished herself. The warm and homey effect had not only transformed Bonnie's perspective, but everyone who entered the office, causing her coworkers to mill and linger more often, chatting with Bonnie and each other over coffee and donuts Meg brought in on Fridays.

She released a satisfied sigh. *A lovely transformation, indeed. But not as lovely as Miss Bonnie Roof when I'm done!* The hint of a smile squirmed on Meg's lips. Poor Bonnie should've never confessed George was her crush, because if there was anything Meg loved more than reading, chess, and math, it was matchmaking. Quite certain she'd never have a romance of her own, she'd taken great joy in masterminding connections for girls in her class. Other than being the chubby child genius who won almost every spelling bee or science fair from first grade on, matchmaking had been her only claim to fame, and now she had the chance to do it all over again!

If I can just get Bonnie to agree . . .

She paused to appraise the back of Bonnie's severe bun—a knot so taut and tight over the crown of her head that she might have been bald if one squinted—and felt almost giddy over the transformation she had in mind. Rimless eyeglasses—popularized by Teddy Roosevelt himself—would replace Bonnie's heavy horn-rimmed style, allowing her graceful cheekbones to be the focal point while the spectacles almost disappeared on her face. Meg's fingers itched to unravel that severe bun, softening her friend's appearance with lustrous ebony hair piled loose and high in the graceful Gibson Girl style. Her gaze traveled the length of Bonnie's lanky frame, certain a few tucks here and there with some of Alli's stylish hand-me-downs and a lengthened hem would give her far more confidence than the matronly blouses and skirts she'd inherited from her maiden aunt. And with the makeup tips Meg had learned from Mr. Poiret, she had no doubt that Miss Bonnie Roof, self-proclaimed old maid, would not only turn a certain executive assistant district attorney's head, but astound herself as well, infusing her with confidence both inside and out.

"I brought you coffee," she said, causing her friend to lash around with a squeal. Meg grinned. "We really should work on that," she said with a chuckle, assessing Bonnie's desk with a pensive eye. Handing the cup to her friend, she blinked at the bright wash of sunlight streaming through the windows. "Goodness, doesn't the afternoon sun bother your eyes now that we've permanently opened those blinds?"

"A little." Bonnie glanced over her shoulder at the windowsill where a potted plant she'd brought from home proudly sat. "But I do enjoy watching my philodendron grow and the seagulls glide, so it's worth it." Her full lips curved in a crooked smile while a blush stole into her cheeks. "Although I do tend to daydream a little more now, so maybe that's not so good."

"Mmm . . ." Meg strolled the perimeter of Bonnie's desk with folded arms, studying it with a squint. "Well, since we don't want your productivity to suffer," she said with a crooked smile, "why don't we move your typing table to the opposite side of the desk so the glare's to your back? That way you won't vault in the air when somebody comes up behind you. And . . . ," she said with a smile, "you can focus on your work instead of your daydreams."

Bonnie set her coffee down to wheel her chair around, contemplating Meg's suggestion before she popped up. "Oh my goodness!" She was suddenly breathless with excitement, her five-foot-eight height easily towering over Meg. "I don't know why you want to be a lawyer or doctor when you are so brilliant at decorating and design!" Eyes sparkling, she immediately tackled the typing table, repositioning it on the other side, then stood back to admire the new arrangement. With a pleased clap of her hands, she promptly bundled Meg in a grateful hug. "Goodness, is there anything you *can't* do?"

Meg laughed. "Well, I can't make coffee like Linda Marie, but it's better than Conor's, I hope, even if just barely."

Pushing her horn-rimmed glasses back to the bridge of her nose, Bonnie took a sip. "Oh, bless you, Meg—it's perfect! I've been trying to decipher George's chicken scratch all morning, and I'm near comatose, so I needed this badly." She glanced at the elegant mahogany wall clock that Meg had also filched from Mother's attic and set the coffee down, plopping back into her chair with a sigh. "I'll need all the energy I can get when

Mr. Turner and the others get back from City Hall with copious notes." A shadow darkened the bubbled glass door, and Bonnie sat straight up, nervously patting the back of her bun. "Uh-oh . . . Mr. Turner's afternoon appointment is early."

"Well, I guess it's back to work for me too," Meg said, the squeal of the door sending her scurrying down the hall to pour another cup of coffee before returning to her research. Humming to herself, she stood on tiptoe to retrieve a mug from the cabinet over the sink, then filled it with the steaming brew. She doctored it with plenty of cream and sugar and leaned back against the counter to take a sip, eyes closed as she savored its rich flavor.

A low whistle jolted her, eyelids snapping open while coffee sloshed in her cup.

"Saint Peter's Gate—I'm in heaven," a husky voice said, a hint of tease in a rich baritone that Meg would have recognized anywhere. Unable to breathe or blink, she could only stare, her eyes dry sockets of shock as Devin Caldwell strolled into the kitchen and butted a hip to the counter not two feet away. His commanding presence forced her gaze up while he all but dwarfed her, assessing her with a cross of arms while he scanned head to toe with a boyish smile. "Sweet thunder, and I thought this internship would be boring."

A harsh gasp caught in her throat. *Internship??* The breath in her lungs refused to comply, diminishing her air. She started to hack, and he promptly relieved her of her cup, scorching her body when he patted her back. "Are you all right, Miss . . . ?"

Her heart ricocheted against her rib cage as she jerked from the massage of his hand on her back, her words stuttering more than her pulse. "Y-Yes, I'm f-fine," she rasped, ignoring his quest for a name.

The grin that had haunted many a dream rolled across wide

lips while his gaze of approval traveled like a caress from the crown of her loose chignon, down her lavender silk shirtwaist to her form-fitting cream skirt. "You certainly are," he whispered, his tall winged collar bobbing the slightest bit. Rubbing his palms on his dark tailored suit, he extended a hand with an engaging smile, and she instantly recognized that mischievous twinkle he'd bestowed on all the pretty girls in her class. "Devin Caldwell at your service, and you are . . . ?"

"L-Late," she stuttered, frantic to flee anywhere that took her far away from the one boy with a talent for both engaging and enraging. She started for the door, only to be halted by the touch of his hand.

"Wait—you do work here, don't you?" A wedge appeared between dark brows that matched thick chestnut hair combed back, which seemed prone to thwart the Brilliantine he wore. His smile dimmed as concern deepened the dark brown of his eyes. "Oh, *please* tell me you work here," he said softly, fingers stroking the silk sleeve of her arm.

She stumbled back with a shaky nod, his touch heating both her skin and her cheeks.

"Oh, thank heavens," he said, his mouth relaxing into a smile once again. "You're a breath of fresh air after the prim schoolmarm at the front desk and the dull intern they hired."

Meg froze, heart thudding to a slow beat. "D-dull in-tern?"

With a cock of his hip, he casually slipped his hands in his pockets, his expression almost sheepish. "Yeah, Megan McClare, a girl I know—long on brains, short on beauty, if you know what I mean."

"Yes, I know what you mean," she whispered.

Painfully so.

"I have an orientation meeting with Andrew—uh, Mr. Turner, my godfather—when he returns from City Hall, so when I saw you making coffee . . ." He exhaled slowly, flashing the same dazzling smile that had mesmerized every girl and nun at St. Vincent's. "My day just got a whole lot better." He nodded to Linda Marie's desk where her nameplate was prominently displayed. "So, this is your desk, I presume, Miss Finn?"

She blinked, tongue pasted to the roof of her mouth.

"Mr. Caldwell?" Bonnie hovered in the doorway with shoulders hunched and head bowed, barely meeting Devin's gaze. "Mr. Turner just returned, and he's ready for you now."

Devin beamed, his easy smile pinking Bonnie's cheeks. "Thank you—Miss Roof, is it?"

"Yes, sir." Bonnie's face was now aflame, a typical reaction where the handsome Devin Caldwell was concerned. Meg's lips compressed.

"Will you tell him I'll be right there?"

"Yes, sir," she said with a quick nod, disappearing faster than Meg could blink.

He shifted to focus on Meg again, the blush in her cheeks going head-to-head with Bonnie's. "I look forward to getting to know you better, Miss Finn." He warmed her with a roguish smile. "And I would love a cup of coffee, if you don't mind, delivered to Mr. Turner's office?" He had the audacity to give her a wink on the way out. "Black if you will."

Oh, I will. She stared as he disappeared down the hall, stunned as always by the bold confidence of Devin Caldwell, the runt in the sixth grade whose life changed forever when he started to grow. "Black as night," she muttered, rattled by his good looks and towering height, which were exceeded only by his cockiness. "Right around the eye . . ."

Megan Maureen McClare! Meg winced, imagining her mother's gentle scold while her cheeks throbbed from both anger and

132

guilt over such vile thoughts. She'd survived years of ridicule by following her mother's wise counsel—love your enemies, do good to those who hate you, and pray for those who insult and persecute you. But this! The bane of her existence, here in the flesh, in the middle of the internship she'd prayed and hoped for—belittling her!

Just like always.

Body rigid, she slowly released the breath she'd been holding, ashamed over the hostility Devin Caldwell provoked.

And the attraction?

No! She stood up straight, shoulders square and head high. If Paris had taught her anything, she'd learned to give insensitive people like Devin Caldwell a wide berth, treating them with the respect due any of God's creatures, certainly, but nothing more. No matter how much he had raced her pulse in the past, she would steer clear of those feelings—and the man who provoked them—as much as possible. Lips pursed, she poured his cup of coffee, shocked when visions of spilling it in the buffoon's lap trickled through her brain. With a quick prayer of repentance, she prayed for him and marched down the hall to Mr. Turner's office, sucking in a deep breath before she quietly knocked on his door.

"Come in."

Meg poked her head in, offering Andrew a penitent smile. "Coffee for Mr. Caldwell," she said with as much humility as she could, purposely avoiding the "buffoon's" grinning gaze.

"Ah, Meg—just the person I wanted to see!" Andrew rose and waved her into the office with a bright smile, pride fairly shimmering in his tone. "Devin, this is Miss Megan McClare, my first intern and one of the brightest young women I have ever seen, so you've got your work cut out for you, my boy, if you hope to keep up with her."

Meg blushed, not daring to peek at Devin lest her cheeks burn even more. "Thank you, Mr. Turner," she whispered, careful to set the cup on the edge of the desk and not in Devin's lap.

Where it belongs.

"Meg's mother, Caitlyn, is the president of the Vigilance Committee and a very dear friend." Andrew rounded his desk to place a protective arm around her shoulder while Devin shot to his feet. "Meg, meet my godson, Devin Caldwell, who expressed interest in this internship just the other night at dinner, so I hope you don't mind—I suggested he join you this summer."

Meg fought the rise of a gulp. "No, sir, I don't mind," she lied, her gaze slowly climbing to meet Devin's. Before she could stop it, her jaw sagged open, nearly unhinged. *Never* in eleven years of school events had she *ever* seen Devin Caldwell blush before. And not just a ruddy, masculine shade, but the deepest, brightest pink she'd ever seen on a human being's face, instantly tipping her lips into a delighted smile. She extended her hand. "Goodness, what a surprise," she said, his blatant humiliation buoying her spirits.

Devin cleared his throat, fingers sweaty when they grasped hers. "H-Hello, Meg." He pulled away to shove his hands in his pockets, obviously flustered. "It's been a long time."

"You two know each other?" Andrew asked, gaze flicking from Megan to Devin.

Another clear of a throat, gruffer this time, before Devin's response came out in a near croak. "Yes, Meg and I competed in every competition, spelling bee, and science project from first grade through eleventh."

"No kidding?" Andrew squeezed Meg's arm with a low chuckle, still bracing her shoulder. "And who usually won?"

Meg grinned, the sight of a scarlet Devin Caldwell doing wonders for her confidence. "Well, I suppose that depends," she said with a teasing tilt of her head, unable to thwart the squirm of her lips. "If humility was the prize, then I believe Mr. Caldwell holds the crown."

Andrew's laughter rolled through the office, bloodying Devin's cheeks, if possible, even more than before. "What'd I tell you, Dev? This young woman is a force to be reckoned with."

"Yes, sir," he said with a tight clamp of a smile. He reached for his coffee and acknowledged her with a stiff raise of his cup. "Thank you for the coffee, Meg, and I apologize for not recognizing you in the coffee room earlier."

Giving her a final pat, Andrew resumed his seat. "Don't feel too badly, Dev, none of us recognized her after she returned from Paris, not even her own brother. She's certainly blossomed into a beauty, eh?"

"Yes, sir." A knot jerked in his throat, near the size of the fist pinched on the handle of his cup.

Andrew checked his pocket watch and cut loose with a low whistle. "Dash it, I almost forgot." He reached for his leather attaché from a credenza in front of the large window and fished out a manila envelope. "Meg, I was supposed to drop this off at the Barbary Volunteer Legal Services on my way back from City Hall, but it slipped my mind." He glanced up with a conciliatory smile. "Would you mind delivering it for me? You can call Hadley or take the cable car out front—it goes right by their building on Washington. Then just feel free to head on home early since it's Friday, all right?"

The Barbary Volunteer Legal Services? Excitement scurried and scampered within, completely obliterating any thought of Devin Caldwell and his snide opinion of her. Ever since Bram had mentioned a law-school classmate of his had an uncle who'd opened a free clinic for legal services on the edge of the Barbary

Coast, Meg had longed to volunteer there. But Mother had put the kibosh on it, telling her she was too young. And yet, that was exactly the type of lawyer she wanted to be, accessible to those poor souls in the Coast, especially women and children. And now, to be able to go there and see it firsthand—and via cable car no less! A slow grin slid across her face at the very thought. *My first cable car ride!* Goodness, Mother never allowed them on the cable cars before, citing germs and unsavory characters as reason enough.

"If you'd rather not, Meg, I understand . . ."

She blinked, Andrew capturing her attention when he laid the envelope aside.

"No!" With a catch of her breath she snatched it up and hugged it to her chest, beaming so brightly she could have been the blinding sun blazing through Bonnie's window. "I would love to do this for you, Mr. Turner, truly! Sweet heavens, I've been dying to see the Barbary Volunteer Legal Services office for years now, so this is perfect."

He chuckled and scratched the back of his neck. "Well, I can't say a brownstone storefront on the edge of the worst part of town would be *my* first choice for something I've been 'dying' to see. But I've already figured out that you are no ordinary young woman, Meg, so I am happy to oblige a long-held dream of yours." He jotted the address and the name of the man to whom she was to deliver the file, then handed it over. "Marcus Wilson is the director and a good friend, and this is the file on one of his clients that he asked me to look at. Tell him I'll be happy to assist in any way he needs and I'll be in touch."

"Oh yes, sir, and thank you! I may even take advantage of your generosity to take the afternoon off and stay awhile to observe if they'll let me."

With a shake of his head, Andrew sat back in his chair, arms relaxed on its sides. "I'll tell you what, Meg, you so remind me of your mother, and that's high praise, indeed."

Her cheeks warmed with pleasure. "Thank you, Mr. Turner, and I agree—my mother is everything I aspire to be—a woman of deep faith and gentle compassion." Mischief flickered at the edge of her smile. "With enough steel in her spine to accomplish whatever she wants and withstand anything she doesn't."

Andrew grinned. "Ah, yes—something I've learned quite well." Elbows propped on the arms of his chair, he tented two fingers to his mouth, affection lacing his smile. "Well, enjoy your observation then, Meg, and come Monday, I'll expect Devin to be observing *you* as an example of just what a legal intern should be."

Meg chanced a peek at Devin, who was still standing with the cup in his hand, more awkward than before. She nodded at him with a polite smile, not exactly sure what to say. *I look forward to working with you?* Hardly. *Nice to see you again?* Goodness, that would be perjury, and in a district attorney's office, no less. She clutched the folder like a shield. "I ... hope you enjoy it here as much as I do," she finally said, relieved she didn't have to lie because she certainly enjoyed the experience thus far. Of course that was before the scourge of St. Patrick's had arrived to torment her ...

His head bobbed up and down as if he didn't know what to say, and his smile was as strained as their working relationship was likely to be.

"Have a great weekend, Mr. Turner, Mr. Caldwell." And with a spin on her heel, she darted for the door, halting at the nervous clear of a throat. She glanced over her shoulder at a very wooden Devin Caldwell as he once again lifted his cup in the air. "Uh ... thank you for the coffee, Meg—you brew a very decent pot."

His nervous compliment seemed to dissolve all the years of

ridicule she'd suffered at his hand. Tubby. Four eyes. Wallflower, and more. Hurtful names she now realized were nothing more than the barbs of an insecure little boy. And a bully who would *never* bully her again.

"Why, thank you," she said with a flash of a perfect smile afforded by three years of braces at great expense to her mother. She felt almost giddy as she gave him a wink. "Not too shabby for somebody long on brains, short on beauty, eh?" And with a toss of her newly hennaed hair, she turned on her heel, the taste of vindication sweet solace, indeed.

14

"Next stop, please!" Megan raised her voice over the clatter of the cable car rails. The gold lettering on the storefront window shaded by a tattered green awning tripped her pulse as much as her excitement over her very first cable car ride. Her gaze scanned up in awe at the three-story brick buildings that lined the narrow streets of Jackson Square. Here the charm of hodge-podge buildings with cast-iron shutters from the 1850s offered a glimpse into the California Gold Rush that gave San Francisco its start. Meg gripped the step pole, feet straddled, and her heart jolted along with her body as the car lurched to a stop, the *clang-clang-clang* of the bell announcing her arrival on what could be the threshold of her future.

The Barbary Volunteer Legal Services.

Cheeks flushed, she hopped off half a block from her destination, landing on the cracked sidewalk with a wobbly thump. Her eyes homed in on the green awning flapping in the breeze, the sagging material rippling as much as her stomach. Adrenaline coursed as she clutched the manila envelope to her chest, barely able to contain her excitement.

"I said get out and stay out—don't need no soiled doves chasing business away."

Soiled dove? Meg halted, the sight of a storekeeper shoving a young woman out of his drugstore stealing her air. The poor thing stumbled, falling headlong onto the sidewalk while the disgruntled store owner slammed the door behind her.

Meg rushed to help her up, pulse pounding over the cruel treatment this woman had just encountered. "Oh my goodness—are you all right?" she whispered, scanning the lady's frayed shirtwaist and worn black skirt that appeared to have been washed till it faded to gray. Furrowed gaze flicking to the drugstore and back, Meg picked up the shabby cloth purse at her feet, looping the tattered strap over the young woman's arm. "What an awful man—I'm so very sorry."

Light brown eyes blinked back, so shadowed with fatigue that Meg's stomach cramped. "Thank you for your kindness, miss," the girl whispered, averting her eyes to the hem of Meg's skirt as if too ashamed to meet her gaze, "but I can't say I blame 'im."

With a quick nod, she moved to pass, and Meg stayed her with a gentle hand. "Is there . . . something you needed in the store?" Her stomach constricted at the sudden gloss of tears in the woman's eyes, the sag of bony shoulders appearing weighted with grief. "Something I can get for you, perhaps?"

"No, miss," she said with a small shake of her head, her thin body trembling beneath the touch of Meg's fingers. She nodded toward the drugstore window, the saddest of smiles tilting at the edge of full lips rouged with red. "Not unless you can rustle me a better job."

Meg's gaze followed hers to a help-wanted sign propped against the glass, and comprehension dawned, as cold and sharp as the icy pinpricks that skittered her skin.

Soiled dove.

"Where do you work now?" Meg asked, almost an ache in her tone.

The girl looked up, a world of sorrow in eyes that had seen far too much pain for one so young. "Six-twenty Jackson Street," she whispered, her words barely audible and yet deafening with a shame that shivered Meg's soul.

Six-twenty Jackson. The Standard Lodging House.

Meg's eyelids flickered closed. Otherwise known as the Municipal Crib. The very building that her mother, Andrew Turner, and the Vigilance Committee labored to shut down. In a single stutter of her pulse, painful memories of the suffering souls of the Pigalle district invaded her mind. And, as always, they riveted her resolve to the steel of intent. She opened her eyes, her gaze moist with compassion. "And you want to move," she said quietly, her tone a statement rather than a question as she clasped the girl's hand.

Scarlet lips quivered closed, as if to stifle a sob that rose with the swell of tears in her eyes. She gave a jerky nod, gripping Meg's hand so tightly, the ache in her fingers matched that of her heart. A heave broke from the woman's mouth. "Y-yes, m-a'am, I surely d-do . . ."

Hope surged through Meg's limbs as she squeezed her hand, her smile tender. "As so you shall. My name is Meg—what's yours?"

"Ruby. Ruby Pearl," she said with a swipe of her eyes, a watery giggle wobbling from her lips. "My mama told me she called me that 'cause I was her precious jewel and needed a name to show it." Water slithered down her cheeks on another heave. "She died when I was eight. Been in the cow-yards ever since, but seems there's no hope of gettin' out."

Pain constricted in Meg's chest. *Cow-yards.* Brothels cramped with women and rats. She ducked her head, her own face damp with tears. "Ruby, you believe in God, don't you?"

Ruby's eyes reflected the same broken despair Meg had seen

141

on the streets of Pigalle. "No, ma'am, I don't 'cause I ain't never seen no proof afore."

"Well," Meg said with a final press of her hand, "you're about to see it now." She rifled through her purse for her ink pen, quickly scratching her name and phone number on a scrap of paper she tore off the corner of Andrew's envelope. Digging some more, she tugged a half dollar from her purse and tucked both into Ruby's hand, ignoring the drop of the woman's jaw. "I know this is not much help right now, but in about five months or so, my cousin and his mother and sister will be opening a boardinghouse, so here's my phone number and money to stay in contact until then, all right?" Meg leaned to give her a hug before pulling back with a soggy smile, her hands still braced to the woman's arms. "Because you see, Miss Ruby Pearl, your name will be at the very top of the list."

Ruby's face blanched white, making her rouged lips all the darker. "B-but I don't have m-money for a boardinghouse, miss, and no one will give me a better job to earn it."

Meg nodded toward the ragged green awning down the street. "Do you have time to accompany me to the Barbary Volunteer Legal Services? Because that's where I'm headed, and I understand they have resources to help."

Ruby glanced over her shoulder, calling Meg's attention to a patched hole on the back of a collar that partially hid an ugly bruise. "I wish I did, ma'am, but I've already been gone so long I'm scared Molly might ditch my little Charlie."

"Charlie?" Meg said, a slight pucker in her brow.

The brown of Ruby's eyes softened to a lovely shade of hazel. "Charlie's my boy, you know, just turned six on Tuesday, and Molly and I trade watchin' babies while we work."

Work. Meg fought the rise of a gulp.

Patches of pink stained Ruby's pale face as her gaze dropped to her feet. "I know what you're thinkin', ma'am, but I'm one of the lucky ones who don't have to do that a whole lot anymore unless some of the girls take sick. Mostly I just work in the office since I'm one of the few who can read and write." Her gaze lifted to meet Meg's, softening at the mention of her son. "And then, of course, there's Charlie . . . which is why I cain't go today, ma'am—"

"Meg. Call me Meg, Ruby, please."

More tears pooled in Ruby's eyes. "Meg, then," she said softly, attempting to return Meg's money. "You're a kind woman, but I cain't take your money neither."

Meg pushed Ruby's hand away. "Yes you can—you'll need it to call me from a phone booth, remember? And you don't need money to live in my cousin's boardinghouse, at least not until you can afford to live on your own." She clasped the girl's hand with a gentle smile, money and all. "My cousin grew up in a cow-yard too, you see, so all he wants to do is help women like you escape the Barbary Coast." With a light touch of her hand, she gave Ruby a misty smile. "Women like his mother used to be, Ruby—"

As if frozen to the sidewalk, Ruby stared for several chaotic beats of Meg's heart before she shot into Meg's arms, and there was no stopping the stream of tears that flowed from both of their eyes. "Oh, Miss Meg—you've given me more hope than I've known in a lifetime."

Meg's joy bubbled up in a chuckle, her own hope soaring to the blue of the sky. "Not me, Ruby," she said with a quick hug, "the God of Hope." She pulled back to smile into Ruby's red-rimmed eyes with an affection only God could supply. "Because you see, He *is* real and so is His love for you. In fact, this God of Hope promises to fill you with all joy and peace in believing, that your hope may abound." She patted Ruby's arms. "So you pray to Him, you hear? And be sure to stay in touch with me too. In the meanwhile, I'll talk to the director of the Barbary Volunteer Legal Services today, to see what resources they might have for you. Then you check back with them as soon as you can, okay?"

Drawing in a deep breath, Ruby nodded, her hesitant gaze flicking toward the green awning and back. "Do you work there?"

"No, I work at the district attorney's office, but I'm hoping to volunteer for the Barbary Legal Services soon, so if you come back on a Saturday, I might even see you."

Ruby laughed and held out her hand. "It's a deal, Miss Meg, and you'll hear from me, I promise." Her light brown eyes warmed like melted caramel while muscles wobbled in her throat. "Don't know how I can ever repay your kindness, ma'am . . ."

Meg's smile quivered. "That's easy, Ruby—just seek the One who gave His to me."

The young woman nodded, apparently unable to speak lest she unleash the pool of emotion in her eyes. With a final shaky smile, she continued on down the street, turning a quarter block away to offer a farewell wave.

"God bless you, Ruby Pearl," Meg whispered, watching her fade from view. Turning on her heel, she made her way toward the green awning, noticing several unsavory men loitering in the doorway of a tavern nearby. Salacious whistles heated her cheeks, burning away some of the joy of her encounter with Ruby, but she kept her gaze straight ahead. She quickened her pace to the paned glass door, its chipped black paint and smudged glass a testimony to a lack of funds.

"Hey, girly, can I buy you a drink?"

Blood scorching her cheeks, she jerked the door so hard, swirls of dust and air whooshed in along with her trembling body. Her breathing was labored when she closed it again, pulse sprinting as she sagged against the glass with eyes closed.

"May I help you?"

Meg's eyelids flipped open to yet another jolt of surprise, expanding the whites of her eyes. "Jess?"

The girl behind a battered oak desk blinked wide, golden brown eyes and ebony curls so like Jamie's Meg had no doubt she was his sister. A faint haze of pink dotted creamy porcelain skin while dark brows knit in question. "Pardon me, miss, but do I know you?"

Meg laughed and strolled forward to extend her hand. "I'm Megan McClare, Cassie's cousin. We met briefly at Jamie and Cassie's wedding?"

Jess's eyes flared in recognition, the pink in her cheeks engulfing her face. "Oh, forgive me, of course! I feel so silly not recognizing you . . ."

"Don't," Meg said with a chuckle. "Nobody recognizes me these days, not even my family. I studied in Paris for a year and underwent quite a transformation."

A smile lifted Jess's gaping mouth. "Good heavens, I'll say—you look wonderful!"

"As do you," Meg said softly, remembering all too well Jamie's agony over his sister's painful lot in life—being nearly housebound with a crippling condition he blamed on himself. The radiant glow in Jess's face indicated a young woman who now enjoyed life to the fullest, no longer the "cripple" that children ridiculed, but a godly young woman who was as beautiful as she was bright. Blinking hard to deflect a sting of tears over the miraculous turnaround in Jess's life, Meg offered a shy smile. "It would appear the hip operation brought about a wonderful transformation for you as well, if those papers in your hands indicate you work here."

"Indeed!" Jess's smile could have lit up the room, the only bright spot in a bedraggled waiting area boasting two rickety chairs and sallow walls. "In fact, I volunteer here because I hope to become a lawyer someday, and this seemed like a logical step."

"Me, too!" It was Meg's turn for a sagging jaw. "In fact, I'm working at the district attorney's office this summer on an internship."

"Really?" Jess's eyes sparkled. "Mmm ... seems we have more in common than our ties to my brother. Maybe we should chat about joining forces to take the legal field by storm."

Meg chuckled, fingering the manila envelope in her hand. "I would love that, Jess. In fact ..." She surveyed stacks of files lining the desk and floor, noting a battered steel filing cabinet whose drawers yawned wide. "The district attorney asked me to personally deliver this envelope to Mr. Marcus Wilson, but if you don't mind, I'd love to stay and help in any way I can."

Jess laughed and extended her hand with a throaty giggle. "Oh, go ahead—twist away!" She scooted around the desk to give Meg a hug. "Trust me—it will bless the socks off both Megan Joy and me."

"Megan Joy?" Meg tilted her head in question.

"Yes, Megan Joy Burdzy—the full-time secretary here Monday through Friday and quite appropriately named, I assure you. I'm only filling in today because she's sick, but that sweet girl is a pure joy to clients and employees alike. Unfortunately, she's so inundated with filing and typing that she'd barter her firstborn for extra help." She nodded to the mountains of papers that obviously needed to be filed. "Volunteers are scarce and I'm usually only here on Wednesdays and Saturdays, so trust me—we'll have you chin-high in files, briefs, and legal paperwork so fast, you'll think you're in law school."

Their laughter was disrupted by another swish of air when the front door flew open, admitting a young woman with a squall-ing baby.

"Abbi—right on time!" Jess bounded over to greet the woman with a warm hug. "Meg, this is Mrs. Abbi Hart, one of our very favorite clients, along with her absolutely adorable baby girl, Ellia Paige."

"Not so adorable at the moment, I'm afraid," Mrs. Hart said with a worrisome smile, jostling the crying baby to no avail.

Jess tugged the fussy infant from her mother's arms. "Not to worry, Abbi—Mr. Sherman is waiting for you in his office, so you go on in, and I'll take care of Ellia for you, all right?"

The woman clutched a ragged reticule, her dark eyes moist with gratitude. "Oh, thank you so much, Miss MacKenna—Ellia is not herself today because she's teething, and I'm not either, I'm afraid, with the poor dear up half the night."

Jess happily bundled the baby in her arms, patting her bottom while appearing quite unfazed by her cries. "Don't you worry—my mother mixed cloves with olive oil for me after I told her how unhappy Ellia was on your last visit. Mama claims it's just the thing for her sore gums, so I plan to give that a try, along with a piece of crusty bread she'll love to gnaw, so you go." She slipped the young mother a wink as she rounded her desk, her bouncy pats already working wonders on Ellia's poor disposition. "I think Mr. Sherman just may have good news for you."

"Goodness, you're a natural with children," Meg said with true admiration, the hurried click-click-click of Mrs. Hart's shoes echoing down the long hallway. She snuck a peek at the little girl in Jess's arms who now appeared ready to doze. "But I have to admit—I didn't think watching babies would be part of the job."

Jess pressed a soft kiss to little Ellia's downy head. "Well, I'm afraid you'll quickly learn this isn't McClare, Rupert and

Byington. The clients here have no money to pay legal fees much less hire someone to watch their children for an hour or two." Settling in her chair with a contented smile, Jess nodded to the hallway. "Mr. Wilson's office is at the end of the hall, so you can deliver your envelope, then come back and I'll get you started with a brief orientation."

"Sounds good, thanks." Several steps into the hall, Meg did a quick half pivot, her smile dimming when she remembered Ruby Pearl. "Oh, and Jess—can you tell me if you have resources here to help people get jobs? I met a young woman coming out of the drugstore who is in dire need of finding a new job to support her and her little boy."

Jess smiled, her legs still bouncing along with the baby in her arms. "As a matter of fact we do, so tell her to come in, all right?"

Meg grinned, her gratitude channeling into another rush of adrenaline. "Oh, that's wonderful! Her name is Ruby Pearl and she promised to come in when she had more time, so thank you." Offering a shy smile, she hesitated with a nervous chew of her lip. "Jess?"

The bouncing stopped for a moment as Jess blinked, eyes wide in response. "Yes?"

Meg took a tentative step closer, hoping she wasn't being too forward. "Ruby currently lives in a—" the muscles in her throat contracted—"brothel," she whispered, the very sound causing her heart to cramp. "So I was hoping that maybe . . . well, maybe she could stay at—"

"Absolutely!" Jess's tone rang with a certainty that caused Meg's limbs to go weak with relief. Jess's gentle gaze—so like her brother's—softened in understanding rooted deeply in her own painful past. "That's what MacKenna's Boardinghouse is all about, Meg—Jamie's dream to offer a way out of the Barbary

Coast for women just like Ruby." A sheen of moisture glistened in Jess's eyes like a glimmer of hope while her voice tapered into a whisper. "Just like Jamie did for Mama and me."

Meg nodded quickly, unable to speak for the emotion in her throat.

"We hope to open in five or six months, and I'll tell Mama and Jamie to put Ruby at the top of the list, all right?"

Unable to stem the tears in her eyes, Meg shot back into the waiting room to swallow Jess and Ellia in a collective hug. "Oh, God bless you, Jess, for all that you're doing."

The warmth of Jess's chuckle feathered Meg's neck. "He already has, Meg," she said softly, a reverence in her tone that echoed what Meg felt in her heart. With a firm pat of Meg's arms, she pulled away, a twinkle glittering in her hazel eyes. "As He's about to do through *you*, my friend . . ." She winked while she caressed little Ellia's soft curls. "For a precious soul named Ruby."

"Thank you—so much." Meg's whisper drifted out in a rush of gratitude.

"My pleasure." Jess eased into her chair with a sleeping baby in her arms.

"And mine," Meg whispered to herself, leaving Jess to hum quietly to the little girl. She almost tiptoed down the long wooden hallway while a silly grin tickled her lips.

And sweet, sweet Ruby's . . .

15

$\mathcal{T}$hat's it, then, Joe—the next time we meet, it'll be for a settlement check long overdue." Bram circled his desk to grip Joseph Monteleone's hand as if they were old friends instead of merely attorney and client. He cuffed Joe's frail shoulder, grateful the retired factory worker would finally be compensated for the limb he lost due to his employer's negligence.

"Thank you, Mr. Hughes—I don't know how we can ever repay you."

"Your well-being and restitution is payment enough, Joe, and I already told you—we're in this together, so it's Bram, not Mr. Hughes."

"Yes, sir," Joe said with several bobs of his head, twisting a dog-eared hat in his hands. "Well, then, you can bet your last dollar that Helen and I will be praying for you, Mr. Bram, that God will bless you for all you're doing for us."

"He already has, Joe, but I welcome any and all prayers. Give Helen a hug for me, all right?" With a protective palm to Joe's back, Bram ushered him to the door, pausing to squint at the shadow of a young lady in the dark hallway where the only light to be found was that which filtered out of open offices. His mouth sagged in surprise. "Meg? What are you doing here?"

150

She halted not ten feet away, eyes wide and the hallway shadows unable to hide her shock, which was clearly equal to his. She wagged the envelope with an open-mouthed smile. "I have a delivery for Mr. Wilson, but I could ask you the same thing, Mr. Hughes."

Bram cleared his throat. "I'll be in touch, Joe, when I receive the settlement."

"Thank you, Bram. God bless."

Joe shuffled down the hall and Bram grinned, posturing a hip to the wall. He folded tan arms beneath rolled sleeves that were clearly out of character for his meticulous dress at McClare, Rupert and Byington. "On official business for the DA's office, are you? Pretty impressive, Bug, for two weeks on the job."

Flashing a grin that was a mirror reflection of his, she matched his casual stance with a plunk of hands to her hips. "Yes, as a matter of fact, Counselor Hughes, it is. What isn't impressive, however," she said with a jag of her brow, "is how my best friend failed to tell me he volunteers at the one place I've been dying to work."

He steered her into his tiny office with a chuckle, tweaking her neck before seating her in a rickety wooden chair in front of an equally scuffed and scarred desk. "Jealous, are you? Bored with the pastoral views of Portsmouth Square, I suppose." He waved his hand at a dirty window that overlooked a brick wall. "Longing for the urban charm of the city, no doubt."

She laughed, eyeing the room's dingy bare walls yellowed with age and the planked wooden floor that hadn't seen a waxing in many a year. "Indeed, but teasing won't get you off the hook, Bram Hughes, for shutting me out of this most important aspect of your life."

He tossed her a grin. "I didn't think so." He circled his desk to sit down, then flipped Joe's file onto a stack of others next to a rusty typing table with an antiquated Remington. His lip quirked at the stark difference between his job at Logan's prestigious firm and the volunteer hours he worked here, where pro bono attorneys typed their own files.

Shimmying to the edge of her seat, she leaned in with a fold of hands on his desk. "So, counselor, just when exactly did you start working here?"

He glanced at his pocket watch, then straightened his tie before he slanted back in a wooden swivel chair that squealed unmercifully. A half smile played on his lips as he studied her. "Since you deserted us for Paris. Had to do something with those empty Saturdays once you left." Humor laced his tone. "Nobody mans the sails like you, Bug, on those weekend treks to Sausalito, or takes me to task in tennis or chess."

A wispy sigh feathered her lips as she settled back in her chair like him—appearing relaxed and comfortable, as best friends should be. "Goodness, I miss those days," she said softly, her faraway look conjuring memories of the old Meg.

Bram drew in a quiet breath, suddenly missing that shy little girl whose eyes glowed whenever he'd partnered with her in tennis against Alli and Blake. Or the flush of her sun-kissed cheeks when he'd dubbed her first mate on his prized sailboat during family sails on the bay. He exhaled slowly, his smile sad. "Me too, Bug."

"So . . . ," she said with a tip of her head, "do you love it here? You're a volunteer, not salaried, right?" Her nose wrinkled in that adorable little-girl way that had always called attention to freckles now hidden beneath rice powder and rouge. "And for goodness sake, Bram Hughes—what on earth are you doing here during the week?"

He laughed and pinched the bridge of his nose. "Yes, I like it here and no, I'm definitely not salaried. Marcus has his hands full with the rent on this storefront, I'm afraid, so he has a pool of lawyers like me who volunteer their time." Resting his head on the back of the chair, he watched her through a lidded gaze, his faint smile warm with affection. "Logan has graciously allowed me one free afternoon a week of my choosing in addition to the Saturday mornings I've committed to here. And although it's pro bono work, in some ways the pay is greater than what I receive in your uncle's firm—giving back to a community I love, helping the less fortunate, makes me a richer man in more ways than one."

"Oh, Bram, that's what I want too!" she breathed, hands clasped to her chin. "Would you . . ." Her teeth tugged at her lip. "I mean . . . would you . . . mind if I filled out an application to volunteer here too? You know, to help out on Saturdays like Jess?"

Here? Bram's heart stopped for a split second, but he never let on, too practiced in the courtroom to allow his true feelings to show. Just like he'd done since Meg returned from Paris. Yes, they'd both embraced this new friendship plagued by the undercurrents of attraction—at least for him—but it had been more difficult than Bram expected. All the sweet gentleness and little-girl playfulness he'd enjoyed with Meg over the years was still there, but now it was coupled with an outer beauty that Bram found hard to resist as a man. Oh, he still battled her in chess and partnered with her in family gatherings, be it pinochle or badminton, but always with others around. Since her return, he'd taken great pains to avoid being alone with her, evading the private conversations that had once been the mainstay of their friendship.

But here? Working side by side with her every Saturday? He fought a gulp. The one place other than the firm where he'd been able to lose himself in other people's lives and forget about this annoying attraction to his best friend?

"Bram? If you rather I wouldn't . . ."

He blinked, Meg's face blurring back into view, the gentle slope of her brows a clear indication he'd hurt her feelings. His chest constricted at the thought of causing Meg any pain at all, and with a noisy squeal of his chair, he sat straight up, fingers latched to the edge of his desk. "Of course I don't mind, Meg. I think it's incredibly noble of you to want to give of your time to volunteer, and heaven knows we—*they*—need you." He hesitated, battling the urge to jump up and round the desk to pull her into his arms. He offered a conciliatory smile instead, head bowed as if to nudge her lips into a smile that would chase the hurt from her eyes. "I'm just wondering if you don't already have a pretty full agenda working five days a week for the district attorney." The edge of his lip tipped. "Hear tell he's as big a slave driver as your uncle."

It worked. Her eyes crinkled with a smile. "Oh, Mr. Turner has been wonderful, Bram, and I will admit that I come home pretty worn out, but I dearly love it." She paused, a flicker of concern in green eyes that held him captive. "Or, at least I did."

He peered at her, eyes in a squint. "Did? Has something happened to change your mind?"

She sighed, a wavering sound that always tugged at his protective instincts. Her gaze locked on the hands in her lap while she picked at her nails, a nervous habit she'd obviously inherited from her mother. "I hope not, but I won't be sure until I see how it goes ..."

His brows arched in a frown. "How what goes?"

Another shaky sigh escaped, drawing his gaze to the fullness of her mouth before he forced his eyes to meet hers. "How my relationship with the new intern goes ... ," she whispered, teeth scraping the edge of her lip in another nervous habit with which he was intimately familiar. The dark lashes swept up to reveal that

154

innocent stare that had always gut-punched him with the need to protect her, encourage her.

Love her.

"Devin Caldwell."

Bram blinked, barely able to believe he'd heard correctly. *Speaking of gut-punched!* He leaned in, jaw sagging low. "As in that annoying little twit who used to make your life miserable—*that* Devin Caldwell?"

She nodded, a tiny smile peeking through despite the thumbnail she chewed.

Facial muscles slack, Bram slumped back in a stupor, hands dangling over the arms of his chair. "Well, I'll be," he muttered, his lips sliding into a grin. "Talk about the chickens coming home to roost—or maybe I should say, 'vultures.' Did he recognize you?"

A giggle escaped as she shook her head, her grin going head-to-head with his. "Not even a little. Flirted with me outrageously, then asked me to fetch him coffee . . ." A twinkle lit her eyes. "Right after proclaiming the 'other intern' to be 'long on brains and short on beauty.'"

He stared open-mouthed, assessing her reaction for hurt before he cut loose with a hearty laugh, grateful she seemed as tickled by the dolt's ignorance as he. "Oh, that is rich, Bug. What did he say when he found out who you were?"

Her grin was pure sunshine. "Told me I brewed a very decent pot of coffee."

Bram laughed out loud, the sound as joyous as the pride that pumped in his chest. "A scalding pot, if I have my guesses right."

She gave a little shrug of her shoulders, a bit of the imp in her eyes that reminded him so much of her sister Alli. "There may have been some singeing involved, I suppose—possibly in the vicinity of both his cheeks and his pride."

Bram chuckled and snatched a pen from his desk, twiddling it as he watched her closely, his smile sobering. "And how do you feel about working with him? Are you . . . ready?"

Meg paused, Bram's sensitivity to the pains of her past nudging her, as always, to consider the true state of her heart. Was she? Ready to face the person who had wounded her more than any other? The main person responsible for her deep-seated feelings of shame and self-deprecation? Her heart thudded to a stop as her eyelids wavered closed, her mind whirling back to the time he'd shattered her confidence once and for all . . .

"Congratulations, Miss McClare," Sister Margaret had announced that final day of junior year, "your exemplary academic record has earned you the honor as Queen of the Junior Prom." A ripple of titters had circled the room, pinking Meg's cheeks, but they hadn't daunted her joy one bit. Because everyone knew who the King would be—St. Patrick's finest and every girl's dream: one Devin Caldwell. Her pulse skittered with anticipation at the prospect of dancing away the most important night of her life in the arms of the one boy for whom she pined.

Never had she taken greater pains with her appearance than the day the girls of St. Vincent's and the boys of St. Patrick's decorated the gym for the prom. Alli and Cassie helped Meg pick out a new dress and Mother had labored over her hair, making her feel like a princess for the very first time. Both her face and her mood had been aglow when she'd hurried into the storage closet for a box of bud vases Sr. Margaret asked her to retrieve. Hefting the box in her arms with a grunt, she'd turned to leave . . .

"Excited?" Devin Caldwell's voice drifted in from the hall, halting Meg's breath. "To be stuck dancing with Megan McTubby?" Laughter echoed through the corridor as she pasted herself to the wall, her cheeks aflame along with her confidence. "I'd rather dance with a hog—more personality and smells better too." A round of chortles filtered into the dark coat closet where Meg's heart had bled as thoroughly as the tears from her eyes.

"Cheer up, Dev—maybe she'll step on your foot and break it, so you won't have to dance at all," Ryan Morrow had snickered, making Meg wish she could disappear and never come out.

"Or maybe being that close to her ugly puss will make you nauseous and you can sit most of the dances out," Neil Mayfair said with a chuckle.

"I hope she's too nauseous to come at all so I can dance every dance with Lu-Ann—"

Crash! Meg's heart and lungs had seized when the box slipped to the floor, the sound of breaking glass halting both her air and the conversation in the hall.

"What the . . . ?"

Never would she forget the sound of their laughter when Devin Caldwell had whooshed open the door, exposing Meg to more shame and humiliation than she'd ever known before. The deep hurt she'd experienced that day had shattered any confidence she had as thoroughly as the broken vases on the floor . . .

Sitting there in Bram's office, the old anguish throbbed like a reinjured wound, as raw as that day in the closet when her prayers had been dashed and Devin's had been answered. No one ever knew it wasn't the flu that kept her home from that dance. No one but Bram . . .

"Meg?"

With a harsh catch of her breath, her eyelids snapped up. "Wh-what?"

She saw a flash of worry in blue eyes so tender that tears stung in her own. "Aw, Bug," he whispered, his voice husky with concern, "Devin Caldwell was a moron then and apparently still is, and a blind one at that." He leaned in, so close she could see the blond bristle beginning to pepper his jaw. "You have always been one of the most beautiful people I have ever known—both in your heart and your soul—and now your face and form match perfectly. Don't let the pain of your past color your future, Meg, because God has blessings in store." He reached to skim the edge of her face with his thumb, worry clouding his eyes. "You have forgiven him, right?"

She nodded, grateful for Bram's mentorship over the years, especially in things of the spirit. He'd convinced her long ago that the only way to stop the pain that people inflicted was to let go of the hurt and give it to God, allowing forgiveness to unleash the blessings of heaven. And it had—immeasurably—until Devin Caldwell had once again darkened her door.

"Good." He leaned back in his chair, arms folded and gaze warm.

Shimmying back into her chair, she absently chewed on her thumbnail. "But from the shock and embarrassment I saw on his face, I suspect he's more nervous than I, which is certainly a new scenario." She sucked in a deep draw of air, releasing it slowly. "The way he ogled me in the coffee room, I just hope he doesn't try and win me over with his charm," she said with a shaky sigh. "Heaven knows he's always had a disastrous effect on me."

Bram gave a gruff clear of his throat and tossed the pen onto the desk. "Well, don't let him, it's as simple as that. Be professional and nice, but keep your distance."

"You're absolutely right." She lifted her chin, mouth firming with resolve. "And trust me—I plan to. Ever since his growth spurt, he's been every girl's dream, and I have no desire to become another notch on his oversized ego."

Bram's smile tightened. "Good girl," he said with his usual calm, which somehow appeared at odds with the troubled look in his eyes. Clearing his throat again, he fished his watch out to check the time. "Just see to it that you don't. I'm enjoying the fact that the days of picking up the pieces of Megan McClare's heart appear to be over." He rose and skirted the desk to help her to her feet, ushering her to the door where he gave her a side hug. "I don't know about Caldwell being "every woman's dream," but I do know you'll be Marcus Wilson's dream if you apply for a volunteer position."

"Oh, Bram, thank you!" She spun to face him, hugging him so hard that he chuckled as he ushered her into the hall. "To the dogs with Devin Caldwell," she said with a giggle. "You're the one who's every woman's dream!" She stood on tiptoe to deposit a kiss to his cheek, smiling at the ruddy color that suddenly crept up his neck. "*Especially* as a dear friend, Counselor Hughes." And waving goodbye with the file in the air, she hurried down the hall to Marcus Wilson's office, her pulse racing as fast as her thoughts.

Devin Caldwell—every woman's dream?

"Ha—in *his* dreams, maybe, but not mine." Warmth invaded her cheeks when she realized she'd spoken out loud and peeking over her shoulder, she was relieved to find the hall empty. All at once, she halted dead in her tracks, jaw sagging into a gaping smile of shock. *Wait*—it finally dawned—*Devin Caldwell is no longer my dream.* Her smile slowly bloomed into a grin. Eye on the bubbled glass door at the very end of the hall, she straightened her shoulders and continued on, thankful she was finally emotionally free without danger of anything more. Because Devin Caldwell may think he's every woman's dream, but since Paris? A smile flickered at the corners of Meg's mouth as she softly rapped on the door.

She was not "every woman."

16

"Are you serious?" Bonnie stared at her through her horn-rimmed glasses, eyes as large as the gape of her jaw. Gaze locked with Meg's, she lifted her mug to take a sip of the coffee she'd just brewed for their early-morning prayer chat and almost missed her mouth. "*He's* the boy who pestered you all through school?"

Meg nodded, cheeks too full of Rosie's homemade banana muffins to even speak.

"Oh, that's a real shame." Bonnie huffed out a sigh before stuffing her mouth with the rest of her muffin. A lump bobbed in her skinny throat as she swallowed. "He's dreamy."

"*And* knows it, which makes him not so dreamy if you ask me." Meg took a drink of her coffee, nose scrunched at the thought of falling for anyone like Devin Caldwell. No, he'd cured her of trusting flirty, double-tongued men like him, so she supposed she owed him a debt of thanks. After all, that very distrust had protected her heart in Paris. She took another bite and chewed. Just like it would protect her heart at home.

"You're right," Bonnie said with a hike of her chin. "I think Conor's handsome too, but he knows it as well, so I prefer the intellectual type who have no idea they're appealing."

Meg chuckled. "Mmm . . . I wonder who that might be?"

"I have no earthly idea," Bonnie said with a dainty tip of her cup, one pinky in the air.

Meg grinned despite the muffin bulging in her cheeks. She swallowed it in a gulp. "So . . . when do I get to redecorate?" She set her cup down and leaned in, arms folded on the table.

"What do you mean?" Bonnie blinked, adorably reminiscent of a baby owl. "The waiting room looks perfect—what more can you do?"

Meg's tongue rolled in her cheek. "Oh, I don't know—shine up the receptionist maybe?"

Heat surged in said receptionist's cheeks, causing her to fan her face as furiously as the rapid blink of her eyes. "Oh my, let me save both of us a lot of embarrassment and assure you I am hopelessly dowdy and quite certain any effort to 'shine' will be futile."

Meg huffed out a sigh, gaze thinning with determination. "Close your eyes."

"I beg your pardon?" Bonnie's long, slender fingers splayed to her sunken chest.

"I said 'close your eyes'—*please.*" Meg swished her hand at her good friend, prompting a bewildered flutter of Bonnie's lids before they finally slammed closed. "Now . . . I want you to envision Evelyn Nesbit in that Coca-Cola ad, you know the one where her hair is piled loosely on her head except for the two banana curls down her back?"

Bonnie nodded slowly, the pinch of her brows undeniable proof she saw no connection.

"All right, now I want you to replace Evelyn's face with yours in your mind's eye, seeing yourself without glasses . . ."

"But I can't see without my glas—"

"Humor me," Meg said in a firm tone, giving Bonnie's fingers an affectionate pinch. "Now remember the dress I had on last week, the blue silk that you loved?"

Bonnie caught her breath, eyes still closed. "You mean the one with the gold piping?"

Meg grinned, satisfied she'd hooked her interest. "Yes, that's the one, and my sister Alli has one just like it." She paused for effect. "In red—"

A gasp parted from Bonnie's lips. "Like a rich scarlet red?"

"Yes, ma'am—with black piping . . ." Meg let that settle in, her grin growing at the lengthy sigh that trailed from Bonnie's lips. "*Except* she tossed it in the rag basket just last week."

Another gasp, this time harsh enough to pop her eyelids. "No!"

Meg clasped Bonnie's hands. "Yes! And if I lengthen the hem, it will be perfect for you."

"Oh, Meg!" Bonnie sagged back, hand clutched to her chest once again. "I couldn't . . ."

"Yes you can—Alli insists, and so do I. Except there *is* a catch . . ."

A lump bobbed in Bonnie's long neck, as big as the muffins Meg brought in for the staff meeting. "What?" she whispered.

"You have to come to dinner so you can try it on *and* let me fix your hair and makeup."

"Oh goodness, I don't know . . ."

"No, but I do, and I'm telling you right now that when I am done with you, George Crane will say, 'Peggy who?'"

The fullness of Bonnie's normally lush lips flattened into a thin scowl. "Peggy O'Keefe is an insatiable flirt who ogles anything in pants."

"Ah-hah! You know that and I know that, but sweet, deluded George thinks Peggy is the marvel of the mailroom, a veritable angel from heaven."

"Humph . . . the fallen kind." Bonnie's hand flew to her mouth as if she'd just realized how awful that sounded. Her cheeks flamed. "Oh, I'm a terrible person."

Meg's smile was soft. "No, just a human one, Bonnie, who has a bit of the mama-bear mentality when it comes to George Crane. And Peggy is human too, just like us, so only heaven knows what painful trials she's endured to make her demean herself so much. I think we just need to pray for her, don't you?"

Bonnie nodded, her manner considerably humbled. "It wouldn't hurt to pray for me too, I suppose, after that catty remark." Expelling a noisy sigh, she peered at Meg with a tilt of her head. "Goodness, Meg, we've been working together for almost a month now, and I've never heard a negative word from your lips about anybody. Do you *ever* talk badly about anyone? Because it seems like you are near perfect when it comes to the feelings of others."

Heat broiled Meg's face. *Near perfect? Ha!* She thought of all the terrible names she'd secretly called Devin Caldwell over the years and vehemently shook her head. "Trust me, Bonnie, I've profaned Devin Caldwell's name till it's lower than dirt, so don't—"

"What's this? 'Lower than dirt'—is that what I heard?" Conor strolled into the conference room with a steaming cup of coffee and a grin. He tossed a glance over his shoulder past Teddy and George to target Devin with a curious gaze. "I'm not sure, but I think our Meg just relegated you to the worm family, Dev . . ."

Megan's jaw remained frozen, heat blasting her cheeks at the sight of Devin Caldwell in the doorway, his face an even ruddier shade of shock than her own.

George chuckled and set his coffee cup on the table, easing into his chair with a broad smile. "Either that or she thinks you're pretty down to earth."

Hearty laughter filled the room, coaxing a sheepish smile from Devin's face, which was as crimson as his red paisley tie. Its four-in-hand knot bobbed along with his Adam's apple as he buried one hand in his pocket, his coffee mug held stiffly in the other.

Despite an impeccable navy suit, gold cufflinks, and stylish high-collar pinstripe shirt, his posture was as wooden and unsure as an awkward little boy—one obviously not used to being the butt of anyone's jokes.

Sympathy squeezed in her chest despite all the years Devin had ridiculed her. A silent sigh feathered her lips. *Not a very nice feeling, is it, Mr. Caldwell?*

"So, what exactly did you do to our sweet little Meg anyway, Dev, to elicit such 'mud'-slinging?" George took a sip of his coffee, one of his mammoth ears twitching the slightest bit.

Avoiding Meg's gaze, Devin pulled his chair out from the table too quickly, bumping George's shoulder. "Sorry," he muttered as he placed his mug on the table with a wobble, splattering coffee onto the polished surface. His face scorched scarlet.

Bonnie launched from the table faster than the skyrockets at Uncle Logan's Napa Estate on the Fourth of July. "I'll wipe it—"

"No!" Devin halted her with a raised palm and a very tight smile. "I mean, no need, Miss Roof, but thank you." He fished a folded handkerchief from his suit coat and proceeded to mop up the spill, jaw compressed despite a smile as starched as his collar.

Bonnie skidded to a stop, her cherry-red cheeks a close match with Devin's. "More coffee, then?" she offered, obviously noting that half of his cup had ended up on the table.

Devin shook his head, wadding his handkerchief before burying it into his pants pocket. "No thank you, I'm not sure I can be trusted." His eyes met Meg's briefly, a touch of that famous Caldwell charm shadowing his smile. "No need to test manners already in tatters."

"Yeah, if he needs more coffee, he can just squeeze it from his handkerchief, right, Dev?" Conor strolled over to take a seat next to Meg. "And as far as manners go, Meg can teach you all you need to know. She gives me the evil eye every time I snitch one too many cookies or donuts." He eyed the plate of muffins. "Hey, Teach—are those for us?"

"Oh—yes!" She shot to her feet, anxious to move beyond her embarrassment and Devin's. Offering a schoolmarm smile, she rounded the table, dispensing the stack of plates she'd brought in. "And only one per person, Mr. O'Neil, so don't get greedy or I'll send you to the principal, understood?"

"Me?" Conor said in mock offense, hand splayed to his beige silk vest. "What about Dev—he's the one you called a worm."

Heat swarmed the lacy collar of Meg's silk blouse, most likely making her powdered face and auburn hair a perfect match. "Conor O'Neil, I did *not* call Mr. Caldwell a worm . . ."

Conor shrugged, cheeks chunky with muffin. "Worm, lower than dirt, same difference."

"Actually, Con," Teddy said in a low, tentative jest, "in a court of law, Meg would win." Stretching across the table with a soft grunt, he took a muffin, his full face a perennial shade of pink except for the spray of freckles across a surprisingly delicate nose. "Lower than dirt doesn't necessarily constitute a worm, you know. It could mean a grub, crickets, ants, termites—"

"Snakes, rats, tarantulas—" George offered, licking crumbs from his fingers.

"Hey, now you're getting personal," Devin said with a chuckle.

Conor licked a splotch of chocolate from his lip. "Well, it sure sounds personal." He angled back with a quick brush of hands, scrutinizing Devin with a curious gaze. "Our Meg—one of the sweetest, kindest people I know—thinks you're lower than dirt?" He shook his head, ignoring the finger Meg pressed to her lips. "I for one would like to know why."

She inwardly groaned as she resumed her seat, quite sure she had no need of rouge today. "Conor, please—can't we just change the subject?"

"I agree," Devin said, gaze flicking to hers. "But *not* before I even the score."

Meg's fingers froze, paralyzed on the coffee cup halfway to her lips.

With exasperating calm, Devin took another bite, gaze thoughtful as he chewed, eyes locked with hers. He upended his cup, then slid it in her direction, a twinkle gleaming in warm eyes the color of his coffee. "And since you know how I take it, Meg—do you mind?"

She vaulted to her feet despite wobbly legs, instantly submitting to the same hypnotic control Devin Caldwell wielded over her and every other girl at school. "Oh, not at all—"

"I'm teasing," he said softly. His eyes shone with a sincerity that shocked despite the mischief in his tone. "Besides, Miss McClare, do you really think it's wise to let the girl to whom I was always a snot-nosed hooligan doctor my coffee?"

All she could do was stare, paralyzed by the gentleness of his tone and his penitent smile. "Will you forgive me, Meg, for treating you so poorly over the years?"

She swallowed hard and nodded, barely able to believe that Devin Caldwell was making amends. "Of course I forgive you," she whispered, "if you'll forgive me for—"

"Saying he's lower than dirt?" A smile twitched on Conor's lips.

"Implying he's a worm?" Teddy volunteered.

"Calling him a snake and a rat?" George popped the rest of his muffin in his mouth.

Meg laughed despite the burn of her cheeks. "I did *not* call him either of those nasty names, George Crane, and you know it." Her throat constricted as she met Devin's gaze across the table. "Although I suppose I did say something about being . . .

lower than dirt, possibly implying you're a worm, but I apologize, Devin, because it was wrong . . ."

His eyes softened. "Yes, it was, because we both know I was *not* a worm." Inhaling deeply, he expelled a sigh laden with regret, scanning the table as if to offer a group apology before he focused on Meg once again. "The truth is, I was *lower* than a worm to Miss McClare in school, and I just hope she can find it in her heart to let me make it up, especially now that we have to work together so closely."

She opened her mouth to respond, but nothing came out. *For the sake of sanity, Meg, say something . . .* She ingested a deep draw of air to regain her confidence before she managed a hint of a smile. "Maybe . . . if you'll forgive me for trampling your pride in every spelling bee and science fair from first grade through eleventh."

The others chuckled, easing the tightness in her chest as Devin extended a hand. "Deal . . . if you promise to forgive me when I outshine you as the DA's star intern."

She laughed and shook his hand. "Ah . . . now *there's* the Devin Caldwell I know and love—a competitor to the core."

"Love?" The brown eyes gleamed with mischief. "Don't toy with my emotions like that, Miss McClare."

"Ha! She toys with mine all the time, so what makes you think you're any different?" Conor clunked his empty cup on the table, grin widening when Linda Marie appeared at the door. "As does the lovely Miss Finn, who, I might add," he quipped, hamming it up by clutching his cup to his chest, "I hope will have pity on us with another pot of her truly miraculous coffee."

Linda Marie strolled in with a sassy smile, arms folded across a particularly snug shirtwaist. "I'll have pity all right, Conor O'Neil," she said with a pretty toss of her head, her chestnut pompadour sporting a navy bow to match her form-fitting skirt. "On poor

George and Teddy, that is, for having to work with the likes of you." Awarding Conor a playful smirk, her attention instantly lighted upon Devin with a coy smile. "And, of course, poor Devin too," she said in a voice too sultry for an office, "whose cup I will gladly refill along with yours when I return with Mr. Turner's."

"Sure, fawn over all the heartbreakers," George said in a good-natured grouse, "while Teddy and I are forced to get our own."

Heartbreakers. Meg gulped when Devin flirted back with Linda Marie, employing his trademark flash of teeth.

Coffee. I need coffee. She bolted to her feet. *And distance . . . lots and lots of distance.* "Uh, I need a refill before our morning meeting, so I'll be happy to replenish coffee all around."

"Oh, no you don't." Devin snatched her cup and rose with great fanfare, hand splayed to his chest. "I'm the new kid on the block, so I'll help Linda Marie. I'm sure she knows how these jokers take their coffee, but how 'bout you?"

"No, really, Devin, you don't have—"

"Yes, he does, Meg—let 'im." George jotted notes with the paper and pencil he'd brought.

"Yes, Meg, let me." Devin's smile weakened her resistance. "It's the least I can do after acting like a buffoon last week, expecting you to deliver *my* coffee." He winked. "Besides, it might win me points with Andrew for top-intern status." He paused, one dark brow cocked in question. "I'm guessing you're a cream-and-sugar type of girl?"

"Uh . . . yes, please—heavy on the cream, light on the sugar, thank you."

He followed Linda Marie to the door, shooting a grin over his shoulder. "Thought so—sugar to feed that sweet disposition and cream to enhance the peaches-and-cream glow." He gave a quick salute. "Sit tight, ladies and gentlemen—we'll be right back."

Sit tight? No problem. Meg's body was so rigid now, she could barely breathe, the notion of Devin Caldwell flirting with her—Megan McTubby—unraveling any poise she may have had. Her eyelids fluttered closed. *Lord, please—do* not *let Devin Caldwell reduce me to one of his simpering, love-struck females!*

She tried to settle her nerves with a deep inhale, smiling as she pretended to listen to the good-natured ribbing between Conor and George. Idly snatching her pen from the table, she rolled it between her fingers while forcing her body to calm. She needed to evaluate the situation through intellect, not pulse rate. The very last thing she wanted was attraction to a sweet-talking, overconfident rogue like Devin Caldwell. A "pretty boy," as Cassie had dubbed Jamie early on in their relationship. Only Jamie had a heart for underdogs like Meg had once been, where Devin had made a practice of ridiculing them. How could she ever trust a man like that or even feed his ego, which was already well overfed? Meg sighed. The truth was she couldn't, especially not one bent on "top-intern status."

Her jaw went slack. *Top-intern status . . .*

She blinked. Oh my goodness, that was it—the way to protect herself from Devin Caldwell. The same way she'd protected herself all these years from his ridicule, only now she would use it to protect herself from his charm.

A slow smile inched across her lips.

She would challenge him.

Because as sure as the dimples in those chiseled cheeks, if there was one thing Devin Caldwell possessed in great abundance other than charm, it was pride.

And *everyone* knows that pride goeth before the fall.

Her teeth tugged on the edge of her grin.

His.

17

*L*ogan resisted a scowl as he escorted Cait across the posh marble lobby of The St. Francis Hotel, thinking Turner's new residence matched him perfectly—stuffy and overstated.

"Goodness, Logan, it's a welcome-home party for your niece, not a funeral." Caitlyn's glance held a hint of a tease, her beauty far surpassing anything The St. Francis had to offer. A calming mix of lavender with a hint of spicy clove roused his senses as she leaned close, obviously hoping to keep her jest discreet. They both nodded at a cluster of society matrons chatting in the pillared lounging area, where gilded ceilings and crystal chandeliers provided a lavish setting for scarlet sofas and gold Tiffany lamps. Cait's smile was a whole lot warmer than his, but then Andrew Turner showing off at a $2.5 million-dollar hotel designed to rival the great hotels of Europe was nothing to smile about. Not when it upstaged Logan with *his* family.

"Mezzanine," he muttered to the elevator attendant, lips compressed as they stepped into the ornate gilded conveyance that would take them to the second story. He drew Cait back to allow others to enter behind them, his body stiff against rich wood-paneled walls graced with expensive artwork. The doors closed, and she bent near once again, voice low. "Well then, can you at least *pretend* you enjoy my company, Mr. McClare?" she said softly

170

in his ear, a definite smile in her tone. "I'd rather my self-esteem not suffer quite as much as you."

He peered at her out of the corner of his eye, the humor in her face coaxing a faint smile to his lips. "Your self-esteem is safe with me, Cait," he said, wishing she didn't look so blasted beautiful in that form-fitting jade satin dress that heightened the green of her eyes. His mouth crooked. "Which is more than I can say for Turner's face if he lords it over me tonight."

"Mezzanine level." The attendant opened the doors, and all occupants quickly filed out, desperate, evidently, to get to *the* place to be and be seen in San Francisco these days—The St. Francis's Mural Room. Logan nodded his thanks to the attendant as he herded Cait out, miffed that Turner was not only upstaging him with his family, but trumping Logan's Palace Hotel residence as well. His jaw began to grind.

"Logan." Cait halted him in the hallway with a gentle hand, all humor in her eyes softening into quiet understanding. "I appreciate you coming tonight despite your dislike of Andrew because you are incredibly important to our family and we all want you there. Please know I would've never agreed to this if Meg hadn't been so excited, but she was, so I could hardly say no." The green satin of her bodice shimmered with a soft sigh in the glow of the crystal chandelier overhead while she peeked up with a tentative smile. "Promise me you'll try—please? Try to be civil to Andrew? Who knows—maybe you'll even enjoy yourself. This is important to Meg because Andrew is her manager, and he's invited her co-workers as well. So, please—" She cupped his jaw, stilling his body with that little-girl smile that always melted his heart. "For Meg, for me, *and* for you—promise you'll try to enjoy a lovely dinner in a beautiful hotel with people who love you very, very much."

Palming her hand on his cheek, he expelled a weighty sigh,

his eyes conveying a promise he hoped he could keep. "I promise, Cait, but only because my love for you and your family runs deeper than my disdain for Turner." In natural reflex, his gaze lowered to her lips briefly before his eyes reconnected with hers. "Much, much deeper," he whispered.

"Cait—you're here! I was beginning to think Logan absconded with you." Andrew strode across a vibrant Oriental rug to greet them in the hall, calcifying Logan's jaw when the man took Cait's hands in his own. "You look exquisite, Cait, as always." His smile shifted to Logan, the warmth in his eyes more than evident as he extended his hand. "Thank you for joining us, Logan. I know it wouldn't be the same for Cait and her family without you."

My family. A nerve flicked in Logan's cheek as he shook Andrew's hand, wondering if they would still be best friends today if Cait hadn't entered the picture. He felt the firm press of Andrew's palm, saw the sincerity in pale-blue eyes that had always held affection and humor when they were boys, and suddenly knew that they would. He and Andrew had weathered every storm from grade school through law school, be it disgruntled teachers or brokenhearted girls, and Logan almost regretted the rift.

Almost.

Andrew appeared ready to escort Cait into the Mural Room, and Logan grazed the small of her back before firmly offering his arm instead. This may be Turner's party, but Logan intended to claim the lion's share of Cait's attention tonight.

Andrew acquiesced with a quiet nod before leading them into the room to which San Francisco society flocked.

And no wonder. Logan bit back a growl when Cait actually paused with a faint catch of her breath as she took it all in—an exquisite ballroom, alive with Old World charm and sophistication. A gold-filigreed coffered ceiling was resplendent with an ornate balcony that wrapped three sides of the room. One entire wall boasted an exquisite mural depicting a Tuscany countryside while stately palms, flowering trees, and potted bougainvillea added a garden effect that would charm every single female in the room.

"Oh, Andrew, it's lovely," she breathed as they made their way along the edge of a lustrous oak dance floor where the crème de la crème dined and danced to a waltz performed by a ten-piece orchestra in tails and tie.

Dash it, Cait, he doesn't own the blasted hotel. Logan's grip on her arm tightened as he offered stiff smiles to several friends and acquaintances.

Andrew had secured a somewhat private area beneath the far balcony where Meg sat at the head of a long linen-clad table flanked by Bram and family on one side and coworkers on the other. Crystal vases heavy with pale-pink roses—Meg's favorite—spanned its length, infusing the intimate space with a heady scent while candlelight lent a soft glow to his niece's smiling face. He could hear her laughter amid the chatter and music as she grinned at something Bram said, and in that moment Logan knew he could do this for his family—put his feud with Andrew aside for one night to celebrate a niece who was more like a daughter.

"Mama, Uncle Logan—you're here!" Maddie hopped from Jamie's lap with a squeal and bounded toward them, giggling when Logan swooped her up in his arms. "Bram let me sit in the front seat of his car," she gushed, obviously thrilled she'd been allowed to accompany her older siblings and cousin.

"Did he now?" Cait said, standing on tiptoe to press a kiss to Maddie's cheek, her upturned face so near that Logan's pulse skipped a beat.

Maddie wiggled from his arms to Cait's, allowing Logan to stroll over to cuff Jamie, Blake, and Bram on the shoulders while giving George, Teddy, Conor, and Devin a friendly nod. "Consorting with the enemy, I see," he said with a wink at Meg, greeting Bonnie and Linda Marie before bending to kiss both Cassie's and Alli's cheeks.

Jamie grinned. "Just lulling them into a false sense of security by showing an interest," he said with a lift of his glass, a definite note of levity in his tone, "satisfying our curiosity as to just how they win any cases at all."

Logan laughed. "Well, don't swap trade secrets—curiosity killed the cat, you know."

Bram grinned. "I'm afraid they already have an unfair advantage, sir. They've got Megs while all we have are Blake and Jamie."

Jamie squinted at Bram, ignoring the laughter over his remark. "Hey, Hughes, we're on the same team, remember?"

"Not if you don't win the Hyde case," Logan quipped with a ruffle of Jamie's dark curls, leaving the revelry behind to return to his place next to Cait. Andrew had placed her at the opposite head of the table as Meg with his seat to her right and Logan's to the left.

Clinking his spoon against his water goblet, Andrew introduced his staff before raising a toast to Meg, welcoming her home from Paris and as a new member of his team.

Despite his enmity with Turner, Logan actually found himself enjoying both dinner and then dessert. Andrew had them all laughing over humorous stories of Meg's rivalry with Devin Caldwell in the office, where she seemed bent on surpassing the upstart in every task Andrew assigned. Logan's gaze flicked to the intern who'd made Meg's life miserable for so many years, and a proud grin stretched across his face. *That a girl, Megs.*

Pushing his dessert plate away, Logan eased back in his chair and unbuttoned his jacket, his heart surprisingly content on Andrew's dime. He enjoyed the friendly sparring between Andrew's staff and his and, of course, Cait divided her attention evenly between Andrew and him, gracious to a fault. With little or no effort, she drew them both into conversation she obviously deemed safe enough to neutralize ill feelings. And she'd succeeded, he was reluctant to admit—all without a drop of alcohol to take the edge off, due to Andrew's teetotaler ways. Logan upended his iced tea, wondering just when Andrew gave up the liquor they both so readily consumed in law school. Since Cait, perhaps? Well, no matter—somehow she'd managed to make the evening enjoyable, the time spent between Andrew and him almost cordial.

Until the lowlife asked her to dance.

Every nerve in Logan's body twitched as Turner took Cait in his arms—too close to suit and too blasted confident while he whirled her into a waltz. Grilling them with a glare, he bolted his water, aware he'd been grinding his teeth because his jaw ached as much as his pride.

"Uncle Logan . . . may I have this dance?"

He glanced up to see Meg watching him with a tentative smile, not missing the hint of concern in her eyes. Expelling a silent breath, he rose and forced a bright smile to put her worries at ease. "It would be my pleasure, Miss McClare, and a true honor when you can obviously have your pick of partners." Tucking her hand over his arm, he led her to the floor, as far from Turner and Cait as he could possibly get.

"So," he said with an easy spin, "I understand Devin Caldwell is still coming in a distant second these days." A pretty blush burnished Meg's cheeks, bringing a grin to Logan's face. He laughed as he twirled her again, feathering the wispy auburn curls at the back of her neck. "Good work, Megs. Make that rascal pay for every obnoxious thing he ever said or did."

Her imp of a smile told him she enjoyed putting Caldwell

in his place. "I'm just doing my job, Uncle Logan, to the best of my ability, that's all." Her chin notched up, a definite sparkle in emerald eyes so like her mother's. "And if Devin can't keep up, well, then I'm sorry."

He grinned. "No you're not, you're enjoying every single moment, and I'm glad." His smile faded to soft. "Nobody deserves it more than you, sweetheart." He drew her close with a hand to her waist, depositing a kiss to her head.

"Uncle Logan?"

"Mmm?"

Meg's voice was barely a whisper. "Devin Caldwell's not the only one lagging behind," she said softly. "Mr. Turner's not even a distant second—he's so far behind that Mother can't see him for you."

He swallowed hard as he gave her a final spin. "One can only hope."

"And pray," she whispered as the music ended, the love in her eyes thickening the walls of his throat. She stood on tiptoe to deposit a gentle kiss to his cheek. "We all love you so very much, Uncle Logan, and we're all praying you win."

He fought the sting of moisture in his eyes, quickly looping her waist to lead her from the floor. "Then I don't see how I can fail, Megs, with the love and prayers of my family."

"Am I up next, I hope?" Bram's smile tilted off-center. "Although I don't have Logan's finesse on the dance floor, Bug, I promise not to step on your toes."

She took Bram's hand then smiled at Logan, her gaze flicking to the dance floor and back before she gave a short nod in Cait and Turner's direction. "I've never known you to be shy about cutting in, you know." She gave him a wink so out of character for the shy niece he knew and loved that he grinned, shaking his head as Bram led her to the floor.

With a faint smile, he tugged on the cuffs of his sleeves and rebuttoned his jacket while scanning the couples, looking for Turner and Cait.

"Uncle Logan? Will you dance with me?"

He paused to look down, heart melting as always when Maddie gave him that innocent blink of blue eyes. Without a moment's hesitation, he swept her up and dove for her neck, giving her a snuggle kiss that unleashed a peal of giggles. "I'd be delighted, Miss McClare, and the envy of every man in the room, I assure you." Holding her close, he took to the floor with her snug in his arms, holding one of her tiny hands in waltz position as the other curled around his neck. Maddie rested her head on his chest, and he closed his eyes, breathing in her sweet scent of talcum powder and Pear's soap while slowly moving to the sound of the music. This is what he craved, what he lived for—perfect moments like this, loving those who possessed his heart so completely. Spoiling nieces he adored and bonding with nephews he loved, longing to restore the love they'd lost with the death of his brother. His eyes opened, lighting on Cait across the room. *And, God help me, please—aching to love their mother . . .*

"My turn, squirt." Jamie tickled Maddie's waist before tapping Logan's shoulder. "May I cut in, sir? It seems my wife has disappeared, so I'm looking for a pretty woman."

Maddie giggled and lunged into Jamie's arms. "Thanks, Uncle Logan—I'll dance with you later."

"Mmm . . . deserted three times tonight," Logan said with a mock scowl. "Must be losing my touch."

"I doubt that." Jamie winked, giving Logan a knowing smile. "All it takes is cutting in, sir."

Logan grinned, eyes perusing the couples crowding the floor. "I'm going, I'm going," he muttered with a slap of Jamie's shoulder, tugging a lock of Maddie's auburn hair before turning to stroll the perimeter, eyes in a squint. He searched the dance floor, stomach as jumpy as a kid with a crush on a first date. "Where the devil are you, Cait?" he mumbled under his breath.

"Why, Logan McClare, as I live and breathe, are you back from the dead, I hope?"

A groan trapped in Logan's throat as he turned around, gut cramping at the sight of Ann Miller, one of the beautiful social-ites he'd been involved with before he dropped from the social scene for Cait. "Ann," he whispered, a rare surge of heat ringing his collar. "It's good to see you again."

"Now if that were true, Supervisor," she said coyly, "I doubt it would've taken this long." She cocked her head, a vision in blue crepe. "Dare I hope we might share a dance?"

He hesitated, reluctant to turn her away so abruptly like he had before.

Because of Cait.

Her hand lighted on his arm, her coax as soft as the hope in her eyes. "One dance, Logan—not a proposal of marriage, after all. Just a moment to catch up between old friends."

Old friends. Logan inwardly winced. Old lovers would be more apt. He drew in a shaky breath, painfully aware just how much Cait—and God—had changed his life for the better.

He exhaled his resignation with an inaudible sigh. "Why not?" he said quietly, calmly leading her onto the floor.

Why not? His smile was stiff as he took her in his arms, wish-ing he were anywhere but there. *Because the next dance—and my heart, Miss Miller—belongs to Caitlyn McClare.*

18

"Now, honestly, Mrs. McClare—isn't this worth stealing away for a few moments?"

Caitlyn expanded her lungs with the crisp night breeze on The St. Francis veranda, hoping to calm the nervous skitter of her stomach. The glorious scent of the sea was heavy in the air along with that of night-blooming jasmine, which spilled from planters along the perimeter of the stone balustrade. The wind ruffled stray tendrils against her cheek as she expelled a tentative sigh. "Indeed. Union Square is one of my favorite spots in the city, Andrew, and to see it at night with the Dewey Monument all aglow is truly a breathtaking view."

The air in her chest stalled when he moved in close. His arm shored the small of her back as they stared out into the night together, the isolated veranda lit only by moonlight that suddenly felt *far* too intimate. "'Breathtaking' is certainly an appropriate word, Cait," he whispered, his fingers grazing the bare skin of her arm before he turned her to face him. His hands lingered at her waist, coaxing with a slow graze of thumbs. "Because you take mine every time I see you." His Adam's apple shifted. "But then you always have."

A silent gasp snagged in her throat while the air sizzled with romantic tension she neither needed nor wanted right now. *Especially* with Logan a mere room away! Heart thudding, she took a step back, dislodging his hold with an awkward clutch of her arms. "Goodness, it's chilly out here. I think it's best we head back in."

Taking his jacket off, he draped it over her shoulders. "Not yet, Cait, please?" He rubbed her arms, and she felt the heat of his hands through the sleeves of his coat. "I need to ask you something."

"Wh-what is it?" she stuttered, cinching his jacket with pinched fingers, his scent enveloping her with a heat she didn't expect.

The intensity of his eyes tightened her stomach. "I think you already know I have deep feelings for you, Cait, although heaven knows I've tried to take it slow."

"Andrew—"

He stilled her words with a slow trace of her lips. "No, Cait—hear me out, please?"

She nodded dumbly, goose bumps pebbling her arms despite the warmth of his jacket.

"I'm in love with you, Cait—deeply, irrevocably, and completely around the bend, despite your best intentions and mine." His eyes probed hers with a longing she'd ignored far too long. "I'm asking you to give me a chance to court you and we can take it slowly if you like—beginning with the Barrister Ball."

She froze, too stunned to move or even object as he moved closer.

"Please say yes . . . at least to the Barrister Ball, and then you can take your time to pray and think about courtship." He stroked the edge of her jaw with a tender touch. "I know it's ridiculously late notice, with the ball only a week away, and I apologize for that, truly I do." He paused, smile sheepish. "But to be honest I didn't think I had a prayer of you saying yes, and then . . ." He grinned outright, his little-boy enthusiasm making her smile. "Well, I'm not supposed to know this, understand, but I just found out that I'm in the running for the Dickherber Civil Service Award—"

"Oh, Andrew," she breathed, tears pricking at the memory of Liam receiving the prestigious Dickherber Award the year before he died. His greatest achievement, he always said, after her and his family. "I am so very proud of you!" she whispered, blinking hard to stem her tears while she hugged him with all of her might.

He pulled back, the look of love in his eyes tripping her pulse. "So the truth is, Cait, I was hoping—praying, really—that you'd consider accompanying me because you see, if I win," his smile faded to tender, "I want the most important person in my life to be there."

She gave a slow blink. *The most important person in his life??*

He tucked a curl behind her ear. "It would mean the world to me, even if we go just as friends for now, so please say yes."

"Andrew, I . . . I'm s-sorry, b-but I c-can't—"

"Can't go to the ball or can't court me?" he whispered.

"B-both, I'm afraid."

Palms suddenly damp, she attempted to pull away, but he halted her with a gentle hold. "Because you don't care for me?"

"Of course I care for you," she said in a rush, her voice a rasp of regret, "but as a friend, Andrew, nothing more."

He stilled, the intensity in his eyes making her squirm. "So . . . you're not attracted to me then, is that it?"

Eyes wide, she beseeched him with her gaze, unwilling to lie. Because in one defining beat of her heart, the truth struck hard, as swift as the hammer of her pulse. *If not for Logan,* she suddenly realized, *I could fall in love with this man.* A man who shared her hopes and dreams for the city . . . *and* a man who shared a faith as deep as her own.

His grip tightened. "Please answer me, Cait," he whispered, the urgency in his tone causing her to shiver. "I need to know if you're feeling what I am, if there's any chance at all."

"An-drew, I . . . I can't say—"

Her gasp was lost in the tenderness of his kiss when he drew her near. She jolted as heat coiled through her so strong that a moan rose within, utterly silenced by the caress of his mouth.

And then in a whoosh of cold air, he jerked back with a violence that iced her skin more than the absence of his touch, as his body sprawled across the veranda with a harsh grunt.

"So help me, Turner, I'll kill you if you ever touch her again." Logan's eyes were those of a madman as he stood over Andrew, fists knotted at his sides.

"You don't own her, McClare." Andrew shot up with the same blood lust in his eyes that she saw in Logan's. "No matter what you think. She's her own woman and can decide for herself."

Logan lunged, two-fisting Andrew's vest and shirt with so much brute force Caitlyn screamed. "I've warned you before, and I'm not going to warn you again—stay away from her!"

"Logan, stop!" Heat pulsed in Cait's cheeks, Logan's violence causing her to tremble.

Andrew shoved back with equal strength. "Why don't you let Cait decide, McClare?" A smile hovered on his lips, obviously meant to goad. "Or are you afraid you'll lose once again?"

Caitlyn's cry pierced the night when Logan slammed a fist into Andrew's jaw. The sickening thud of knuckles to bone curdled her stomach and paralyzed her tongue.

Dazed, Andrew staggered back and swiped his bloody mouth with the back of his hand. Glancing at the scarlet stains splattered across his white shirt, he unleashed a harsh growl with a powerful thrust that sent Logan reeling.

"Nooooo!" Caitlyn blocked Andrew with palms to his chest. "This stops *now!*"

Chest heaving, Andrew singed Logan with a glare before his eyes finally met hers, contrition strong in their depths. "Forgive me, Cait, for ruining your evening," he whispered. He pulled his handkerchief from his pocket to wipe his face.

She nodded mutely and took the cloth from his hand to gently remove the remains of blood that he missed, aware of Logan's seething presence behind her. Relinquishing a weary sigh, she removed his jacket and handed it to him. "Go change your shirt, Andrew," she said quietly, "and we'll try to salvage what has been up till now a most splendid evening."

He drew in a deep breath and nodded, pocketing his handkerchief as he crossed the stone veranda. He turned at the door. "But I won't change just yet, Cait." His eyes lanced Logan with a venomous stare. "I'll wait in the hallway just to make sure you're okay."

Logan jerked forward with a hiss, but Cait halted him with a brutal wrench of his shirt, nails digging into a heaving chest that felt like rock. "No!" she screamed, eyes blazing with anger she seldom displayed. "You lay a hand on Andrew Turner ever again, and it will be the last you see of me, is that understood?"

His silence pounded like the blood in her ears as he stared, gray eyes black with fury.

With a hard yank of his pristine shirt, she shoved him back. "Answer me! *Do-you-understand?*"

A muscle twitched in his cheek as his eyes bore through hers, his temper barely contained. In rigid motion, he retucked his shirt and adjusted the sleeves of coat, his voice little more than a hiss. "Yes."

She turned to give Andrew a stiff smile. "Thank you, Andrew—I won't be a moment."

Andrew nodded and left. The door barely clicked behind him when Caitlyn whirled to face Logan. "How dare you!" she breathed, shallow breaths rasping from her throat.

"How dare *I*?" He bit the words out, eyes seething. "How dare *you* profess to love me and agree to court me not *nine* months ago, then so readily fall into the arms of the one man I despise, letting him paw you like some wanton woman—"

The air whooshed still in her lungs, paralyzing her for several seconds while tears stung in her eyes. And then in a delayed knee-jerk reaction, she slapped him so hard, his head slammed to the side, the crack of her palm echoing loud in the night. She shook with fury that begged release, angrier than she'd ever been. "A fine remark from the man who forced his way on me in Napa and on heaven knows how many other women over the years." She hiked her chin in defiance, voice quivering, but shoulders square. "This-conversation-is-over," she whispered, turning on her heel to bolt for the door.

"The deuce it is!" He spun her around, gripping her arms so tightly, she couldn't move. "We're going to settle this once and for all, Cait." His chest pumped hard as he slowly released her, stepping back as if to give her some air. His harsh tone lowered to the level of calm she imagined he employed with difficult clients, arms stiff at his sides while his fingers flexed and clenched several times. "I love you more than anything in this world, Cait, and you claim to love me, and yet you deny me the hope of marriage." A tic flickered in his steeled jaw. "For the love of all that's decent—how do you *expect* me to react when I find him kissing you, something you go to great lengths to avoid with me—the man you *supposedly* love?"

A weary sigh quivered from her lips, draining all anger. She took a step forward to gently cup his wrist. "Logan, I'm sorry you had to see that, but please believe me—he took me by surprise. It was nothing I asked for nor wanted, I assure you."

A flash of fire sparked in his eyes. "You could have assured me far more by pushing him away, Cait, slapping him silly like he deserved." He distanced himself once again, causing her hand to plummet from his wrist. "But you didn't," he whispered, his words edged with ice.

Her cheeks flushed hot because he was right. She swallowed hard, struggling to respond.

"Are-you-attracted-to-him?" He bit each syllable out, jaw clamped as tight as his lips.

"Logan, this is silly—I have no romantic interest in Andrew Turn—"

He grasped her arms again, giving them a firm shake. "Are-you-attracted-to-him?" he repeated, the hiss of each word hot against her face.

She felt the heat of her blush to the roots of her hair. "I don't have to answer that," she shot back, ashamed to admit the truth to herself, much less to him.

His voice was deadly quiet when he released her. "You just did." Turning away, he slashed blunt fingers through his hair, his broad back appearing to sag.

"Logan . . ." Her heart cramped at the pain she'd caused. Hands shaking, she rubbed his back with a tender touch. "He kissed me, it's true, but I suspect only to coax me to accompany him to the Barrister Ball. But I turned him down, so you have nothing to worry about . . ."

He rotated slowly, his face set in mortar and stone like the very veranda beneath their feet. "You're right, Cait, because after tonight, he's out of your life."

Her body stilled. "Pardon me?"

"Other than Vigilance Meetings at Walter's or elsewhere, I'm asking you to stop seeing him."

Her ire rose along with her voice. "Asking? Or telling?"

A nerve jerked in his cheek. "Demanding."

Icy needles prickled her skin. "You c-can't be serious."

He never even blinked. "Dead serious."

Arms barricaded to her chest, she shook her head, body quivering. "Well, you can demand all you want, Logan McClare, but as Andrew so aptly put it, you don't own me."

He stepped in close, obviously to intimidate her with his towering height. "I may not own you, Cait, but I *am* responsible for the well-being of you and your family, per final request of my brother. So rest assured, I fully intend to protect your interests and those of my family."

"My 'interests'?" she shouted. "Or yours?"

"*Ours*, Cait." He sucked in a breath and stepped back, softening his stance, but not the steely look in his eyes. "I want your word, Cait, that Turner will be out of your life."

Resolve hardened in her bones. She was well aware this was a battle she could not afford to lose. Logan already held far too much sway in her life—and in her heart. She could not allow him to gain any ground. "And if I won't?"

He pierced her with a look so menacing, she fought the twinge of a buckle at the back of her knees. His voice was low, but the threat was loud and clear. "Then you've made your choice, and I'll make mine."

She stiffened her shoulders. "Meaning?"

His jaw began to grind, chilling evidence of an iron will. "It's me or him, Cait—take your pick."

Her stomach seized, and somewhere deep down inside she felt it—the faint rumble of outrage stirring, rising from the same dark tomb in which she'd buried the husband she loved. A soul-quaking fury that had begun after Logan's betrayal years ago and deepened with the death of her best friend and father of her children. Too painful and foreign to entertain, she'd embedded it deep in the recesses of her mind, never to see the light of day.

Until now.

Yes, she loved Logan McClare, but she also knew she couldn't allow him to dominate her again, not like before when she'd been a starry-eyed debutante who opened her heart so completely. So very trusting, so vulnerable. A shiver scurried up her spine. And so very wounded.

But never again.

His breathing was shallow and harsh. "I'll not stand by and lose the woman I love to the man I hate," he said quietly, a pulsing in his temple telling her he would not back down. "So the choice is yours."

She challenged his hard gaze with an unflinching one of her own. "No, Logan, the choice is *yours*," she said quietly, calling his bluff. "Rest assured that I love you and my family loves you, and you are a critical part of our lives. But do not attempt to control me ever again. Please understand I will do anything or see anyone I choose, including Andrew, is that clear?" She spun on her heel, desperate to escape before her limbs gave way.

"Don't do it, Cait," he called, his voice a hoarse command. "Don't fight for a man who will only hurt you and the family I love—I won't allow it."

She halted at the door, his words a flare to the flame of her anger. "You won't *allow* it?" she whispered, pivoting slowly, barely able to comprehend the audacity of his demand. She stared, jaw sagging and anger seething, as close to losing control as she had ever been. "You won't *allow* it?" She seared him with a look before whirling around and lashing the door open. Her eyes scanned the mezzanine lobby until she saw Andrew chatting with several men by the elevator. Scorching Logan with a glare over her shoulder, she opted for rash behavior for the first time in her life, her voice deadly calm. "No, Logan—you just *guaranteed* it."

"Cait—wait!"

But she refused, determined that Logan would never threaten or badger her again. "Andrew," she called, and he glanced up, taking a step forward. Satin skirt clenched in her hands, she literally ran to where he stood, well aware that Logan stalked behind.

"Cait!" Logan's voice echoed, out of breath and a hint of regret for the very first time.

She gripped Andrew's hand. "Is your offer for the Barrister Ball still good?"

Eyes on Logan as he stormed across the lobby, Andrew nodded, smile hesitant. "You know it is, Cait, always."

"Then it's a date," she said with a thrust of her chin. She turned to challenge Logan with a streak of rebellion that felt far better than it should. "And you can thank Logan, Andrew, because he's the one who convinced me to accept."

Logan halted, not five feet away, his look of utter disbelief far less satisfying than she'd expected, not when the pain in his eyes deprived her of all anger.

She opened her mouth to speak, but it was too late. He'd already bolted for the stairwell, slamming the door so hard, it rattled both her bones and her heart. Tears pricked, and she blinked hard to deflect them, hand to her eyes. *Oh Lord—what have I done?* She bowed her head in grief, drawing no comfort from Andrew's gentle touch to her back.

She swallowed hard, regret searing the very walls of her throat. A woman who prided herself on grace and decorum, but tonight she'd lost her temper, her calm, her God-given peace of mind, sacrificing a friendship on the pyre of pride.

The tongue is a fire . . .

She shivered in Andrew's arms, the Scripture she'd read in her prayer book that very morning wrenching a sob from her soul.

And her heart bore the scars to prove it.

19

*M*egan released a sigh of relief as Bram ushered her to the table, the knots in her stomach unraveling when Devin Caldwell was nowhere in sight. Working with Devin day after day for the last week in a professional environment was one thing, but dancing in his arms on a crowded dance floor in front of family and friends was something else altogether. When Andrew had mentioned a family gathering to celebrate her homecoming, she hadn't realized he'd meant the staff "family" as well—a surprise she hadn't expected. Her heart had stuttered when she'd spotted Devin's easy smile, his mention of saving him a dance conjuring memories that slickened her palms.

"I'd rather dance with a hog—more personality and smells better too."

She squeezed her eyes shut, wondering if there would ever be a time when the barbs from her past would wane. She thought they had since Paris, but that was before Devin Caldwell had reentered her life. Now it took everything in her to remain professional and aloof in the workplace, distancing herself—and her heart—from both the man's prior ridicule and notorious charm. She could not—*would not*—let her guard down.

Meg offered Bram a tremulous smile when he seated her next to Alli and Nick, then promptly reached for her water goblet while her eyes scanned the room. She spotted Devin dancing center floor with Linda Marie, who appeared to hang on to his every word while he chatted with George and Bonnie, who danced alongside. Chugging the rest of her water, she set the glass down with shaky fingers, desperately wishing the evening were done.

"Oh!" Hand to her throat, she jumped at Bram's touch.

He nudged his full water goblet next to her empty one with a somber smile, his tone gentle. "I know this isn't what you want to hear, but it may be best to just go ahead and dance with him, Bug. You know, confront your fears and put them to rest?" He slipped an arm around her shoulder to give her a hug, eyes tender. "Not that I don't enjoy dancing almost every dance with you," he said with a crooked grin. His voice veered low. "But you danced with Conor, Teddy, and George, so common courtesy dictates you're going to have to say yes to Devin too. And as much as I enjoy being your excuse each time he asks . . ." His smile was edged with sympathy. "I think you may have to just bite the bullet."

"Or shoot it from a gun," Blake said with a wink, clinking his water glass to Alli's.

Bram chuckled and tugged Meg to face him, settling her nerves with his calm and steady manner. The humor in his eyes faded as he gently brushed a stray curl from her face. "I think you need to—face the past head-on and then put it behind, for your own good and his. Besides . . ." He glanced at the dance floor where the song was just coming to an end. "I'm not fond of him for how he hurt you in the past, but I had a chance to talk with him over dinner and he seems decent enough now, so who knows? Maybe a leopard can change his spots." He tugged on the curl before slipping it behind her ear. "After all, there *is* more than one way to skin a cat."

Smiling despite herself, Meg inhaled deeply, her smile wobbly at best. "I hate skinning cats," she whispered.

He grinned. "Think of it more as taming a tiger—less bloody that way." His manner sobered. "I want to see you leave the hurt behind, Bug, and that can't happen until you confront it—and *him*." He rubbed her arms, as if doing so could infuse her with the courage she needed. When he tipped her chin up, the love in his eyes helped to calm her. "Ask him why he did it. Who knows—you might just find an answer that sets you free—and him."

Expelling a quivering sigh, she felt the old insecurities whirling in her mind like the couples on the floor. She picked at her nails, gaze focused on her fingers. "I'm afraid," she whispered. "Afraid to get too close, afraid he'll charm me like he does everyone else, afraid to be honest." She looked up, voice wavering as her glossy eyes met his. "And terribly afraid to be that vulnerable again." She shook her head, palms sliding her arms like he'd just done. "No, I think I need time, time for the fear to subside before I can let him into my world."

"That's just it, Bug—the fear won't subside. It will never leave until you confront it head-on. The truth is, the things that fear prevents us from doing are the very weapons to dismantle that fear." His lips tipped in the barest of smiles. "Do it afraid, Meg—walk out on that dance floor with Devin Caldwell, knees knocking and heart racing, and just spit in the devil's eye." The lazy smile she loved skimmed across his face while a gleam lit up the blue of his eyes. "But don't make a mistake and spit in Devin's instead."

A tiny giggle bubbled into a half sob, and she threw herself into his arms. "Oh, Bram, what would I do without you?" she whispered, soaking in his strength and stability, an anchor in every storm of her life. Her eyes drifted closed while the peace of his friendship stilled the chaotic beat of her heart. "I love you so much."

His body stiffened for no more than the clip of her heart, and then the solid warmth of his embrace enveloped her as he tucked his head to hers. "And I you, Bug, with all of my heart."

The gruff clear of a throat disrupted the moment. "Excuse me, Miss McClare, but the final set of the evening is upon us, and I've yet to have the pleasure of a dance." Devin Caldwell stood before them with a confident air, hand extended and smile calm. He tipped his head toward the floor. "May I?"

Meg gulped, pulse erratic despite the firm press of Bram's hand. Her frantic gaze darted to Bram's gentle one, pleading for intervention despite the conversation they'd just shared.

Bram smiled and rose. "Excuse me, I believe I spotted an old friend," he said with a final squeeze of her palm, eyes scanning the ballroom. She watched him walk away, broad shoulders and sandy hair disappearing into the crowd, taking her courage with him. *And* her calm.

"Meg?"

She glanced up as Devin waited. A smile crinkled at the edges of brown eyes that held a twinkle. "I suppose that's one way to avoid dancing with me—stalling until the music is over."

Heat skimmed her face as she rose, palm grazing her abdomen to quell the knots in her stomach. She tentatively placed her hand in his, peering up with an apology in her eyes. "Goodness, Devin—we're coworkers—why on earth would I want to avoid you?"

He ushered her onto the floor, deftly sweeping her into a waltz with a pensive smile. "Well actually, Meg, I was hoping you could tell me, because we both know you have—tonight and at the office."

She stumbled and stepped on his foot, but he transitioned smoothly with a steady hand to her waist, shoring her up as if he hadn't noticed. Her cheeks flamed hot as she averted her gaze, feeling every bit of the "Megan McTubby" he'd disdained not so long ago.

"Meg." His voice was a husky whisper, drawing her gaze. The contrition in his eyes took her by surprise. "I was a pompous blowhard in high school and an insufferable cad, especially to you, and I can't apologize enough." He cocked his head to study her as he effortlessly whirled her to the waltz. "You said you've forgiven me, but somehow I doubt that you have."

Blood pulsed in her cheeks. "Devin, I a-assure you, I have forgiven you," she stammered, praying the dance would just come to an end.

"All right," he said quietly, the brown eyes dark with regret. "So then tell me, Miss McClare . . ." He executed a masterful spin that quickened her pulse. "How does a repentant cad achieve absolution from a young woman with whom he very much wants to be friends?"

She peeked up with a chew of her lip, deciding Bram was right—she needed to know why Devin had always been so cruel. Rib cage expanding with an infusion of air, she lifted her eyes to his. "Well, I suppose one could start with the truth, Mr. Caldwell, as to why one would be so hateful to another human being."

A hint of ruddy color invaded his cheeks. "Ah, yes, the truth," he said quietly, shooting a quick glance over his shoulder. Returning his gaze to hers, he inclined his head toward the ballroom door. "Would you mind if we stole away for a bit of privacy and some air?"

She faltered again with a trip over his foot, and heat swamped every inch of her body. "Oh, I'm so sorry," she whispered, not sure which mortified her more—bumbling over his foot or stealing away with the likes of Devin Caldwell.

"You have no reason to be sorry whatsoever, Meg, but I do. It's not a story of which I'm proud, but it is one better suited to fresh air and quiet rather than a noisy room."

"Oh . . . oh, no, r-really, t-that's n-not necess—" Her words came out as jumbled as she.

A smile twitched the corners of his mouth. "I know *you* have never seen me play the role of a gentleman, Miss McClare, but I promise you I can." He paused, awaiting her answer.

Tongue all but glued to the roof of her mouth, Megan could do nothing but nod as he ushered her into the foyer and out onto a stone veranda overlooking Union Square. She released the breath she'd been holding when she spotted another couple beneath the soft glow of a frosted wall sconce. Their presence and the intoxicating scent of jasmine helped soothe the jitters she felt as Devin led her to a quiet corner on the opposite side.

She spied the majestic pillar of the Dewey Monument and for a moment, all nervousness fled as she gazed at the city below, bejeweled with glimmers of light like a lady dressed for a ball. "Oh, it's lovely," she breathed, lifting her face to feel the breeze from the bay.

"I couldn't agree more," Devin said with a smile in his voice, and her jumpiness returned when she realized he was looking at her instead of the view.

Inching away, she faced him with arms tucked to her waist. "So, tell me, Devin, please—why would you show such disregard to another human being and why did you hate me so much?"

His face was somber as he stared at her for several seconds before he leaned over the balustrade, his exhale heavy as he gazed into Union Square with a casual fold of hands. "It's really pretty simple, Meg," he said in a droll tone. "Because you reminded me of my little sister and quite frankly, she's a brat."

Meg's smile was dry. "I see—a family trait?"

He gave her a sideways grin. "Apparently, although mine was by provocation, not heredity." His eyes lapsed into a stare, as if his thoughts were miles away. "I was the apple of my mother's eye, you see, and the bane of my father's existence. So when my mother died—"

Megan gasped, her hand lighting upon his arm. "Oh, Devin—I didn't know. I'm so very sorry," she whispered, desperate to comfort. "How old were you?"

His glance was vague, almost as if he were trapped in the past and not really seeing her at all. "Just turned six," he said quietly, smile sad as his gaze returned to the park. "And would you believe I still miss her?"

Meg's heart cramped, the thought of losing Mother swelling her eyes with tears. She took a step closer, fingers grazing his back. "Yes, I do. I'd be devastated if I lost my mother."

"I was." His tone hardened. "But my father sure wasn't."

His words chilled her skin. "Wh-what do you mean? S-surely he loved her . . ."

"Nope. Married her for her money." He angled to face her, his attitude suddenly cavalier. "An arranged marriage, you know—to fortify two of San Francisco's wealthiest families."

Meg's eyes rounded in shock. "Oh, Devin, I'm so sorry—my heart breaks for you."

He grunted. "Mine did too, especially when he remarried a woman with a prodigy daughter who can do no wrong."

"Prodigy?" Meg tilted her head. "You mean in music?"

His mouth slanted. "I mean in everything. She's all of sixteen and a master at academics, art, music, athletics, you name it. A

196

'wunderkind,' as her private tutor calls her. And as spoiled as the three-day-old fish heads rotting on the pier." His smile went flat. "Which should give you some inkling as to why I hated the smartest girl in the archdiocese."

Megan bit the side of her lip. "It does clarify things, but did you have to be so cruel?"

He buried his hands in his pockets with a sheepish shrug. "What can I say, I was my father's son—the one who couldn't measure up. The one he openly maligned as a mama's boy, lazy runt, moron, troublemaker—whatever title suited his fancy that day." He sighed and cocked a hip against the wall, his brow furrowed with regret. "It's not an excuse, Meg, I know, but I hope it explains somewhat just why I was so harsh with you in school."

Her voice came out as a rasp, heart aching for Devin Caldwell or any son who'd suffer such cruelty at the hand of their own flesh and blood. "Why did he treat you that way?"

He sucked in a harsh breath and released it again, shoulders slumping as if all energy had siphoned out too. "In his defense, I was a pretty whiny child, I guess. My mother pampered me to make up for my father's neglect, and he'd rail at her that she was turning me into a useless, namby-pamby kid, which I suppose she was." He kneaded his nose while his eyes remained closed, and Meg didn't miss the angry quiver in his cheek. "But I suspect the real reason he hated me was he didn't believe I was his son. He used to accuse my mother of having an affair, which was nothing but a bald-faced lie." The hard angles of his jaw calcified. "The man could have spit me out of his mouth, we look so much alike. But he will never, *ever* be a father to me."

Meg stood there, bleeding for the little boy he'd been. Without a single thought to propriety, she flung herself into his arms, crushing him in an embrace born of a sorrow so deep, a sob broke from her lips. "Oh, Devin, I never knew, and I am so very, very sorry."

His low chuckle was warm against her hair as he patted her back. "You should be, Miss McClare—for calling me a worm and all those other inappropriate names over the years."

Her eyes expanded in denial. "No, I promise, I never called you any names, ever . . ." Heat braised her cheeks. "Well, except I may have called you a twerp once or twice . . ."

The adorable smile for which he was famous made an appearance. "And 'lower than dirt,' as I recall . . ."

The blush went full throttle as she squirmed beneath his gaze. "Well, nobody's perfect."

His grin softened as he gently tugged on a loose curl feathering her ear. "You are, Meg, and apparently I'm as big a dolt as my father believes for not realizing that sooner."

Goose bumps popped that had nothing to do with the cold. She avoided his eyes while taking a step toward the door with a brisk buff of her arms. "Brrr . . . I should have brought my wrap, but I suppose as guest of honor of the party, I should probably just go back in anyway."

He whipped his jacket off and settled it over her shoulders, the warmth and scent from his body causing her stomach to flutter. Offering his arm to escort her in, he bewitched her with an endearing smile as warm as his coat. "It is a bit brisk out here, Miss McClare, but I'm hoping our newfound friendship has cleared the air for warmer climes, both here *and* at work."

She peeked up beneath heavy lashes to give him a skittish smile, not sure friendship with Devin Caldwell was a sound idea in the least. But it was certainly better than enmity and far less dangerous than attraction. She hurried through the door, girding herself with a deep ingest of air. Perhaps when it came to Devin Caldwell, the middle of the road was the safest place to be after all. Holding the door, he gave her a wink, and a lump promptly ducked in her throat.

If his charm doesn't run me down first . . .

20

*B*ram pumped the throttle of his Stanley Steamer and slowly eased away from the McClare mansion, heart heavy over Meg's nervous chatter about Caldwell on the drive home. Thankfully, the acrid smell of kerosene dispelled the scent of violets that captured his senses when Meg had been tucked between Alli and him on the bench of his car.

The two girls had jabbered nonstop on the drive home, and although Bram had encouraged Meg to forgive and forget with Devin, something in her giddy tone had needled him more than he liked. Somehow Caldwell had not only managed to change Meg's opinion of him in the span of one dance, but creep into a tiny corner of her heart as well. Oh, she still insisted Devin held no interest for her beyond friendship, but Bram knew Meg almost better than she knew herself. Her face had been too flushed, her voice too high, and her normally shy and soft manner far too keyed up. His jaw tightened as he turned onto his street, screeching to a stop in front of his house. No, his sweet and innocent Bug, despite all denial, had once again become vulnerable to the man who'd stomped on her heart more times than Bram could count.

He closed the drip valve and applied the brake, brow furrowing at the silhouette of his mother peeking out of her bedroom bay window of their two-story Italianate-style Victorian. The house, shrouded in darkness except for his mother's room and a light blazing in the parlour, was one of the more established homes on the hill. Its Old-World elegance testified to his father's rise to wealth as a shipping magnate in post–Gold Rush San Francisco.

His mother's shadow disappeared from the window, and Bram glanced at his watch and frowned, noting the late hour. His parents were always abed by this time, the house usually completely dark except for a dim light left for him in the foyer. He hopped out of the vehicle more quickly than usual, pulse thudding as he loped up the marble steps. Breathing shallow as he reached the arched portico with its marble colonnade, he firmly grasped the lion's-head knob, jolting when one of the mahogany double doors carefully wheeled open.

"Mom, what's wron—"

"Shhh . . ." With a nervous glance over her shoulder, she slipped out the door and closed it quietly, hooking Bram's arm to lead him to the far side of the porch where ivy spilled from glazed potted urns. "Oh, Bram, I'm so glad you're home—your father suffered a setback today."

The blood froze in his brain. "What do you mean, a 'setback'?" he whispered, the words raspy from the emotions closing his throat.

Even in the dim light of the moon, Bram could see the strain in his mother's face, lines of distress etched deep by a son who'd betrayed her and a husband who worried her. For the first time he noticed she wore her robe and sleeping cap, a silver braid spilling over one shoulder. Her voice shook as much as her hand when she laid it on the arm of his suit coat, but he didn't miss the forced humor in her words, something for which she always strove to allay his fears. "Oh, the pigheaded old coot overdid it today, took a notion to rise at the crack of dawn to go into work, on a Saturday, no less. Insisted he needed to oversee a big shipment, as if Darby couldn't handle it with only twenty years under his belt as the best dock foreman in the city." She grunted, almost masking the tremors in her tone. "The man would live on those infernal docks if I let him." She sighed, her casual demeanor slipping somewhat. "He swore me to secrecy because he didn't want to worry you. Claims it was nothing, but Darby said he collapsed on the docks today," she whispered, her humor fading enough to reveal the fear Bram knew she was trying to hide. "Right after he carried a heavy crate, the stubborn old fool. Complained of chest pains and shortness of breath. Darby said he was huffing harder than the steam engines on the wharf."

Bram clutched his mother's arms. "Has Doc Walsh—"

She nodded before the frantic question even left his tongue. "Yes, yes, of course—Darby saw to that, thank God." A hint of tears glimmered in the moonlight, and she hiked her chin, an attempt to thwart them, he knew. "Doc says he's on borrowed time if he doesn't slow down." She glanced toward the parlour before turning back to stroke his cheek with the tips of her fingers. "Which is why he's still up—waiting for you—and we both know what's on his mind."

A faint pall settled over Bram's mood. Yes, he knew.

Her eyes sharpened with an intensity that conveyed a mother's concern and affection. "So I wanted to . . . no, I *had to* . . . find out for sure . . ." The caress of her fingers skimmed to cradle his face like when he was a boy. "You do like Amelia, don't you, Bram? You've told us over and over that this is what you want, but I won't have you laying your desires aside for your father's. It's your life to live, after all."

The awful memory of his father lying in a pool of blood flashed through Bram's mind. *No, Mother, it's my retribution to pay.* "Of course I like Amelia," he reassured her, anxious to put her worries to rest. "I couldn't pick a better wife, and you know it." Meg's image suddenly invaded, and somewhere deep inside a dull ache throbbed in his chest. His resolve hardened along with his jaw as his palm covered his mother's cupped hand on his face, deflecting his true feelings with humor just like her. "Besides, at almost twenty-eight, it's high time I fly the coop and settle in a home of my own, don't you think?" He gave her chin a gentle tap. "After all, I can't let Jamie appear to be the mature, responsible one, can I?"

Her soft chuckle seemed to alleviate tension for them both. "Ha! As if anyone would believe it, Abraham Hughes. Jamie has turned into a fine young man to be sure, but you, my son, were born with a wise and tender heart, a maturity that's always made your father and me proud."

Bram inwardly winced. *Not always . . .*

"From the moment you held your little sister in your arms at the age of five, you were the nurturer, the protector." Her voice wavered the slightest bit as her eyes glowed with love. "Especially with your father and me."

Tears stung, and Bram swallowed her up in a ferocious hug. Prompted by love, yes, but also by guilt and shame over his betrayal of the very parents he respected and adored. A betrayal so heinous, it had altered each of their lives forever. Grief pierced as he tightened his hold.

And they never even knew . . .

"I love you both more than life itself," he whispered, his voice hoarse. "It's my privilege and joy to nurture and protect you in any way I can." His eyelids lumbered closed as he pressed a kiss to her nightcap. *Especially from a truth that would break both of your hearts . . .*

"And we love you, son—more than we can say." She gently patted his cheek before she swiped at her eyes. "Now, that crusty curmudgeon of a father of yours is inside waiting to terrorize you with his plans for your future, so I suggest you speak now or forever hold your peace, understood?" She gave him a kiss on the cheek. "I need to sneak back to bed, but I was hoping you might follow him closely up the stairs, just to help if he needs it. But for heaven's sake, don't tell him I told you, all right? You know what a stubborn crank he can be."

Bram forced a grin. "Yes, ma'am. Although I think it may be a toss-up on who's the more stubborn—my mother or my father."

Tsking on her way to the door, she glanced behind with a finger to her lips. "Shhh . . . it's the secret to our happy home—he just doesn't know it." She tossed an impish grin over her shoulder that gave her the air of a little girl despite the silver hair. "Good night, son."

"Good night, Mom." He smiled as she tiptoed up the stairs, nightgown hiked to her ankles while her long silver braid bobbed back and forth. Closing the front door with enough noise to alert his father, he locked and bolted it with a deep inhale, uttering a prayer for strength. He strode into the parlour and stopped, love welling at the sight of Jeremiah Hughes asleep in his well-worn leather chair, stockinged feet crossed on his paper-strewn desk. Their silver tabby, Mortimer, lay curled in a ball beneath his father's neck, looking like a beard that matched the neatly trimmed moustache. Bram smiled when Mort's ears twitched with his father's every deafening snore, vibrating both the man's sagging jowls and the poor cat.

Shaking his head, Bram made his way to the desk and carefully lifted Mort from his father's chest, grinning outright when the man jerked awake with a noisy flail of limbs.

"Thunderation, wh-what's going on?" his father stammered, obviously in a groggy state.

"It's me, Pop," Bram said quietly, heart twisting over the betrayal that had cost his father nearly all of his sight. "You fell asleep in your chair."

"Well, blue blazes, son, less chance of a heart attack with a soft word, you know." Feet thudding to the floor, he kneaded his temple, his bottle-thick eyeglasses askew on his face. "How was your evening?"

Bram stroked the tabby with a smile meant to mask his concern over the pallor of his father's face. "Good. Andrew Turner knows how to throw a party, that's for sure. Meg was bashfully aglow with the attention and having a good time, I think." He paused, noting dark circles and deep lines of fatigue. "What are you still doing up? Trouble sleeping?"

His father struggled to rise, and it took everything Bram had not to toss Mort aside and assist him. The husky chuckle that rumbled from his father's throat did little to deflect the weary bent of his back or the sag of his shoulders. A rusty wheeze followed that stabbed Bram like a knife. "Apparently not, since Mort and I were both sprawled out like sots in a side alley."

"You sound congested," Bram said, tone casual in deference to his mother's request. "Not feeling well?"

"Oh, pish-posh—never better," he groused. Pushing his heavy-lensed eyeglasses back on his nose, he steadied himself with a weathered hand to his desk, straightening to his full six-foot height to meet his son eye to eye. "Amelia's home," he whispered, as if divulging a secret.

"Is she, now?" Bram turned to place Morty on his favorite chair, heart taking off in a sprint. "I thought she was to spend the year in Europe with her aunt."

A grunt rolled from his father's lips. "That's what Amelia thought too, but some blackguard was sniffing around, apparently, so Henry yanked her home six months early. Which means, of course . . ." His father gave him a wink. "Courtship is in the air, my boy."

"Indeed." Bram adjusted his jacket, smiling despite the churn of his gut. "Then I suppose I'll be calling on the lady soon."

"Sooner than you think if Henry has his way," his father said with a grin, snatching his walking cane, which was never far from his grasp. He slapped Bram on the back with more force than his weakened state warranted, breathing heavily as he shuffled toward the door. "He's hoping you'll honor her with an invitation to the Barrister Ball."

Bram halted midway, jaw gaping before he could stop it. "A week's notice for an invitation to one of the social highlights of the year is hardly an honor, Pop." He casually braced a stabilizing arm on his father's shoulder with a smile that was more of a grunt. "Most ladies would consider it an affront, especially since guest names were required for place settings and printed programs weeks ago."

"Most ladies, yes." His body rattled with a hacking cough that worried Bram so much, he shored him up at the waist, pausing until the spell passed. "But not the Darlingtons," his father continued, seemingly oblivious to Bram's protective hold. "Henry's fortune is relatively new as you know, as is his foray into society." He gave Bram's shoulder a weak squeeze, his breathing becoming more labored. "Merging his small shipping business with mine will go a long way in elevating the Darlington name in Frisco society." His hoarse chuckle carried the threat of another coughing fit. "He needs my name and influence, and I need his youth and vigor."

And his money. Bram's heart twisted over the truth his father refused to tell his own son and probably his wife too. He suspected his mother—intuitive to a fault—harbored an uneasy feeling as well, no doubt suspicious as to why a stubborn shipping mogul would consent to share the helm of his empire. *Especially* one he'd built and managed himself for some thirty-odd years. Drawing in a quiet breath, Bram felt his rib cage constrict by the weight of the secrets he bore—both his own and now his father's. There was no way he would worry his mother with the financial burdens that threatened her husband's health, heavy burdens imposed by steep import tariffs and damaged ships. His mouth thinned as he supported his father through another bout of the croup. But . . . he *could* remedy them by meeting Darlington's key term for the merger—acquisition of the Hughes name, both for his company *and* for his daughter.

"I'd say Henry's youth and vigor is essential the way you're feeling tonight, Pop," Bram said as he ushered him to the sweeping marble stairs. He infused a hint of humor into his tone to battle the guilt that endlessly circled his brain. "Especially given a high-falutin' son who opted for a comfortable law school over learning the ropes of his father's shipping business on the docks of Fisherman's Wharf."

Jeremiah Hughes spun to face him with a speed and power that belied the hollow look of his face. "It was *my* decision to send you to Stanford, not yours, so you can just toss that load of guilt into the ocean where it belongs." His father gripped his arm with a pressure born of a fierce love, the sheen of moisture in his eyes sparking tears in Bram's own. "You fought me tooth and nail, you did, but you were meant for far more than life on the docks, son, far more than my humble beginnings. Seeing the man you've become is worth more to me than all the money I've ever made, all the dreams I've ever dreamed. All of it," he whispered, the sound hoarse with emotion. "So no regrets when it comes to me, my boy—just put them all out of your mind, do you hear?"

Bram nodded, his throat too thick with emotion to utter a single word. *Yes, sir, I hear, and God help me, how I wish that I could.*

His father patted a veined hand to Bram's cheek. "You're our crowning achievement, son, and the only thing that could make us happier is to bounce your children upon our knees." He tackled the first step, then turned to offer a wink. "And heaven knows you won't oblige unless Mother and I give you a little nudge, eh?" He hesitated, his smile screwing into a squint. "You do favor Amelia, don't you? That seems to be Mother's biggest concern, you know, that I'm 'railroading' you into something you don't want."

Bram kneaded his father's shoulder with a reassuring grin. "Nobody's railroading me into anything, Pop—Amelia's a lovely girl."

"Then you'll ask her to the Barrister Ball?" His father stilled on the bottom step, his breathing appearing to halt as well.

Bram's heart lurched at the hope in the eyes of his father, the same man who had slaved and sacrificed to give Bram everything he'd never had growing up. He fought the sting of more tears with a broad grin. "Yes, Pop, I will ask her tomorrow."

The furrows in his father's face dissolved into a smile as he slowly mounted the steps with Bram close behind. "Good boy. She's a pretty little thing, Bram, with a sweet way about her. Mother and I think she'll make you very happy—the perfect wife and mother."

"I don't doubt that for a moment, Pop," he said, concern wedging his brow at the slow pace with which his father lumbered up the stairs. Shadowing him closely, Bram managed a light tone, body poised to catch him should he falter. "After all, what more could a man possibly want?" He expelled a silent sigh.

Except absolution . . .

21

"Soooo . . ." With a touch of the imp, Meg bumped Bonnie's hip with her own, snatching a coffee mug from the cabinet overhead. Flashing a grin, she slid her cup next to the one Bonnie was pouring for herself. "Were you able to get any sleep after Andrew's party, Miss Roof, or did you spend the nights dreaming wide awake?"

Color burned up the back of Bonnie's slender neck, where wisps of ebony curls teased the lacy collar of Alli's pretty hand-me-down suit. Coffee splattered the counter when Bonnie fumbled the pot with bright pink cheeks, casting a nervous peek over her shoulder. "Shhh!" She quickly poured Meg a cup before she clattered the pot back on the burner. "For mercy's sake, Meg, he could walk in here at any moment," she whispered while she cleaned up the spill. "And I'd die if he knew I had a crush on him."

Meg hooked her waist to give her a gentle squeeze. "He won't know because he's already in the conference room for the meeting. He passed me in the hall on his way in."

Bonnie's lanky frame relaxed as a wobbly smile inched its way across full lips the color of berries from Meg's lip rouge. "Oh, Meg, I had the most wonderful time of my life!" she breathed,

209

nudging her new rimless eyeglasses back up her nose. "I could barely catch my breath for all the dancing with Teddy and Conor, and even Mr. Turner was kind enough to ask."

"And George?" Meg wiggled her brows.

Bonnie's teeth tugged at a shy smile. "Only once, but oh, Meg—he told me I looked pretty!"

Meg laughed, the sound as joyous as the glow in Bonnie's eyes. She gave her a tight hug and pulled back, gaze blurring with a sheen of emotion. "That's because you *are*, my sweet friend, and don't you ever forget it." She glanced at the clock on the wall when voices filtered down the hall. "Uh-oh, I'm going to be late for the meeting." Dousing her coffee with cream and sugar, she hurried to the door, then tossed a wink over her shoulder while locking her lips with an imaginary key. "Mum's the word."

Ooomphf! Meg bounced off a brick wall in a brown suit, spilling coffee everywhere.

A deep-throated chuckle broke her silent stun, sending heat pulsing into her cheeks when the "wall" actually winked. "Uh . . . nope, I think the word may be 'damp,'" Devin said, brushing dribbles of coffee off of the front of his tan vest.

Meg wanted to die. "Oh, Devin, I am *so* sorry—I wasn't looking where I was going, and now I've ruined your vest." She whirled around to retrieve a wet dishrag from the sink, but Bonnie beat her to it, handing it over with a sympathetic smile.

Mortified at the mess she'd made, Meg never gave a thought to yanking Devin's vest out and blotting it with the rag, rubbing frantically until the stains disappeared into soggy satin. "There," she said with a shallow exhale, "a little wet, but good as new." She peered up, brows peaked in apology. "Can I get you some coffee to make it up to you?"

"Sure," he said, grinning, "but in a cup this time, Miss Mc-

Clare, if you don't mind." Flapping his vest, he sauntered into the conference room while Meg faced Bonnie with a low groan.

"I can't believe I did that," she whispered, body suddenly as wilted as the rag in her hand.

Bonnie chuckled and refilled two cups of coffee, doctoring them while Meg rubbed a few stains from the front of her blue blouse. "Mmm . . . maybe it's subconscious retaliation for all the insults over the years."

Meg sighed and tossed the wet rag in the sink. "I hope not—he actually apologized the night of the party and gave me some insight as to why he picked at me like he did."

"Ooooo, I want details at lunch, but for now, here—you're late for a meeting." Bonnie handed her the two cups with a mischievous grin. "And when you give Devin his, resist the urge, okay?"

"Yes, ma'am," Meg said with a chuckle, slipping into the conference room where Andrew was in deep discussion with George and the others. No one noticed her late arrival—for which she was most grateful—except for Devin who slid her a wink when she gave him his coffee. She took her seat across the table and sipped hers, gaze pinned to Andrew to avoid Devin, who was directly in her line of sight at Andrew's right. When all cases had been reviewed, discussed, and new ones assigned, Andrew scanned the room with a slap of palms to the table. "That's it for now, but I hope you enjoyed yourselves Saturday night at Meg's party." His eyes sought hers. "Meg and her family are very dear to me, so I appreciate you taking the time to come. Oh, and George, I forgot to tell you the O'Hara case has been moved up, so I'll need recommendations by two."

"You got it, Boss." George stood and pushed his chair in along with everyone else.

Shuffling his papers on the table, Andrew remained seated,

gaze flitting from Meg to Devin. "Meg, Devin—keep your seats because I need a word with you both, if you don't mind. Teddy, close the door behind you, if you will."

"Yes, sir." Teddy obliged while Meg and Devin exchanged glances.

At the ominous click of the door, Andrew stretched back in his chair, arms folded while he eyed them with a pensive air. The muscles in Meg's stomach stretched taut at his serious look. He finally snatched his pen to absently roll it between two fingers. "How much do you two know about the Progressive Movement?"

Meg blinked, blood warming her cheeks over the mere mention of the crusade to close down the brothels and dance halls of the Barbary Coast. Although her mother chaired the Vigilance Committee that fought to put an end to the city's red-light district, never had she divulged the full extent of debauchery to Meg, ever protective of her children. Despite her mother's reticence, however, Meg had read every edition of *The San Francisco Evening Bulletin* since she'd returned home, soaking up Fremont Older's editorials about the civic corruption that tainted the city. With a quiet intake of air, she chanced a peek at Devin, whose face matched the crimson tie he wore.

Andrew's mouth quirked in a sour smile. "I can see that both of you are well aware of what the movement is all about, but how much do you know about Father Terrence Caraher and the battle he waged against the Nymphia brothel?"

Devin cleared his throat, the sound hoarse as he took a fast swig of coffee. "Not much, sir, I'm afraid, other than what I've heard from my father or read in the paper."

Andrew's sharp gaze flicked to Meg, the intensity in his eyes telling her this was a passion he shared with her mother. "And you, Meg? Has your mother divulged anything of the political or spiritual battles we've encountered in our quest to clean up the Coast?"

Meg sat up straight, chin high and voice firm. "Yes, Mr. Turner, some, although naturally Mother spares us the unsavory details. But I've been able to keep up by gleaning as much as I can from Mr. Fremont's editorials."

The faintest of smiles edged Andrew's mouth as he studied her with a look rimmed with pride. "You are so much like your mother, you know that, young lady?"

A brief burst of pleasure warmed in her chest at the comparison, although she didn't believe it for a moment. Her mother was everything she aspired to be, but Meg doubted a frumpy and insecure little girl could blossom into such beauty and grace. *Formerly frumpy*, she reminded herself, forgetting she was no longer that defeated creature who cringed over ridicule from her peers. She returned Andrew's smile with a shy one of her own, uncomfortable with his praise in front of Devin. "Thank you, Mr. Turner—I pray to be half the woman my mother is someday."

"I'd say you're well on your way, Miss McClare, given the stack of summaries you wrote this week, according to George." Andrew's approval fairly shone in eyes so startling blue, she wondered how she hadn't noticed before. "Claims you prepared a record number, identifying laws and judicial decisions he didn't even know existed, an astonishing feat for any member of the bar, Meg, much less an intern fresh out of high school."

Her cheeks flared hot. "Thank you, Mr. Turner," she whispered, careful to avoid Devin's gaze. "I suppose research has always been a love of mine, sir."

"Well, it certainly shows." He laid the pen aside, his demeanor suddenly serious. "Which is why I've decided to assign you and Devin to work on a special project. One that is near and dear to my heart and far more critical than preparing motions and pleadings or writing summaries, as important as that may be." He cocked his head to peer first at Devin and then Meg, his manner all business. "As both of you are aware, the district attorney's office and the Vigilance Committee are now aligned with Father Terence Caraher, pastor of St. Francis of Assisi and chairman of the Committee on Morals of the North Beach Promotion Association." Andrew paused, the note of respect in his voice hard to miss. "Father Caraher is a true man of God, so we are fortunate to be working in tandem with him. It was his relentless crusade that finally shut down the Nymphia last year, a near-impossible feat that brought great joy to a lot of souls, not the least of which are Megan's mother and me."

He removed two documents from his portfolio and handed one to both Devin and Meg. Elbows propped on the table, he steepled hands in a somber pose, worry lines prominent as they fanned from his eyes. "These documents are highly confidential, so I ask for your utmost care and reticence regarding this project while at work. I suggest you lock them or any related documents in your desk drawer at night, understood?" He paused, his gaze fixing on Meg. "I don't mind if your mother or family is aware of this project, Meg, because there will be nights we'll be working late, so they'll need to know why. But no details, please, and I ask the same of Devin with his family."

Both nodded while they scanned the paper before them.

"This is the outline I'd like you to follow as far as the research required, and its points are self-explanatory. Meg, I want you to focus on the Twinkling Star Corporation, delving into every aspect of the company and every whoremonger affiliated with it."

The blood in Meg's face whooshed to the tips of her fingers and toes, leaving her woozy. "The Twinkling Star Corporation?" she whispered. "You m-mean the company that owned the N-Nymphia?"

Andrew's mouth went flat. "One and the same. Once the Nymphia was shut down, its owner Emil Kehrlein transferred operations to the Marsicania, an equally abominable den of depravity *and*," he said with a pointed look, "the target of our covert investigation. An investigation that must be kept under wraps due to the court injunction by the 'vice magistrate,' the dishonorable Carroll Cook." His sigh was heavy as he massaged the bridge of his nose. "An injunction against police interference or surveillance that ties our hands and our investigation."

"Investigation, sir?" Devin asked, dark brows pinched in confusion. "In the legal sense?"

"A presentence investigation report, Devin, to compile both legal and extralegal information about the owners and clients of the Marsicania in order to frame a case for shutting them down." Andrew absently fanned blunt fingers through sandy hair, a habit she'd noticed when he was particularly intense about a subject. *Like cleaning up the Coast*, she thought with an uneasy twinge in her gut, a cause that bonded him to her mother more than Megan liked. His eyes trailed into a faraway stare. "And hopefully stop them once and for all with an airtight conviction that will put them away for a long time to come."

He snapped out of his reverie, his professionalism in place once again. "Of course, heaven knows the political establishment is up to its eyeballs in the Barbary Coast, so there's no telling what kind of dirt we'll find." His smile quirked as he snapped his portfolio shut. "Tongues are still wagging over ex-Mayor Phalen's family owning a gambling den around the corner from the Nymphia, for pity's sake." Andrew winked. "A timely scandal prior to election, of course."

Rising to his feet, he pushed his chair in. "Meg, I want detailed documentation of anything you can dig up on Twinkling Star and the vermin associated with it—investors, clients, even the women who work at the Marsicania. The district court clerk will provide you with files ad nauseum to pore over, I assure you, as will Chief Wittman's office. I'll have Bonnie send a letter introducing you and Devin as my assistants, requesting full cooperation."

He turned to cuff a hand to Devin's shoulder. "Dev, I need you to flesh out profiles on anybody hauled in after the grand vice-squad raid on the Nymphia last year." His tone took a turn toward dry. "Although judging from the lists of names the police turned in, no one except John Smith ever visited the Nymphia." Andrew sighed. "Nonetheless, I want as much information as possible—prior records, pending cases, background, ties to the community, financial circumstances, employment history, education history, you name it. Sniff out as many ties to Twinkling Star as you can and follow the rabbit trail—we need an iron-clad case to nail these moral leeches to the wall, and we'll look under every rock to do it, understood?"

"Yes, sir."

"Good. Since this is highly sensitive, I'd rather you two hole up in your office rather than the conference room to avoid any leakage of what we're doing. I want a status report every Tuesday and Friday evening at close of business." He glanced at Meg. "This will require additional hours for a time, Meg, but I'm well aware you volunteer at the Barbary Volunteer Legal Services on Saturdays, so just plan to work late a few nights a week instead, all right? I'll be monitoring your progress and providing direction whenever you need it." He paused to push in his chair, eyes scanning from Devin to Meg. "Any questions?"

Meg drew in a deep breath, head spinning. "Yes, sir—when

can we expect the files from the district court clerk and Chief Wittman?"

Andrew glanced at his watch. "Any moment now—at least for the first batch you'll be combing through, and you'll need to get started right away." He glanced up. "It's a nice, meaty project for the both of you, and more importantly, one that will make a huge difference in our city for the better." He studied them both with keen eyes that shone with approval. "I'm grateful to have two such sharp interns to tackle something I wouldn't give to just anyone." The edge of his lip tipped up. "Of course you'll be working side by side in very close quarters, so if you're not friends yet—you will be." He smiled. "Either that or you'll drive each other crazy." Portfolio tucked under his arm, he strolled toward the door and turned, a twinkle in his eyes as he slipped a hand into his vest pocket. "Oh, I almost forgot." He tossed two tickets onto the table. "Since you're not drawing a salary, I had to figure out some way to thank you for all the hard work you're going to do."

Devin reached for the tickets, eyes expanding along with his mouth. "The Barrister Ball?" he said with a croak. "We're going to the Barrister Ball?"

Andrew grinned. "Since we're not a fancy, high-priced firm like Meg's uncle's, the DA's office is only allotted two barrister tickets and two guests." He shrugged his shoulders. "I suppose it's downright rude of me to be so chipper about George having to attend his sister's wedding in Los Angeles this weekend, and Conor and Teddy otherwise engaged, but I don't know . . ." He scrunched his nose. "I rather like the idea of attending the Barrister Ball with both my intern and her mother as well as my godson."

Meg stared, jaw distended. *The Barrister Ball? With Devin Caldwell??*

"Holy thunder, Uncle Drew," Devin said with a wide grin,

217

apparently so excited, he slipped into the familiar family name he usually took great pains to avoid. "Are you serious?"

Andrew's rich laughter boomed through the room as he gave them both a jaunty salute. "Oh, don't worry," he said with a wink, "you'll earn it and more."

22

*L*ogan stared out the window of his six-story office, the dark thunderclouds rolling over the pewter bay as vicious and rare as the angst churning in his gut. At least since Meg's party Saturday night when Cait had struck with a little thunder of her own. He absently rubbed the cheek she had slapped as he slumped back in his chair. He kneaded the socket of his eye with the heel of his palm to alleviate the tension that had been brewing between Cait and him ever since. A sharp, divisive tension that kept him working late at the office to explain his absence at dinners. Absence from his family.

And absence from Cait's life.

A silent groan rose in his chest as he rested his head, eyes closed.

Why, Cait? When you love me like I know you do, why turn on me so?

The answer, deep and silent, niggled. It came to him in the dead of each night when he couldn't sleep, and in every hour of every day when he couldn't forget. Painful guilt slithering through his thoughts, confirming what he already knew. Cait loved him, yes, but she couldn't trust him. Not when hate could so easily erupt for the man who was trying to take her away. The man who threatened to shatter Logan's dream a second time. Sweat beaded the back of his neck when he realized something he'd never fully entertained before.

Andrew could do it.

And Logan could lose her.

The look of anger and disgust he'd seen in Cait's eyes that night assured him Turner was making inroads into her heart, rapidly becoming a force to be reckoned with, which chilled Logan's blood. For surely the hundredth time since Saturday night, a thick and heavy malaise settled, convincing him he needed to do something to staunch the flow of Cait's distrust, to stem the bleeding of their love. And yet all the while, rage simmered beneath the surface of reason, an invitation to hunt Turner down and spill some blood of his own. His hands fisted on the arm of the chair as he stared aimlessly into the sea of uncertainty. *Dear God in heaven, what can I do?*

Pray.

The thought, so distant and faint, struck hard like one of those extraordinary bolts of lightning high over San Francisco Bay, a remarkable rarity that left the city in awe. Much like Logan was feeling right now. *Pray?*

The thought seemed almost ludicrous, and he might have dismissed it if it hadn't produced an infinitesimal flash of hope, no matter how brief. A split second of shimmering light in an otherwise dark and ominous sky. Oh yes, he'd certainly made great strides toward God in the last year, actually enjoying church for the first time in his life. And he couldn't deny he'd seen countless answers to prayer in Cait's life and those of Jamie, Bram, and his nieces. But him? Would God even listen to a sinner like him?

A memory drifted in his mind, as quiet as the directive to pray only moments before, the image of the night little Maddie had gone missing almost a year ago. Caitlyn and he had been frantic, unable to find the little girl . . . until God had answered their prayer.

Through Logan.

The sweetness of that moment flooded his soul even now, spilling hope into every crack and crevice Andrew Turner had gouged into Logan's dream to marry Cait. A weight lifted from his shoulders while something fluttered in his chest, and suddenly he knew. His eyelids popped up.

He would pray.

To become the man Cait needed him to be.

The husband he hoped to be.

And the man God called him to be.

Moisture stung as an overwhelming sense of peace purled through his body, dismantling all fear. Throat thick with emotion, he stared up into the sky, no longer seeing the gloom of *what if*, but instead the blazing glow of the Almighty's *I can*. "God, I don't have the right to ask You this, but I'm asking nonetheless. Will You help me? Help me to trust You so Cait can trust me? Will You show me how to be a man worthy of her love? To win her hand and her heart completely?" He squinted at the black, billowing clouds that portended a squall, and his confidence surged like the whitecaps whipped up on the bay. "I promise I'll do whatever—"

Forgive.

Logan's prayer caught in his throat, pride swelling to close off his air. His flat palms clenched into knots on the arms of the chair when Andrew's image invaded his mind. "No, not that. Anything but that."

If I regard iniquity in my heart, the Lord will not hear me . . .

A groan worked its way past his lips as snippets of Father Mulaney's sermon filtered through his brain. He peered up, temple pulsing. "You can't ask that of me—when Turner betrayed me, he robbed me of my very life!" He slammed his fist on the chair. "Cait was meant to be *my* wife, her children *my* children! I've not lived a pristine life, it's true, but what he stole from me is unforgivable, a debt that cannot be paid."

Above all, love each other deeply, because love covers a multitude of sins.

Logan put a hand to his eyes, his breathing shallow. He thought of Cait, and in one stuttered beat of his heart, it became achingly clear—he would do whatever it took.

Even if it meant forgiving the one person he hated the most.

Sucking in a sharp stab of air, he expelled it again in one long, ragged breath of surrender. "All right—You win," he whispered, "but I have no idea how to proceed."

He startled at a knock on the door, and spinning away from the window, he squinted at the antique grandfather clock on the far wall, noting the late hour. *Who the devil—*

Bram popped his head in, the surprise on his face mirroring Logan's. "I thought I saw a sliver of light beneath your door," he said with a tired smile. "I didn't realize anybody was still here." He opened the door and paused, wrinkles in his brow matching those beneath his eyes. "I'm not interrupting, I hope."

"No, no, of course not," Logan said, waving him in. "Have a seat unless you're in a hurry to be somewhere else."

Bram's chuckle helped dispel the gloom of Logan's thoughts. "In my bed, as a matter of fact, but a few minutes to chat will do me good, unbending my mind from the horrors of the McCarron case." He slung his jacket over the arm of one of two chairs in front of Logan's desk and sank in as if all his energy were seeping into the leather right along with him. Resting his head on the back, he loosened his tie. "So . . . what are you still doing here? I didn't think anything kept you from family dinners."

Heat circled Logan's collar, and he quickly slanted back in his chair, one polished shoe propped against the carved wooden handle of his lowest drawer. "Not much usually does, but I'm afraid the Alberici embezzlement case would give the McCarron case a run for its money." He scratched the back of his neck with a wry smile. "Actually thinking of passing it off to Jamie or Blake—whoever thrashes me first in pool."

Bram laughed, the exhaustion in his face easing somewhat. "My vote is Blake, but only because I'm feeling a little sorry for Jamie right now."

Logan settled back in his chair like Bram, head resting. "How so?"

A heavy exhale parted from Bram's lips as he rubbed his temples. "Blake, Jamie, and I have been looking forward to the Barrister Ball since we stepped foot in law school, and now here it is, and Jamie can't take Cass."

The muscles at the back of Logan's neck instantly tightened. "What? Why not? Is something wrong?"

He shook his head, his smile edged with sympathy. "Just a mild case of the flu, we think, but Cass woke up feeling like Blake after a hard night on the town—nausea, congestion, fever." He scrunched his nose. "Kissed Jamie goodbye this morning, then retched all over his shoes."

Logan grimaced. "Thank heavens it wasn't Nick's Italian oxfords—the man is downright obsessive about his shoes according to Alli." He squinted in concern. "Is she okay?"

Bram nodded. "Mrs. McClare insisted on taking her home where she can get around-the-clock care, so Cass is safely tucked in her old bedroom, fawned over by Rosie, Hadley, and her aunt." Bram exhaled. "But Jamie is worried about her, of course, and really disappointed she won't be there to cheer him on as part of the city's new crop of legal counsel." Bram cocked his head to give Logan a wry smile. "So being the genius I am, I suggested Jamie take his sister Jess instead, since she has aspirations to be a lawyer, and he thought it was a brilliant idea."

Logan relaxed, his gaze inquisitive. "Sounds brilliant to me."

Bram's smile went flat. "You'd think so, but then Jamie gets this bright idea to take his mother too, understandably, since she worked herself to the bone to put him through school." He huffed out a sigh. "Unfortunately, he asked me to take Jess so *he* could take his mother."

"Makes sense," Logan said, grateful Jamie would have his sister and mother at one of the biggest events of his legal career.

Bram's mouth took a twist. "He thought so too, since heaven knows I attend every wedding, wake, and whatnot by myself. But . . . unfortunately, for this esteemed affair my father railroaded me into taking Amelia Darlington."

Logan couldn't retain his smile. Ah, yes, Amelia Darlington—the sweet but flighty daughter of Henry Darlington, a self-made shipping tycoon on the rise who'd aligned himself with Bram's father. A merger was in the making, no question, and not just with both men's companies. It was no secret in financial circles that Henry Darlington had his sights set on another merger as well—a marriage between his daughter and Bram. And as an immigrant from the old country, Bram's father's often extolled the virtues of arranged marriages, citing his own as a match made in heaven. In fact, for as long as Logan could remember—at least every Christmas get-together with the McClares—Jeremiah had expressed his desire to see Bram settled with a woman of Jeremiah's choosing, just like his father had done for him. And if that arranged marriage was one of convenience that also expanded the coffers of his company, then so be it.

Logan studied the young man before him with a full measure of respect, knowing Bram would honor his father at all costs. Even if that meant marrying a woman he didn't love. Fortunately, his heart had never been claimed by another, so this marriage of convenience might very well be quite convenient for all. Especially given that Amelia Darlington was both pretty and personable, not to mention a young woman of like faith. Logan nodded with approval. "I like her, Bram. She's young, but she has spunk and heart, and you could do worse."

Bram scratched the back of his neck with a sheepish smile. "Agreed, but it seems Mr. James Foot-in-Mouth MacKenna jumped the gun and asked Jess and his mother *before* he asked me, and now he has to disappoint one of them."

A frown puckered Logan's brow. "What about Blake?" he asked, almost reluctant to subject either Jamie's mother or sister to his wayward nephew.

Bram laughed as he peered at Logan beneath a beetled brow. "Blake the Rake McClare? The man who ushers one woman to a function while he flirts with the waitress and three others?" He shook his head. "No, even if Jamie wasn't averse to asking your nephew, Blake already has a date for the ball, so he's out of the question."

Mouth compressed in thought, Logan stroked his chin, an idea germinating in his brain. Despite the fact he'd heard he'd been nominated for the Dickherber Civil Service Award, he'd considered forgoing the ball this year since Cait had declined his invitation. He preferred to shun the limelight rather than watch Turner escort her to one of the social events of the season, leaving tongues to wag as to the relationship between the two. But . . . at the last minute he'd decided that Jamie, Blake, and Bram were too important to miss honoring them as part of the city's new crop of counselors. So what if he killed two birds with one stone, so to speak—helped Jamie out by taking his mother while showing Cait he had no ill feelings? The idea bore merit, he decided, a fact confirmed by the sudden peace he felt deep inside. He glanced up at Bram. "What if I were to escort Jamie's mother?" he asked, the wild whim settling into a cozy fit, like house slippers warmed by the fire. "And he took his sister?"

Bram's clear blue eyes blinked once and then twice, the statement obviously taking him by surprise. "You mean . . . you'd actually consider escorting Jamie's . . ." His Adam's apple dipped several times. "His mother to the ball?"

Logan's smile wavered, the stark reality of the situation rattling all good intentions. This *would* be the first interaction between Jamie's mother and him—the woman with whom he'd had an illegitimate son back in law school—as well as a painful reminder of his betrayal of Cait.

And yet, the idea took hold, simmering in his mind until it bubbled with promise like Rosie's homemade beef stew, words of consent warm and flavorful on his tongue. A deep satisfaction filled his soul at the prospect of doing this for his son, taking that first step to bring Jamie's parentage full circle, hopefully to move past the shame once and for all. To give Jean MacKenna the moment of pride she so deserved as a mother. Logan exhaled a tremulous breath as his thoughts strayed to Andrew. *And* to give God the moment of forgiveness He so required as a Father. He cocked his head, smile pensive as he gave Bram his answer. "I think so. Jamie's family deserves to be there, and I would do anything for my son." He fought the emotion that stung in his nose. *And for Cait.*

"Well, I guarantee you, Logan, it'll be the greatest gift you can give," Bram said quietly, eyes sober with respect.

Logan cleared his throat. "Yes, well actually it's the perfect opportunity to broach an idea I've had rolling around in my brain anyway." He scratched the edge of his temple, nose wrinkling. "I've always been proud of Jamie, but never more than when he bought that ramshackle Victorian as a boardinghouse down the street from Cait's school." He shook his head, pride welling so fast it threatened to seep from his eyes. "And all to reach out to victimized women like Jamie's mother used to be, helping them escape the malevolent tentacles of Barbary." His exhale was slow and steady. "To give them a future they could never hope for in the cow-yards and brothels." He peered up at Bram with a set of his jaw. "That's a future I think I'd like to invest in, both for those unfortunate women and for Jamie's family."

"It's certainly a noble ambition, sir, and one that will touch your son deeply."

Logan yanked at his tie to loosen it while he settled back in his chair, deflecting his awkwardness with a casual grin. "I can wholeheartedly assure you, Counselor Hughes, that that is the very first time the word 'noble' has ever been used in reference to my ambitions or goals."

"I seriously doubt that, sir." Bram's smile was kind.

"Well, don't." Logan's grin deflated into a reflective smile. His gaze veered into a distant stare while his tone tapered to serious. "I haven't always been the most respectable man in the past, Bram, something I've come to regret."

"I don't know much about your past, Logan," Bram said softly, "but I do know that in the present, you are one of the men I admire most in the world. I count it an honor and privilege to work with you." As if sensing Logan's discomfort, Bram broke his serious demeanor with a chuckle. "And despite my deep affection and respect for Jamie and Blake, I'd like you to know, sir—my threshold for respect is pretty high."

Logan drew in a sharp breath and released it again, a smile easing across his face. "Thanks, Bram—the feeling is more than mutual, I assure you." He paused, feeling a pull to ask Bram a question he'd never asked anyone before, and suddenly it occurred to him just why Jamie and Blake had coined the nickname "Padre Hughes" for this humble man. Yes, Logan knew Bram was the rock foundation of the "Three Musketeers," as the boys called themselves in law school, a true stabilizer for both Jamie and Blake with his keen mind and mild manner. And, yes, he was well aware of Blake's complaints that Bram preferred ginger ale to beer or whiskey and intellectual chats with women rather than idle flirtations. He'd even been privy to the subtle aspirations of Bram's parents, who hoped their son might follow in the footsteps of his Protestant uncle and become a minister. But their dreams had been waylaid by both their son's disinterest and his preference for attending church with the McClares, and for that Logan was grateful. Not only because Bram was a godsend for Meg over the years, but because he'd become a vital and integral part of their tight-knit family. One who, at times, seemed to be the glue that bound Logan's nieces and nephews together.

And yet looking at Bram now, Logan sensed something far deeper, far more compelling when one was alone with him—something that seldom occurred for Logan, either in the office or at family dinners or functions. Although Bram joked and teased with the best of them, he always appeared content to let Jamie and Blake take center stage, which, of course they always did, never allowing Logan to really see Bram's deep connection with God.

Eyes in a squint, Logan studied him now—the calm and caring eyes that seemed to penetrate the hard veneer of Logan's pride and bore straight into his soul. A relaxed composure that was strong, steady, and sure. And somehow, expectant. As if he were waiting for what he knew Logan needed to know . . .

"Bram," Logan said with a gruff clear of his throat, "would you mind if I asked you a question of a rather . . . spiritual nature?"

If Bram was surprised, it didn't register in his manner. Instead, his eyes sparked with interest, dispelling any fatigue that may have been there before. "Have at it, sir," he said with a grin. "I just happen to thrive on questions of a spiritual nature."

Logan leaned in to cross his arms on the front of the desk, fist to mouth in contemplation. "Good, because there's something I want to do—" He grunted. "Well, not 'want' per se, but *need* to do, and I'm not quite sure how to do it."

Bram's sandy brows bunched low while a faint smile played at the edge of his mouth. "What—explain the facts of life to Blake?"

Logan laughed, appreciating Bram's attempt to lighten a difficult subject. He scratched the back of his head with a sheepish grin. "Yes, well, that too—something Cait has been after me to do for a long time now, but no." He glanced up, eyes locking with Bram's. "How do you . . . I mean, are there any . . . well, you know . . . specific steps one takes to . . ." The words strangled as he snatched his cold coffee and glugged until empty, clunking it down while heat crawled up his neck. "Uh . . . forgive?"

To his credit, Bram kept a straight face, the unassuming kindness in his eyes unraveling the knots in Logan's gut. He exhaled slowly, then sat up to brace arms on the sides of his chair. "It's been my experience, Logan, that forgiveness is—like love—a decision, the choice of one's will to override all negative emotion and let go of hate and hurt for the common good—both for you and those you love."

Logan nodded, thinking of Cait, knowing full well she was the only reason he needed to do this, to avoid hurting her again with his temper and jealousy. But on the heels of that very thought, he saw Andrew kissing her on the veranda, and a rush of fury pumped through his veins. "I've made that decision, yes," he said in a clipped tone, "but I'm not quite sure what to do with the urgent need to dismantle this person's jaw."

Bram grinned, rubbing the side of his face as if he felt the clip of a punch. "That is a problem, but . . ." His manner sobered, although Logan could have sworn he saw a twinkle in his eye. "There *are* solutions."

Logan jagged a brow. "Pay someone to do it for me?"

Bram's low chuckles worked just like laudanum, melting the stress in Logan's chest. "No, but if anyone could afford it, sir, it's you." He cocked his head, his gaze almost wistful. "People don't realize just how much energy it takes to hate and hurt someone who's wounded them, nor how destructive that hate can be." His blue eyes were suddenly somber, the gunmetal color of the sky before the storm. "It's like a gun aimed at themselves instead of the offending party," he said in a solemn tone. "It can destroy them and those they love." His chest expanded with a heavy inhale, which he slowly released, eyes never straying from Logan's. "But . . . if one were to utilize the same level of emotion it takes to hate and channel it into God's precepts instead . . ." The faintest of smiles hovered on his lips. "Well, then it becomes like the steam in my Stanley—all that hot air not only has the power to take you where you want to go, but farther, faster, and safer than allowing all that hate to grind on the gears."

Jaw compressed, Logan stared through a slivered gaze, almost reluctant to concur for what it would cost him. He finally huffed out a noisy sigh. "Agreed," he said in a dry tone, "but how exactly does one go about harnessing all this 'hot air' once the throttle is pumped and the tiller's ready to steer?"

Bram assessed him through eyes as serene as Logan's were stormy, a nice complement to the gale raging outside his window. "Well, I've certainly never been able to do it on my own, that's for sure. But, forgiveness is God's precept, and ironically, it's only His power that can accomplish it in our lives." Bram paused, as if searching for the right words to drive his point home. "But first, we have to move over and let Him maneuver the tiller, so to speak, allowing Him to channel all that angry steam into His power, which in turn, will steer us to our dreams."

Logan's lips went flat, tone more of a mumble than consent. "Holy thunder, I don't even let Hadley drive me around, much less somebody I can't see." He slumped back in his chair and mauled his face with his hand, finally venting with a noisy sigh. "All right, I give—and how exactly am I supposed to do that?"

Tone steady, Bram was the picture of patience. "It's pretty simple, really—just ask Him to help you do things His way in everything you do. To help you live according to His precepts instead of your own."

"You mean pray," Logan clarified.

Bram nodded. "Yes, I mean pray. As believers, it's the single most important tool we have outside of God's grace."

Logan considered that, face screwed in thought. "Okay, I've made the decision to forgive and I already prayed for God's help." He glanced up, ready to close the deal. "So, is that it?"

"Uh . . . actually, no." Appearing to stifle a grin, Bram ruffled the back of his hair, disrupting the Brilliantine he wore. "I've always found it quite useful to exercise another key precept in this whole forgiveness process."

A pucker wedged above Logan's nose, his patience as thin as the slit of his eyes. "What? Bonbons wrapped in a bow?"

Bram grinned, apparently unable to maintain a serious demeanor. "Close. You need to pray for the person you want to forgive."

Logan blinked, sure he'd misheard. His brows dipped along with his chin, eyes slivers of heat. "You mean pray he goes to the devil so I don't have to send him there with my fist?"

All humor faded from Bram's face while his eyes softened with understanding. "No, Logan—you pray for God to bless him."

He jolted straight up in his chair and slammed a fist to his desk. "No, I refuse. I will *not* pray for God to bless some backstabbing lowlife whose only ambition is to steal my dream!"

Bram's chest rose and fell. "Well, then I guess you have to ask yourself what's more important," he said quietly, gentle eyes pinning him to the wall. "Your pride or your dream?"

Logan stared, the quiet delivery of Bram's words more effective than a punch to the gut. *Pray for Andrew?* For God to bless him? And what if that blessing were Cait? The possibility sucked the air right out of his lungs, and with a sharp stab of reality, he slumped back in the chair with his head in his hands. "I can't do this," he whispered.

"No, Logan, you can't." Bram paused, the weight of his words confident and resolute. "But He can." Silence reigned for several clips of Logan's heart before Bram finally spoke, his voice a strained monotone that sounded nothing like the man Logan knew. "A lesson I learned the hard way," he whispered, "when my father was stabbed and robbed years ago."

Wincing at the memory, Logan looked up, suddenly aware he'd never heard Bram talk about it before, the day Jeremiah Hughes almost died at the hands of a street thug, left for dead in a puddle of blood. Only fifteen at the time and estranged from his father, Bram had been the one to discover him on the study floor, the room in shambles and splattered with blood. When the ambulance arrived, they'd found Bram weeping convulsively, his father clutched tightly in his arms while the housekeeper ushered his sobbing mother from the room. Logan quietly sucked in a calming breath, watching the man who'd become as much of a nephew as Blake. He marveled at how such a tragedy had triggered a transformation in a boy once so prone to rebellion, now so prone to honor God.

Bram's gaze sought Logan's, the horror of that night still evident in the glaze of grief in his eyes. "For months I dreamed of nothing but a bloody room with my knife plunged into the robber's chest. My hate . . . my hurt . . . was so strong I couldn't even stand to be in that house anymore. Every fiber in the blood-stained carpet, every leather-bound volume ripped from my father's library, a chilling reminder of the damage that demon had done . . ."

"And so you spent the bulk of your time at Cait's." Logan's voice was low, his heart aching over the raw pain inflicted upon this boy and the family they all loved.

A faint smile lifted the gloom from Bram's shoulders. "I did," he said with a slow exhale, his trademark peace and calm returning once again. "Mrs. McClare all but saved my life, Logan, by reuniting me with the God of my youth." A sheen of moisture glimmered in his eyes. "The same God who helped me weather every storm of my life, no matter how heinous, and battle every obstacle, no matter how high." The strong line of his chiseled jaw rose, forged in steel by his unshakable faith in God. "*That* God and His precepts helped me fight the horror of my hate with love, forgiveness, and prayers of blessing for my father's attacker. And you know what?" His smile broadened into a grin. "It worked. He's given me my dream of restoration with my family, Logan, something I lost when my sister died. But it wouldn't have been possible without His help, His grace, and His precepts to lead the way."

With a quick tap of his palms on the arms of his chair, he rose, slipping his jacket back on with an energy that hadn't been there before. "Love your enemies, do good to them which hate you, bless them that curse you, and pray for them which despitefully use you." He puckered his nose in a show of distaste. "A bitter pill to swallow, true, but after it goes down?" He winked as he buttoned his coat. "All that nasty hate goes away and I guarantee—you'll never feel better in your life." He glanced at his watch. "Gotta go—my parents are waiting on dinner, but I've enjoyed this, Logan."

Logan rose and extended his hand, clutching Bram's in a firm shake. "Me too, Bram. You know, I think you may have missed your calling as a doctor or minister—your chair-side manner's pretty darn good."

Bram chuckled. "And let Jamie and Blake grab all the legal glory at the Barrister Ball?" He turned with the flash of a grin. "Not good for the boys' humility, I'm afraid."

Shaking his head, Logan couldn't help but laugh. "I suppose that includes their boss too?"

"Naw, they could take a few lessons from him, I think, judging by our conversation tonight. See you tomorrow, Logan." Turning, he strode for the door.

"G'night, Bram—and thanks."

"Sure thing." He paused to toss a grin over his shoulder. "Oh, and about your dream?" His nose bunched in a tight-lipped smile. "Trust me—it's safer in His hands than yours."

23

"Okay just one ... more ... pin." Meg held her breath while Alli focused on positioning a hairpin in just the right spot in Meg's upswept hair, the delicate cream roses with mossy leaves the perfect complement to her pale-green gown. Her sister stepped back to observe her handiwork and grinned at Meg in the mirror with a waggle of dark brows. "Don't trip over your tongue, Devin Caldwell, she's only yours for one night."

A weak giggle drifted from the canopy bed where Cassie lay in her nightgown, limp as the rag doll perched on top of Meg's chiffarobe. "Yes, siree, Megs—that boy will have drool all over his face for sure."

Alli chuckled while she tugged Meg's lacy scoop-neck bodice up another inch. "And egg, if I have anything to say about it," she muttered, squinting in the mirror at Meg's bosom. "Good heavens, Meggie, how can a girl lose weight everywhere but there?"

Color blasted Meg's cheeks as she eyed the very noticeable cleft in her neckline. She sighed and took a turn at yanking it up, helping somewhat. "I honestly don't know, Al. And Rosie even added some lace."

"Humph, not enough to suit me with the likes of Devin Caldwell around." Palms on Meg's shoulder, she gave her a wink in the mirror. "I guess it's not so bad when you pull it up like that, so just give it a tug every now and then, okay?" She leaned to kiss her sister's cheek, then circled her in a tight hug. "You look absolutely beautiful, Megs, and if Devin Caldwell isn't a perfect gentleman tonight, you just let me know, and I'll send Cassie over to sneeze on him."

"With my stinky rope," Cassie volunteered in a nasal tone, handkerchief dabbing at her cherry-red nose. "Right before I truss him up like a snotty-nosed little calf."

Alli's eyes lit up. "Ooooo, or you can take my skewer-size hatpin or atomizer bracelet!"

Cassie sneezed, then managed a watery grin. "Or hide one of my spurs in your purse."

Meg giggled, grateful for the humor that always helped to settle her nerves, something she desperately needed right now. Although a part of her *did* feel badly over the disparaging remarks about Devin. After all, he'd apologized several times. And his behavior at the office had been nothing but gracious and kind. She peeked up, her smile a bit wobbly. "Poor Devin—maybe we should just let bygones be bygones?"

"*Poor* Devin?" Alli plunked hands to her hips. "Megs—this is the twerp that made most of your life miserable! Have you forgotten all the tears you cried in this very room alone?"

"Well, no . . ." Head bowed, she fiddled with her fingers. "But you know Mother has always taught us to forgive, and well . . ." She gave a tiny shrug of her shoulders, suddenly noting how bare they looked in this off-the-shoulder gown. "I've forgiven him."

Cassie yawned from the bed. "I'm convinced you'd forgive Lucifer if given the chance, but then that's one of the things we love most about you." She blew her nose loudly before giving Meg a tired smile. "Your tender heart."

236

"Cassie's right," Alli said with a gentle cup of her sister's cheek. "You've always been so gentle and soft, we've just naturally circled the wagons to protect you." She squeezed Meg's hand, then angled a brow. "And *most* of the time it was from Devin Caldwell, dear sister, so you'll forgive us if we have an axe to grind when it comes to the man."

"And it's honed to a fine blade," Cassie said, "so you just let us know if he steps out of line."

Meg laughed out loud. "Oh, do you have any idea just how much I love you two?"

"I think we do," Alli said, tugging Meg into a hug. She kissed her sister's head.

"Meg darling, are you ready?"

Meg spun around, heart clutching at the sight of her mother in the door. "Oh, Mother . . ." Her voice trailed off because never had she seen her mother look more beautiful. "You look . . ."

"Amazing," Alli supplied, hurrying to take her mother's hands. She pulled back to survey her head to toe, while all Meg could do was stare. She'd always known her mother was a natural beauty, but this evening she seemed to glow. Her usually flawless skin appeared almost iridescent, a soft blush highlighting graceful cheekbones from rouge she seldom wore. Not one to overly fuss with her hair, tonight the auburn locks had a striking sheen about them, piled higher than usual atop her head in a breathless chignon. Two scarlet curls spilled from the nape of her neck over one shoulder, accentuating the creamy skin of her off-the-shoulder gown.

"You don't think I look . . ." Caitlyn McClare glanced over her shoulder to tug at the back of her gauzy lavender dress, which fit as snug as the Glacé kid opera gloves that ran the length of her arm. "Too . . . too . . ."

"Attractive?" Alli chuckled as she tugged her mother into the room to show her off. "Goodness, Mother, you're a vision!" She whirled her around, mouth ajar as she gently patted the lustrous pompadour atop her head. "And sweet heavens, you used a rat, didn't you?" she said, as surprised as Meg that her mother had resorted to the hair pads she never wore, designed to create the high Gibson Girl style of the day.

Meg grinned. "'Ooh là là, Madame McClare,' as Lily would say, 'très belle!'"

Her mother's blush deepened, heightening the dewy effect of her rouge as she nervously patted her hair. "Thank you, girls, but I'm afraid it was Rosie's idea, all of it—the hairstyle, the pearl-white powder, the rouge, the dress—and I simply couldn't dissuade her." A pucker popped above her nose as she attempted to pull up the wispy off-the-shoulder sleeves. "It's not too . . . revealing, is it?"

A hoarse chuckle rolled from the bed where Cassie lay, a mischievous grin on her face despite her sluggish manner and puffy eyes. "Oh, absolutely, Aunt Cait—'revealing' once again that you are one of the most striking women in San Francisco."

Obviously uneasy with the compliment, Caitlyn rushed to Cassie's side. "Oh, Cass—all this silly primping has stolen my brain! How you are feeling, darling?"

"Pretty much like I look," Cassie said, voice stuffy. She punctuated it with a sneeze, which she promptly stifled with her handkerchief. "But I'm hoping the fever will break soon."

"Bless you!" Caitlyn pressed a kiss to Cassie's forehead. "It's down, I think, but there's still a smidge." She stroked her niece's face, eyes soft with regret. "I'm just sorry you won't be there to see Jamie's big moment, but we promise to tell you all about it tomorrow, all right?"

Cassie sniffed and blew her nose. "Yes, and I'll be wanting all the delicious details from both of you, understood? So take notes."

Looping an arm around her sister's shoulder, Alli bumped Meg's hip with her own. "Well, I know *one* person who'll take note when Mother walks into the room, don't you, Megs?"

"Allison Erin McClare!" Her mother's cheeks bloomed bright red, a shade that rivaled her hair. "For heaven's sake, how many times do I have to tell you girls that your Uncle Logan and I are dear friends and nothing more?" She seemed flustered as she moved toward the mirror, turning to study the back of her dress with a crimp in her brow. "And he won't even be there, thank heavens," she muttered under her breath.

Alli fluttered her lashes. "Why, Mother, how your mind does wander—I was talking about Mr. Turner."

Plainly choosing to ignore Alli's remark, her mother hurried over to clasp Meg's hands, stepping back to scan her daughter's dress. "Meg darling, look at you—you're absolutely stunning!" The sparkle of excitement in her emerald eyes was contagious. "Are you nervous?" she said, her shaky giggle hinting at her own butterflies about the evening. "Because it's nothing to be anxious about, so just enjoy, all right?" She touched the silk rose pins in Meg's hair, then cupped her face with a sheen of moisture in her eyes. "I'm so very proud to show you off, sweetheart, and so grateful Andrew invited you and Devin." Voice breathless, she swiped at her eyes and grinned. "This is really an honor, you know, young people such as yourselves attending one of the crème de la crème social events of the year. It's quite lavish, as I recall, although I haven't been since . . ." Her voice trailed off while she busied herself with adjusting Megan's dress, her mood dimming from memories of Megan's father, no doubt.

"Oh, Mother, you have no idea how grateful I am *you* will be there too." Meg gave her a hug, then pulled away, slowly grazing the soft kid leather of her mother's gloves, voice hesitant. "I know you've regretted accepting Andrew's invitation, not only because of Uncle Logan, but because of Father and the memories the ball evokes. But maybe this can be a special mother-daughter memory between you and me."

"Oh, yes!" Her mother laughed and gave her a squeeze. "I think that sounds wonderful."

"And who knows?" Alli said with a joyous clap of her hands. "Tonight could end up being one of the most perfect nights of your lives, like a cloud with a silver lining."

Meg's eyes locked with her mother's and saw the same nervous anticipation she felt, yes, but also the same trepidation that now tightened Meg's chest. *A cloud with a silver lining?* A knot ducked in both their throats before each sucked in a deep draw of air, blowing it out at the same time.

As long as it doesn't rain . . .

Caitlyn blinked, unable to budge. Hand welded to Andrew's arm, she stood on the two-storied arched threshold of The Palace Hotel's magnificent Garden Court, as stiff as the ice sculptures scattered throughout the room. She tried to swallow, but nothing worked. Apparently the muscles in her throat were as paralyzed as her feet, which remained rooted to the plush scarlet carpet as if her satin heels were hobbled to the floor. Although they were late and appetizers were just being served, she could barely hear the tinkle of silverware and murmur of voices for the pounding of blood in her ears. Laughter floated above the tables like a specter, as if taunting her for putting herself in this uncomfortable position. The ball was a blur of lush palms, white linen-clad tables, and flickering candlelight, luring Caitlyn's glassy-eyed stare up seven stories of columned balconies to a massive skylight the full breadth of the room.

Sweet heavenly hosts—what had possessed her to say yes? To agree to accompany a man—one of the most eligible bachelors in the city, no less—to the social event of the season? To all but shout to the world that she and Andrew Turner were smitten? Wooing, even? Her palms started to sweat. Oh, sweet angels in heaven, next it would be courting and then . . . Her eyelids slammed shut, her breathing shallow and fast as the magnitude of what she'd done struck hard. She swayed on her feet, nails digging into Andrew's arm. *Lord help me—I can't do this . . .*

"Cait?" Andrew's breath was warm in her ear, and she vaguely sensed the gentle kneading of his thumb on her glove. "Everything's going to be fine, Mrs. McClare," he whispered, the scent of Bay Rum doing nothing for her composure. "Just take a deep breath."

Oh that she could!

It seemed she had used all her deep breaths up at home, where her frazzled nerves had caused them to be late when she misplaced first her wrap and then her purse, necessitating a duck into the powder room to collect her wits. She gulped. Something *else* she'd apparently misplaced at the moment . . .

"Mother? Are you all right?" Meg shored an arm to Caitlyn's waist, and her touch instantly slowed the frantic pace of her pulse. The concern in her daughter's wide green eyes gave her pause, dosing her with the realization she could ruin this special evening for Meg if she didn't regain control. Inhaling deeply, she nodded. "Yes, darling, just a wee bit overwhelmed by all the people and splendor, but I'll be fine." She forced a shaky smile, swallowing the dread that clogged in her throat.

In about five or six hours . . .

"Andrew! Good to see you again—it's been way too long." An elderly gentleman rose from his seat to pump Andrew's hand while others approached, men eyeing her with interest while ladies offered coy smiles, their unspoken curiosity as loud as the twenty-piece orchestra just tuning up. She nodded and smiled when Andrew made the introductions, head swimming with names and invitations to dinners she was certain she'd never remember. Devin and Meg fetched their table numbers, and Andrew firmly steered her forward.

It was a sea of glittering tables seated with even more glittering people dining on shrimp cocktail and champagne. A watercolor blur of silks and satins and enough diamonds, gems, and gold to feed every downtrodden person in the Barbary Coast for the rest of their lives. Someone stopped Andrew every few feet, and Cait's face grew stiff with smiles. She wondered if they would ever make it to their table. She breathed a silent sigh of relief when Andrew spotted their number in a prime and cozy location to the right of the stage, where the orchestra played soft dinner music Cait had yet to enjoy. All at once he stopped so abruptly, she nearly plowed into his back, Megan and Devin close on her heels.

"Thank goodness you're finally here. We thought you decided to sit elsewhere." Jamie's voice reached Cait's ears, and she peeked around Andrew's broad back, surprised to see him and Bram rising from Andrew's table, both very handsome in tails and tie. Jamie's grin sloped uphill. "Figured it was because of Bram."

Megan sidled around her mother with a gaping smile, gaze immediately zeroing in on the object of Jamie's tease. "Goodness, we're all sitting at the same table? I didn't know that."

Andrew extended a handshake to both Jamie and Bram with a smile as broad as his reach. "Neither did I," he said with his usual boyish charm, "but it certainly makes everything nice and cozy." If he was shocked they were sitting with her family, he never let on, simply greeted everyone at the table with equal grace. "Mrs.

MacKenna, Jess—it's wonderful to see you both again." His smile was genuine as he seated Caitlyn in the chair designated by her name holder while Devin did the same for Meg.

Caitlyn immediately offered her hand to Jamie's mother with a warm smile, pleased to see her and Jess here in Cassie's absence. "Jean, I'm sorry Cassie is sick tonight, but I must say it's lovely to see you and Jess again, especially on this big night for your son."

Jean MacKenna gave Caitlyn's hand a cordial squeeze, the glow of excitement in her cheeks lending a delicate blush to near-flawless skin that belied her age of forty-four. Hazel eyes so like her son's sparkled with pleasure as she patted his arm, the pride in her voice unmistakable. "Well, I have to admit, I'm feeling a wee bit guilty about Cass home in bed, but I'd be lying if I didn't say this is one of the happiest and proudest moments of my life."

Hooking his mother close, Jamie gave her a kiss on the cheek, their dark curls almost identical. "Mine too, Mom, having you and Jess here."

Caitlyn turned to greet Jess and Bram, eyes lighting on the pretty girl by Bram's side who appeared a little older than Meg. "Amelia Darlington, I presume? It's a pleasure to finally meet you—I recognize you from the paper."

The girl's smile could have lit up the room. "Oh, likewise, Mrs. McClare," she said. A bejeweled hand pressed to the pale-yellow bodice of her elegant organza gown, a near match to the flaxen wisps that framed her heart-shaped face. Sequined flowers twinkled in her curly chignon that rivaled the sparkle in wide blue eyes. For all her apparent affluence, she reminded Caitlyn of a starry-eyed little girl anxious to grow up. "Why, you're an icon in San Francisco society, ma'am," she gushed, tone tinged with awe, "and I count it an absolute honor to be seated at your table."

Settling her napkin on her lap, Caitlyn chuckled, cheeks warming as she speared one of the shrimp on her plate with her fork. "Good heavens, an 'icon'—well, there goes eating shrimp with my fingers."

"Uncle Logan!" Meg's voice shimmered with excitement. "I thought Mother said you weren't coming."

Out of the corner of her eye, Caitlyn saw a tall tuxedo-clad man bend to buss Meg's cheek. The shrimp swelled in Caitlyn's throat, blocking her air.

Logan? Here???

She started to choke, disgorging the half-eaten shrimp in her napkin when a palm slapped firmly on her back. "One bite at a time, Mrs. McClare," Logan whispered in her ear, the heat engulfing her face hot enough to fry the shrimp. With a casual air, he leaned to shake both Devin's and Andrew's hands before claiming the empty seat between Jean and her. "Couldn't miss a ceremony honoring three of my best counselors, could I?" Shaking his napkin, he placed it in his lap, then slanted a hair closer to Cait with a sideways smile. "Good evening, Mrs. McClare—you're looking lovely as usual."

Forging a smile as stiff as the starched napkin she pressed to her lips, she bent near. "What on earth are you doing here?" she whispered, her voice a soft hiss.

His handsome profile shifted slightly her way, their chairs so close she could see the dark lashes hooding gray eyes that sported a hint of a twinkle. "It's the Barrister Ball, Cait, and I'm a member of the bar, remember?"

Her smile went flat beneath the napkin. "You know what I mean—you implied you weren't coming and now here you are, and it's rather . . ."

"Awkward?" he supplied.

She lunged for her water and bolted it half down.

He turned to face her, palm quietly slipping over her hand beneath the table, which was tensely splayed to the seat of her chair. "No, Cait," he said for her ears alone, "my abominable behavior the night of Megan's party was awkward, not this. This is merely my clumsy attempt to apologize for losing my temper and trying to bully you around. It was stupid and bullheaded and I've already sent my apologies to Andrew as well." His weighted pause slowly drew her eyes to his while the pleated shirt of his tuxedo rose and fell with a heavy sigh. "But most of all, I'm sorry for erecting a wall between us that should never, *ever* be." He gave her hand a gentle squeeze. "Am I forgiven?"

"Andrew, you made it!" Claudia Marsh sailed over to their table with a wispy sweep of pink chiffon flowing behind, her regal bearing marking her as the president of the planning committee for the Barrister Ball. "I hope you don't mind, but I took the liberty of switching your table seating from the Pembrook table to the McClares' when I saw who your lovely guest would be." She extended a gloved hand to Caitlyn, her smile as gracious as the lady herself. "Caitlyn, it's so very good to see you again—we've missed you at all the various functions, I assure you." Her brown eyes were warm with concern. "How are you, my dear?"

Caitlyn clasped Claudia's hands in hers, fighting a sting of moisture over the welcome manner of the woman who had been so very kind at the time of Liam's death. Ever mindful of the needs of others, she had quietly absolved Caitlyn of the many committee obligations she'd carried before grief struck a painful blow. "Wonderful, Claudia, especially now that my family is all together again and growing." She nodded toward Meg with a proud smile. "Meg just returned from a year in Paris, and my daughter Alli is engaged to a wonderful man we all adore." Her eyes glowed with pride as she nodded to Jamie. "And as you're well aware, my niece married Mr. MacKenna last December, so things are definitely looking up."

"Oh, I'm so glad, my dear." A bit of mischief shadowed her smile as she patted a gloved hand to both Andrew's and Logan's shoulders at the same time. "And I would certainly say things *are* looking up, being seated between two of the most influential and eligible men in the room." She leaned in as if to whisper in Caitlyn's ear, but her voice carried well around the table, heating Caitlyn's cheeks. "You're the envy of every woman in this room tonight, my dear, so enjoy it." She tweaked the men's shoulders with a wink before moving toward the next table, but not before tossing a smile over her shoulder. "After all, it's not often we see Supervisor McClare and the district attorney so cozy outside of the courtroom, eh?"

Cozy? Caitlyn gulped. *Not exactly the word I would have chosen.* Appetite greatly diminished, she absently poked at her shrimp, smiling and nodding when Andrew asked her a question. She was grateful Logan was engaged in a conversation with Jamie and his mother—

She froze, a shrimp instantly lodged at the back of her throat. Jamie. His mother. *And* his father.

Together as a family for the very first time.

Napkin to mouth, she started to hack, mortified when all conversation ceased around the table. Logan instantly tapped on her back once again while Andrew offered a glass of water.

"Mother, are you all right?" Megan asked, the concern in her eyes matching the stares of all those seated.

She nodded, eyes watering. "Yes, dear," she managed in a hoarse voice before downing the water in one, long unladylike glug. She placed the empty goblet back on the table and took a deep swallow of air, hand to her stomach. "Went down the wrong pipe, I'm afraid, making me a bit nauseous."

"I'd be happy to fetch you some ginger ale from the bar to settle your stomach, Mrs. McClare," Devin offered, and Andrew promptly popped up.

"Excellent suggestion, Dev, but no need, I'll take care of it." Hand on her shoulder, Andrew leaned in, worry edging his tone. "Do you need anything else other than ginger ale, Cait—crackers, perhaps, or a bromide?"

"Ginger ale would be lovely, Andrew, thank you so much."

"Coming right up," he said with a knead of her shoulder, and then promptly wove his way through the crowd to the bar.

"Sorry about the shrimp," Logan said at her side, nudging his untouched water goblet toward her, "but then I'm sorry about a lot of things when it comes to you, Cait."

She drew in a deep breath and slowly released it again, fiddling with the napkin on her lap. *So am I, Logan, more than you'll ever know . . .*

"You never answered my question," he continued, voice low while he pushed his appetizer plate away. "Am I forgiven—for my outrageous behavior over Andrew?"

Her gaze lifted to meet his. "Yes, forgiven," she whispered, "always." Her eyes flicked past him to Jean, who was laughing over something with Jamie and Jess, and a horrendous ache cramped in her chest. *But, regrettably, never forgotten . . .*

As if reading her thoughts, he exhaled slowly, his voice private and low. "I wasn't planning on attending, as you know, but Jamie needed an extra escort," he said quietly.

She attempted a smile and failed, wishing she could offer a casual response, but jealousy rose like bile, tainting her tongue. Loathe for Logan to read her pathetic response, she snatched his water goblet and took a fast drink, fully aware she had no earthly right to feel this way. She and Logan were friends, nothing more, and for goodness' sake, it was just the favor of an escort for one single evening. No more than a courtesy to Jamie so his family could attend, both his sister *and* his mother. Her eyelids flickered closed.

The mother of Logan's child.

"Cait."

Exhaling a quivering breath, she glanced up, desperate to convey an air of nonchalance despite the racing of her heart. She forced a polite smile. "Yes, Logan?"

His eyes bore into hers with an intensity that laid low her mask of calm, stripping her bare with a whisper that literally pulsed with emotion. "You need to know, Cait, that you are the only woman I have ever loved, and that will *never* change."

"Excuse me, miss."

She startled as a waiter reached to remove her appetizer plate, replacing it with a Caesar salad just as Andrew returned. He placed her ginger ale before her, then leaned close with a look of concern. "How are you feeling, Cait?" he asked.

"Better," she said with a smile she hoped was convincing, but it was hardly the truth. Seldom had she felt worse. Her hand shook as she reached for the ginger ale, well aware that Logan had returned his attention to Jean. "Thank you, Andrew," she whispered, taking a quick gulp. "This should help immensely in keeping my nausea down." Her eyelids flickered closed.

While my heartache, unfortunately, appears to be on the rise . . .

24

*S*o . . . are you enjoying yourself, Bug?"

Meg glanced up at Bram, truly comfortable for the first time all night as he spun her in his arms, the firm hold of his palm against her shoulder blade more potent than laudanum in settling her nerves. Breathing in a calming breath, she smiled up at him, wishing she could stay in his arms for the rest of the evening rather than just this one dance. She was quite sure Abraham Hughes was not only one of the most gentle and caring men in the room, but certainly one of the most handsome. She'd always thought so from little on, but tonight he seemed especially so—completely dashing in his charcoal double-breasted waistcoat with tails. His crisp white shirt with high-necked collar and white satin bow tie were the very height of fashion, which made Meg smile all the more. For a man who didn't seem to care about society, he sure knew how to dress well. "I am now," she said with a tremulous grin.

One sandy brow jagged up, his wide smile unable to hide the crinkle of concern at the bridge of his nose. "Why, Megan Mc-Clare—are you practicing your wiles on me, the oldest friend you have?"

Her cheeks warmed. *Not likely, for all the good it would do.* She tipped her head to study him, smile ebbing when she realized they might not always be able to share this deep friendship they had. Her gaze flicked to Devin and Amelia just a few feet away, and the same dull ache she'd experienced when she'd first met Bram's date struck again, clouding her good mood.

"What's wrong?" Bram's quiet question brought her eyes back to his, and she fought an involuntary shiver, yearning for one of their private games of chess right now where she could spill all the trouble brewing in her soul. Instead, she had only this one dance with her best friend before returning to the company of a man whose subtle flirtations made her downright nervous. She swallowed hard. While her best friend returned to a woman who did much the same.

She braved a tenuous smile. "Oh, I'm just being silly, Bram, don't mind me, truly."

Their eyes connected with a familiarity that told her he would not let her off so easily, and halting mid-dance, he promptly ushered her toward the terrace door. "I could use some air," he said with a flat smile, "and so can you, apparently."

Before she could utter a word, he'd whisked her through the crowd outside to a stone terrace lined with palms and people, where he promptly seated her on a wrought-iron bench. Settling in beside her, he faced her, the casual lay of his arm over the back of the settee belying blue eyes now dark with concern. "What's the problem, Bug?"

She nodded, feeling all of thirteen again and more than a little foolish. "It's silly, I know, but being with Devin makes me nervous, unsettled somehow."

"Because . . . ?" He tilted his head, calm tone coaxing her to confess.

Her gaze dropped to her lap where she picked at her nails.

"Because . . . I think he may be, well, flirting with me, and I'm not sure I trust him."

"Perfectly understandable, given your history, but he seems like a nice enough fellow from the conservations we've had." He lifted her chin with his finger, voice brimming with affection. "And of course he's flirting with you, Bug—you've grown into a beautiful woman, and he's a man. That's a natural progression, I think."

She glanced away. *Except with you* . . . "Well, you see, he's been hinting that he'd like to . . ." Her throat parched dry at the very thought of becoming close with any man but Bram.

He skimmed a wisp of a curl away from her face. "To what?"

Her bodice quivered with a shaky breath. "Well . . . you know . . . to date."

A shadow of a frown flickered before he quickly covered it with his usual serene composure. "Hinting? Or asking outright?"

She peeked up. "No, not asking outright or even blatant hinting, I suppose, but subtleties that make me nervous all the same."

Exhaling slowly, he tipped his head with a tender smile, his gaze meeting hers. "Well, there's no need to worry yourself with this tonight, is there? How 'bout we tackle your concerns over a game of chess tomorrow and just try to enjoy the rest of the evening?"

Oh, that I could! Offering a slow nod, she lowered her gaze lest he see the truth in her eyes. *But I'm not with you* . . .

"So . . . is that all that's bothering you, then?"

She peeked up. *No, but if I bring up Amelia, you'll think I'm a spoiled brat.* "Well, I suppose I am a bit concerned about Mother," she said quietly. "She doesn't seem herself tonight either, and I'm concerned she's feeling awkward being with Andrew while Uncle Logan's right beside her." She expelled a heavy blast of air. "Not to mention how Uncle Logan must feel."

He nodded, lips compressing enough for her to notice. "I have to admit, I was surprised when Logan changed his mind about coming to escort Jamie's mother, but Jamie was thrilled, naturally, and of course none of us thought we'd all be sitting at the same table."

"No, I suppose not." She paused to stare at him with fondness, embarrassed at the wetness in her eyes. "Thank you, Bram, for always being there for me. I honestly don't know what I would do without you."

He squeezed her hands, his solid touch infusing her with strength. "Well, hopefully, you'll never have to—"

"Pardon me, Meg, but Amelia has been looking for Bram."

Meg all but jumped, eyes round at the sight of Devin not ten feet away, his manner stiff despite the smile on his face. When his eyes flicked to the clasp of Bram's hands with hers, she shot to her feet, her stomach taking a tumble. "Oh . . . yes . . . of course, Devin, thank you." She spun to face Bram, fingers quivering as she fumbled with the lace of her gown. "You should go."

Bram rose slowly, gaze fixed on Meg while directing his comment to Devin. "Thank you, Devin. If you'd be kind enough to tell Amelia I'm on my way, I'd be most grateful."

Devin didn't respond, and Meg stole a quick glance, mortified at the stony look on his face. She bit her lip. "No, Bram, really—"

Despite the patient smile on Bram's face, his tone carried an air of authority. "We won't be a moment."

Devin gave a gruff nod and turned on his heel, stealing Meg's wind. "Oh, Bram, I'm so sorry—"

"No, Bug." His look was gentle despite the arch of his brow. "I am not letting you go back in there frazzled, and that's all there is to it. Now . . . both you and I have enough faith in prayer to know that everything will work out, both in your situation with Devin and between your mother and Logan, right?"

She nodded, so very grateful her mother had raised her with a deep faith.

"Good girl. Always remember, Meg, with faith, we're not in this alone." He sighed and took her hands in his, lowering his voice. "Now close your eyes and take a deep breath, then let it out slowly, repeating several times."

After she did, he gave her a brief hug, pulling away as if to assess her mood. "Feeling any better, I hope?"

She peered up, realizing that she actually did. "I think so."

"Good. Exactly what I wanted to hear." He offered his arm. "There are some things that are just more important than parties and dances," he said with a quirk of a smile, "and the well-being of friends is definitely one of them. Ready?"

"With a dear friend like you by my side? Always!" She took his arm, holding on more tightly than she should, expelling the softest of sighs. Always, indeed.

And God willing . . . forever.

It was the best of times, it was the worst of times. Logan's smile was melancholy as he listened to Henry St. George Tucker III, esteemed president of the bar association, introduce the newest members of the bar. Watching his own flesh and blood standing on the same platform where he himself once stood as a newly graduated attorney so many years ago, made this evening one of the best of his life.

And one of the worst.

Eyes trained on Jamie, Logan leaned back with arms folded, keenly aware of the presence of two women on either side of his chair who, in the light of his son's glowing success, only reminded him of his own dismal failures. He'd been a vain and selfish young man who wasn't half the man his son had turned out to be. A stark truth accompanied by grief over the blunders he'd made, neatly colliding with the joy of his most grievous mistake—a son who filled his heart and his days with more joy and pride than he deserved.

Oddly enough, reconnecting with Jean tonight, if only for Jamie's sake, had brought both grief and joy full circle in regard to his son. Although conversation had been stilted at first, laughing and joking with Jamie, his sister, and Jean had been good for them all. Somehow it seemed to allow the painful past to quietly slip away while they focused on a future that stirred passion and pride and peace within a not-so-conventional family. Rising to his feet to clap loudly at the mention of Bram's name and then Blake's and Jamie's, Logan knew that despite his initial reservations about coming tonight, God had ordained this evening. Out of the ashes of his mistakes would rise a noble calling that could very well heal them all—a partnership with Jean MacKenna where he could give back to women like she used to be. First by funding her, Jamie, and Jess's boardinghouse for disadvantaged women. And then through a foundation headed by Jean MacKenna herself to provide training for jobs that would rescue women from the brothels of the Barbary Coast.

From the stage, Jamie smiled their way, and Logan grinned while Jean commenced to weeping. As natural as rain, he promptly slipped an arm around her shoulder while Jess shored her up on the other side, uniting the three of them in a show of solidarity that brought a broad grin to Jamie's face.

The men returned to their tables, and Logan pumped Blake's and Bram's hands as Jean and Jess fawned over Jamie. Bram grinned and nodded toward his best friend. "Not too bad for a pretty boy, eh?"

Logan laughed, his pride chasing all melancholy away. "No, sir, not at all. And I'm feeling pretty smug I snatched the three of you before anybody else could, I can tell you that."

Henry St. George Tucker III tapped a spoon on a water glass at the podium to recapture everyone's attention, and Logan turned to shake Jamie's hand as any employer might do with an employee. Jamie and he had opted to keep Logan's paternity a secret from everyone except the family. A decision not made lightly to shield Jean MacKenna from scandal. Heart near bursting with pride, Logan finally threw caution to the wind with a bear hug that brought tears to his eyes. "I love you, son, and I couldn't be prouder."

Jamie clasped his arm with a stoic smile, his jaw tight as if staving off the same emotion swelling inside of Logan. "I love you too, sir, and likewise, I assure you."

With a firm clasp of Jamie's shoulder, Logan returned to his seat, grateful Cait was occupied talking to Andrew.

"Our next order of business is a true highlight for me and the bar association of San Francisco. Tonight we gather to honor our new attorneys, yes, but also the counselor that the committee feels has contributed the most to the betterment of this great city." His gaze traveled the room, his dark moustache twitching with the motion. "Although only one of our fine barristers will walk away with the Dickherber Civil Service Award tonight, without question, mere nomination is the highest honor and achievement in our profession. So, without further ado, let me offer my sincere congratulations to the following three gentlemen."

Logan shifted, never completely comfortable with recognition in front of his peers, especially in front of Cait. Henry McEuen, a good friend married to Brittany McEuen, Claudia Marsh's co-chair, had alerted him he was on the short list. He was honored, of course, particularly since his brother Liam—one of the few men he'd revered and respected—had won the award the year before he died. Logan still remembered the glow of pride on Cait's face. His jaw inadvertently tightened. But there was no way he deserved such recognition in her eyes, not compared to his brother. He massaged the back of his neck. Not when one considered the failings of one of the most notorious members of the Board of Supervisors.

"I will list the gentlemen in alphabetical order, and I'd like to ask each to stand if they're here." The president cleared his throat. "Mr. Richard Barrows."

Applause broke out throughout the room as the president continued.

"Mr. Logan McClare."

Jamie and Bram applauded louder than anyone, and Logan couldn't help but squirm.

"And, finally . . . Mr. Andrew Turner. Let's give a hand to each of these extraordinary counselors, and I'd like to commend each of them for many tireless hours devoted to this city."

The room erupted in applause, and Logan extended a hand to Andrew, keenly aware of Cait's gaze. Exhaling, he sat back down, palm twitching as it cupped the edge of his chair.

"And, now, the moment we've all been waiting for—this year's Dickherber Service Award goes to . . ."

Logan startled at the touch of Cait's hand, lighting discreetly over his on the seat of the chair, his heart clutching at the gentle press of her palm. Their eyes locked.

"Logan McClare!"

A thunderous ovation rose to the glass ceiling as everyone stood to their feet, eyes fixed on him. But all he could see was the love and pride in green eyes that bore a sheen of tears when

Cait squeezed his hand. "Oh, Logan, I'm so very proud, and I know Liam would be too."

"Mr. McClare," the president boomed, "if you'll kindly make your way to the stage, I believe we have a plaque with your name on it, sir."

"Go!" Cait prodded with a swipe of her eyes, standing to join the others in their clapping and cheers.

Generally a man of the utmost confidence, Logan had never felt more awkward. This was something every attorney in this room aspired to and yet, it shocked him just how shallow it felt reaping men's praises when it was no longer the most paramount thing in his life. Accepting the plaque, it pained him to stand by while the president lauded his accomplishments—his work on the Board of Supervisors and his philanthropy to Cooper Medical, Lane Hospital, and Stanford. He cited Logan's leadership on the city's Civil Progress Committee—which to him, in the face of all Liam had accomplished—paled in importance.

Never more eager to escape the limelight, Logan bolted for the table the moment the president shook his hand, declining to give a speech other than a quick heft of his plaque and a hoarse thank-you. Blake was there with Jamie and Bram, the three of them taking turns shaking his hand and slapping him on the back while Meg vaulted into his arms, clinging with all of her might.

"Congratulations, Logan," Andrew said, offering his hand in a show of friendship. "Well deserved, my friend."

Logan shook his hand, the sincerity in Andrew's eyes giving him pause. "Thanks, Andrew—I suspect with all you've contributed to this city, the next one is yours."

Andrew laughed. "With you out of the running, McClare, one can only hope."

The orchestra began to play, and Jamie rose to escort his mother to the dance floor while Blake and Jess followed behind. Logan's gaze settled on Cait. "Andrew, if it's all right with you, I'd like an opportunity to dance with Cait if I may."

"That's up to Cait," Andrew said with a light squeeze of her shoulder. He retrieved her empty ginger ale glass from the table and bent forward. "Cait, I saw someone I need to speak to across the room, so I'll get you a refill on the way."

"Thank you, Andrew," she whispered, picking at her nails as her eyes trailed him into the crowd, as if she were reluctant to meet Logan's gaze.

His voice was low as he grazed the soft skin of her shoulder. "Shall we, Mrs. McClare?" Seldom had Logan seen Cait more nervous, biting the edge of her lip as she rose. He heard the catch of her breath when he skimmed her arms with his palms. "If you'd rather not . . ."

She glanced up then, lips curving in a shy smile that reminded him so much of Meg. "And miss the chance to dance with the man of the hour, easily becoming the absolute envy of almost every woman in this room?" She looped her arm through his. "I think not, Mr. McClare."

He grinned as he escorted her to the floor. "There's only one woman whose opinion I care about, and I'm about to dance with her." Hand to the small of her back, he guided her past the crowd to a less congested area, the distant glow of chandeliers overhead lending an intimate feel to a room lit by candlelight. Taking her into his arms, his chest ached at having her so near, the feel of her hands in his as natural as breathing. Hundreds of people crowded the room, but for him, there was only one.

One person.

One woman.

One love for the rest of my life.

"Have I told you yet just how handsome you look tonight?"

He grinned, her stilted attempt at flirtation so out of character that he knew she was flustered. "Are you flirting with me, Mrs. McClare?" he asked with a jut of his brow, laughing out loud when her cheeks fused bright pink. He neatly executed a wide spin, as fluid as if they were one. "And have I ever told *you* just how adorable you are when you're nervous?"

"I am *not* nervous," she said with a thrust of her chin, a flicker of a smile at the edge of her lips. A familiar spark in those mesmerizing green eyes told him he'd struck a nerve.

"Ah, now *there's* the Caitlyn I know and love." Palm grazing her shoulder blade, he swept her in a wide arc, her body as graceful and light as the chiffon folds of her dress as they fluttered in the breeze. His smile faded to tender. "This is me, Cait, remember?" he said quietly. "No need to be nervous."

She looked away, the muscles in her throat contracting as if she didn't know what to say, and his heart stalled for a split second. Suddenly she seemed as if she were a million miles away, so distant in her emotions that they might have been mere acquaintances. Her gaze roamed the room, lighting on anything but him, and instantly a hint of alarm curled in his belly.

He gripped her closer, palm firm against her back while his voice came out hoarse and low. "Don't do this, Cait," he whispered, "don't leave me. I can feel you pulling away, and I don't know why."

Anyone else might have missed the almost imperceptible quiver of her lip, but not him, not in a face that haunted his dreams day and night. When she finally lifted her gaze to his, her face held a shadow of sadness despite a wellspring of affection misting her eyes. "I'm not going anywhere, Logan," she said softly, briefly cupping a gentle hand to his face. Her fingers quivered noticeably against his jaw, and it took everything in him not to place his hand over hers. Her expression was tender. "You and I share a friendship and love that will last forever."

Her bodice expanded with a quick inhale, as if she were desperate to change the subject. "You and Jean certainly make a handsome couple," she said casually, her gaze roaming the room, looking everywhere but at him. "It's easy to see where Jamie gets his good looks."

He fought the rise of a gulp, any and all nervousness suddenly his. So *that* was the reason for her detached behavior—Jean MacKenna. Sweat licked the back of his collar. But was it jealousy . . . or something else? Swallowing hard, he whirled her wide before his sober eyes met hers. "I'd rather not talk about Jean, Cait, any more than I imagine you want to talk about Andrew."

The heightened color in her cheeks told him he'd struck his mark.

He continued before she could speak, tempering his words with the same logic, calm, and confidence he utilized in his profession. "Jamie was in a bind because he obviously couldn't escort both Jess and his mother, so I bailed him out, Cait, nothing more."

The blush in her cheeks deepened. "Logan, really, it's none of my busi—"

"Of course it is," he said, cutting her off with a pointed tone. His face softened when she peeked up at him with a sheen of tears, a shadow of grief haunting her gaze that near shredded his heart. The volume of his voice dropped to husky. "I'm in love with you, Cait—when are you going to realize that means forever?"

"Sorry, old boy, but your second dance just ended."

Both he and Cait startled, obviously so focused on each other neither noticed that the song had stopped and another was just beginning.

"The orchestra just indicated last dance of the night, Supervisor," Andrew said with a clap on Logan's back, his smile kind, but the jest in his tone getting on Logan's nerves. "So despite your lucky win tonight, I believe a court would rule in my favor since the lady *is* my date."

Date.

His. Not Logan's.

Salt in a wound that had just begun to heal.

Employing the unruffled demeanor for which he was known, Logan stepped back and graciously offered Cait's hand to Turner along with an easy smile that wasn't easy at all. But not before caressing her palm with the pad of his thumb, squeezing lightly before finally letting go. "I defer, old boy, but I think a jury would concur, counselor, as to which of us is luckier tonight." With a slight bow, Logan turned to make his way through the crowd, fielding a flurry of handshakes on the way, masterful at hiding the awful jealousy that clawed in his chest. All around him, people offered congratulations, cheering and praising him for the award he had won. A coveted wooden plaque with a brass inscription—the prize he'd take home tonight.

While Andrew took Cait.

Changing his course midstride to the table, he made a beeline for the terrace door instead, skimming his fingers inside his collar to loosen his tie. No question about it—the Dickherber Award recipient definitely needed privacy and distance and a whole lot of air. He shoved through the French doors, the sharp blast of sea breeze doing little to cool his temper.

Because despite the polished brass plate carefully etched with his name? A swear word teetered on the tip of his tongue. He wasn't the winner at all.

25

"*I* had a wonderful time, Bram."

Bram stood on the Darlington marble portico with Amelia, wishing he were anywhere but here. Not that he didn't like her—he did. But the conversation with Meg had unsettled him more than he wanted to admit—especially to Meg. He cared too much about her happiness and peace of mind, he realized, and the threat of Caldwell hurting her again disturbed him as much as it did her. He frowned. Not necessarily a good thing now that she was all grown up and poised to live her own life. And he, his. He refocused on Amelia, noting the doleful slope of brows and the two tiny creases above her nose, and guilt instantly cramped in his chest. *You're an idiot, Hughes.*

"But *you* didn't, did you?" The quiver of hurt in her whisper shot straight to his heart.

"Of course I did," he assured her, taking her hands into his own. "I'm just a little distracted right now, that's all, and I apologize for that."

"Distracted because of . . . Meg?" There was a childlike quality to her voice, soft and unsure, overriding any shock he might have experienced over the pointed question she asked.

He exhaled slowly. "Actually, yes, but only because Meg is like a sister to me, so when she's upset, I'm afraid I revert to being her big brother, protective to a fault."

"But you're not," she whispered, a glimmer in her eyes that hinted at tears. "Her brother, that is, which makes it all the harder to accept the fact that . . ."

Her lower lip began to quiver, and he tightened his grip. "Accept what?" he asked softly, fighting the urge to pull her into his arms and comfort her like he'd always done with Meg.

She gave a tiny lift of her shoulders while she stared at the floor, looking far more like a little girl than a woman of almost twenty. "Well, you know . . . accept the fact that men aren't . . ." Her voice broke on a tiny heave. "A-Attracted to me."

He bit back a groan, regretting that his preoccupation with Meg had affected Amelia's evening as well. Desperate to appease, he lifted her hands to graze her fingers with a tender kiss. "That's ridiculous—you turned many a head tonight, Amelia, and I was proud to be your escort."

"You were?" Her eyelids flickered several times, lashes spiky with tears, and then his stomach clenched when her lip started to tremble again. "But if th-that's true, then wh-why did Antonio b-break my heart . . . ?" Her voice trailed into a quiet sob.

Bram blinked, paralyzed for half a heartbeat before he gathered her in his arms, soothing with a gentle caress of her back. "Okay, young lady, just who is this Antonio?" She hiccupped in his arms, and a faint smile tipped the edge of his lips at the soft little girl hidden so carefully beneath the perky veneer. The notion that she was like Meg in this respect seemed to calm him, unleashing the caretaker in him. He gave her shoulder a squeeze while tease tempered his tone. "The truth, Miss Darlington, if you please—do I have competition to worry about?"

She pulled away, eyes wide and wet, and the nervous peak of

her brows made him want to hug her all over again. "Oh, no, Bram—I didn't mean to imply that, it's just that . . . that . . ."

More moisture pooled in her eyes, and before she could utter another word, he steered her to an ornate wrought-iron chaise on the Darlingtons' rock patio at the side of the house. Gently prompting her to sit, he joined her while the gurgle of a marble fountain filled the night air, hoping it would mask any conversation—or weeping—that might occur. He took her hands in his, voice as tender as his smile. "Amelia," he said softly, "I want you to start at the beginning and tell me who Antonio is, and I promise you will not offend or hurt my feelings. Yes, there is an unspoken understanding between our families and us, I realize, but that doesn't preclude others we may have cared for in the past." He tucked a finger to her chin, lifting her swollen gaze to his. "And frankly, Miss Darlington, you're way too pretty and young to know heartbreak, so I want to know the source of your grief, all right?"

She nodded, sniffling while she groped in her reticule for a handkerchief that appeared to be lost in a dark hole. Battling a smile, he slipped his own freshly starched handkerchief into her hand and placed her beaded purse between them. "Okay, I assume you met Antonio in Rome?"

Blond curls bobbed in agreement while she blew her nose in a dainty manner.

"And you obviously cared for him a great deal."

He tempered a smile when a loose flower in her hair flopped with another jerky nod. "So what happened?" he whispered.

A tiny shudder traveled her body before she finally released a wavering sigh, head bowed and shoulders slumped, handkerchief limp in her lap. "I . . . met h-him at a g-gathering Aunt Flora's dear friend Isabella gave to welcome me to Rome. He was her daughter Gia's friend, actually, and we . . ." She dabbed at fresh tears. "Hit it off beautifully . . . even magically, you might say." Her gaze rose to meet Bram's, tragedy welling in her dark eyes. "We spent . . . so much time together . . . with Gia and her friends, and h-he . . ." A muscle spasmed in her throat. "H-he told me he loved m-me, Bram . . . that he wanted to m-marry me . . ." Her voice cracked on a heave. "And then . . . then h-he . . . w-was gone."

"Gone?"

The flower that dangled in her hair flapped unmercifully, but Bram found no humor in it now, aching for this young woman whose heart had been shattered. "To Milan, he s-said, a family matter h-he needed to attend to." Her eyelids weighted closed, sending a trail of tears down each sodden cheek. "Only he . . . he . . . ended it after he left."

Bram reached for her hand, palming it between his. "What do you mean 'ended it'?"

She sniffed, handkerchief blotting moisture in what appeared to be a valiant attempt at composure. "A . . . brief n-note a few days later, saying he was s-sorry to lead me on but that it was nothing m-more than an innocent f-flirtation . . ."

Her broken words trailed into weeping so anguished, Bram could do naught but cradle her in his arms. "Amelia, I'm so sorry," he said quietly, feeling her pain in every shudder. "But it sounds as if God may have spared you from a shallow relationship."

"That's wh-what Auntie Flo said, b-but it d-doesn't make it h-hurt any less . . ."

"No, it doesn't, but we're going to do something about that."

"We are?" she said with a soggy sniff, luring a smile to his lips.

"Yes, we are."

She pulled from his embrace to peer up with puffy eyes. "What?"

He pressed a kiss to her nose and tipped her chin up. "Well, first we're going to get your mind off of it."

"How?" His heart softened at the somber blink of blue eyes that appeared far too innocent to have been dealt such a blow.

He deposited a kiss to her head. "By getting to know each other as friends until you're ready to court."

She pulled back, fissures of strain melting away on a lovely face that now glowed with hope. "Oh, Bram, do you mean it? You're not upset that I still harbor feelings for Antonio?"

"Nope." He carefully removed the precarious flower from her hair and tucked it into the pocket near his lapel, dispensing a smile edged with tease. "I'm an old-fashioned type of man, Miss Darlington, who believes friendship is the most solid foundation a courtship can have."

She flung herself into his arms as a giggle escaped. "Oh my, Bram, you are truly the best friend a girl could ever have!"

Meg's image flashed in his mind, and heat stormed up his neck at the attraction he so vehemently denied, buried so deep he prayed no one would ever know.

The best friend a girl could ever have?

Maybe. His eyelids lumbered closed as a muscle jerked in his throat.

And then again . . . maybe not.

With a squeaky twist of the tarnished brass knob, Meg entered the district attorney's office, near exhausted from an afternoon at the district court hunting documents to complete her report. No question it would be another late night, but Meg didn't mind. She thrived on the research that would bring Andrew—and her mother—closer to the goal of shutting the Marsicania down.

Her mouth twitched with a near smile despite the fatigue in her bones. *Not to mention the satisfaction of completing my report before Devin completes his . . .*

"Uh-oh . . . looks like somebody's feeling pretty smug." Bonnie glanced up from her typewriter, appearing far more energetic than Meg felt at the end of this grueling day. With a smile as fresh as her crisp pinstripe blouse, she jerked a piece of paper from the platen and placed it on a stack of letters while assessing Meg over the rims of her stylish new glasses. "Something tells me Devin's day just got a whole lot worse, which I didn't think was possible."

Meg couldn't help but grin as she quietly shut the door, the thought of besting Devin once again bringing a little too much pleasure. A chuckle broke loose as she waggled her brows, attaché case in hand. "Why, whatever do you mean, Miss Roof? I'm only doing my job."

Bonnie's lips quirked, her short nod down the hall indicating Devin was working late too. "A little too well if Devin's crabby mood is any indication." She shook her head. "Goodness, Meg, how did a shy and sweet little thing like you ever become so bloodthirsty in business?"

Meg plopped the attaché on the edge of Bonnie's desk with a clunk, a touch of guilt overriding her victorious mood. "Survival of the fittest, I suppose," she said with a weary sigh. Her gaze flicked from the clock on Bonnie's desk that registered six to the office where she knew Devin would be the only other one still present, and seriously considered taking her work home.

Their evening at the Barrister Ball had been nice enough if you discounted the jittery feeling in her stomach whenever he held her in his arms for a dance. The real problem, however, had begun when Devin had interrupted her conversation with Bram on the terrace. It seemed from that point on, something had changed in Devin's mood, his manner almost grumpy. Meg had been relieved when her mother declined the dessert and coffee Andrew suggested after the ball. And when Devin arrived for work this morning with little more than a curt greeting that came off more as a grunt, Meg had silently rejoiced she'd be spending her day at district court. Goodness, she was barely comfortable working and teasing with the old flirtatious Devin, much less this cranky, sullen one. Her gaze darted toward their office and back. "So he's still in a crabby mood, then?" she asked, feeling a sudden urge to chew on a hangnail.

A drawer slammed down the hall, causing one side of Bonnie's lip to swerve up. "Oh, I think we're well beyond crabby." She carefully covered her typewriter, then rose and slipped the strap of her purse over her shoulder with a sympathetic smile. "What on earth did you do to him, anyway? He's been in a huff all day."

She blinked. "Nothing, I promise."

Bonnie delivered a wink. "Well, there you go. Or . . . I suppose it could be the fact Andrew changed the deadline for your reports from next Friday to *this* Friday."

Meg's eyes went wide as she pressed a palm to her lips, a disbelieving smile peeking through. "Oh, no—poor Devin!"

"Yes," Bonnie said with a touch of drama, delivering a hug before she sashayed to the door. She threw a sassy grin over her shoulder. "But not as 'poor' as *you*, I'll wager, when he learns *yours* will be finished tonight." She blew Megan a kiss. "Don't stay too late."

"I won't," Meg whispered, debating whether she should just hightail it home now or face the dragon head-on. A second drawer slammed, harder than the first, and empathy won out, nudging her down the hall on tiptoe. Sucking in a quiet breath, she peeked around the corner and couldn't stop the tiny tug of a smile. Eyes closed, Devin lay sprawled in his chair like a man who'd been shot, a sheet of paper dangling limp in his hand. Normally meticulous and stylish to a fault, he appeared as wilted as his once freshly starched shirt, which now sported a loosened collar and tie. His dark hair, usually so neat and precise, looked like he'd tangled in a catfight, no doubt from the constant gouge of his fingers, a habit she'd noticed whenever he was stressed. His crack-of-dawn arrival this morning—unusual for a man who enjoyed late hours with women and friends—meant that the dark stubble on his face was now more pronounced than usual, coaxing her smile into a grin. With an impish grate of her lip, she just couldn't resist a tiny, little tease. "Ah, so *this* is your method of study and research," she said in a mock serious tone, hoping to rib him into a good mood. "I wondered why I always came in first."

The eyelids snapped open with a scowl that assured her the attempt at humor was a total bust. Dark coffee-brown eyes normally stirred with mischief and tease now boiled hot, indicating a mood brewing that was bitter and black. "If that's your sad attempt at cheering me up, Miss McClare, you'd have better luck with a cup of Conor's three-day-old sludge." He crumpled the paper and aimed it for the wastebasket, scowl deepening when it bounced off the rim to plunk on the floor. "Figures," he muttered, snatching a fresh sheet from the credenza by his desk.

Meg's heart softened as she watched him jerk his tie even more off-kilter before he hunkered down to begin his report again, brows beetled and eyes squinted like that determined little boy she'd known growing up. Thumping the attaché case on her desk, she paused, tempering her smile. "Well, then, how about a freshly brewed cup of coffee with a sprinkle of cinnamon and half of my famous peach cobbler left over from lunch—would that cheer you up?"

"Nope."

She folded her arms, determined to make him smile in spite of himself. "All right, then. How about a nice, hot cup of peppermint tea—guaranteed to soothe the grouchiest of bears—along with some of Bonnie's leftover sugar cookies to sweeten the deal?"

"Not interested," he snapped. The sullen press of his mouth tightened.

She pursed her lips in thought. "Well, then I'd be happy to help you with—"

His dark gaze lifted to singe her with a glare. "No-thank-you, Miss McClare," he said in a clipped tone, "I am perfectly capable of finishing my own report." He paused, eyes thinning considerably. "But I'll just bet you're done, aren't you?"

Fire scorched her cheeks as she grabbed the attaché and hugged it to her chest. "Uh . . . no," she fibbed, backing toward the door with a nervous slope of brows. "I have a lot to do tonight, so I think I'll just . . . spread out . . . in the next room." Bolting into the conference room, she placed her attaché on the table with an extended exhale, thinking she'd never seen anyone so grouchy. A veritable grizzly bear. Goodness, was this how he'd felt every time he'd competed with her over the years? No wonder he couldn't stand her!

Coffee, I need coffee! Once her papers were carefully spread out in order, she quietly snuck into the coffee room, not even sparing a glance in Devin's direction. Heaven knows she didn't want to risk another growl from a man she now nicknamed Grizz. Her mouth curved in a tiny smile at the thought as she scrubbed the pot and filled it with fresh water. Finishing up, she hurried back to the conference room until she sniffed the aroma of fresh-brewed coffee. On her way to the coffee room, she chanced a peek at Devin, and immediately her heart squeezed in her chest. The poor guy appeared utterly defeated, shoulders hunched over his desk and tousled head buried in his arms. Releasing a wavering breath, she poured him a cup of coffee just the way he liked it, taking extra care to include a sprinkle of cinnamon from the cabinet. She caught her breath when she spotted half of George's Hershey bar wrapped and tucked in the back—Devin's favorite as well. In no time, she had a pretty plate arranged with her muffin surrounded by several sugar cookies and pieces of chocolate fanned around the perimeter. Eyeing it with approval, she carried both his coffee and his snack into their office and laid it on the desk beside him, the fragrant steam rising over his rumpled head. Satisfied, she left him to his nettlesome behavior, returning to the conference room to finish her task.

While proofing the fourth page, she sensed his presence hovering at the door. Body completely still, only her lashes lifted as she peered up with gentle eyes. "Are we better, I hope?"

A ghost of a smile flitted across his lips as he stood cocked in the door, arms folded and shoulder braced to the jamb. "Some."

She rumpled her nose. "I knew I should have gone with the peppermint," she said with a shake of her head. "Mother always said cinnamon for energy and peppermint to calm a mood."

Hard eyes defied the quirk of his mouth. "And what does she recommend when someone annoys you to no end?"

She blinked, lips parting when his barb found its mark, the old, familiar hurt and rejection stinging in her eyes. "Devin, if I annoyed or offended you in any way, please forgive me . . ."

"Not *you*, Miss McClare," he said with a voice that was more of a growl, "your so-called best friend." He strolled in and straddled the corner of the table, arms stiff across his chest.

"Bram?" She peered up, totally confused. "What on earth has this got to do with him?"

His scowl compressed. "He claims to be your friend, but I've never seen a man fawn over a woman more, or vice versa for that matter, and him with another girl, for pity's sake."

Her jaw literally dropped, a rare flash of anger gilding her tone. "Pardon me? *Fawn?* Not that it's any of your business, Devin Caldwell, but Bram Hughes is my very dearest friend." She huffed out a raspy breath and bowed her head, eyes closed while she counted to ten. Expending a quiet sigh, she lifted her gaze, voice gentle. "Why are you acting like this?"

She jumped when he slammed a hand to the table. "Because I'm jealous, blast it!"

He couldn't have shocked her more if he'd tossed cold coffee in her face. Her lips parted to emit shallow breaths while her eyes circled wide. "Of what?" she whispered. She suddenly noted the moody look in his eyes, and immediately she sensed a thread of that same insecurity he'd expressed when he'd told her about his family. Sympathy stabbed, along with more than a little twinge of her own shame and regret. "This is about the competition between us, isn't it?"

Mouth open, it was his turn to stare in disbelief as the merest trace of a smile formed on his lips. "See? This is only one of a million things that drives me crazy about you, Meg—you have no earthly idea what I'm talking about, do you?"

She stared, barely able to blink. "Uh . . . no?"

He shot up from the table and began to pace, hand slashing his hair until it fell across his forehead in reckless abandon. "Dash it all, that's because you aren't like other girls. You're beautiful and smart and so blasted naïve you have no idea the effect you have on men." He halted to expel a harsh breath, bowing his head to swab his face while his voice trailed to a whisper. "Especially me."

The blood iced in her veins while her body froze in the chair.

His shoulders slumped as he continued on, hands buried in his pockets. The fury faded from his voice along with the rakish confidence that was so much a part of who he was. "I suppose I've been spoiled—I've always seemed to have the upper hand with women," he said quietly as if talking to himself, "most of them easy pursuits and no challenge at all." With a loud exhale, he faced her, his eyes as humble as she'd ever seen. "Until you." He assessed her from several feet away, his gaze intense as if studying every hair on her head, every curve of her face. And then those full lips tipped into a semblance of a smile so reminiscent of the rogue that he was. "Do you have *any* idea what that does to a man?"

A knot jogged in her throat as she shook her head.

"It makes him crazy," he said softly, stalling the beat of her heart with his slow approach. Nudging the chair next to hers out of the way, he perched on the edge of the table with arms loosely crossed, one leg braced to the floor and one cocked at the knee, so close she could see the pattern of thread in his slacks. "Day after day I have to work beside you," he whispered, "drinking in your smile, breathing in your scent, flirting my fool head off to no avail because you're not even remotely aware. For once I've met a girl whose beauty on the inside is so powerful and deep, the surface beauty is almost secondary, which is something I've never experienced before." He shook his head, gaze roaming her face as if she were some priceless work of art. "You're irresistible, you know that? And I have never been more jealous of a man than I am of Hughes right now." She caught her breath when he reached to fondle a wisp of her hair, knuckles grazing her neck in the process. "I want to know you the way he knows you, Meg—be an important part of your life the way he is. Please say you'll go out with me," he whispered, "please."

"Devin, I . . . don't think that's . . . such a good idea," she said weakly, her breathing erratic. "We're colleagues, after all, so it wouldn't be right . . ."

He rose, lifting her to her feet along with him while he gently clasped her arms, thumbs grazing her sleeves. "No, Meg, what wouldn't be right is denying the feelings I have—"

She tried to step back, but his hold was as firm as the cut of his jaw. "I don't deserve it based on our past, I know, but I'm asking you to give me a chance to get to know you better."

"I . . . I . . ." Her voice came out as a squeak as she tried to lean away, her words hampered by a gulp. "C-can g-get to know you b-better h-here . . . at w-work." She swallowed hard, the motion almost painful. "As f-friends."

A twinkle of the rogue lit in his eyes as a hint of a smile shadowed his lips. "I was rather hoping for a wee bit closer than that, Miss McClare." His gaze flicked to her lips and back, stealing what air she still had in her lungs. "*Much* closer, as a matter of fact," he whispered, bending his head to slowly lean in.

No! She lunged free of his hold, heart pounding so hard, her palm instinctively flew to her chest. Good night, if the man could quiver her belly with what felt like a near kiss, what could he do with the real thing? Totally disarm her, that's what, leaving her defenseless and vulnerable to the charm of the most notorious flirt in St. Patrick's history. A shiver whispered down her spine that compelled her to take yet another step back. And she was far, far smarter than that.

Aren't I?

"Meg?"

She sucked in a deep breath and glanced up, blinking several times in a row as if that could clear the daze from her mind. Her response was little more than a rasp. "Yes?"

A trace of a boyish smile played on his lips, the same smile she'd seen him use on many a girl in her class . . . right before he stole their hearts. "Will you?" he asked softly, the hope in his eyes weakening her defenses. When she didn't answer, he slipped his hands in his pockets with an awkward hunch of shoulders, indicating a hesitancy and uneasiness she'd never seen in him before. "Say something, please, because you've got me off-kilter here." He cuffed the back of his head, mussing his hair even further while he mumbled under his breath. "Which frankly, has never happened before." His sigh was heavy as he buried his hands in his pocket once again, glancing up with a transparency that revealed the lost little boy inside, so desperate for love. "Will you . . . go out with me, please? The theatre and dinner, perhaps?"

She stared, pulse pounding while worry and wonder warred in her brain. Heaven help her, those subtleties she'd fretted over at the ball had apparently been valid, early warnings she should have heeded and nipped in the bud. But who would have thought it possible—Devin Caldwell, nemesis of old, seeking *her* company and favor! She studied him now, and for the first time ever, she felt her body relax in his presence, this tiny glimpse into his soul proving he was really no different than she. The self-esteem of both had been badly bruised—his by his family, and hers by his hand and others. She expelled a reedy breath, her reluctance dissipating in a swell of compassion that made her long to know him too. To impart a touch of the healing balm of God's love, just like God had done for her. But . . . if there was one thing she'd learned in her life and learned well, it was that every decision she made—especially those of the heart—needed to be weighed on the scale of God's will. At the thought, a familiar peace settled, coaxing the trace of a smile to her lips.

He waited as if the very air suspended in his lungs, lips parted and a mix of hope and dread in his eyes. "Is that a . . . yes?" he whispered, the sound of his breathing suddenly shallow.

Her soft laugh lured a grin to his face as she shook her head, her smile resigned. "I'd say it's more of a maybe, Mr. Caldwell, contingent upon several very important things."

"And those would be . . ." He took a step forward, the dimples in his cheeks deepening like his voice, which sounded hoarse and low.

She folded her arms, head cocked to assess him with candor. "I'll need to pray about it, of course, since God has a much better view of these things than I . . ."

He gave a short nod, his Adam's apple wobbling. "Fair enough. What else?"

She paused, her smile hesitant. "I don't know if you're a prayerful man or not, Devin, but if you are," she said quietly, "I would hope you might pray about it as well."

His grin bordered on dazzling. "Yes, Miss McClare, I am a prayerful man, especially of late in the hopes of making inroads with a certain brilliant and beautiful girl who has stolen my heart. But rest assured, if it means lighting candles until kingdom come, Megan McClare, I will pursue the Almighty until both you and He agree to say yes . . ."

Her smile tipped off-center as she lowered her head a smidge, peering up beneath sooty lashes. "Well, regrettably for you, your dangerous reputation precedes you, Mr. Caldwell, as does your flirtatious nature, neither of which give me the comfort level I desire in a relationship."

The tendons in his throat convulsed. "All right, that's perfectly understandable, and a situation I am more than ready to amend." He cleared his throat, offering a tight smile. "That is, if you would kindly clarify exactly what that means."

She tugged at her lip with her teeth, a grin peeking through. "It means, Devin, I'm not of a mind to engage in wrestling matches, something I'm told is prone to happen where you are concerned. The devil in your eye, so to speak, like I just saw a moment earlier."

A flush swallowed him whole while he skimmed a finger along the inside of his collar. "Yes, ma'am, you have my word I will keep my distance." He blew out a long shaky breath, a dimple winking when one edge of his mouth quirked in a crooked smile. "Unless, of course, I have your permission to express any ardor that's sure to occur."

She grinned, his statement shoring up her trust considerably. "I certainly appreciate that, I assure you, so except for those points, there's only two others."

His smile faded while serious brown eyes fixed on hers, squared shoulders and the swell of his chest telling her he was preparing himself for her answer. "And those are . . . ?"

She drew in a deep breath, hoping to make the next point in a firm but gentle manner. "Bram is my dearest friend in the whole world," she said in a tone as soft as her gaze, "which means it would make me very happy if you and he were friends as well."

His jaw tightened a smidge before he gave a short nod. "All right, Meg. And the other point?" He lifted his head, body straightening as if bracing himself for her final request.

Containing her smile, she elevated her chin in a sober pose, mischief twitching at the edge of her mouth. "You have to tell Mr. Grizz to stay away."

He blinked, a ridge in his brow. "Mr. Grizz?"

"The bear I saw this morning *and* tonight." She wrinkled her nose. "He's a grouch."

Her words apparently unleashed the scamp in him once again, given the dangerous twinkle in his eyes. He placed a palm to his heart with a flash of white teeth. "You have my word, Miss Mc-Clare, that Mr. Grizz will never show his face around here again."

She chuckled, her grin as wide as his when she shimmied back into her seat. "Well, let's just test that out, shall we?" she said with a coy tilt of her head, every bit the imp as she imparted a wink. "Because, you see, Mr. Caldwell . . . *my* report will be finished tonight."

26

The doorbell rang, and Caitlyn jolted in her cribbage chair, pulse racing as her gaze darted to the brass clock on the mantel. *Six-thirty.* She gulped. *Merciful Providence, Logan is early!* Her hands started to sweat as Hadley crossed the foyer to the door, the sharp staccato clip of his heels on the marble matching the painful thud of her heart. "Lord, help me please," she whispered, eyelids fluttering closed when she heard the deep timbre of Logan's voice, his husky laughter signaling a merry mood. A reedy breath quivered from her lips.

But not for long . . .

"This house is far too quiet, Mrs. McClare." He strode into the parlour for the Monday family dinner—his first since the altercation at Meg's welcome home party—striking as always in a stylish charcoal suit with striped crimson tie. His handsome face and commanding presence seemed all the more powerful given what she needed to do. A chill slid down her spine. *And* given that after tonight, his presence might be as scarce as the air in her lungs.

He bent to kiss her cheek, and her stomach did a little flip as always when he was near, her heart acquiescing to his charms like she so wished her mind could. If only her trust in him hadn't been damaged over and over, Logan McClare would be kissing his wife right now instead of a sister-in-law who longed to be more. Melancholy struck hard. And yet, the very reason that had kept her from accepting his proposal in the first place—lack of trust—was now compounded by a barrier even more daunting.

Her body warmed when he kneaded her shoulders, fingers lingering before he claimed his seat across the table with a smile that fluttered her pulse. "What, did you kick everyone out of the house except Hadley, including Rosie, I hope?"

The jest eased the tension in her neck as she returned his smile with a precarious one of her own. "I'm afraid your luck isn't holding tonight, Mr. McClare," she said in a tone that clearly conveyed her deep affection. "Although the children have been whisked away to dinner and game night at Cassie and Jamie's, Rosie is still among us. And none too pleased, I might add, that I requested a special dinner and dessert only for you."

His teeth gleamed white in the glow of the milk-glass tulip lamp that arched over the table. "Thank you for the kind hospitality, Mrs. McClare, but I'm sure you'll understand if I wait to taste it after you."

Her soft chuckle chased her melancholy away, at least for the moment as she watched him shuffle the cards. "It's your favorite, you know—lobster linguini and Boston cream pie. *And* to enhance your enjoyment, I even asked Hadley to serve rather than Rosie."

He dealt the cards with a deft hand, one dark brow jagging high. "Mmm . . . all alone, my favorite meal and dessert, and your pit bull on a leash?" The smile eased into a grin as he gave her a wink. "Anyone would think you have ulterior motives, Mrs. McClare."

Her face flashed hot, clear up to the roots of her hair.

He laughed out loud and slid his hand over hers, thumb grazing the side of her fingers. "I don't mind, Cait," he said softly, voice husky with tease. His smile gentled along with his eyes. "In fact, it would be an answer to just about every prayer I've ever said."

She shot to her feet. "I'll just check on dinner . . ." Limbs as limp as the linguini Rosie was preparing, she bolted into the foyer and down the hall, pausing with a palm flat to the kitchen door. "Oh, Lord, I can't do this," she whispered, kneading her temple to massage the dull throb in her head.

"Oh!" She jolted when the swinging door smacked her hard in the face, causing her to jerk back with a hand to her nose.

Poor Hadley stood on the other side, a tray with iced beverages in hand and surprise in his eyes. "Mrs. McClare, my deepest apologies, miss—are you all right?"

"Yes, Hadley, I'm fine," she said, forcing a smile as she rubbed the tip of her nose, but it was perhaps the greatest untruth she'd ever told. All semblance of "fine" had fled the moment she'd seen Jean MacKenna on the dance floor in Logan's arms at the Barrister Ball. Her pulse had paused for several painful beats at the picture they presented—he with his teasing eyes and heart-melting grin, and her with a shy smile that told Caitlyn all she needed to know. She knew then that Jean MacKenna was still smitten with Jamie's father. But even that wouldn't have changed the course of Cait's heart had it not been for the look she'd seen in their son's eyes. A look of regret and longing that spoke to Caitlyn loud and clear. *They* were a family in the most spiritual sense of the word—Logan, Jean, and Jamie—and the conviction that had settled upon her soul that night and each day thereafter could not be ignored.

And the two shall become one flesh: so that they are no more two, but one . . .

One flesh.

One family.

One fiat from God.

Except for the one thing that stood in the way. Her eyelids fluttered closed for the briefest of moments as reality struck a painful blow.

Me.

The realization had shattered her. Not only had she led Logan on with a friendship that might never be anything more, but she denied him the very chance to be happy with anyone else. Heart buckling, she silenced the demons of guilt with a calm façade and a tremulous lift of her chin as she smiled at Hadley. "I wanted to save you a trip with the drinks."

"Yes, ma'am," he said in his perennially poised manner, and promptly handed over the tray. But not before she'd noted the hint of concern in his eyes, clearly indicating her odd behavior had not gone unnoticed.

Pasting a bright smile on her face, she reentered the parlour, eyes on her task as she placed Logan's iced tea before him. "Here we are," she said in a cheery tone as she sat down across from him.

Too cheery.

Logan's hand stilled hers. "And where's that, Cait?" he whispered. She stiffened, gaze fused to the glass in her hand. Breathing shallow, she compelled her eyes to meet his, and immediately her stomach plunged to her toes.

"Something's desperately wrong," he said quietly, the sobriety in his tone matching that in his eyes. His lips compressed as he tightened his grip. "And I want to know what it is—*now.*"

Involuntarily, her eyes flickered as she battled the urge to lie, to let this evening pass without telling him so she could revel in his company one last time like the coward she was. Her voice shook as she attempted a smile, opting to put off breaking his heart until another day. *And mine.* "Honestly, Logan, there's no need for melodrama—"

"Let me be the judge of that." His tone was sharp as he rose from his seat to circle the table. Without warning, he hauled her to her feet, hands locked to her arms as he held her at bay. "You've got bad news for me, Cait, and I want it now. There's tragedy in your eyes, and apparently it's bad enough to send the children away, so give it to me straight."

She stared up at him while tears welled, unable to speak for the quiver of her lip.

"Tell me *now!*" he repeated, jarring her with an urgent shake. "Or so help me—"

"I've agreed to see Andrew," she blurted, no control over tears that slipped from her eyes.

The blood instantly leached from his face while his hands fell to his sides. "I see. So it's to be a contest then, is it?" His jaw hardened to granite while a tic flickered in his cheek. "You'll forgive me, Mrs. McClare, if I assumed this was a contest already won."

"It's *not* a contest," she whispered, her voice raspy with regret. She laid a hand to his arm, but he only shook it off.

"Then what the devil is it?" His gaze bore into hers, sparks of fury all but singeing her raw. "You claim to love me—"

"I *do* love you," she cried.

He rattled her with another harsh shake of her arms. "Then prove it! Stop all this infernal nonsense and marry me."

Agony slashed as she shook her head, his face little more than a blur through her tears. "I can't . . . ," she whispered.

He released her and stepped back, adjusting the sleeves of his coat as his eyes pinned her in place. "All right, Cait, we'll do this your way, then. I suppose I should thank Turner because somehow he managed to do what I couldn't—open your eyes to the prospect of courtship again." He extended his hand toward the cribbage table. "Shall we sit and decide when our first outing will be because I assure you, Mrs. McClare, I intend to give him a run for his money."

She didn't move, feet rooted to the blue-and-gold Persian rug along with her gaze. When she spoke, her tone was laden with grief. "I . . . love you, Logan, I do—more than you will ever know." Her gaze rose to meet his, heart twisting at the raw love she saw in his eyes. "But it's because of that very love that I must do what I'm about to do." She sucked in a deep breath and leveled her chin. "I've given this a great deal of thought, and I feel strongly that God has a wonderful plan for us both." She paused to swallow the lump in her throat, voice fading to a whisper. "J-just not together."

His color drained once again. "What are you saying, Cait?" he whispered, the hoarse sound as ragged as the beat of her heart.

"I'm saying . . ." Words trembled on her tongue, and she was certain the agony in his face mirrored that in her own. "The two shall be one flesh: so that they are no longer two but one . . ."

Confusion clouded his gaze. "I don't understand, Cait—speak clearly."

A wavering breath expired on her lips . . . like her hope. "I'm saying . . . I feel strongly that . . ." Her throat contracted. "You and Jean were meant to be together."

"*What?*" His tone lashed out like a whip, stripping the flesh from her heart.

"I saw it at the Barrister Ball," she said in a rush, desperate to convey the truth revealed to her that night. "The joy and hope in Jamie's eyes when he saw you and his mother together, as it *should* be."

"No!" Shaking his head, he moved close, his breathing harsh.

"Blast it, Cait, I am *not* in love with Jean MacKenna, I'm in love with you! For all that is holy, I barely know the woman!"

She faltered back before he could touch her again. "It doesn't matter—I believe in God's eyes, you are one, and I will not be a hindrance to His will for your life."

His jaw dropped a full inch while he stared, those gray eyes almost black as they flared in shock. "This is *crazy*! You and I were meant to be together." He slashed his arm toward the foyer. "This house, this family—is *our* house, *our* family! You and I have everything in common, and Jean and I are nothing but strangers."

She shook her head, the motion spilling moisture onto her cheeks. "Strangers who share a bond far stronger than ours, Logan, no matter how deep our love. A bond born in flesh through your son and more importantly, a bond mandated by God Himself when you and Jean became one."

A low aching groan parted from his lips as he turned away, fingers quivering while they gashed through his hair.

"You and J-jean have so much in c-common," she stuttered, the fractured words souring her tongue. "Jamie, the boardinghouse, the foundation—this makes sense, this is right."

"No," he shouted, "this is wrong!" He rammed her chair into the table, then spun around, the fire in his eyes glittering like molten steel. "For the love of decency, Cait, I made one lousy mistake when I was no more than a boy—doesn't God mandate forgiveness as well?"

"Yes, and I *have* forgiven you," she cried, clutching her arms to her waist as a barrier against his wrath. "Truly I have."

His chest expanded with a heavy intake of air before it seeped out again, lips pinched white. "I see. It's just that your forgiveness comes with a tally, is that it? Forgiven, but never forgotten?"

She rubbed her arms against the cold chill of his words. "Maybe it wasn't supposed to be forgotten, Logan," she said quietly, "to ensure God's will."

"No!" Fingers taut on the back of her chair, he rammed it again. "You and I were always meant to be together, and nothing you can say will convince me otherwise." He jabbed a fist to his chest, eyes burning with fury. "Blast it, Cait, you're in love with me, not Turner, and you're attracted to me, not him."

She squared her shoulders, more to shore up her strength than to defy. "Attraction is the very last thing I'm concerned about, if you must know. Andrew and I have a solid basis for a deeper relationship, both in our faith and in our common goal to clean up the Coast, and to me, that's more important than the race of my pulse."

"Really, Cait?" Mouth slack, he slung hands low on his hips, disbelief gouging deep into his expression. The bite in his tone fairly vibrated with sarcasm. "You're going to stand there and talk to me about God's will while you lie through your teeth?"

Her indignation rose along with her chin. "I am not lying, Logan McClare—I don't give a whit about physical attraction at this point in my life, so it's a moot point."

He gripped her so fast, she stumbled against the coffee table in an effort to back away, the granite set of his jaw trapping all the air in her throat. Her eyes circled wide when she read the intent in a steely gaze that quivered her belly. "Logan, no, ple—"

But her words only faded into his mouth when his lips took hers, conquering her with a passion that eclipsed her will with his own. She made a feeble attempt to lash away, but his arms were a powerful vise, swallowing her whole. Heat pulsed when he devoured her with a kiss so deep, it weakened her limbs. He pulled back, voice hoarse with desire as his palm locked at the base of her neck with a possession that was firm and sure. "Face it, Cait," he said, eyes burning hot, "the attraction between us never has nor ever will be—a moot point."

A moan faded on her lips when his mouth traveled her jaw to suckle her ear, confirming to her heart—if not her mind—that she was his, body and soul. "Logan, no . . ." But her will to fight spiraled away into a whirlpool of desire when his mouth consumed hers with a low groan, their ragged breathing merging into one.

"Cait, I adore you," he whispered against her mouth, his kisses gentling with a tender passion that twisted her heart. "Don't do this to me, please—don't push me away."

Her eyes fluttered closed to breathe in his scent, to embed in her mind the memory of his arms one final time. When she spoke, her voice heaved with a grief she hadn't experienced since Liam. "I'm not pushing you away," she rasped, "I'm loving you the only way I know how." Her palms trembled against his chest as she held him at bay, agony bleeding from both her soul and her eyes. "Logan, *please*—I'm asking you to stay in my life as my friend and an integral part of my family. But I'm begging you—give your heart to the woman who has more claim to it than I." Her body shuddered when she broke from his hold, words quivering into a fragile whisper. "The mother of your child."

He took a step forward, eyes crazed. "It's *not* meant to be, Cait—we are!"

Blocking his approach with a stiff palm, her insides trembled more than her hand. "I've made my decision, and I'm asking you—no, *begging* you—to respect it and our friendship by letting any romantic notions between us go."

"*Romantic notions?*" His words were little more than a hiss as he stared, his fury barely contained by a twitch in his cheek. "You are my lifeblood, Cait, the reason I get up in the morning, the soul mate I have waited a lifetime for. You are the *only* woman I will ever love, and if you're demanding I let romantic notions go, then you need to be aware of what you're asking me to do." That formidable jaw rose while his shoulders broadened, eyes glittering like jagged quartz. "I will not stand by and watch you give your heart to another, especially the man I despise above all others."

"Logan—"

"No!" It was his turn to halt her with a blunt hand. "I've done things your way for the last two years, agreed to friendship despite the fact that I ache inside whenever you're near. I've laid my desires aside in the hope that someday, somehow, you'd come to your fool senses and see what I've known all along." His chest expanded as his eyes pierced hers, an urgent appeal glimmering in their depths. "We're good together, Cait," he whispered. "You and I—we're the restoration of the family you lost when Liam died, a blood connection with your children that binds us all together." His lips pinched tight, calcifying his jaw. "If you do this, you will not only destroy everything we have, but you will damage our family."

Her heart thundered to a stop, breathing shallow over his veiled threat. "Logan, please—it doesn't have to be that way—"

"Yes, Cait, it does," he emphasized in a clipped tone, "because if you think I'm going to stand by and watch while you give yourself to Turner—"

Blood scalded her cheeks. "For heaven's sake, I have no intention of 'giving' myself to anyone. My relationship with Andrew will be purely social."

He stared, temple throbbing as his eyes narrowed to black. "Then your relationship with me will be purely over, Mrs. McClare, it's as simple as that. It's me or him, Cait."

"You don't mean that," she whispered.

A tic twittered in his jaw. "Try me."

Panic threatened to sever her air. "You can't do that to the children, Logan, please . . ."

He jerked hard on the sleeves of his jacket, eyeing her with a coldness that chilled her to the bone. "Rest assured I will see my nieces and nephew on a regular basis, but it won't be in your home, Mrs. McClare—ever again."

"N-no . . ." The word escaped her lips in a broken cry.

His face appeared sculpted in rock. "The decision is yours—Turner or me."

Her eyelids flickered closed, grief welling in her heart as quickly as water welled in her eyes.

Love suffereth long . . . it seeketh not its own . . .

"So, what's it going to be, Cait?"

Oh, Lord, I can't bear to live without him . . .

A feeble sob wrenched from her lips as she pleaded with her eyes. "Don't do this, Logan, please . . ."

His face blanched white as stone. "I'm not, Cait—*you* are."

And with a violent hitch of her breath, she watched him stride from the room, her heart shattering with the brutal slam of the door. The awful sound echoed in the house like anguish echoed in her brain.

"Oh, no, please . . . ," she whispered, her body numb as she made her way to the divan.

Love never fails.

A deep ache rose in a guttural groan, consuming her with its awful grief. Because she knew then, more powerfully than ever before—she would give her life for Logan McClare. Her heart fisted as her body crumpled onto the sofa, her weeping raw with the gut-wrenching truth.

And she just did.

27

I'm worried," Meg whispered, the sound of her frail voice filling the usually cozy parlour with the same unease reflected in each of the somber faces around her. Mother's lacy sheers billowed with a sea-scented breeze normally so welcome on a late summer day, but today it served only to chill Megan's skin. She chewed on her thumbnail until it was little more than a nub, wincing when she bit too far and drew blood. Peering up from the cream brocade sofa she shared with Bram, a gloss of moisture blurred her vision, distorting the faces of those she loved.

Just like Andrew Turner is distorting our family.

Lifting her chin, she fought the rise of more tears, desperate to remain strong in a situation that had turned their world—and their family—upside down. "It's been a month and a half since Uncle Logan stopped coming for dinners, and neither Mother nor he will even talk about what happened." Her whispered words trembled despite her best efforts. "And I w-worry it will last f-forever."

Bram's gentle touch breached her defenses, and before she could stop herself, she crumpled into his embrace with a broken heave, weeping as he stroked her hair. "Shhh . . . it's okay, Bug," he said quietly, "Logan won't stay away forever—he loves this family too much."

"I just hate this!" Arms clenched at her waist, Alli paced in front of the game table where Cassie and Jamie sat with Blake and Nick, an interrupted game of whist all but forgotten. A spark of anger flashed in her eyes as she kicked at one of Maddie's dolls lying on the floor, sending it flying into the air until it landed in a heap on top of Nick's polished shoes. "Why would Mother do this to Uncle Logan when she knows how much he cares? How can she be so heartless?"

"Maybe she's sparing Logan's feelings because she doesn't love him that way." Nick's tone was quiet but direct.

"Horse feathers," Cassie snapped. She slapped a palm on the table so hard, cards bounced in the air. "Aunt Cait loves Uncle Logan as much as he loves her, but she's just too stubborn to admit it." She folded her arms with a huff of noisy air, green eyes narrowing. "Sweet thunderation, I'd give anything to know what's going on, but she won't talk to me either."

"I'll tell you what's going on—she doesn't trust him," Jamie whispered, a thread of sadness in solemn words as his eyes trailed into a faraway stare, as if sifting through his own memories of forgiving his father. "He told me awhile back that she feels like he's betrayed her throughout their lives—first with my mom, and then with covering it up all these years." He released a weighty breath. "And although part of me understands her lack of trust, it rips my heart out to see what she's doing to my father and this family."

"Have you tried talking to him, asking him to come back?" Meg asked, holding out hope that as Logan's son, Jamie might have more sway with their uncle than any of them.

Jamie's lip took a slant. "Over and over, but he's a lot like me, unfortunately—sealed tighter than a vault when it comes to opening up about anything too painful."

"Amen to that," Cassie said in agreement. "May as well beat a dead horse." Her mouth quirked as she ruffled Jamie's dark curls. "No, make that a deaf and dumb mule."

Meg smiled in spite of herself, then dabbed at her eyes with the handkerchief Bram had given her. "I just wish we could get through to either Mother or him," she whispered, the smile fading from her lips. "Convince them to at least talk to each other, so maybe we can get things back to normal."

Cassie grunted. "I think we may have seen the last of 'normal' for a while, at least with Andrew here two and three times a week instead of Uncle Logan."

"Well somebody needs to talk to Uncle Logan." Meg twisted around to train her gaze on her brother Blake, stretched back in his chair at the game table with hands behind his neck. "What about you, Blake? You see Uncle Logan every day at the office."

Her brother's brows shot high. "Are you kidding? The deepest conversation I've ever had with Uncle Logan was which hair color I prefer on a woman—blond, brunette, or redhead."

"Requiring lots of research on your part, no doubt," Nick said with a chuckle.

Blake grinned. "Yes, well I like to go deep in some areas, but meaningful conversations is not one of them, Detective, with either Uncle Logan or women."

Alli tossed a pillow at Blake's head. "You are such a rogue, Blake McClare! Heaven knows the trouble in store for any woman who falls in love with you."

"I doubt heaven would have anything to do with it, Al, if the Rake is involved." Jamie nudged Blake's shoulder with a grin.

Blake jutted his chin, gaze zeroing in on Bram. "I vote for

Bram to talk to Uncle Logan. After all, Jamie's too close and I'm too far, but Bram's just right—barely related and one of Uncle Logan's golden boys at the firm." He grinned. "Not to mention the Padre is the most serious of us three, with a propensity for deep conversation."

Meg spun around, beseeching Bram with anxious eyes. "Oh, Bram, would you? Blake's right—Uncle Logan trusts you more than anyone."

"Hey!" Jamie feigned offense, his handsome face pinched in a frown. "I can be trusted."

Drawing air through a clenched smile, Cassie patted her husband's hand. "Yes, you can, darling . . . especially if there's a lasso in the room."

Blake chuckled. "Ah, now that I would like to see—Mac all tied up, especially during one of our pool tournaments."

Sporting a crooked smile, Jamie gave him a jaunty salute. "Hate to break it to you, Rake, but I can win against you with my hands tied behind my back."

Cassie's fingers playfully nipped at her husband's waist. "It can be arranged, darling, just give me the word."

"Oh, yeah," Alli said with a rub of her palms, "maybe with a poke or two from a cattle prod."

"Hey, who voted me the fall guy?" Jamie said with a trace of hurt in his tone. "My wife wants to hog-tie me, Alli wants to prod me, and Meg implies I can't be trusted."

Meg's smile was apologetic. "You know what I mean, Jamie— you said yourself that Uncle Logan refuses to talk to you, so Bram is our last hope." She turned to Bram, a plea etched in her face. "Will you, Bram? Will you talk to Uncle Logan for us, help clear the air between Mother and him?"

Bram hesitated.

"Come on, Padre," Blake said. "Meg's right, we need somebody Uncle Logan trusts since I'm too shallow and Jamie's too inept."

"I beg your pardon," Jamie said with dagger eyes.

Meg ignored them to clutch Bram's hand. "Will you, Bram, please?"

Bram expelled a heavy sigh. "Sure, Bug," he said with a tender smile. "I want to see this family back together as much as anybody, although I can't promise much. Logan and I have talked before about sensitive issues, but that's no guarantee he'll open up on this."

"Sensitive issues?" Jamie said with a squint. "What sensitive issues?" A slow grin traveled his lips. "How and when to fire Blake?"

A grunt parted from Blake's lips. "What are you talking about, MacKenna—I clocked more hours than you this month."

"Sure you did—at the Blue Moon, not the office." Jamie grinned. "Sorry, old buddy, but I'm just giving you a taste of your own medicine."

Cassie glanced at the clock on the mantel and hopped up, tugging Jamie along too. "Uh-oh, Aunt Cait and Andrew'll be home any minute now, so I'd rather vamoose before they come." She pushed in her chair with a heavy sigh. "I like Andrew well enough, I suppose, but not for Aunt Cait, so it's best we leave lest I'm tempted to sink a spur into his ankle."

"Ooooo, I like the way you think." Alli gave her a hug before tweaking Jamie's neck. "Is that how you keep this one in line?"

Jamie's dark brows peaked high. "Hey, I run the MacKenna household, not the little missus, right, Cowgirl?" In a flash of his arm, he dipped Cassie back for a kiss.

She broke free with a giggle and pinched his cheek. "Depends—with or without my lasso?" she quipped, sauntering over to give both Meg and Alli a hug. She shot Jamie a lazy smile over her shoulder on the way to the door. "I can still hog-tie steers—or Jamie MacKenna—in under fifteen seconds flat, so don't you forget that *either*, Pretty Boy."

"How can I, Mrs. MacKenna, when we practice every night?" Jamie wiggled his brows and gave his wife a wink, laughing out loud when her face flushed beet red.

Her eyes thinned as he joined her at the door. "I should hog-tie you for real, just to teach a lesson, you little brat."

"Awk, Jamie's a rat, Jamie's a rat." Miss B. danced sideways on her perch, squawking the phrase Alli taught her when Jamie had broken Cassie's heart before they were married.

"She said 'brat,' not 'rat,'" Jamie called, doing a little squawking of his own.

"Oh, I don't know." Bram rose to shove his chair in with a lopsided grin. "Miss B. usually gets it right, and everybody knows that is one intelligent bird."

Cassie all but preened, her smile a gloat. "Face it, MacKenna—both titles fit upon occasion." She blew kisses before making her way into the foyer. "Good night, all."

"It will be if I have anything to say about it," Jamie winked as he followed her out.

The front door closed, and Blake shot up with a chuckle, eyeing Nick and Bram as he pushed in his chair. "Well, that's my cue to disappear before Mother gets home as well, so anybody up for a game of pool—Bram? Nick?"

Bram buttoned his jacket, smile edged with regret. "Love to, old buddy, but I'm in court in the morning, so I need an early start." He shot Nick a grin. "But I'd sleep a whole lot better, Nick, knowing you're feeding this guy a little crow to keep him humble."

"Will do," Nick said with a chuckle. He set his empty ginger ale down and rose with a stretch. "As long as Al cheers me on."

Alli stood on tiptoe to give him a sweet peck on the cheek. "For my big, hulking fiancé? You bet." She looped her arm through Nick's and gave Blake a smug smile. "Besides, somebody has to make sure Blake doesn't cheat."

"Awk, Blake cheats, Blake cheats—"

"Oh, put a sock in it," Blake said, aiming a pillow at Miss B. to rattle both her and the cage.

Alli laughed. "Bram's right—that is one smart bird." She tossed the pillow back, bouncing it off of Blake's head. "Maybe even smarter than you." She shot a glance Meg's way. "Coming Megs? I'll need help keeping my eye on Blake."

Blake tickled the back of Alli's neck on his way to the door. "Yeah, Megs, and you can keep your eye on Alli, sort of like a chaperone."

Hands on her hips, Alli stuck out her tongue. "For your information, I don't need a chaperone," she said with a toss of her head.

Nick surprised her with a hard tug to his chest, his half-lidded gaze settling on her lips. "And just what makes you think you don't need a chaperone, Princess, when your future husband gets a notion to steal a kiss?"

Alli patted his cheek with a pretty blush. "Because the room is full of cue sticks, Detective Burke, which I understand work just fine in a pinch."

"Ouch." He grinned and kissed her forehead, hooking her arm to lead her from the room.

"G'night, Bram," she called on her way to the door, "be sure to let us know as soon as you talk to Uncle Logan, all right?"

Bram gave her a two-finger salute. "Yes, ma'am, full report."

Laughter faded up the stairwell as Meg released a wispy sigh. "I wish you didn't have to go," she whispered.

He gently rubbed her arms, the warmth of his palms seeping into her body. "It'll get better, Bug, I promise. Logan's just angry right now, but between your prayers and mine, he'll come around, you'll see."

"I hope so." She worried her lip, another subject suddenly weighting her mind. She peeked up. "Can I ask for your prayers on something else as well?"

"Always," Bram said quietly, willing to do almost anything to remove that sad look in her eyes.

She expelled a wavering sigh. "I need to know if I'm . . . well, doing the right thing."

His pulse stopped for a fraction of a second before it kicked back in, faster than before. "About what?"

She blinked up at him, a child's tender heart in a woman's body. "Devin wants me to . . ."

Paralysis struck as Bram's body went completely still. Inhaling a quiet draw of air, he grazed a finger to her chin. "Devin wants you to what . . . ?"

The dark sweep of lashes flickered over enormous green eyes, revealing the skittishness of a graceful doe. "Well, we've been seeing each other as friends in group situations as you know, ever since he told me he wanted to get to know me better after the Barrister Ball."

He remained completely calm despite a rare twinge of annoyance. "Yes, and a very wise and safe compromise on your part, Bug, for the long term, so I'm proud of you."

A muscle shifted in her throat as she peeked up at him with a hesitant look, as if tongue-tied in his presence for the very first time. She cleared her throat. "Uh . . . only now that casual arrangement of friendship . . . well, it seems to be . . . ," her cheeks glowed pink, "more short-term," she said softly, her eyes appearing to seek his approval. "You see, he wants to start dating me."

He chafed, his initial annoyance flaring in his gut. "Why? So he can stomp on your heart more effectively?" He closed his eyes to knead his temple, exhaling his shame over his snide remark. "I'm sorry, Bug, I guess I'm just a bit overprotective when it comes to you." He placed his hands on her shoulders like he'd done so often over the years, only this time it was more to stabilize his own unsettled feelings than hers. "And how do *you* feel about it?"

She hedged with a tiny hunch of her shoulders, but he detected a glimmer of excitement in her eyes that bothered him more than it should. "I've always liked Devin, you know that, but it's been a safe crush since he never liked me back. But now that he does . . ."

Bram's lips went flat. "I thought you didn't trust him."

A deep russet curl dangled against her neck when she tipped her head in thought. "Well, I didn't before, it's true, but since we've been praying about it like you suggested the night of the ball, well, I think maybe I could trust him now. You know . . . *that way.*"

That way. Bram's jaw hardened against his will. Subject to Caldwell's admiring gaze, she meant—his tender caresses, the touch of his lips . . . Bram dropped his hands from her shoulders to massage his neck, hoping to shake off the tension mounting within.

"You see, he promised me after the Barrister Ball he'd always be on his best behavior," she continued in a soft tone that told him she was way too innocent for the likes of Devin Caldwell. Her trusting gaze searched his, almost as if she deemed this his decision rather than hers. "So I told him I would pray about it, which I did, and that's when I came up with the compromise of doing things together as friends in a group, but lately . . . well, lately I've been thinking dating Devin just might be God's will for me, so I've been praying in that vein."

He folded his arms and studied her with an impassive look that hid the turmoil roiling inside. "And you think you got your answer?"

She nodded, that infernal tress bobbing against a creamy throat he craved to kiss. Heat blasted his cheeks at the renegade thought, and he quickly cleared his throat, his voice a hoarse whisper. "So what's God telling you to do, Bug?"

A sad smile shadowed her lips while she studied him for several seconds, almost as if she were committing his face to memory. And then she seemed to snap out of her soulful reverie with a quivering exhale when her eyes sought his. "I think He's telling me it would be a good thing," she said quietly, a hint of melancholy in her tone. "What do you think?"

That I'd like to toss Caldwell into the bay. He nodded, swallowing the jealousy that tasted like bile. "Well, it might be, then, as long as he treats you with respect and regard."

The tightness in her face instantly eased, reminding him once again of the heavy responsibility he carried as Meg's mentor and friend. "Oh, thank you, Bram!" she said with that little-girl glow she always reserved for him. She arched on tiptoe to kiss his cheek, the soft touch of her lips thudding his pulse. "You seem to be my rock in every storm." Her sweet smile dimmed somewhat, shadowed by the same trace of sorrow he'd sensed before. "But it won't always be that way, will it?"

Her words sliced through him, brutal in the reality they bore. Against his better judgment, he pulled her close, head bent to hers as he breathed in her scent. "No, Bug—not when you become another man's wife. There will come a time when he'll be the mentor and man to guide and protect you, not me. As it should be."

Her eyes were misty when she pulled away. "I know. Just like you'll protect and love Amelia," she whispered, and the impact of her statement all but sucked the air from his lungs.

His breathing shallowed as he caressed her face with a gentle palm, the silky touch of her skin making his mouth go dry. "I have to go." His voice was gentle but firm, his intent for the moment to escape with his calm intact. "I'll let you know as soon as I talk to Logan, all right?"

She nodded and followed him to the door, her demeanor as somber as his. "I'll see you for dinner on Wednesday?" she whispered, as if their sober conversation had instilled a fear that hadn't been there before.

He smiled and tapped a finger to her nose. "I suspect I'll be coming for dinners long after you're gone from this household, Miss McClare."

Blinking hard, she shot into his arms with a feeble cry, jolting his senses when she clung with all of her might. As natural as breathing, he engulfed her with his arms, shocked at the tender passion she stirred. "I love you, Bram," she whispered, the breathless tone of her voice rife with emotion, "and I pray you will always be in my life."

He held her close, infusing a touch of tease to deflect the awful ache in his heart. "I will, Bug. Whether it's as big brother to you or Uncle Bram to your kids, I'll be here—always." With a final hug, he opened the door and strode down the steps, avoiding the wobble of that one loose brick as she still watched from the door. He rounded his roadster, and she waved, her silhouette so tiny and lost in the light. Gaze straight ahead, he pumped the throttle and eased the tiller down, finally steering his vehicle toward home.

"I love you, Bram," she'd said, just like she'd said a million times

before. Only this time, the declaration came from the lips of a woman, unnerving him all the more.

"I love you too, Meg," he whispered, the words rising in the air like the steam drifting skyward, as out of reach as his dreams to always be there for one lost little girl. He exhaled a silent sigh. "More than you'll ever know."

28

*L*oosening his tie, Bram glanced over his shoulder at the gold antique clock on the credenza in front of his window, the ominous black of the night sky confirming the late hour of eight-thirty. He mauled his face with his hands, wishing he were out with Jamie or Blake or home with Mom and Pop rather than staying late at the office for one of the hardest things he'd ever had to do.

Confront Logan McClare.

Certainly a task too difficult to do at the family dinners Logan now held at The Palace and to which Mrs. McClare was never invited, or even throughout the day when the man worked like a fiend. But in the silent hours of the night when everyone else had gone home? Oh yes, of late one could always find Logan bottled up in his office till the wee hours of the morning. Bram's mouth compressed as a heaviness settled like the dense fog over the bay. "Bottled" being the operative word, it seemed—at least these days—for a man who'd all but abstained from liquor over the last two years.

Exhaling a weary sigh, Bram rose and skirted his desk, the silence of the dark hallway only accentuating the deafening thud of his heart. He ducked in the kitchen area to retrieve two cups of the coffee he'd just made along with the half sandwich he'd saved from dinner. Uttering a quick prayer, he sucked in enough oxygen to hopefully fortify him for an encounter with a man who'd bitten off everyone's head in the office at least twice over the last month and a half.

Steaming cups in one hand, he tucked the paper-wrapped sandwich under his arm and knocked on Logan's cherrywood door, a thin slice of light bleeding beneath the wood threshold like all the joy had obviously bled from Logan's life.

"Who isss it?" a voice snapped on the other side, and Bram didn't miss the slur that indicated Logan was already well into the bottle.

"It's Bram—can I come in?"

"Go away—I'm busy."

Bram expelled a weighty breath and opened the door, his eyes scanning from Logan's rumpled shirt and loosened tie to the disheveled dark hair sifted with gray. Sullen circles beneath glassy eyes testified to sleepless nights and a daily bout with the bottle, restricted to after-hours so no one would know. "I can see that, sir—misery can be a full-time job."

"What the devil are you still doing here?" Logan said, his fatigue dissipating somewhat when he sat up to singe Bram with a glare.

Bram strolled in and set the cups of coffee on the desk, sympathy warm in his eyes as he tossed the sandwich to Logan. "I'd ask you the same thing, sir, but I think I already know." He nodded toward the coffees and the sandwich. "Figured you could use something warm in your belly and sustenance that doesn't come from a bottle."

Issuing a grunt, Logan snatched a half-empty bottle of Chivas and replenished his drink with a sneer, the golden liquid swirling into the glass like unease swirled in Bram's gut. "Sorry, Bram, but this is the only sustenance I need right now, so you can just pack up your good intentions and take 'em on home."

"That's just it, sir—it's not just good intentions," he said quietly. "There's a great deal of respect and admiration involved, along with a heavy dose of compassion and love."

Logan spun around to stare out of the window, but not before Bram saw the flash of moisture in his eyes. His words came out hoarse and low. "I appreciate what you're trying to do, Bram, really I do, but I'm just not ready to talk about this yet."

"I understand, sir. What's going on between you and Mrs. Mc-Clare is a very private and obviously very painful situation, and normally I would honor that." He slowly perched on the edge of the leather chair in front of Logan's desk, muscles tight despite his casual clasp of hands. "But I'm afraid the pain extends much farther than just to you and Mrs. McClare, and your family has asked me to talk to you."

A harsh laugh erupted from Logan's throat as he gouged a trembling hand through his hair. "Yes, I'm sure there's more than enough pain to go around, but I'm afraid it can't be helped right now."

Bram hesitated, girding himself with another deep swell of air. "Well, pardon me, sir, but I think that it can."

Logan turned, his eyes glittering like slivers of black diamonds. "Really." Acid coated his tone. "Well, tell me, Bram—have you ever had your hope shattered into a million pieces? The light in your life snuffed out in a single night? Your heart so battered that it's bleeding raw?" He bludgeoned the desk hard with his fist, spilling the coffee. "Well, have you?"

Meg's image lighted in his mind, the same image that haunted his dreams every night since she'd returned from Paris, a festering ache deep inside over a woman who would always possess his heart, but never be his. His sorrowful gaze locked with Logan's, and he suddenly realized that at this very moment, he needed Logan every bit as much as Logan needed him. "Yes, sir, I have," he said quietly, "not to the extent that you have after loving Mrs. McClare for so many years, I realize, but then pain isn't particularly partial to either time or depth, is it, sir?"

Logan stared, confusion softening the hard planes of his face. "Who?"

Bram swallowed hard, unwilling to put voice to his feelings for Meg. "Let's just say as much as I respect Amelia Darlington, she's not the woman with whom I long to spend the rest of my life."

The fog in Logan's eyes seemed to clear. He more than anyone was aware of Bram's commitment to his father in honoring a marriage forged over a fortune. "Meg?" he whispered.

Bram exhaled and nodded, the very sound of her name causing his heart to cramp. His gaze lagged into a distant stare. "You see, I owe my father a heavy debt, sir, one of which he's not even aware and one that I can certainly never repay." He glanced up, the resolve in his gut as keen as the determined look in his eyes. "But you understand, sir—I have to try."

All fight seemed to leave Logan as he sagged forward, facial muscles slackening into grief while he put a hand to his eyes. "I'm sorry, Bram—I've been so focused on my own problems that I never realized you cared for Meg in any way other than as a friend."

"Quite frankly, neither did I, sir, until she came home from Paris." He expelled a ragged breath of air while he massaged his temple with the heel of his hand. "But I believed it was just an initial attraction to the new Meg, one that would surely right itself once we returned to the safety of our close friendship." He glanced up in somewhat of a stupor, a little dazed himself over the full extent of his reaction to Meg's statement the other night that she was considering dating Devin. He released a cumbersome sigh. "So I've just worked hard to bury any attraction, which is difficult, but doable."

Logan dropped back in his chair, watching Bram beneath heavy lids, his gaze dark with sympathy. "So . . . tell me then—how do you do it? Spend time with Meg like you do when you know friendship is all you can ever have? Especially since she told me at dinner at The Palace last night that she has a date with Devin this weekend."

Bram winced, unaware of this latest development since he and his family attended dinner at the Darlingtons' last night. "I didn't realize that, sir, although she'd told me she'd prayed and decided to start seeing him in a more . . ." His Adam's apple ducked hard. "Personal way."

Logan was silent for several seconds, assessing Bram through pensive eyes. "So, how long have you been in love with her?" he asked quietly. "And I don't mean in a brotherly way."

Heat suffused Bram's cheeks, and suddenly he didn't want to pursue this conversation any more than Logan did, but apparently he had little choice. "I didn't say I was in love—"

Some of the rancor returned to Logan's tone. "Don't mince words with me, son. You just implied my niece is the woman with whom you long to spend the rest of your life, did you not?"

Bram's throat constricted as he tried to swallow, hoping to mask the bitter emotion that tainted his tongue. Hearing the statement out loud was like being gut-punched, and almost as agonizing as knowing he could never have her. He was a man who preferred to face things head-on, be it in business or in his personal life, but these deeper feelings for Meg had broadsided him. He'd known he was attracted to her that first night home, certainly, but the thought had been so preposterous—and so utterly impossible— he'd pushed the feelings away. Traitorous feelings buried deep inside, just lying in wait.

His gaze dropped. "Since shortly after she came home from Paris, I suppose," he whispered, stunned at the words coming out of his mouth. "Meg and I have always shared a closeness, a respect and regard, but I saw myself as a mentor, sir, a brother and dear friend who'd protect and cherish her for the beautiful person she was." He glanced up, revelation piercing his very soul. "I swear, sir, I never intended for this to happen."

Logan looked up, a wistful smile on his face. "None of us do, Bram. There's not a man alive I know who falls in love on purpose. Affairs of the heart have a way of sneaking up on you, taking you by surprise." He mauled the back of his neck while a bitter laugh tripped from his lips. "Trust me, my love for Cait took me by surprise when I first laid eyes on her twenty-nine years ago, and then it knocked me upside the head when she broke our engagement and married my brother." His gaze veered off as the smile dissolved on his face. "But the biggest surprise of all was how it lay dormant all these years until the day my brother died, and then it reared up and kicked me right in the gut." He kneaded his temple and released a heavy sigh before his gaze met Bram's, a rare sense of defeat in his eyes. "The blasted woman has ruined me for any other, Bram, and for the first time in my life, I really don't know what to do."

Bram sat forward, eager to help alleviate Logan's grief. "Logan, you want to know how I do it—spend time with Meg when I know friendship is all we'll ever have? I never really thought about that until you asked the question just now . . ." A sheepish smile slid across his face as he scratched the back of his head. "Okay, truth be told, I never really allowed myself to think about how deep my feelings for Meg really were until the shock of the other night when she told me she was thinking of dating Devin." He peered up beneath a furrowed brow, his manner reflective. "But now that I'm fully aware of the situation, the only option I can employ—and the only one that will really work—is a directive from the Bible I call the Abraham Factor."

Logan squinted, the tug of a smile on his lips. "You're telling me you have a biblical directive named after you?"

Bram laughed. "Hardly, but he is my namesake." He sat back with hands on the arms of the chair, fingers limp over the edge. "I'm speaking of Abraham in the Old Testament, of course, the father of the Hebrew nation and proclaimed 'friend of God.' The man of whom God required the sacrifice of his only son on an altar in the region of Moriah. It's not a comfortable story by a long shot, but an important one for two men faced with heartache such as you and I."

He propped his elbows on the arms of the chair and steepled his hands, staring out the window over Logan's shoulder, the gloom of night the perfect backdrop for the subject he broached. "You see, I've learned the hard way that when it comes to the most precious things in my life, the safest place to keep them is in God's hands. To trust Him to do for them and me the very best thing." His eyes met Logan's. "No matter *what* that is." He expelled a weary sigh. "Because if I love someone—really and truly love them—I'll always want to give them God's best, not my own."

Rising from his chair, he nudged Logan's cup of coffee toward him before he picked up his own. "Abraham loved his son fiercely, waited decades for God to honor His promise to give him a son in the first place. And then one day, God—Abraham's 'friend,' mind you—asks him to lay that precious son on the altar and give him up. Sacrifice him—just like that. And you know what?" Against his will, tears glazed Bram's eyes as his gaze locked with Logan's. "That man didn't balk or miss a beat. Nope. Because Abraham's trust in God was so strong, he actually told his traveling companions to 'abide ye here and I and the lad will go yonder; and we will worship, and come again to you.'" Bram shook his head, overwhelmed as always at the strength of Abraham's faith, the certainty that somehow, some way, God's best would prevail. "And you and I both know what happened, Logan. God stayed the knife in Abraham's hand, giving him his son back because of his remarkable trust."

"Trust," Logan whispered in a low drone, "the very reason I've lost Cait."

Bram nodded, his tone quiet but sure. "And the very thing that will help you find God in a way you've never experienced Him before. He wants you to trust Him, Logan, to put your love for Mrs. McClare on the altar where God can do with it what He wills for your good and hers. And whether He stays your hand or not, your sacrifice of obedience will be rewarded with more peace and joy and hope than you ever believed possible."

Logan's brows dipped, the deep wedges indicating his skepticism. "And you really believe that?"

Bram smiled, remembering his own lack of faith before God had proven it true. "I do. And I not only believe it, I've experienced it firsthand after my sister died. As you know, she and I were very close because I'd waited for a sibling for a long time. I know now that it had been a heart's desire of mine, so to speak, so I was pretty angry with God when He took her away. Even rebelled for a season, of which you are all too well aware. I'd been raised to have a strong faith, so basically, I resigned myself to God's will like Job had. You know, 'The Lord giveth and the Lord taketh away'?" His gaze drifted past Logan again, mind wandering back to the pain of his loss. "Only I missed something very important in all of that. The next line Job speaks is, 'Blessed be the name of the Lord.' I realized then I had only resigned myself to God's will, not accepted it."

"What do you mean?" Logan asked.

Bram glanced up, offering a silent prayer he could reach Logan like God had reached him. "I mean that I discovered there's a huge difference between *acceptance* and *resignation*—one is positive, the other is negative. Acceptance opens the door of hope wide, while resignation slams it shut. One says God is good and loves us, and the other says He is harsh and doesn't care. Abraham chose to 'accept' God's will, knowing full well that God loved him and not only wanted the best for him, but knew exactly what that 'best' would be. Neither is easy when it means relinquishing the desires of our heart, but 'acceptance' promises that God will bless our obedience with a greater good. 'Resignation,' however, can sever our relationship with God, which leaves us on our own, resulting in darkness and despair."

Bram breathed in deeply, then released it in one long, steady sigh. "Once God revealed the lesson of the Abraham Factor, I learned to put my trust in Him despite Ruthy's death—no matter how painful it had been. I chose to believe God loved me and would bring good from it, even replacing my heart's desire." He smiled, the warmth of his gratitude seeping through his body to chase the chill of his past away. "And He did—through Meg and your family, both of which have given me more love, peace, and joy than I ever dreamed possible."

Logan tilted forward, eyes homing in on Bram with a new clarity. "So, let me get this straight. If Cait is the desire of my heart and I lay her on this altar, God may or may not give her back to me, but either way, I'll be happy—lousy with love, peace, and joy, so to speak."

Bram grinned. "Not the word I would have chosen, but yes, eventually you would be 'lousy with love, peace, and joy' in this situation."

A grunt rolled from Logan's lips. "Yeah, well 'lousy' is something I seem to have a talent for, at least in the past." He eyed Bram with the same do-or-die look he wore in their weekly strategy meetings. "So, since you're the experienced one here, counselor, just how exactly does one go about implementing this Abraham Factor?"

Bram grimaced while rubbing the back of his neck. "It won't be easy, but it's certainly possible, especially with lots of prayer."

Logan's lip took a slant. "'Easy' has never been my style, so I'm up to the task, but I need a game plan."

"Well, for starters, we both need to put our money where our mouth is regarding those we love, meaning we love them unconditionally, not selfishly, putting their best interests before our own." He hesitated, well aware his next statement might further fan the flame of Logan's fury. "Which for me is being there for Meg as a friend and big brother as long as she needs me, no matter what or no matter whom she marries. And for you?" His gaze flicked to Logan's and held. "It means coming back to the family, being there for them no matter what or no matter who is in Mrs. McClare's life. It's knowing that your feelings have to come second to those you love, choosing their happiness over your own." He leaned in for emphasis, making sure he had Logan's full attention. "And let me be clear here, sir—their happiness depends on you being a vital part of the family, because right now I've never seen a more miserable lot of people, including Mrs. McClare." His mouth tipped. "And I can't be sure, of course, because one can never really tell with Rosie, but it seems to me she's been somewhat crankier too."

Logan actually grinned. "Good. At least something positive has come out of this."

Bram chuckled, the sound and feel of it releasing most of the strain at the back of his neck. His smile ebbed. "I mean it, sir—it's not the same without you, and although you think you can't be happy while Mr. Turner is in Mrs. McClare's life, the truth is, you will be far more miserable without her friendship and so will she."

Face in a scrunch, Logan's eyes narrowed the barest amount. "How on earth did you get so smart?" he whispered. "And how on earth am I not paying you more?"

"You're paying me plenty," he said quietly, tone soft but intent sharp. "Especially if you return to the family and love Mrs. Mc-Clare the way she deserves."

Logan flinched before he looked away. "You don't pull any punches, do you, Hughes?"

"Not when it comes to people I love, sir, among whom you are paramount, I assure you."

A faint smile curved on Logan's lips as he bowed his head, gaze fixed on the floor. Several moments passed before he finally nodded. "I will, Bram—soon." His eyes flicked up with a dry slant of his mouth. "When I can do it without spitting in Turner's eye."

Bram gave the arms of his chair several pats and rose, feeling the pull of a grin. "Well, then, my work here is done."

Logan's eyes narrowed, belying the ghost of a smile on his face. "Not yet, counselor—I refuse to do this alone," he said with a pointed look that told Bram loud and clear Logan McClare was asking for prayer. "You and I have talked prayer and forgiveness before, and I thought I had a handle on it then, but I was wrong." His smile faded as his gaze trailed into melancholy. "I never meant to turn on Cait like I did," he whispered. "I thought I was bigger than that, stronger, especially since your and my last talk." He glanced away, but Bram didn't miss the moisture that glazed in his eyes. "But bitterness and anger took hold, and I . . ." His Adam's apple jogged. "I hurt her, and everyone else in the process." Expelling a weary breath, he looked up then, a quiet resolve sharpening his features. "I'll need God's help and your prayers," he said with a deep draw of air, slowly releasing it again in one long, tenuous sigh. "And some more time and prayer on my own to prepare for the toughest trial of my life."

"You have it," Bram said quietly.

"As do you, my friend." Logan rose to extend his hand across the desk, their grip one of solidarity and faith. "Thanks, Bram."

"You're welcome." He nodded toward the wrapped sandwich on Logan's desk, hoping to dispel their sobriety with a touch of humor. "Tuller's pastrami—your favorite." With a casual salute, he headed toward the door before flashing a few teeth over his shoulder. "And I'd take it if I were you, sir, 'cause you're going to need all the sustenance you can get."

29

$\mathcal{E}$yes closed and face lifted, Meg breathed in the crisp sea air of San Francisco Bay while she lunched on the veranda of the San Francisco Yacht Club. The summer music of seagulls and lapping waves harmonized with the gentle squeaking of weathered docks that bobbed in the salty breeze, and for once she was grateful to spend a rare Saturday afternoon with her family rather than volunteering at the Barbary Volunteer Legal Services. A contented sigh floated from her lips as she sat back in her chair on the upper terrace of Sausalito's most prestigious venue, full from the lobster she'd just finished with her family, Nick, and Bram. A gust of wind billowed the sentry of flags overhead, causing the gentle snap of material to punctuate the laughter and chatter of diners below. Her eyes flicked to the blue of the sky where not a cloud could be found earlier, and her mood dimmed somewhat at the darker haze on the horizon. The threat of thunderclouds, most likely, portending gloom. The smile on her lips suddenly lagged. Not unlike in my family, she reflected with a tug of her heart, barely aware that ridges now furrowed her forehead.

She startled at Bram's touch. "You all right?" he asked, the crimp in his brow no doubt matching her own. "You're not seasick, are you?"

"No, of course not," she said softly, gaze dropping to the nautical napkin on her lap while she absently toyed with the nubby seam of its edge. "I was just thinking of Uncle Logan, that's all." Her solemn gaze flicked up. "You know, about how he'll feel when he finds out."

"Mother needs to tell him soon." Alli's quiet statement across the table stilled everyone's chatter, all laughter dying along with the breeze to leave the air suddenly sticky and hot. "The last thing he needs right now is to learn from someone else that she and Andrew are engaged."

"A little hard to do when they haven't spoken to each other in almost two months." Cassie hurled her napkin on the table, the hard bent of her jaw suggesting a rare frustration with both her aunt and her uncle. Her green eyes narrowed on Bram. "I thought you said Uncle Logan agreed to come back to family dinners soon? That was over two weeks ago."

Bram rubbed the back of his neck, fatigue quickly edging his tone. "Yes, that's what he implied, once he gets his anger under control, that is, which I imagine is considerable given how long he's stayed away." His lips went flat. "Which means his 'soon' may not be the same as ours."

Alli slammed the water glass she'd just guzzled back on the table. Her green eyes seemed to churn as much as the foam slapping against the rock-embedded seawall that meandered the shore. "Well, if Mother doesn't tell him soon, I'll . . . I'll . . ."

"Hit her with a stick?" Nick volunteered, obviously trying to lighten the mood with a lazy smile, referencing the countless times she'd whacked him with a stick when they first met.

She grinned, breaking the tension at the table. "No, but I'd like to, trust me."

"Me too," Cassie said with a slump of shoulders, chin in hand.

Her lips quirked as she peered around the table through slitted eyes. "I suppose a cattle prod is out of the question?"

Alli fluttered her lashes. "You mean it still works? I thought you broke it on Jamie."

"Funny, Al." Jamie pushed away from the table to stretch arms high as he gave Cassie a wink. "Might have thought twice about marrying into this family if I'd known the women were so violent."

"I could have told you that," Blake said, his manner casual as he tossed the last of Alli's dessert in his mouth. "But I wasn't about to let that cat out of the bag because face it—misery loves company."

"You are such a mooch!" Alli slapped his hand.

"Hey, you gave me a bite before."

Alli popped him lightly on the back of the head. "No, *you* helped yourself to a bite as I recall, you little brat. I swear, Blake, give you an inch, you take a mile."

Jamie flashed a grin. "In more ways than one."

Blake gave him a drop-jawed smile. "Now there's the rogue calling the rake a flirt. You had enough rope and cattle-prod injuries to qualify you for the burn unit at Cooper Medical."

"Ha! Irrefutable evidence to strengthen my case," Jamie said. "You just proved my point, counselor, that McClare women can be hostile."

Cassie gave him a quick kiss. "Only when provoked, darlin'. Besides, Meg's not violent."

Bram grunted as he retrieved his wallet. "You've obviously never played chess with her," he quipped, mentally calculating the bill before he tallied the tip.

"Uh, it appears correct," Meg said softly, enjoying teasing Bram with her knack for numbers.

"Of course it is, showoff." He slid her a sideways smile that put heat in her cheeks, then tossed money down to pay for the lunch, waving Nick, Jamie, and Blake off. "My treat, gentlemen—I invited you to go sailing, remember?" He glanced at his watch, then peered at Jamie across the table, who was taking his time with the rest of Cassie's uneaten torte. "Better head back soon if you all have dinner and the theatre tonight, so make it snappy, Mac."

"Hey, one does not rush dessert, Padre—it's a sin."

"So is eating everyone's dessert." Alli sent Jamie a smirk. Leaning in with a contented sigh, she folded her arms on the table. "It's been a fun day, Bram, so thank you for both sailing and lunch," she said while everyone echoed her sentiments. The sparkle dimmed in her eyes. "But I wish you were coming with us tonight, and Meg too." She managed a pout that came off with the barest hint of a smile. "This was supposed to be a group event tonight if Devin's parents hadn't invited Meg for dinner and Amelia's parents hadn't invited you." She sighed, her voice forlorn. "Why do families have to change so much?"

Cassie hooked an arm to Alli's waist. "Families growing because of love is never a bad thing, Al, so we just need to adapt and enjoy." She focused her attention on Bram, steering the subject in a teasing direction as she was often prone to do. "And, yes, Mr. Hughes, to answer your prior question, I have played chess with Meg." Her nose scrunched in an impish grin. "She just lets *me* win all the time because she likes me better."

Bram eyed Meg with a mock glare. "Is she saying that half the wins I accrue are simply at your mercy?"

Meg battled a grin, grateful for the banter that helped chase her prior melancholy away. "Uh . . . why, no—"

"Yes!" Everyone shouted.

"Face it," Alli said with a wink, "Meg's a marshmallow genius—too sweet and soft to trounce anyone in games of skill or mental acuity, although we know she can do it in her sleep."

"Except Devin Caldwell," Cassie said with a dance of brows.

"Speaking of which," Alli continued, "is it my imagination or have you been letting that poor boy win at chess now that you two are not sparring anymore?"

Meg felt sunburn on her cheeks that had nothing to do with the sun. "Maybe . . . but it's more likely to keep the peace while we're working so closely on Andrew's special project."

"How's that going, by the way?" Cassie asked.

Adrenaline surged through Meg like the billowing breakers against Sausalito's shore. "Oh, worlds better than I expected," she said with a delighted giggle, the progress she and Devin were making in building a case against the Marsicania exceeding her wildest expectations. She sent Nick a grateful smile. "Thanks to invaluable help from my truly talented partner in crime, Chief Detective Burke—a veritable wealth of information."

Alli peered up at Nick, smile gaping. "*My* Detective Burke? The man whose jaw I have to pry open to talk about his day?"

Nick gave her a lidded smile out of the corner of his eye as he slowly sipped his coffee. "Murder and mayhem are not exactly what I want to talk about when I'm with my fiancée, Princess." He finished the last of his cup and nudged it away. "Not that I'd have the chance."

Alli poked his arm with her utensil. "Are you saying I talk too much, Nicholas Burke?"

Snatching the fork from her hand, he tossed it on the table and pulled her close, his lips hovering. "Am I going to have to hide the silverware as well as the sticks once we're married?" he whispered, voice husky while his gaze fused to hers.

"Naw, she'll just talk you to death," Jamie said with another bite of dessert. "Everybody knows Alli always has to have the last word."

"I do not," Alli said with another open-mouth smile, still locked against Nick's chest. "For your information, Mr. MacKenna, I am a drama teacher, so allocution is my profession, and one, I might add, at which I am quite good."

Nick bent to graze a lingering kiss to the side of her neck, effectively silencing her with a soft gasp of air. "I happen to think you're pretty good at quiet too," he whispered.

"Speaking of 'quiet'. . ." Jamie pushed the empty dessert plate away and rose. "I agree with both Nick and Bram." He tugged Cassie to her feet, locking her in an embrace with a wicked smile. "I'd like a little quiet time right about now."

Blake slid Jamie a sly grin. "I'll tell you what, Mac, marriage sure hasn't slowed you down."

Jamie latched an arm to Cassie's waist as everyone headed for the door. "Nope, it's downright criminal how fun it can be, Rake—you oughta give it a whirl sometime."

Blake shivered as he clunked down the creaky wooden steps. "Bite your tongue."

A shrill whistle pierced the air, signaling the next ferry to San Francisco, and Meg whirled around, halting Bram while the others continued ahead. "I know everyone else has to get back, but Devin's not picking me up till seven. What time is your dinner at Amelia's?"

Bram studied her, as if sensing she had something to discuss. "Seven-thirty. Why?"

"Maybe one more sail to Angel Island and Alcatraz?" she whispered. "Since we won't be together tonight?" Her brows sloped in a gentle plea. "Please—there's something I'd like to talk to you about."

He glanced at the horizon where the sun peeked through mounds of gunmetal clouds scudding the sky, and his lips curved in a slow smile. "You guys go ahead," he called to the others. "Meg and I'll take the last ferry home."

They waved as they filed on to the ferry, and she grabbed his hand, as giddy as if she were celebrating her birthday. "This is a first, you know—you've never taken me sailing by myself."

He grinned, the sparkle in his blue eyes matching the gleam of sun in his summer-streaked hair. "Then, I'd say it's about time, don't you?"

She squealed with a clap of her hands. "Oh, this will be so much fun!"

His laughter, warm and low, made her dizzy with delight as he ushered her back to where he moored his sloop. "Just one sail to the islands and back, all right?"

He had them out on the water in no time, an experienced sailor who'd competed in a number of San Francisco Yacht Club sailing events, and Meg thrilled at watching him man the sails. Her heart fluttered along with her hair in the briny breeze when he stripped off his jacket and tie and tossed them aside, unbuttoning his shirt to further loosen the collar. Mist molded his rolled-sleeved shirt to hard muscles that bulged and strained with every move. He trimmed the sail until the front edge stopped luffing, and she saw his body finally relax when the vessel stayed its course, his hand steady on the tiller. All at once, he turned to give her a wink, white teeth flashing in a chiseled face tanned to a golden brown. Comfortably propped on the rim of the boat, he motioned with his head for her to come closer, long legs stretched out as he manned the tiller.

She slowly picked her way to where he sat, plopping down when he spread his jacket for her across the wooden bench. "So, what's on your mind, Bug?" he asked, those piercing blue eyes warming her as much as the sun before it ducked behind a tumble of steel-tipped clouds.

You, Bram . . . always you . . . She quickly looked away, grateful for the wind that whipped her hair against her face, obscuring the burn in her cheeks. She closed her eyes and lifted her chin to the leaden sky, drinking in the beauty of the day. The pungent scent of the sea, the gentle swoosh of the water, the plaintive call of the gulls overhead—a longing in their cry that seemed to match her own. She breathed in deeply, chest swelling and dipping like the waves, wishing this moment could last forever. Her exhale was lost in a sudden gust of wind, sweeping her wishes away with a bluster of reality as cool as the spray of seawater chilling her skin.

Bram is committed to another.

And Devin is committed to me.

Her reluctant gaze rose to meet Bram's. "Devin has asked to court me," she said, so softly she thought he mightn't have heard except for the sudden pallor in cheeks so ruddy before. "And I don't know what to do."

He looked away, squinting at the ashen sky where sooty clouds slithered and surged like a serpent sulking on the horizon. "Do you love him?"

No, I only love you . . . "I certainly enjoy his company," she said slowly, hoping to convince herself as much as him, "and we have so much in common, especially if I pursue the law." She stared at his profile, the duck of his Adam's apple drawing her eye to his open shirt where wisps of blond hair fluttered against gilded skin. "And I do care for him . . ."

He faced her again, his demeanor clearly in mentor mode—wise eyes, kind manner, and scalpel-precision comfort to heal whatever ailed. Only now the healer was the wounder, and oh, how it would wound him if he ever knew . . .

"Can you see yourself spending the rest of your life with him, Bug, as man and wife . . . ?"

She closed her eyes to ponder the question, but all she saw was the gentlest of men, a friend and mentor who had never left her side from the moment he'd tucked her in a hug at the age of seven. A man who would certainly make the most caring of husbands and a tender lover . . .

Her eyelids popped open and she turned away, horrified he might read that brazen thought in her eyes. She focused on his question. Could she see Devin as the man she'd love for the rest of her life? Live with? Grow old with? Her heart stuttered. And have children with? The very thought was not unpleasant and even stirred at the memory of that "almost" kiss in the conference room at work that one day. Over the last month they'd dated, she'd found herself growing more comfortable, more attracted than she ever expected. He seemed to work hard to put her at ease, keeping his word and his distance with only occasional chaste kisses on the cheek despite the desire she saw in his eyes. "I think so," she said quietly, knowing that was what he needed to hear even if it wasn't what she wanted to say.

"Is he a prayerful man, Meg? A man who reveres God as much as you?" As always, Bram's voice was steady and strong, in direct contrast to the rolling waves that matched the turmoil in her stomach.

"Rest assured, if it means lighting candles until kingdom come, Megan McClare, I will pursue the Almighty until both you and He agree to say yes . . ."

"I believe he is," she said with a faint curve of her lips, the memory of his humble ardor that night making her smile.

"Well, then, do you trust him?" Eyes intent, he posed a question she couldn't have said yes to before. But in the last month, Devin had proven his allegiance, his credibility, his restraint.

She peered up, realizing that the impossible had finally happened—she was learning to trust Devin Caldwell, of all people, the very one who had robbed her of trust and confidence all those years. A trace of a smile flickered on her face, along with a tiny flame of hope. That was certainly a beginning, wasn't it? The smile grew. "I do, actually, something I never thought I'd say. But he's a good man, Bram, and I think I could grow to care about him a great deal."

For a split second, the calm in Bram's eyes wavered, revealing a spark of hurt so imperceptible that it mightn't have been there at all. His smile grew to match hers. "Then I suppose there's only one question left, Bug." He adjusted the tiller and shifted back, tipping his head to study her. "What is God telling you to do?"

Delight thyself also in the LORD: *and He shall give thee the desires of thine heart.*

A trembling began in the very pit of her stomach that produced a keening in her soul so mournful, it brought tears to her eyes. *Oh Lord, if only . . .*

She turned away, unwilling for him to see the grief hidden within. Her gaze snagged on the jagged shore of Angel Island and she pounced on the diversion, jutting straight up in her seat. "Oh, I just love Angel Island," she breathed, "both the name and the fact that it's a military post, like an angel watching over San Francisco." She spun around, her excitement bringing a grin to Bram's face. "Did you know the Army first set up camp on Angel Island during the Civil War?"

He nodded, lips pursed in amusement. "But it's merely a discharge camp now, Bug, for processing those returning from the Philippines, not a line of defense anymore."

She teased with a jut of her chin, gaze returning to the vibrant green hills that seemed to roll into the restless sea. "I don't care. It's the largest island in San Francisco Bay and home to Fort McDowell, so that alone elicits a feeling of power and protection.

And," she said, turning to give him a look of wonder that coaxed another grin to his lips, "did you know that some say the island is so large you can see Sonoma and Napa on a clear day?"

He chuckled, his gaze following hers. "You may have missed your calling, Miss McClare—perhaps you should be a tour guide."

"Perhaps I should," she said with a giggle."

A faraway rumble drew Bram's attention and he frowned, the sun lost in a swirl of dingy clouds that seemed to consume the sky. "We better head in—looks like weather might be brewing."

Her heart lurched, not wanting their excursion to end. She glanced at the watch pinned to her blouse before she raised frantic eyes to the man with whom she felt safer than any other. "Oh, Bram, just a while longer, please? The darkest clouds are so far away, and we still have a good hour and a half before the last ferry. Can't we sail to Alcatraz first?"

He hesitated, gaze flitting to the horizon and back with a sober look. "I don't think so, Bug—weather in the bay is unpredictable, and I want to get you home safe and sound."

"All right, Bram," she whispered, unable to hide the disappointment in her tone.

He stared for several moments, a twitch in his jaw indicating she was asking him to do something of which he didn't approve. And then with a sharp rise of his chest, he blasted out a noisy sigh that told her she'd won. He aimed a blunt finger, tone harsh for a man so gentle. "One quick pass, and we head back, understood?"

Her brows circled high over wide eyes. "I've made you angry," she whispered—something he seldom displayed. Clutching her hands in her lap, she dropped her gaze to the floor, feeling absolutely awful. "No, please—let's go back."

She flinched when he dropped the tiller to squat before her. "Meg," he whispered, "look at me."

Her throat worked as she slowly raised her eyes. "I'm s-so sorry, Bram, truly—"

He cupped her face, thumbs feathering the line of her jaw. "Meg, I couldn't be mad at you if my life depended on it. What you heard in my voice, sensed in my manner, was fear and concern because I would never—*ever*—want to put you in harm's way."

She blinked, swiping the moisture from her eyes. *Oh Bram— you already have . . .*

His heavy sigh carried away on a breeze as he clasped both of her hands between his. "Forgive me—please. You're a woman full-grown, but I sometimes forget just how tender you are inside." He swept stray curls from her face, his smile shadowed with tease as he shook his head. "No doubt about it, young lady—you're a heartbreaker with those tears in your eyes." He squeezed her fingers and jumped up, gaze traveling to a moody horizon darkening by the moment. "I'm more than fair with a sail, Miss McClare, but even I'm running out of time, so we best get moving." He grinned. "Duck when I tell you, aye?"

Hands braced to the tiller, he steered the boat through the wind, jerking the jib sheet out of its cleat. "Duck!" he yelled and Meg dropped flat on the bench, hands over her head as the boom swooped across the boat, self-setting the mainsail on the other side. With lightning speed, Bram hauled in the jib sheet until the sail grew taut. Meg grinned as it bloomed in the breeze, skimming the sloop across the water with astonishing speed. She laughed out loud when the wind whipped the pins from her hair, curls streaming while sea spray tingled her face.

Excitement pulsed in her veins like the bay beneath the keel. Heart swelling with pride, she watched Bram straddle the tiller, so incredibly solid and male and tall. He emanated a strength that swirled heat in her belly as much as the wind swirled the waves, and when he tossed a grin over his shoulder, her heart soared along with the pelicans overhead. "Alcatraz at your service, milady," he shouted, sandy hair lashing in the breeze like some tawny-haired pirate who had truly pirated her heart. She clapped her hands in delight as the island loomed with its Cape Cod lighthouse, rising from the sea, a sinister presence that seemed to grow before their eyes. A nervous thrill bubbled in her chest at the memory of Bram's comment earlier in the day. "The Evil Island," he'd told them, an appellation bestowed by Native Americans who believed the island accursed until the Spanish wisely renamed it. Alcatraz—Island of the Pelicans.

Boom! She screamed when a horrendous crack of thunder stole the air from her lungs, leaving her dazed and breathless until a bolt of lightning split the sky. It splintered both the heavens and her peace of mind, causing her heart to thud to a stop. Bram jerked to look behind, and danger flashed in his face. One hand on the tiller, he snatched two life preservers stowed in the bow and tossed one to Meg, grappling to don the other with his free hand. "Tie it around your waist as tight as you can," he yelled, another growl of thunder almost drowning him out.

Sweat beaded beneath her bodice despite the sudden chill in the air, and fingers trembling, she did as he said, tying the strings of the cork-filled preserver as quickly as she could. Unbidden, thoughts of the horrific tragedy in New York two and a half months prior came to mind—over 1,000 men, women, and children perishing after the PS *General Slocum* sank in the East River. Her mouth went dry while she fumbled with the ties. *Oh Lord, please—protect us!*

"Meg!" She jolted at the shout of her name, Bram's voice barely audible with the angry rattle of the wind snapping at the sails. "I need you to crawl—not walk—to the stern and retrieve a coil of rope beneath the bench, all right? Bring it to me, please, while I reef the sails."

Casting a worried look at the horizon, she dropped to her knees and scrambled to the stern, skirt soaked by a pool of water blown in by vicious waves. She shivered while her frantic gaze flicked to the skyline. Her blood iced at the grim sight of ink-stained clouds undulating like some ravenous monster. When she returned with the rope, she waited while Bram secured the boom, fingers flying with half hitches as quickly as lightning slashed the sky. Whitecaps surged when water slammed against the hull, dousing them both with icy sea spray that molded Bram's shirt to his chest.

"During a storm, you want to flatten the mainsail," he said loudly, as if talking it through might help ease her fear. But his fluid movements possessed an urgency while he explained each motion, moving to the aft to pull the clew near to the end of the boom. His gaze darted to Alcatraz, mouth thinning and jaw tight. "I think we can make it to the shore if our speed holds, but I need you to tie the rope around your waist, Meg, then hand it to me."

Sleet slithered through her veins. "You think we're going to sink?" she cried, hysteria creeping into her voice while she clutched the rope to her chest.

His gaze met hers, unflinching while wind battered his body, willing her to calm. "It's standard safety procedure, Meg, nothing more." Before she could speak, he'd tugged the rope from her hands and tied it to her waist, leaving a good length to loop around his own. A crack of thunder exploded while jagged veins of electricity spidered overhead, and Bram wasted no time securing his end of the rope to the mast. He grabbed for the tiller, eyes mere hollows of black as they flicked to the island and back. "Almost there . . ."

A deafening roar pounded in her ears and in a hard slam of

her pulse, the heavens disgorged, icy pellets and frigid rain assaulting so violently, she could barely see Bram three feet away. "Meg—down!" he screamed, but she had no time to comply. A rogue wave bludgeoned the boat, blinding her with saltwater when another whitecap knocked her down. A cry gurgled in her throat as the boat began to heel, and with a hellish howl, a wall of water broadsided the sloop, heaving Meg into the air with a final shriek before blackness swallowed her whole.

"Meg!" Bram's cry was lost in a slash of seawater while he pummeled the waves, eyes burning as he frantically searched over the raging foam. Beside him, the shattered sloop bobbed on its back, its hull broken and battered. Violent sheets of rain continued to gush from a sky dark as pitch, and fear constricted Bram's chest until he couldn't breathe. *"Meg!"*

Something dark and fluid floated several feet away, and his heart shot to his throat, his sudden gasp choking him with icy brine. "Meg!" he rasped, hands numb as they groped along the sodden hemp. His blood froze to ice at the horror of her facedown, auburn tresses black while they snaked through the dirty froth. Within two painful throbs of his pulse, he had her in his arms, fingers shaking as he swept sopping hair from her face. Her head lagged back with eyes closed, and for several paralyzing seconds he couldn't breathe or move or think. And then with a violent gasp of air, he shook her hard, fingers digging into her frigid flesh. "Meg!"

Her body hung slack in his arms, and his wild gaze darted to Alcatraz. Relief surged through him when he saw that the thrashing waves had almost washed them to shore. With renewed energy, he braced her rib cage from behind and swam with one arm, her body pinned to his side while he focused on the rocky shoreline. His silent petitions were as fractured as his breath, terror striking like the thunderous waves that battled his body. Legs pumping as fast as his heart, he refused to give sway, inching his way to safety. *God, please—don't let me lose her—please!*

It seemed like eons, but he knew it was only moments until he crawled into a crevice at the base of the bluff, barely large enough to shelter them both. Warring against panic, he wrenched her frigid body into his lap and briskly rubbed her arms before pushing a thumb to her wrist. His heart leapt at the faintest of beats. Chilled and exhausted, he struggled to remember life-saving techniques he'd learned on the sailing team. *God, help me please . . .*

In a wild whip of the wind, it all came rushing back like a dictum from God, guiding him as he elevated her legs higher than her head. Lips moving in silent prayer, he applied pressure to her abdomen, hope flaring when water gushed from her throat. "Come on, Meg," he whispered, and cradling her head, he covered her mouth with his own, blowing in long, slow breaths that caused her chest to rise. He intermittently massaged her arms, then breathed in again and again, pulse slamming to a stop at the gargle of a wet, guttural cough.

Bluish eyelids flickered on her waxlike face before they slowly lifted, as if made of lead and too heavy to bear. Tears stung while he caressed her pale cheeks, fingers trembling with the motion. "Oh, Meg," he whispered, voice hoarse and broken, "I thought I lost you." His body heaved as he clutched her close, tears streaming instead of saltwater. "God help me, I thought I lost you."

"B-Bram?" It was no more than a frail breath on her lips, but he craved to taste it for himself, this precious whisper of life. With unrestrained laughter bubbling warm against her icy skin, he caressed her mouth with his own, skimming joyously to every

part of her face, overcome with wonder and awe over the priceless gift of God in his arms. "Oh, Meg," he rasped, kissing her
forehead, her temple, her cheek . . . "My life would be so empty
without you." He lost himself in the joy of touching her, mind
dazed while his lips explored a treasure too long forbidden. The
delicate line of her cheekbone, the soft flesh of her ear, the curve
of her throat—his for the moment at least—a miracle that wrung
more tears from his eyes. Besieged by gratitude, he found himself
bewitched by wonder, undone when her lips moved warm beneath
his. *Oh Meg, I love you more than life itself* . . . Gratitude swelled
like a riptide, and cocooning her close, he took her mouth with
a passion long, long overdue, deepening the kiss until his moan
melded with hers.

"I love you, Bram . . ." Her tender words were no more than a
breath against his skin as her body slowed and melted in his arms.
Her eyelids weighted closed while exhaustion claimed her with
a final rustle of air before sleep stole her away. "So happy . . . ,"
she whispered, voice fading when her porcelain face stilled like a
child abed, the faintest of smiles shadowing her mouth.

Bundling her close, his gaze trailed into the storm that had
already abated, his euphoria dissipating as quickly as the rain. She
loved him. And he loved her. Pain slashed, more brutal than any
tempest that could ravage the sea. He tucked his head to hers,
jaw firm while he fought the tide of more tears. Because he knew
to the depth of his being.

Although one tragedy had been averted.

Another yet remained.

~ 30 ~

*L*ogan sprinted up the brick steps of Cait's house, throat parched and heart pounding while he kneaded a dull ache in his chest with the ball of his hand. It'd been like an electric shock when Cait had called, a dizzy sensation as if he were falling when he'd first heard her voice.

"Meg and Bram capsized in the bay . . ."

Everything important before—the Board of Supervisors, his law firm, even his relentless pursuit of Cait—suddenly meant nothing in the face of losing one of his own. He'd been nauseous, then chilled, then numb, rushing from his apartment without even a tie, barely aware of traffic as he sped to Cait's house.

Breathing hard, he didn't even bother to knock, but thrust the door open with a loud crack to the wall. "Where is she?" he shouted to Hadley, his tone barely contained. "Where's Meg?"

Hadley stepped aside, his expression grim. "In her room, sir, second door on the left."

Without so much as a glance in the foyer, Logan raced up the staircase like a man half his age, the muscles around his heart cramping as hard as when Cait had first called. He literally ran down the hall, barely knocking before he burst into Meg's room, body heaving to a stop when he stared at her bed. Even in the dim light, her face was like chalk, dark circles sinking beneath translucent lids while matted hair splayed on her pillow. She seemed so small and frail, barely a bump under the covers, and when he spied the bruises on her cheek, tears sprang to his eyes. "Meg."

He noticed Cait for the first time when she rose from a chair by the bed, eyes and face swollen as quivering fingers flew to her mouth. "Oh Logan . . ."

Within three powerful strides, he swept her into his arms, clutching so tightly, they became as one, trembling together over the terror that might have befallen them all. The feel of her in his arms was so natural, so right, that he groaned with relief to be here for them both—the woman he loved and the niece that he cherished. He pressed a kiss to Cait's hair, and immediately a calm settled on him as he focused on her and how he could help. "How is she?"

Her shiver rattled them both, and he gripped tighter while she did the same, her voice congested with tears and fluid and grief. "Sleeping soundly on a dose of laudanum, although she wouldn't have needed it as exhausted as she was. Dr. Miller just left, but he said she's bruised and in shock, but should be fine."

"And Bram?" He hated the waver in his tone.

"Unscathed, thank God." She pulled away, her gaze traveling to a chair in the dim corner of Meg's room where Bram appeared comatose, head back while he slept and as haggard as Logan had ever seen. "At least physically," she whispered as more tears sparked in her eyes. "I think he blames himself although he saved her life. But he refuses to leave."

Logan swept a palm the length of her back, his voice a whisper. "How did this happen?"

She related the details in a mechanical tone, espousing it as a miracle that the lighthouse authorities at Alcatraz had spotted the wreckage close to the shore. An investigation led to Bram and Meg's discovery in the cleft of a rock. Her voice cracked when she mentioned that the others had been sailing with Bram and Meg earlier. "Oh Logan," she whispered, fear quaking her words, "the storm could have happened when they'd all been in that boat. Cassie, Alli, Jamie, Nick—"

"But it *didn't*," he stressed, maintaining a firm grip. He gently brushed a stray hair from her eyes. "Everything's fine, Cait, our family is intact."

She nodded and averted her gaze, taking a step back. "Thank you for coming so quickly, especially given the strain between us lately . . ."

He nudged her chin up. "This is my family too, Cait. And no matter what happens between us, I will love you and them until the day that I die."

With a jerky bob of her head, she returned to her daughter's side and cradled her hand while Logan circled the bed to press a kiss to Meg's forehead. Exhaling a halting sigh, he made his way to where Bram lay sprawled in the chair, a half-day's growth of blond bristle beneath hollowed eyes. At the sight, a deep-seated gratitude surged in his chest for this man, this friend, who had enriched his life—and so many others—with his wisdom and love. *As much of a son as my own*, Logan thought with a burn of moisture. He lightly shook his shoulder. "Bram—wake up. You need to go home."

Jerking up from a deep sleep, Bram stared for several seconds, eyelids sputtering with shock before he slumped back in the chair. His facial muscles sagged as much as his body. "How is she?" he rasped, his voice creaking like a rusted winch from his boat.

"Sleeping soundly in her own bed—like you should be." He

braced a hand beneath Bram's arm and carefully drew him to his feet. "I'll have Hadley drive you home."

"No, I don't want to leave . . ."

Logan steadied him with two hands to his shoulders. "That's not an option, Bram. Your parents will be worried sick—go home. Doc gave Meg laudanum, so she'll be out till morning."

Glassy eyes rose to meet Logan's, the naked pain in Bram's face twisting Logan's gut. "I . . . almost . . . k-killed her . . ."

"No, you *saved* her," Logan emphasized. "And us in the process. Words can't express our gratitude, nor the deep love and respect we all have for you." Blinking away the wetness in his eyes, Logan wrenched him into a fierce embrace, finally releasing him with a gruff clear of his throat. "It's not a suggestion, Bram, it's an order. I'll have Hadley drive you home, no argument. Blake will return your car."

Bram finally nodded, his restless gaze seeking the object of his affection, the woman that only Logan knew that he loved. With the slow, halting steps of a sleepwalker, Bram made his way to Meg's side, bending down to graze a light kiss to her forehead before he skimmed his thumb across her bruised cheek. Logan recognized the despair in the hunched shoulders and haunted eyes as Bram moved to the door, not uttering a single word.

Logan ushered him to the landing and called for Hadley, who immediately appeared at the base of the steps. "Hadley, would you be kind enough to drive Bram home for me, please?" At Hadley's efficient nod, Logan patted Bram's shoulder, watching as he hobbled down the steps like an old man, bent over the banister as if to hold himself up.

"God help him, please," Logan whispered on his way back to Meg's room, knowing all too well the hidden heartbreak Bram carried, loving a woman he could never have.

Heart heavy for both Bram and himself, he reentered the room, and Cait immediately shot up, avoiding his eyes as she grazed a kiss to Meg's brow. Adjusting her daughter's covers, she caressed a hand to Meg's cheek before meeting his gaze. "Can I speak to you for a moment? Downstairs?"

His rib cage immediately contracted. "Absolutely," he said in his courtroom voice, the cool and steady lawyer, always in control. *Except in love.* Placing a lingering kiss on Meg's head, he turned and followed Cait from the room, silent until the door clicked behind them. "What's wrong?" he said quietly, grateful he could read her so easily, this woman too honest and transparent to ever cloak her feelings for manipulation or deceit. "Something's on your mind, and it's more than Meg and Bram."

She managed a skittish look over her shoulder, moving quickly as if she dare not risk his touch in escorting her down the stairs. His gut tightened. *Dear God, what now?*

Rosie waited in the foyer, hands clasped to her apron and worry lines etched in her face, looking far older than Logan remembered.

"Rosie, would you be a dear and bring us some fresh tea, please?"

The crusty housekeeper gave a curt nod, her steely blue gaze flicking to him.

He ground his jaw, bracing for verbal assault.

"It's good to see you again, Mr. McClare," she said in a genuine tone that literally halted him halfway down the stairs. Her chin rose, the silver threading her dark hair appearing more pronounced than a mere nine weeks ago. "I whipped up some of those ginger snaps you're so fond of, so I'll serve those too, hot from the oven." Logan fought the drop of his jaw when the woman's chin began to quiver before she clamped it, shoulders squaring with the motion. "Had to do something to keep this old shrew from going crazy while Doc Miller took his sweet time." She spun on her heel and barreled down the hall before he could even open his mouth, still grappling with the impossibility of Rosie's strange welcome.

"She's missed you," Cait said quietly, permitting a shy smile over her shoulder as she entered the parlour. She hitched to a jarring stop so fast that Logan almost ran her over, swiftly shoring her up with a grip of her shoulders. "Andrew," she breathed, her words hoarse with shock, "you're still here . . ."

He was already up on his feet, hat tossed on the sofa behind him as he stared at Cait with a tender look that made Logan sick to his stomach. "I couldn't leave, Cait, not with all this going on." A muscle in his throat jerked hard. "I . . . wanted to be here for you."

Logan bit back a curse, his eyes all but welding Turner to the spot. *Blast it, I'm here for her, Turner—family!*

As if privy to Logan's thoughts, Andrew faced him with humble respect, a definite apology in his eyes. "But I can see Logan's here now, so I'll just head out." He reached for his hat, then nodded to Logan as he approached Cait. "I'll call you tomorrow," he said quietly, "unless, of course, you'd like me to bring dinner from The St. Francis in lieu of dining out?" She shook her head vehemently, and he nodded, fingering the nubby brim of his hat. "All right then, Cait." Gaze flicking to Logan and back, he bent to brush a light kiss to her cheek before making his way to the door. "Good night."

Neither Logan nor Cait responded, as stiff as ice until they heard the final click of the front door. Bowing her head, Cait put a hand to her eyes, voice raspy with pain. "I'm so sorry, Logan. I thought he had gone."

Hands to her shoulders, he gently turned her to face him. "It's all right, Cait, I've had almost two months to accept that Andrew is a part of your life now, as difficult as it's been."

The green eyes welled with tears, and she nodded, allowing

him to usher her to the sofa where he sat down beside her. She took the handkerchief he offered and dabbed at her eyes. "I hope you know, Logan, that I never meant to hurt you."

"I know," he said, unable to keep the grief from his tone. "But that's what happens when two people love each other as much as we do."

His heart seized when a sob broke from her lips and she thrust herself in his arms, her body shuddering them both as he cocooned her close to his heart. "Oh, I . . . d-do, Logan . . . m-more than you w-will ever know."

A sad smile lined his lips while he stroked her hair, chest cramping at the scent of lavender and clove that evoked a lifetime of memories. Drawing in a deep breath, he braced himself for the words he was afraid to hear. "What's on your mind, Cait?" he whispered, not really wanting to know and hardly ready to hear, but hoping to purge her pain. He forced a levity he didn't feel. "Give it to me straight, Mrs. McClare. I'm a big boy—I can take it."

She only sobbed all the harder, so he let her cry till she was spent, soothing with a tender caress of his palm against her back. When the weeping slowed, he pressed a kiss to her hair and took the handkerchief from her hand to blot the tears before holding it to her nose. "Blow," he said with a shadow of a smile, wishing more than anything he could do this forever—comfort her, protect her, be the man who would love and cherish her all the days of her life.

Sniffing, Cait took the handkerchief and blew her nose again, quite certain she hadn't cried this much in twenty-four hours—or ever—since Liam. Her eyelids shuttered closed when she realized no, that wasn't true. She'd cried for a solid week after Logan had walked out of her life almost two months prior, and she'd been in virtual mourning until she'd accepted Andrew's proposal mere days ago. With very little effort, he'd convinced her once and for all that theirs was a match made in heaven and that he'd loved her from the first moment he'd seen her all those years ago, a starry-eyed girl on the arm of Logan McClare.

"Cait—tell me what's on your mind." His tone, so gentle and kind and almost paternal, unnerved her, because the last thing she wanted to do was to hurt the man she loved most in the world. The man she would sacrifice everything for. The handkerchief flew to her mouth as another sob broke from her throat.

The man I am sacrificing everything for.

His low chuckle rumbled against her ear when he pulled her back into his arms, hugging tightly before letting go. "As God is my witness, Caitlyn McClare—you are a little girl in a mother and woman's body." The smile remained as he tucked a stray curl over her ear, in total contrast to the painful sobriety in his eyes. "I can't stand to watch you suffer, Cait, so let me make this easy for you." He took both of her hands in his and exhaled a slow, steady breath. "Andrew has asked you to marry him."

Her jaw dropped along with her stomach, which plunged clear to her toes. "You know?" she whispered, palm to her chest to calm the awful thudding of her heart. "But how? Who?"

His mouth slanted. "Mag Johnson, of course, ever the gossip monger. Cornered me after a board meeting, simply 'ecstatic' that Andrew was seen purchasing a diamond ring at Shreve & Co." The smile went flat despite a twinkle in his eyes. "Apparently she was 'absolutely thrilled' to offer congratulations on behalf of my sister-in-law's pending engagement."

Cait covered her mouth with his handkerchief, only this time to hide the seed of a smile. "Oh, Logan, I am so sorry, but you know she's been dying to get her hooks into you forever."

His mouth pursed into a mock scowl. "It's bad enough I have to lose you to Turner, but now rumors will be rampant that I'm back on the market again."

Her heart lurched at his offhanded comment, well aware it might be the answer to her prayers. A dull ache throbbed in her chest. *My prayers for him, certainly, but not for myself . . .*

She fought the urge to stroke his unshaven cheek, apparently having caught him at home on a Saturday evening, before stepping out for a late dinner with any one of a hundred willing women. *One of which might be Jean MacKenna, perhaps?* Her thoughts flitted to the dinner with her children a few days earlier, the one that had confirmed her decision to say yes to Andrew.

"So . . . ," she'd asked as she passed a bowl of shredded cheddar cheese to Alli, her tone as casual as the chili Rosie had prepared for her day off, "how is your Uncle Logan?"

Dead silence ensued before a cacophony of eager conversation erupted around the table, each and every one of her children anxious to talk about the person foremost on their mind.

"Oh, Mother, you wouldn't believe what Uncle Logan has done for Jamie, Jess, and their mother," Alli gushed, obviously hoping to extol her uncle's praises to a mother she silently blamed for ruining their family. She passed the cheese and swooped into her chili with gusto, more sparkle in her eyes than Cait had seen in a while. "The boardinghouse wasn't slated to open till after Christmas due to cost and time needed for refurbishing, was it, Jamie?"

Jamie buttered a Saltine with an off-center smile. "Nope. Not with Blake helping . . ." He popped it into his mouth and grinned. "If that's what you wanna call it."

"Hey!" Blake's hurt tone didn't match the mischief in his eyes. "Can I help it if I was born in the lap of luxury where professionals handled all repairs? Besides," he said with a toss of an oyster cracker high in the air, snapping it with his mouth, "my talents lie in other areas."

Alli slapped his hand when he stole a cracker from her plate. "Yes, annoying women."

He chuckled and popped the cracker in his mouth. "Come on, Al, you know I prefer the term 'toy' to 'annoy.'"

"Blake doesn't annoy me," Maddie said with a slope of tiny brows. "I think he's fun."

"That's because you and he are the same age, sweetheart," Bram said easily, "and a lot alike." He grinned at Blake while he spooned chili into his mouth.

"Shhh . . ." Cassie covered Maddie's ears. "You want to scar the child for life?"

"Blake? With a hammer?" Caitlyn patted the napkin to her lips, resorting to humor to steer the conversation back to Logan without her children knowing how much she missed him. "Does he even know which end is up?"

"No," Jamie said with a smirk, "not at the boardinghouse *nor* at work."

"Funny, Mac." Blake sling-shot an oyster cracker at Jamie with his spoon, slipping his mother a smile that barely deflected the concern in his eyes. "And despite the dig, Mother, it's nice to see you smiling again—it's been a little glum around here the last couple of months."

Caitlyn blinked, the spoon buried deep in her mouth. She swallowed and sighed. *Well, so much for fooling my children.* Opting for more cheese, she sprinkled extra on her chili, determined to ignore Blake's subtle observation. "So . . . what has Logan done for the boardinghouse?" She made an attempt to look as politely interested as possible given the tumbling in her stomach that Logan's name always produced.

"Well, for starters," Meg volunteered, "he's made it possible for my friend Ruby Pearl to leave her job at the Municipal Crib sooner than we hoped, and all because Uncle Logan paid his workmen around the clock."

Cait tried to swallow the chili beans wedged in her throat.

"And," she continued unabated, "he set up a foundation that Jamie's mother will personally oversee, not only to provide job training for needy women but for the purchase and administration of additional boardinghouses as well."

"Oh my." Caitlyn lowered her spoon to her bowl, too overcome to take another bite.

"Yep," Jamie said with no little pride. "He and Mom have been working on this for months now, meeting regularly to ensure everything is handled in the most proficient manner."

Meg grinned at her mother, her face positively radiant. "Isn't that wonderful?"

"I'll say." The glow in Jamie's face rivaled the candles on the table, eyes dancing with excitement like the flames on their wicks. "I've never seen my mother happier, laughing and humming all the time. I can't tell you how grateful I am to my father." He blinked several times, apparently to ward off the mist in his eyes. "Never have I been prouder of anyone in my life than him, and my mother too, of course." His grin lit up the room more than the tapers. "They make quite the pair."

Yes, Jamie—I know . . .

"Cait?"

She caught her breath, Logan's voice jerking her back to the parlour where the die would be cast and their fate settled forever. "I'm sorry, Logan . . . what did you say?"

"I said, I need to hear it from you." There was no humor in

the gray eyes now as they laid her bare, blazing with love and the very faintest glimmer of hope. "Did you say yes?"

Her heart ached inside like it had when she'd lost Liam, as if she were losing Logan too, and she couldn't fight the need to caress his cheek one more time. A woman in love with a man she could not have. Her fingers trembled as they glided the strong line of his jaw, quivered at the touch of dark stubble that shadowed his skin. With sorrow welling in her eyes, she slowly laid her hands in her lap. "I did."

It was as if he'd flinched—although he hadn't—so strong was the shock in his face. Seconds ticked by like thundering heartbeats before he shifted a few inches away, his demeanor retreating to where they both knew it must. A muscle flexed in his cheek as he straightened, the motion separating them from the safe intimacy they'd always shared in the past. The polite lift of his chin could have been a courtroom maneuver save the cleft that darkened with beard too long from a razor. "So . . . have you set a date?"

She stared, amazed at his sense of calm when her heart lay shattered in pieces. "No, b-but we've . . . talked about the Saturday after Thanksgiving," she whispered, the words reluctant to leave her tongue. Unable to meet his eyes, she lowered her gaze to her lap while she absently picked at her nails. "He . . . doesn't want to wait."

His heavy sigh broke the awful silence. "Well, whatever faults I've laid at Andrew's door, stupidity has never been one. Congratulations, Cait—I wish you both well."

Her gaze jerked up, her body stunned over his almost casual acceptance of the path she'd chosen. "Thank you, Logan," she whispered, eyes awash with tears. "You have no idea how very much that means to me . . . and to Andrew."

One side of his mouth tipped. "Yes, well, I'm not doing it for Andrew, I'm doing it for you and this family." He chafed the back of his neck, his smile dry. "And for me, I suppose." His eyes met hers, suddenly solemn and so very tender. "I can't live without you, Cait, and if that means loving you as a sister-in-law like I did with Liam, then so be it. This is God's decision, not mine." His eyes narrowed while his jaw began to grind ever so slightly. "But if Turner thinks I'm out of your life, he's dead wrong. We are the very deepest of friends who share an unbreakable bond, and your new husband will just to have to get used to it. In fact . . ." He adjusted his sleeves with a wicked smile before rising to his feet, tugging her up as well. "I think I'll rather enjoy letting Turner be the one who frets for a change, over how close the woman he loves gets to another man." His embrace was tender but firm before he released her with a soft kiss to her head, his roguish smile going head-to-head with a wink. "And trust me—he will." Inclining his head toward the door, he offered his arm. "Shall we check on our girl, Mrs. McClare?"

Too overcome for words, she nodded dumbly, hardly believing that relief could share a bed with such grief. Taking his arm, she paused, peering up at him with a wonder that bordered on awe. "My heart is broken, Logan, so I don't know how you're doing this with such grace."

A trace of a smile edged his lips, shadowed with sorrow. "You're closer to the mark than you know, Cait, because the truth is, without the grace of God, I couldn't." With a deep inhale, he cradled her hand on his arm, finally releasing it with a heavy sigh. "But I decided if Abraham could do it, so can I."

She halted, squinting up in total surprise. "Bram?"

Logan's smile twisted. "No, an uncle of his a few generations back. You see, he let go and gave it to God, Cait, because it was the right thing to do." He patted her hand, his smile at odds with the regret in his eyes. "But don't let the mood fool you, Mrs. McClare, because sometimes it's nothing more than a front." He inclined his head toward the foyer. "Shall we?"

She nodded, her respect for Logan McClare soaring as high as her love.

The right thing to do.

It was, she knew it, for Jamie and him and maybe even her down the road. Even so, a dull ache throbbed as a question remained.

Then why did it feel so wrong?

31

She'll be right down, Bram. Would you like coffee or tea?"

Hunched on the sofa with head in his hands, Bram glanced up as Caitlyn McClare entered the parlour, the dark circles under her eyes not much better than his. He rose, sliding sweaty palms against his charcoal suit pants despite the cooler temperatures that prevailed. "No, thank you, Mrs. McClare—I can't stay long, but I need to see Meg." He searched her face for any sign of a problem. "How is she?"

"Well, she's still pretty shaken, a little sore, and sporting a few bruises, of course, and certainly not willing to step foot in a sailboat anytime soon . . ." She issued an unsteady sigh, offering a half smile as she gave him a hug. "But Doc Miller claims she'll make a full recovery."

Bram's eyelids shuttered closed. *Well, that makes one of us . . .*

Pulling back, she held his arms, affection brimming along with a few tears. "You have always been a godsend to our family, Bram, but never more so than now."

Heat circled his collar at the discomfort of her praise. Not with what he was about to do. "I assure you, Mrs. McClare, the feeling is more than mutual. I love M-Meg too," he said in a halting manner, heat blasting his cheeks at the way it had sounded.

Like a man in love.

He plunged his hands in his pockets, desperately wanting to see Meg, but wishing with everything in him that it was already over. "As a big brother and mentor, of course."

She paused, the almond shape of her eyes thinning a hair, slight enough most people mightn't have noticed. But Bram was so gun-shy about Meg right now, heat tracked up the back of his neck. Her eyes softened with a shy grin. "Of course. I just wish your positive influence had rubbed off on Blake as well, but I suppose there's always hope with you as his friend."

That brought a smile to his face as he scratched at his temple, grateful for the humor that helped loosen his nerves. "Well, not much, Mrs. McClare, but I am a prayerful man."

Her grin mellowed into a quiet smile. "I know," she said softly, "and therein lies one of my greatest comforts."

"Bram!" Meg was little more than a blur as she dashed into the parlour and flung herself toward him. With a tiny gasp, she lunged back, fingers clenched to his arms. "Wait—you're not hurt anywhere, are you? You know, too sore to hug?"

He managed a chuckle, the sound muffled in her hair as he drew her close. "No, Bug, the only thing sore on me is my pride." The familiar scent of violets caused his heart to stutter, followed by a keen stab of regret. Desperate to return to big-brother mode, he patted her shoulder and pulled away, grateful Mrs. McClare had left them alone. "I should have never put you at risk like that, sailing during questionable weather."

"It wasn't questionable when we left," she said, her green eyes probing his. "So you can't blame yourself, especially when I coerced *you* to stay out against your will, remember?"

Against my will. A theme of late.

He expelled a heavy blast of air, his tone laced with regret. "Bug . . . we need to tal—"

"No . . ." She backed away before he could even loose the word from his tongue, shaking her head. "Don't do this, Bram," she whispered, voice hoarse as she rushed to close the double burlwood doors. Whirling around, she hurried back to tug him down on the sofa, panic flaring her eyes. She crushed his hands in hers. "Don't push me away . . ."

Body stiffening, he carefully untangled his fingers from hers and palmed her cheek instead, like the near brother he intended to be. "I'm not pushing you away, Bug," he said in the soothing tone he'd always reserved for skinned knees and hurt feelings.

"You are!" she cried, shocking him when she wrenched his hand from her face to clutch it to her chest. Panic swam in her eyes. "You kissed me, Bram—deeply—when you thought you'd lost me."

His face flamed hotter than the fire in the hearth. "Yes, but with 'deep' gratitude only—"

"Horse apples!" she bellowed, borrowing a pet phrase from Cassie. She leaned in, tears sparking her eyes. "I knew this would happen, I knew you'd deny the attraction—"

He shot to his feet. "We are *not* having this conversation, Bug—" He made a move for Logan's favorite chair a few feet away.

"Oh, yes we are!" she said loudly, seizing his arm to jerk him back around. She caught her breath, brows rising in shock when she realized what she'd done. "I . . . I . . . m-mean, we *are*, Bram," she stuttered, obviously as startled as he at a volatile outburst more indicative of Alli than her. Her lower lip trembled, and Bram knew he was a goner when more tears welled in her eyes. "You have never lied to me once, Abraham Hughes, so please tell me you're not going to start now . . ."

Stifling a groan, he pinched the bridge of his nose before meeting her gaze. "All right, Meg," he said quietly, "you win." With a gentle hook of her arm, he seated her on the sofa and perched beside her, head in his hands. "Yes, I did kiss you deeply, but I wasn't lying about my deep gratitude as a primary motivator because it was. But then . . ." He tunneled fingers through his hair, unable to muzzle the groan this time. "I . . . suddenly realized if I lost you, my life would never be the same and my . . . *gratitude* . . . got the best of me."

"Your '*gratitude*,'" she whispered, a hint of sarcasm threading her tone.

He opted for a show of authority, tone firm as he kneaded his temples. "Yes, my gratitude, young lady. A deluge of humble thanksgiving that may have *possibly* had a drop or two of . . ." He exhaled a shaky sigh. "Attraction."

Her soft giggle melted his heart. "A drop or two?"

He forced a sober tone, determined to nip this in the bud. "It doesn't matter, Bug, I was a fool for letting my emotions get away from me when we both know it can never be."

"Why?" It was a frail question, posed by a woman he no longer saw as a little girl.

"You know why," he said softly, finally meeting her gaze. "I told you when you came home from Paris that attraction is not the problem, Meg—it's simply a matter of what's meant to be." He eased away, straightening his coat to give his hands something to do. "Which means you and I can never be—that way—together."

"Because of Amelia," she whispered. She paused to swallow hard. "Do you . . . love her?"

"I love my father," he emphasized with a dip of his head, eyeing her with a pointed gaze. "Amelia's a wonderful girl, but I'm not in love with her." His inhale was shaky. "It's simply a debt that I owe."

She peered up with troubled eyes. "What debt?"

The oxygen stalled in his lungs before it finally escaped in one long surrender of air. It was time, he realized. Time to confess to someone other than God just what a failure he'd been as a son. Mauling his face with his hand, he finally rested his head on the back of the sofa, gaze lagging into a cold stare. "I'm not the noble and good person you think I am," he said quietly. "At least not when I was a young man."

"I don't understand—what do you mean?"

His eyelids clamped shut, all the memories whooshing back like those turbulent waves that had splintered his sloop into hundreds of jagged pieces. Shattering all hope and promise.

Just like he'd done to his father.

"I mean," he said in a halting tone riddled with grief, "it's because of me"—he squeezed his eyelids tighter, as if he could somehow block out the horrific guilt that lived in his mind—"my father is in poor health and . . . almost blind."

Her gasp was like a physical blow, driving the shame that much deeper into his soul. Avoiding her eyes for fear of the revulsion he might see, he forged on, unyielding in his quest to unveil the truth for the woman who needed it most. "You see, before I became a part of your family, Meg, I was a lost soul, destroyed by bitterness over the death of my sister."

"Yes, Ruthy—I remember," she whispered. "She died of bronchitis at the age of six—"

A harsh laugh broke from his lips that sounded nothing like him at all. "Or so the death certificate said."

"I . . . don't understand . . ."

He turned to her, face sculpted in stone so no tears could escape. "She didn't die of bronchitis, Meg—she died of an overdose."

Her breath caught in a harsh inhale. "Wh-what? What do you mean?"

There was no turning back. No cushioning the blow. Meg—
more than anyone now—needed to know. He steeled his jaw, but
it did nothing to quell the quiver of his voice. "I mean I killed
my sister when I gave her too much medicine while she was in
my care." His head listed forward, heavy with the weight of his
grief as he labored on. "I was only eleven, but my parents trusted
me—'a responsible boy,' they always said, wise beyond my years."
His glossy gaze trailed into the past, seeing his tiny sister deathly
pale in the bed, crying because her throat hurt, raw from coughing up blood. "Pop was at work and Mom went to bed with a
migraine, and I only wanted to help." An involuntary shudder
twitched his body as he bit back a heave, water welling until he
could see nothing but his guilt. "We gave her cough medicine
to help ease the pain of her cough, only I didn't know it was an
opiate," he whispered in a broken voice, "didn't know it could kill
her . . ." His eyes glazed into the past, to where a boy sobbed as
he rocked his baby sister, limp in his arms.

"Oh, Bram . . ." Meg tried to hug him, but he warded her off.

"No, let me finish—you need to understand the debt that I
owe." Rising to collect himself, he paced several feet away to blot
a handkerchief to his face, only returning to the sofa when he was
composed enough to continue. "My parents were devastated, of
course, and our close-knit family, destroyed. My father treated me
differently after that—critical, harsh, riding me hard—so I knew
he was angry at me." Bram laughed, his voice brittle. "Dash it all,
Meg, I was angry too—at myself, at my parents for leaving an
eleven-year-old with a sick little sister, even at the blasted Doctor's
Best Company for marketing their confounded cough syrup."

He jumped up, too restless to sit. His facial muscles ached
from the strain of reliving this nightmare while he continued to
pace. "So I stayed away from home as much as I could from age

eleven to fifteen. Fell in with a group of older boys—hoodlums all." He paused midstride, mouth thinning into a caustic smile. "And believe me, they gladly welcomed an angry rich kid with pockets deep enough to buy them booze and smokes and a brothel or two." He hung his head, dazed at the memory, his diatribe trailing into a lifeless whisper. "Especially a kid who would steal from his parents."

The soft catch of her breath made him feel like the lowest of low. He put a hand to his eyes, guilt racking his soul. *And I was.*

"Oh, Bram . . . I'm so sor—"

His head jerked up as he pierced her with tragic eyes. "I know, Meg, but *please*—just listen and let me get this all out." Needing his space, he moved to the front window, welcoming the cool sea air on his face. Beyond the billowing sheers, seagulls screeched and cable cars clanged as children's laughter sailed high on the breeze. Outside all was at peace with the world while inside the horror remained in his mind.

But not for long.

He turned, his glossy gaze meeting Meg's from across the room. "I'm responsible for my father being robbed that night," he whispered, almost hoping she hadn't heard.

But the proof came in a feeble cry as her hand flew to her mouth.

And yet—somehow—his shoulders felt lighter, his guilt less cumbersome than before, and moisture swelled beneath his lids. Because he knew, in God's eyes if no one else's, he was a man redeemed by a humble carpenter from Nazareth who had given His all. A man who had lain His life down so Bram could be free. A Son who'd sacrificed His will for His Father's.

Just like Bram hoped to do for his.

And the woman I love.

His voice droned on. "One might argue I was no more than a child, embittered and broken by life, exploited and coerced, and I suppose I was. But I was also completely aware. You see, my father had cut off my funds, forbidding me to see my so-called friends. But I knew where the safe was hidden in my father's study, knew my father kept payroll there on Thursday evenings." He swallowed the bile that rose in his throat. "Knew where he'd hidden the combination should Mother and I ever need to know." Bram sank down on the love seat across from the sofa, his father's image filling his thoughts. An image of a man he thought he hated, but one who had earned his respect that awful day. He hung his head.

And every day since.

"I'd been particularly angry that night, drinking more than I could handle." Bram squeezed his eyes shut. "Enough to rail against my father to the others, threatening to steal the allowance he owed. And enough to unwittingly divulge about the safe, apparently." His laugh was acidic, his words as painful as a deathbed confession. "An angry boy, too stupid and too drunk to know my hooligan friends had wheedled the hiding place from me before I passed out."

A shudder spasmed through his body, rattling his soul. "They woke me when the deed was done," he whispered, "telling me to go home . . ." His voice broke, along with the grief in his heart. "That's when I . . . f-found him . . . in a p-pool of blood." He put a trembling hand to his face while repentance flowed from his eyes. "A brave man, a good man, who—unlike his son at the time—battled injustice no matter the cost. And he did, paying the price with his sight and his health."

"H-how . . . ?" The shocked disbelief in Meg's voice seemed no more than a distant echo, but he heard it nonetheless, the same word he'd asked himself over and over since he'd discovered his father facedown on the crimson-stained floor.

How could a son do this to his father?

How could a man fight no matter the cost?

How could a father forgive in the face of evil?

Bram's throat worked hard, fighting the shame that threatened to strangle his words. "In the . . . fight that ensued, my father sustained a blunt trauma to the back of the head, resulting in cortical blindness . . ." His voice choked. "And then a . . . knife w-wound to the upper chest, which j-just missed his heart." He exhaled and bowed his head. "He's been diagnosed with what the doctors call secondary spontaneous pneumothoraces—decreased lung reserve, shortness of breath, and chest pain."

"Oh, Bram . . ."

He looked up then, craving to hold Meg in his arms, to allow her sweet balm to heal his heart like he'd tried to do for her over the years. But that wasn't to be. Not when he had a debt to pay. He recharged with another intake of air. "My father's an astute businessman, Meg, so despite his blindness and increasingly frail health, his shipping business hadn't suffered. Not until he lost several ships in a typhoon a few years back." His heart twisted as always over the tragedies his father had faced. *And survived.*

"But I had no idea the true extent of his debts—that bank-ruptcy loomed—not until I had lunch with an old friend who works at my father's bank." He girded himself against a shiver. "Because you see, Meg, my parents would never tell me, would never inflict guilt on a son who'd chosen his own path as a lawyer. A selfish son who had no interest in joining ranks with his father in a business where he was desperately needed."

There. It was finally out.

The reason he could never love Meg the way that he longed.

For the first time since she'd entered the room, Bram felt a pinprick of peace. A tiny fleck of hope. A resolve that he and the woman before him could someday soon be nothing more than friends. "I asked Amelia to marry me this morning before I came over here," he whispered, his eyes fused to hers. "Not because I love her, Meg, but because I love my father. Because you see—his health, his fortune—ride on this marriage, and I simply cannot let him down once again."

From across the room, he saw those green eyes crest with tears, but even so, he held his ground, keeping his distance. The season for comfort and open arms had ended. At least until they both could put these feelings behind. Before "the kiss" had been difficult enough, but now, it'd be excruciating, and Bram had no desire to inflict further pain on Meg or himself. To his logical, legal mind, he saw only one recourse, and somewhere in the vile gloom of night, he'd decided to take it. "I plan to stay away for a while, not because I want to, but because I need to."

Her body flinched as if he had struck her, but he pressed on. "It's for the best, Meg, trust me, and it won't be forever. Amelia and I need time to get on with our lives, and you need time to get on with yours." He paused, ignoring the wrench of his gut when two tiny tears slithered down her cheeks. "Andrew seems to think highly of Devin, and I think highly of Andrew—he's a godly man and pillar of our community—so I think you can trust his judgment. I'd like to think he and Devin are cut from the same cloth, so I hope you give him a chance." He leaned in, his gaze bonded to hers. "Court him, Meg, get to know him, and see where it takes you, but one way or another, I believe God has a wonderful man who'll love and cherish you all the days of your life."

Meg furiously blinked back her tears, suddenly unable to breathe. *Yes, I know . . . but he plans to marry somebody else.* Panic struck, whether from the heartbreak that fisted in her chest or the emotions that swelled in her throat—either way, neither air nor sound could pass.

He paused, brows knit tight. "Meg? Are you all right . . . ?"

No. "W-will . . . you come . . . for Th-thanksgiving?" she whispered, the words halting and heavy with heartache, unable to imagine a holiday without him.

He hesitated, and she knew from the ridges that furrowed his brow just what his answer would be. "My parents will be expecting me to have Thanksgiving with them . . . at the Darlingtons'."

"But you've always eaten with them at three and come here at seven—"

"Not this year," he said quietly, voice strained.

Her eyelids flickered, lips parting to emit shallow breaths like a fish out of water, goggle-eyed by unfamiliar surroundings. She pressed a hand to her temple as if that might dispel the dizzy whirl in her brain, but to no avail. Her body began to tremble as utter agony clawed in her chest, and desperate for composure, she valiantly fought it back, the worry in Bram's face swimming into a blur. It wasn't until a guttural sob broke from her throat that she knew she'd failed, and with a siege of painful heaves, she crumpled onto the sofa.

"Aw, Bug," he whispered, gathering her in his arms and stroking her hair, "I will always love you, and someday—soon—our friendship will be restored."

"N-no," she whispered, head lagging side to side, "you've always been there, Bram, and I can't imagine my life without you."

He swept a stray curl back before skimming the line of her jaw with the pad of his thumb. "You won't have to—I'll always be there, in my love and in my prayers, and soon," he ducked to offer a smile, caressing every inch of her face with his eyes, "this torment between us will fade into a timeless friendship that will bring us—and our families—much joy." Pressing a lingering kiss to her hair, he kneaded her shoulder as he slowly rose to his feet, pausing to tuck a gentle finger to her chin. "I want you to know, Megan Maureen McClare, that I love you and I will storm heaven night and day for God to give you the desire of your heart." A sheen of moisture glimmered in his eyes. "And His."

"Even if it's you?" she whispered, peering up with eyes rimmed raw.

He stared, all the tragedy of their love stark and naked in his eyes. A muscle convulsed in his throat. "Especially if it's me."

32

THREE MONTHS LATER

"Oh, Bonnie, I just love this time of year, don't you?" Flinging her red plaid woolen scarf around her neck, Meg buttoned her taupe moleskin coat with one hand while burying her nose in a bouquet of mums with the other. She closed her eyes to better enjoy the crisp, woodsy scent of fall from the gold, scarlet, and burnt-orange blooms Devin delivered just moments ago. Back in school again, he often dropped by the office after college classes to "chat with the working stiffs," he said. *Including* Meg, who'd accepted Andrew's extension of her internship until January, when her Cooper Medical internship began. Husky male laughter laced with Linda Marie's sultry giggle drifted into the conference room from Andrew's office where the group was celebrating the onset of a four-day Thanksgiving holiday.

Bonnie's rose-tinted lips quirked off center, her gaze warm with affection. "I do, although I can see how attending your mother's magical wedding over Thanksgiving weekend—with a handsome man you're courting, no less—just might make it a wee bit better." Sobriety tempered her smile. "And *nobody* deserves it more than you, my friend." She dipped her head, compassion soft in her eyes. "That beautiful smile has been far too scarce the last three months."

At Bonnie's words, the so-called beautiful smile faltered a tad before Meg thrust her chin high in an uncharacteristic show of bravado. "Yes, it has," she said, giving the flowers a rather decisive sniff. "But my period of mourning over Mr. Bram Hughes is over, you will be happy to know, and I've resolved to turn over a new 'leaf,' as appropriate for the season." Bouquet in hand, she slung the silver chain of her hinged leather reticule over her shoulder. "It's time I stop mooning around and start enjoying all the blessings I have."

Bonnie pinned her velvet broad-brimmed hat in place with a gleam in her eyes. "Not the least of which are the handsome boss and beau clowning around with the others down the hall." With a dreamy sigh, she buttoned her own black woolen coat, dark brows sloped in longing. "Goodness, talk about fairy-tale romance! Mr. Turner has done nothing but glow since your mother set the wedding date for this Saturday, and Devin Caldwell has been sporting a lovesick look in his eyes ever since you agreed to court three months ago." She peeked down the hall, obviously making sure George wasn't around. "I just wish *someone* else would follow their lead."

"He will," Meg soothed. Turning out the light, she followed Bonnie down the hall, grateful for the four-day weekend Andrew had graciously given them all. "You're making great strides. Why, I think he spends more time at your desk than you, doesn't he? And he *did* ask you to assist him in purchasing his sister's birthday gift on Friday, did he not?"

Bonnie glanced over her shoulder, a silly grin on her face. "Yes and yes!" A tiny giggle slipped out. "Thanks for the reminder. I guess I do have a few blessings of my own, don't I?" They paused at Andrew's open door, both grinning outright at a combative game of darts in progress.

"Who's winning?" Meg asked, scanning the faces with a smile.

"Why, the man you adore, of course," Devin said with a grand bow, jacket off and shirtsleeves rolled. He quickly abandoned the game to hook an arm to Meg's waist, sliding her a wink. "So, what's my prize, Miss McClare?"

"The back of your hand if you're smart, Meggie girl," Conor called, squinting at the dartboard before he sailed the point dead center.

"Care to join us, ladies?" Andrew sat comfortably perched on the edge of his desk, a coffee cup hoisted in invitation. "Linda Marie could use some moral support against these ruffians."

"And I can walk you home after," Devin insisted.

"I wish I could," Meg said, the jovial camaraderie of her co-workers a powerful temptation. "But I promised to meet someone on my way home."

"Uh-oh, Dev . . . a tryst with another beau, perhaps?" Linda Marie arched a brow, tucked between George and Teddy on the large leather couch Andrew utilized for catnaps during late nights at work.

"Hardly, Miss Finn," Devin said. He lifted Meg's hand to his lips, the tease in his tone tempered by a smoldering look he usually kept at bay. "I can vouch from personal experience that Miss McClare is moral to a fault."

Cheeks hot, Meg whirled around, eyeing her best friend. "But Bonnie can stay, can't you?"

Bonnie's eyes circled wide, generally too shy to join after-hour gab fests. "Uh . . . uh . . ."

"Come on, Bonnie." Conor elbowed George while giving Teddy a wink. "George'll walk you home, won't you, Boss?"

George's narrow face flushed scarlet, which made Teddy's normally pink complexion pale by comparison. "Uh . . . uh . . ."

Andrew chuckled, eyes twinkling over the rim of his coffee as he took a sip. "In case you're not fluent, Miss Roof, that's assistant district attorney talk for 'yes,' so I hope you'll join us." He glanced at his watch. "Trust me, one more game, and I'll be sending everyone packing since I need to stay a little late anyway to make up for a honeymoon." He gave Megan a wink. "That is if I can keep my mind on work rather than succumbing to the urge to visit my fiancée." His gaze flicked to Bonnie. "So, what do you say, Bonnie?"

Bonnie peeked at Meg out of the corner of her eye. "Should I?" she whispered, as if she didn't think anybody else could hear.

"Oh, take your coat off, Bonnie." Linda Marie's smile was coy. "These boys won't bite—much."

Meg grinned. "Have fun," she whispered to her friend, giving a wave to everyone else. "Happy Thanksgiving, all—see you at the wedding." She slipped Devin and Andrew a smile. "And I'll see *you* two gentlemen tomorrow night for the best turkey and dressing you will ever taste."

"Count on it," Devin said.

Andrew glanced over his shoulder into Portsmouth Square, where a pale sun hovered over a horizon of mostly bare trees, indicating about an hour and a half till sunset. He turned, eyes narrowed in concern. "You'll be home before dark, right?" he asked, his paternal instincts making her smile.

"Yes, sir, I promise."

Devin began unrolling his sleeves. "Nope, that's it—I'm walking you home." He buttoned his cuffs and reached for his coat.

"No!" Palm raised, Meg offered her sweetest smile. "You're having way too much fun, Dev, and I promised Mother and Rosie I'd help with Thanksgiving preparations tonight, including my famous peach cobbler, so I'll be home long before dark, truly."

360

He paused, clearly torn, coat dangling in hand.

Andrew rose and slapped him on the back. "Come on, Dev, give the woman a night off. You can't monopolize all her time." He grinned, a sparkle in blue eyes aimed right at Megan. "Something I learned the hard way with her mother."

Devin paused, finally tossing his coat over the chair. "All right, Meg, but at least I can walk you to the elevator."

"Dev, that isn't necessary, really—"

"I want to," he said quietly, tugging her through the waiting room and out into the dim hallway. He gave her hand a light squeeze before pressing the button for the elevator. Hooking her waist, he slowly reeled her in, the desire in his eyes quickening her pulse. "I'm crazy about you, Megan McClare, you know that?"

"I . . . care for you too, Dev," she whispered, the groan and grind of elevator gears and pulleys unable to drown out the throb of blood in her ears.

His thumb grazed the edge of her jaw, gliding to fondle the cleft of her chin before skimming the curve of her lips, his eyes following the motion. She could hear his shallow breathing when his gaze met hers. "No other girl makes me feel the way you do, Meg—crazy, delirious, jealous." His Adam's apple ducked as his gaze skipped to her lips. "Heaven help me, Meg, I'm in love with you," he whispered, bending to slowly brush his mouth against hers while he drew her in, his passion climbing as the seconds ticked by.

The elevator doors squealed open and Devin jerked away with a low groan, chest pumping as he slashed a hand through his hair. "Holy thunder, woman, do you have any idea just how hard it is not to kiss the daylights out of you?"

She stared, her breathing as ragged as his. "I think so," she whispered, throat dry at how Devin had just made her feel. In all the time they'd spent together, he'd honored his pledge to keep his distance, with only a kiss on the cheek at the door. But this? Meg's eyes flickered closed. This might just work, she suddenly realized—Devin and her, the key to erasing thoughts of Bram from her soul.

"You're not mad, are you?"

She opened her eyes and smiled. "No."

He expelled a heavy sigh. "Let me walk you home—please?"

"No," she said with a palm to his face. "Go. Have fun with our friends, and I'll see you tomorrow, all right?"

His chest rose and fell. "Okay." He pressed a tender kiss to her forehead, then pulled her close. "As sure as I breathe, Megan McClare, some day you will be my wife."

She grinned. "A distinct possibility, Mr. Caldwell." Standing on tiptoe, she deposited a kiss to his cheek, then stepped into the elevator with a smile. "Now go take Conor down a peg or two." She scrunched her nose before the doors rattled closed. "He's a little too cocky to suit."

Pulse surging, Meg literally leapt from the cable car before it screeched to a stop, bounding toward Ruby Pearl, who waited on a rickety bench outside the Barbary Volunteer Legal Services. "Ruby, I've missed you!" she squealed, crushing the frail young woman in a tight hug before pulling back with a grin, hands clutched to the sleeves of Ruby's paper-thin jacket. Her heart suddenly cramped when she realized Ruby wore neither hat nor gloves, her delicate ears as cherry red as her nose.

"Oh, Ruby, why didn't you wait inside?" Meg jerked off her woolen scarf and wrapped it around Ruby's neck, heartsick she hadn't suggested a meeting spot closer to where the young woman lived. "Thank you for coming, my friend, and I hope to make it worth your while." Meg quickly ushered her into the office, the warmth of a blazing potbelly stove a welcome sight.

Rising from her battered desk, Jamie's sister Jess hurried around to give Meg a sound hug. "Goodness, Meg, what are you doing out on a raw day like this?"

"Ruby and I decided to meet here because I have a present for her." Hooking Ruby's arm, Meg drew her forward. "You remember Ruby, don't you, Jess? I introduced you two about five months ago after we asked Jamie to put Ruby on the boarding-house list."

"Yes, of course." Jess embraced Ruby and stepped back with the flash of a perfect smile, one ebony curl dangling by her ear. "We were able to provide medical care for your little Charlie when he broke his arm. How is he doing?"

A rare joy softened the haggard look of Ruby's face. "Oh, he's fine, Miss Jess, and his arm appears good as new."

Jess chuckled and gave Ruby's back a pat. "That's wonderful." She paused, hazel eyes glimmering like gold. "And guess what else is wonderful?" She wiggled perfectly shaped brows, then clapped her hands together. "We're all ready for you and Charlie to move in tomorrow!"

Tears pooled in Ruby's eyes, causing an ache in Meg's chest. Lips trembling, Ruby flung herself into Meg's arms. "Oh, M-Miss Meg, y-you told me there's a God, and now I know it's true!" She pulled away, a beautiful glow in her face that seemed to transform her before Meg's very eyes. With a catch of her breath, Meg suddenly realized why.

Hope.

Ruby pushed the tears from her cheek and grinned, pumping Meg's hand like she was drawing water from a well. "Because if there's angels like you and Miss Jess on this here earth, then there's sure in heaven gotta be a God who sent you."

Meg grinned, her eyes as soggy as Jess's. Rifling through her purse, she held up a shiny brass key and envelope. "This, my friend, is the brand-new key to your very own room at the equally brand-new MacKenna Boardinghouse. And this," she said, waving the envelope, "is a stipend for a new wardrobe for Charlie and you when he goes to school and you go to work."

The hope in Ruby's eyes dimmed. "But I ain't never had a respectable job, Miss Meg, so I'm not real sure—"

Meg gripped her hand, halting her midsentence. "Well, I am, because not only will you receive all your meals and necessities from Miss Jean until you can pay your own rent, but you'll also receive training for a job of your choice."

Ruby blinked, the motion scattering more tears down her cheeks. "Oh, God bless you, all," she whispered. "I don't know how to repay your kindness . . ."

Moisture pricked as Meg gave her a hug. "Seeing you and Charlie happy is payment enough, my friend." The rickety clock on the wall chimed the hour and Meg glanced up with a start. "Uh-oh, I promised Mother I'd help with preparations, so I need to scoot."

"Wait!" Ruby stopped her, and for the first time, Meg noticed a small gunny sack looped over her friend's arm, out of which she drew a package wrapped in newspaper and string. She pushed it into Meg's hand.

"What's this, a gift?" Meg took the offering, a pucker between her brows. "Oh, Ruby, I hope you didn't spend any money on me."

Ruby ducked her head. "No, ma'am, it's something I made myself, and it's not much, Miss Meg—just a little something for all you've done for Charlie and me."

Meg weighed it in her hand. "Mmm . . . not too heavy, so hopefully you didn't spend too much time, my sweet friend." She started to untie the knot, and Ruby stopped her. "No, open it at home, Miss Meg. The cable car just stopped, so you need to hurry if your mama's waiting."

Meg glanced out the window. "Oh dear, I do need to go." With a quick hug for both girls, she rushed to the door, wagging a finger at Ruby. "But I'm coming to the boardinghouse next week to check on you, Miss Pearl, do you hear? And I plan to take you shopping and treat you to lunch, no argument. Happy Thanksgiving to you both."

Closing the door, Meg dashed to the cable car, head bent against the cold, but heart warm over the joy on Ruby's face. She handed her money to the driver and found an inside seat where she snuggled in to study the package in her lap. Curiosity got the best of her, and she tugged at the string. Peeling the newspaper away, she found a handwritten booklet bound together with more twine and a letter on top:

Dear Miss Meg,

Nobody has ever treated me with respect and kindness like you, so I prayed to God just like you told me, begging Him for some way to say thank you. And then one night when I was saying good night prayers with my boy, I remembered you said something about your mama being on the Vigilance Committee and wanting to shut down the brothels in the Coast. That's when the Lord gave me an idea. It's taken five months, but I copied the client log for the Municipal Crib a little bit each day while the owner was out for lunch. Then last month, I discovered a hidden ledger of payments, most to names I don't recognize except for two. I pray these names will help you and

*your mama do God's work. Please keep this list safe and never
mention my name.*

Sincerely,
Your grateful friend

Meg's breathing was shallow and fast by the time she finished
Ruby's note, and with quivering fingers, she slowly turned the
page, eyes skimming the log of dates, times, services, and names.
Page after page of vile transactions that caused Meg's lunch
to roil in her stomach. Until she came to the section labeled
"Payments to Investors." Body trembling, she scanned top to
bottom, entry after entry, last names and initials only. Her body
went numb.

E. Schmitz

A. Ruef

Chest in a vice, Meg tried to breathe, but air wouldn't come.
Her eyelids flickered in spasm before they sealed tight, trying to
shut out the awful truth burning in her mind.

Eugene Schmitz and Abe Ruef.

The mayor and his political boss.

Bile rose in her throat as shock waves rolled through her body.
The mayor of San Francisco and his political boss—investors in
the most evil scourge on the city.

Clang, clang, clang!

Meg's thoughts jolted back to the frigid cable car, gaze darting out the window while her mind strained to determine just
exactly where she was. "I have to tell somebody," she whispered,
heart hammering as she stumbled to her feet. She yanked the
cord with all of her might while her chaotic thoughts crystallized
into only one.

I have to tell Andrew!

Clutching the book to her chest, she flew down the step while the car still slowed on the rails, running blocks until she had a stitch in her side. Muscles twitching, she stopped to catch her breath, lungs about to burst. She peered down the next block where the pink and purple shadows of dusk were just beginning to cloak Portsmouth Square. *Please, God, let Andrew be there . . .* She picked up her pace and sprinted hard, gaze glued to the second window on the second story of the Hall of Justice, where a dim light shone. With a final burst of energy, she took the front steps three at a time, bolting into the lobby to where the elevator stood open. Despite the chill of the day, sweat beaded the back of her neck as she rode up to the second floor, and when the doors parted, relief flooded at the glow of a faint light beyond the bubbled glass door. Gasping for air, she turned the knob and groaned when it jiggled in her hand.

Locked!

Palms damp, she fished a key from her purse, the one Andrew had given her and Devin for the nights they worked late. She held her breath as she eased it in, grateful when the door wheeled open. The light from the kitchen area beckoned and she darted down the hall, skidding to a stop before Andrew's closed door. A muffled groan sounded, and ear to the wood, alarm coiled in her belly at the rasp of another. She had visions of Andrew sick or even bleeding on the floor from an accidental fall. Her pulse throbbed in her ears as she banged on the door, hysteria all but strangling the words in her throat. "Andrew? Are you all right?"

Ice slithered down her spine at the hiss of a curse, and heart in her throat, she heaved the door wide, eyes squinting to adjust to the shadowy light. "Andrew? Where are—"

She froze with a violent heave as if she'd been shot.

No air.

367

No pulse.

No sound save the ragged breathing of two people on a couch. Shirts untucked and clothes disheveled.

"Meg . . ." Her name issued forth on a broken groan. "What are you doing here?"

She couldn't speak or move, her mind in a stupor while Linda Marie fumbled to straighten her blouse. Tears of horror swelled in Meg's eyes and her muscles began to jerk, limbs like boulders as she slowly backed away.

"Meg, wait!" The male voice was gruff, rattled.

But she didn't. She couldn't.

More curses rent the air as a flurry of motion ensued—someone grappling to put on his shoes, button his shirt. And then Meg—running for her life, stumbling down the stairs, blinded by tears as she bludgeoned through the building's front doors.

Gashes in new-fallen frost followed as she fled across the lawn, and this time, she didn't even feel the stitch in her side. Shades of sunset whorled through the blur of her tears, a macabre kaleidoscope, where betrayal bled within from shards of broken glass. Like a woman who had lost her virtue, Portsmouth Square suddenly changed, the soft blush of day seduced by the sinister hues of night as dusk had its way.

Just like Devin.

"No other girl makes me feel the way you do . . ."

She heard his frantic shouts as the cable car pulled away, and then in a whir of the cables, he was left behind, the specter of a pale, broken man growing smaller and smaller in the street until it was all gone, completely stolen away.

Just like her confidence . . .

Not good enough for Devin Caldwell as a child, and apparently not as a woman either.

"For once I've met a girl whose beauty on the inside is so powerful and deep, the surface beauty is almost secondary . . ."

Almost. Meg sobbed. Not nearly close enough.

The cable car jerked and jostled as it climbed the hill to home, and for the first time since she found Devin entangled with Linda Marie, she drew a breath that soothed rather than seared.

Home. Where betrayal didn't exist and virtue shone with the peace of God.

Mother. She caught her breath. *And Andrew? Oh, dear God, please, yes!*

Her frozen fingers suddenly burned beneath the papers in her hands, their feel light, but their truth heavier than Devin's betrayal.

"True confidence blooms in the soil of relationship with God, in following His path rather than one's own, pursuing His truth rather than the world's."

Mrs. Rousseau's words seeped through her mind like healing balm, their warmth thawing the icy shackles around her heart until it burned with the only thing that really mattered.

God's truth.

Her pulse leapt at the sight of Andrew's car parked in front of her house, and with a frantic jerk of the cable-car cord, she hurdled the lone step and hit the pavement hard, streaking up the brick steps to her house as if Satan's demons nipped at her heels.

And maybe they were, because when her foot sank into the familiar crevice of that lone loose brick, her body took flight with a stunned cry, scattering her and her belongings across Mother's slate porch.

And that's when she saw it.

The final sheet of the book, infested with demons wrought by hell. But only one name wrenched the air from her lungs.

A. Turner.

~❧ 33 ❧~

*A*rms clutched to her waist, Caitlyn stared out the weeping windowpanes of the conservatory, every piece awash with endless rivulets of water much like the tears that slithered down her face. All around her, the palms and ficus seemed as stoop-shouldered as she, their limp fronds and leaves drooping with an unrelenting grief as heavy as that which poured from the bleak granite sky.

Hardly a day to celebrate Thanksgiving, she mused, dabbing at her eyes with a handkerchief that was now as soggy as the puddled backyard.

And yet, so very much for which to be grateful . . .

A shiver pebbled her skin that had nothing to do with the plummeting temperatures outside, and she tucked her arms closer to her body even yet, praying that the laudanum she'd given Meg to sleep last night would keep her abed, still peacefully slumbering like the sun apparently, on this truly desolate day. A painful desolation that could hardly be blamed on the weather. No, this desolation would be laid at the foot of something far more unpredictable.

Betrayal.

Bitterness soured her tongue, the taste of betrayal all too familiar. First in the past with Logan, and now in the present with

Andrew. Her lips compressed with a rare stab of anger. A man now relegated to her past as well.

Buffing her arms, she absently wandered the conservatory, wondering why the end of her relationship with Andrew didn't bother her more than it did. In the brief span of two days, she would have been his wife, helpmate, and lover for the rest of her life. And yet, despite her deep feelings for him—or the man she'd believed him to be—and the attraction that had certainly been real, she was almost . . . relieved. She paused at the revelation, stunned at how close she'd come to marrying the wrong man.

Again.

Her eyelids fluttered closed as the breath thinned in her lungs, thoughts of her daughter's pain foremost on her mind. *Oh, Meg!* The gentle and innocent daughter who deserved far more than a man who would lie and cheat. Ire boiled in Cait's chest like a crater about to erupt, few things able to spark her mild temper like someone inflicting pain on her children. No, Meg deserved someone who loved and cherished her, a man who'd protect her all the days of her life. Cait's eyelids lifted with resolve while her lips tamped down.

Someone like Bram.

"Cait? What on earth are you doing back here? It's freezing outside."

She spun around, warm chills replacing cold ones at the sight of Logan standing in the door, his handsome face still ruddy from the nasty weather. "Oh, thank God you're here!" she whispered, rushing to give him a brief hug before quickly stepping away. "I'm sorry to disturb you so early, but thank you for coming at the crack of dawn."

His gaze sharpened, flicking from her tear-mottled face to the sodden handkerchief limp in her hand, and in two powerful thuds of her heart, he stood before her, gripping her arms. "What's wrong?"

Peace instantly purled through her body, as if the warmth of his hands possessed the power to heal all of her hurts and those of her children. "It's Meg," she said, her words quivering despite the calm of his touch. "She found Devin," her voice cracked, ". . . in the arms of another woman."

A questionable word hissed from his lips, and he slashed fingers through the damp hair at the back of his head. "I'm sorry, Cait, but blast it, how is it that my nieces attract so many charlatans and cads who wreak heartbreak and despair?"

Cait battled the tug of a smile, heart swelling as always for this man who loved her children as if they were his own. "Jamie and Nick aren't charlatans and cads," she said softly, taking his arm to lead him to the settee, "although Cassie and Alli certainly met their fair share in the past."

Logan grunted, allowing her to prod him to sit. He hunched on the edge of the seat with that lovable scowl she adored, loose hands clasped over his knees. "I'd say that's an understatement," he muttered, exhaling loudly before he peered at her out of the corner of his eye. "How is she?"

"Heartbroken and in despair, as one would expect." She paused, shifting to face him while she picked at her nails. "But . . . not over Devin."

His gaze narrowed. "What do you mean?"

Cait bit at her lip, praying that between Logan and she, they could find some way to heal her daughter's hurting heart . . . and Bram's. "I mean that after a long bout of tears last night," she said carefully, unwilling to divulge just yet that some of those had belonged to her, "Meg confessed that it's actually Bram she has deep feelings for, not Devin."

Logan's jaw went slack. "Holy thunder," he said, his tone almost reverent. "You mean Meg's in love with Bram as much as he is with her?"

Cait blinked. "How did you know Bram is in love with Meg? Why, Meg herself only suspected it since the boat accident when he implied—"

"Implied nothing," Logan said, underscoring his response with another grunt. "The man is certifiably head over heels because he told me so himself."

The drop of her jaw was at least equal to Logan's. "When?" she breathed, ashamed she'd dismissed suspicion about Bram's true feelings the day he visited Meg after the accident.

Logan's lips took a twist. "After you told me you were planning to see Andrew and I stayed away to lick my wounds." His look was sheepish before it veered into dry. "Bram was delegated by *your* children to guilt me into rejoining the family, as I recall, and in the process I discovered his true feelings for Meg."

Cait pressed a hand to her mouth, Logan's playful barb unleashing a twitch of a smile. She shook her head, the absurdity of the situation confirming her motive for asking Logan to come by before work at the unholy hour of six a.m. It was one thing for Bram to suffer through an arranged marriage to save his father's company, as Meg had woefully explained. But knowing Bram loved her daughter as much as she loved him, well, that was just too heartbreaking to bear. For Bram, for Meg, *and* for her mother! Steel fusing her spine, Cait sat up with a stiff fold of arms. "Well, I for one cannot sit idly by while two people I love are kept apart by something as vile as money. Something has to be done, Logan, to amend this unfortunate situation."

Easing back, he appeared relaxed for the first time, arm draped over the back of the settee. "I agree," he said with a faint smile, head cocked as he studied her through pensive eyes. "Which is why I am now primary shareholder in Hughes Shipping." He gave her a sly wink. "Fifty-one percent, a sight better than old Darlington was willing to go, I can tell you that."

A family of flies could have set up house in the gape of her mouth. "B-But . . . but . . ." She swallowed her shock, the dawn of a smile slowly rising on her lips. "Merciful Providence—Meg implied Bram's father was nearly bankrupt, so that had to cost you a fortune!"

He feigned a scowl. "Well, what else could I do when I was so rudely informed phase two would jeopardize my investments?" He folded his arms. "I sold and reinvested elsewhere."

Her jaw took another tumble. Good heavens, the man may as well have informed her he'd decided to enter a monastery! She blinked, eyelids flickering so fast, she felt the chill of a breeze. "Oh . . . oh . . ." Unable to form a coherent thought, she simply flung herself into his arms. "Oh, Logan, I don't deserve you . . . !"

His chuckle blew warm in her hair. "No, you don't," he said with a gentle knead of her back. He pulled away and cupped her cheek, his tender gaze suddenly devoid of all humor. "You deserve a man you can trust," he whispered, "a man who'll cherish you for the treasure you are."

"Oh, Logan . . ." She bit on her lip to keep it from trembling.

With an awkward pat of her shoulder, he quickly distanced himself to the other side of the settee, throat working while he reached in his coat. "I have to head to the office, Cait, but I have something to give you first." Eyes averted, he handed her a small velvet pouch. "A wedding present, if you will," he said in a gruff tone, "and a symbol of the trust I hope to inspire as your friend." A nerve pulsed in his cheek as his gaze rose to meet hers. "And *only* your friend."

The bag trembled at her touch as she removed the contents inside, a frail gasp parting from her lips. Her fingers quivered as much as her stomach when she held up a man's gold ring emblazoned with a lion and Celtic cross over black onyx—the signet ring passed down from centuries old to the McClare family heir. The very ring Liam had given her when they'd married. Her heart stuttered. And the one she'd pried off her finger when Liam died, reluctantly returning it to the rightful heir. The gleam of gold swirled into glittering black when tears blurred in her eyes. Shaking her head, she handed it back. "No, Logan, this belongs to you—"

His chest expanded with a shaky draw of air before he released it again. "Yes, it does, Cait," he said, taking the ring from her palm. Piercing her with a solemn gaze, he slipped it on her right index finger before she could retract her hand. "But unfortunately for me, my heart belongs to you, so if I can't grace your left hand with my love, then I'd like to grace your right with a friendship just as deep."

She fought the rise of a sob while tears pooled in her eyes like the rain in the yard. "No, Logan, please . . . save this for your wife . . ."

"There won't be a wife, Cait. At least not for a long, long time."

Her rib cage tightened as visions flashed in her mind—Jean in his arms at the Barrister Ball, Jamie's joy over strides his parents were making together on behalf of the poor. She gave a jerky shake of her head, attempting to remove the ring. "No, Logan, really—save it, please. For J-Jean, perhaps? Why, the children tell me you two have been spending quite a bit of time together, and I couldn't be—" the word tripped on her tongue—"h-happier." She tugged on the ring to no avail. "Oh, drat! I can't imagine why it's so tight—it used to swim on my finger."

Logan stilled her agitation with a firm fold, the gentle cup of his palms engulfing her hands in a dangerous heat that traveled her body. "I had it sized and polished for you, Cait," he said with careful deliberation. The command of his tone softened while he fixed her with a solemn stare. "I gave you this ring that night in Napa, when I was too much of a fool to know what I had. Too much of a fool to know that I needed God. So I'm giving it back—not as a pledge to marry this time, but to love you as a friend." A muscle twitched in that strong, chiseled face—a face she had both kissed and slapped too many times to count. With a shift in his throat, he forced a smile, the intensity of his eyes revealing the true depth of his love. "I adore you, Cait, and by the grace of God, I will be the best friend you have ever had, beseeching Him forever to give you the marriage you deserve."

She slumped into a sob, heart aching over the way it had to be. "B-But . . . Jean . . . ," she whispered. "J-Jamie said you make quite the pair, that he's never seen her happier . . ."

He shoved a handkerchief in her hand before skimming her tear-slicked face with his thumb. "That may be, Cait, but I'm not the one putting the smile on her face."

She paused mid-heave, her confusion punctuated by a hiccup. "I . . . I don't understand . . . Jamie says she's laughing and humming all the time, so I just assumed—"

His mouth tipped as he snatched the handkerchief from her hand and blotted her tears. "Thunderation, Cait, assumptions would end my career as a lawyer." The tease in his eyes turned tender. "How many times have I told you they'll just get you in trouble?"

She blinked, feeling like a little girl as he dabbed at her eyes. "So you're not . . . seeing her?"

He issued a grunt as he pocketed the handkerchief. "And risk the ire of my head contractor who's renovating our boardinghouse? I don't think so. The man is dangerously smitten, and I'm pretty sure Jean is taken with him as well." He leaned in with a conspiratorial smile. "But don't tell Jamie—I think she wants to wait till Bruce actually makes a move." Logan shook his head. "Whenever *that* is. When it comes to construction, the man is a bullet, but with women?" He winced. "Let's just say the old Logan could teach him a thing or two."

The old Logan. Her pulse took off in a sprint. *Not nearly as dangerous as the new!*

He rose. "Gotta go, Cait—Jeremiah's coming to the office at eight to set his son free, and I have a few preparations yet to do. *Then* I have to convince Bram that marrying my niece is better than losing his job." He tweaked her neck and made his way to the door. "See you at six."

"Logan, wait!" She shot to her feet, legs suddenly as unsteady as her heart, which floundered in her chest like a fish swimming in spirits. Heart racing, she picked at her nails, arms all but glued to her sides, knowing she needed to tell him about Andrew, but terrified where that might lead. She clutched the edge of the settee to steady the sway of her body.

He turned at the door, eyes in a squint. "Yes?"

Her breathing accelerated as she stared, tremors skittering through her limbs at the striking figure he cut, framed in the door. His charcoal suit and cranberry tie, broad shoulders and chiseled chin—every bit as handsome as the night he proposed some twenty-eight years ago. *No, more so*, she realized, because now the man's heart was as beautiful as his appearance. Fear iced her spine. But could she ever trust him again?

"Trust your heart, Cait, not your fear. Isn't that what Liam always tried to drum into our brains, no matter the situation?"

Logan's words drifted down like a whisper from God. The very words he'd spoken the night Andrew told her Father Caraher wanted to focus on the Marsicania rather than the Municipal Crib. She knew now that that had been a lie—it was Andrew who'd wanted the Municipal Crib off the table, and he'd probably convinced Father Caraher that it was her.

Logan shifted in the door, a wedge popping between dark brows. "Cait?"

She opened her mouth, but nothing came out, her tongue as paralyzed as her mind. Her eyelids fluttered closed while the memory of last week's homily caused her heart to thud. *He that feareth is not made perfect in love.*

"Cait? I'm sorry, but I really do need to go . . ."

Oh, God, I am so very afraid to make a mistake . . .

"Cait? You're starting to worry me . . ."

My unfailing love is with you, beloved, even as you put your hope in Me.

Logan slacked a hip. "I'll tell you what—I'll come a little early tonight, and you can tell me then, all right?" He turned to go, and her voice finally scraped past the lump in her throat.

"Stop . . ." It was a frail whisper, strained by a fear she suddenly realized had kept her in chains far too long. And one Logan obviously had not heard. The staccato clip of his shoes faded in the marble hallway, the crisp sound fainter and fainter as he neared the front door. With a panicked clear of her throat, she ran to the door and bellowed a hoarse command that actually hurt her lungs, pulse throbbing over what she was about to do. "I said, 'stop'—*please!*"

He turned, hand on the knob, silence filling the foyer with nothing but the hammer of her heart. They stared at each across the length of the marble hall, his thick brows dipped low. "Look, Cait, if you've got something to say—"

"I will only accept this ring on certain conditions, Logan Mc-Clare, and certain conditions only, is that understood?"

He blinked, gaze thinning as he dropped his hand from the door. "Pardon me?"

Pulse racing, she moved forward with chin high, peace slowly melting away the very fear that had kept her from what she now knew was God's will for her life. God's will—not Logan and Jean, but Logan and her, a path once obscured by so much fear, she hadn't seen it till now. For the first time since Liam's death, *this* felt right—she and Logan together, at the helm of a family they both dearly loved, trusting God while trusting each other. Tears stung. *Oh Lord, how can I ever thank You for the freedom You give?* Tempering the grin that tugged at her lips, she casually raised her hand to assess the ring he'd placed on her finger, almost giddy over what she intended to do. "I love it, of course, Logan, but I'm afraid it's been sized for the wrong hand, so that'll have to be fixed."

He stared, eyes in a squint. "All . . . right, Cait," he said slowly, the barest shade of annoyance in his tone. "For which finger would you like it sized?"

"If you'll follow me, please." She marched into the parlour, battling the squirm of a smile at the look of utter confusion on Logan's face.

He followed her in, his tone suddenly more curious than annoyed. "What exactly is going on here?" he asked, arms folded while he slanted against the opening of the burlwood doors.

"A little patience, if you will, Mr. McClare, and you may just think it's worth your while." She moved to the mantel where Andrew had placed the diamond ring she'd returned to him last night after she'd broken their engagement. He'd been stunned, of course, demanding to know why, but all she said was she didn't feel they were suited for each other. Refusing to accept her decision, he'd insisted she keep the ring, obviously hoping she'd change her mind.

Not likely. A shiver scurried within as she picked it up, striding to where Logan stood, brows in a scrunch. Tugging at the fold of his arms, she placed the diamond in his palm. "Here, hold this," she said, issuing little grunts while she attempted to remove Logan's heirloom ring from her right hand.

He stared at Andrew's ring like it was one of those nasty slugs that always invaded her garden.

"Oh, fiddle!" she said when the heirloom ring wouldn't budge, and whirling around, she moved to the drawer where she kept the lotion. Dabbing a little on her finger, she worked it beneath Logan's ring, finally twisting it off before hurrying back to plop it into his palm. She awarded him a bright smile, biting back a giggle at the befuddled look on his face.

"And what exactly am I supposed to do here?" he asked, nose in a pinch.

"Really, Logan, it's not that difficult." She wiggled her empty ring finger of her left hand, using the same patient tone she might use with Maddie. "Simply size your signet ring according to the measure of Andrew's ring, all right?"

He slacked a hip. "Andrew's ring," he said, his tone more of a statement than a question.

She smiled as if he had the wherewithal of one of those awful slugs. "Of course."

His eyes shuttered closed for a moment before they opened again to sear her with a piercing gaze. "All right, Cait, I'll play along." He bobbled both rings in his hand. "Won't you need Andrew's ring for the wedding on Saturday?"

"Oh, heavens, no," she said with a shiver, her tone teasing, but the shudder more than real. "I'm afraid you'll have to get me a gold band instead." She stood on tiptoe to look closely at the rings in his palm, then picked his up to study it against her finger. "I think this'll look fine with a wedding band that's simple and thin, don't you?" She peered up with an innocent smile, totally unprepared for the hard grip of his arms.

His breathing accelerated considerably, and his voice was almost a growl. "Don't toy with me, Cait—what the devil are you talking about? Why was Andrew's ring on the mantel?"

Her eyes softened, diminishing the playfulness of her manner. "Because I gave it back to him last night," she said quietly.

The blood leeched from his cheeks. "And why exactly would you do that?" His words came out hoarse, and as vulnerable as the pale look in his face.

Cradling a hand to his jaw, she allowed the full measure of her love to swim in her eyes. "Because he lied to me, Logan," she whispered, "and I don't know if you're aware or not, but I can't abide a man who lies."

Seldom had she seen such moisture in Logan McClare's eyes, but she saw it now, shining brightly as his Adam's apple jogged twice in his throat. "And what exactly does that mean for me, Cait?" he rasped, grip tightening and voice as ragged as her pulse. "Speak it out plain—are you getting married or not?"

"Oh, I'm getting married all right." He was still as stone as she lifted on tiptoe to brush her mouth against his, her lips an invitation she'd waited years to extend. "Just not to Andrew."

One deafening heartbeat thudded before either of them even breathed, and then his mouth took hers with a passion so fierce, it coaxed a frail moan from her throat. Like a man parched from thirst, he drew deeply from the well of her love, the taste of him shimmering her skin with a heat that left her weak and warm.

"Oh, sweet God in heaven," he rasped, his husky laughter vibrating against her mouth before he skimmed the length of her jaw to nuzzle the tender flesh of her ear. "As God is my witness, Cait, I will cherish and love you all the days of my life."

She gasped when he hoisted her up and whirled around, his deep chuckles making her giggle until he silenced her with a kiss that left her dizzier than the spin. Like a child with a new toy, his mouth explored the wonder of their love, from lips to jaw, temple to lids with such excruciating tenderness that Caitlyn wanted to weep. Gratitude soared in her heart while tears pricked in her eyes. *Oh, Lord—the first tears of joy in such a very long time!* Wending his fingers into her hair, he held her face in his hands, leaving her breathless with a teasing sway of his mouth against hers. "You are a minx of the highest degree, Caitlyn McClare," he whispered, his breath warm against her skin, "toying with my affections like you just did with that ring."

An impish smile eased across her face. "Oh, I don't think so, Logan. Heaven knows you've toyed with mine more times than I can count."

A boyish grin lit his handsome face. "Really?"

She laughed, her eyes softening as she feathered her fingers through the hair at the nape of his neck. "I love you deeply, Logan," she whispered, "and truth be told—from the first moment we met—I've never stopped."

"Oh, Cait . . ." He crushed her in his arms, the rapturous race of their hearts beating in time till they slowed and melded into a rhythm steady and strong. "I am never going to let you go," he rasped, and she giggled when he swooped her up and settled her on the divan, taking his time with a barrage of kisses on every inch of her face and throat. With a final kiss to her nose, he settled back in his seat and took both of her hands in his. "Now. I want to know exactly how this happened, because this is an amazing answer to my prayers."

She smiled. "You don't have much time, my love, but I'll give you the gist now and tell you the rest later." She quickly relayed everything, from the shocking Municipal Crib ledger that bore Andrew's name, to Meg finding Devin in Andrew's office with another woman. "So I put Meg to bed, and then I broke the engagement," she said with a staunch lift of her chin, earning another passionate kiss from the man who was now nibbling her ear.

He jerked back, eyes dark with concern. "Wait—you didn't tell Turner about the ledger, did you?"

"Oh, heavens no!" She looked at him aghast, stomach clenching at the danger involved if anyone discovered the secrets they knew. "I simply told him I had a change of heart."

"And he didn't question that?"

Cait grunted in the grand fashion of Logan. "Of course he did, but he had no choice." She jutted her chin, her anger at Andrew flaring once again. "I was as kind as I could be under the circumstances, telling him as nicely as possible that I felt he'd rushed me into this relationship and I was not a woman to be rushed."

His grin resurfaced as he leaned in to nuzzle some more. "I could have told him that."

Her eyes languished closed while his mouth suckled the lobe of her ear. "Logan," she whispered, dazed by the warmth he provoked, "it's getting late, and I thought you had to go."

"I do," he said with a low groan, his reluctance evident from the smoky look in his eyes. He sighed and brushed several stray tresses from her face, pausing to gently caress her lips. "You are the love of my life, Caitlyn McClare, and all I can say is thank You, sweet God in heaven . . ." A grin slid across his face while his voice rose with a fervor. "And Abraham too."

She pulled back, brows in a scrunch. "What does Bram have to do with this?"

The look he gave her was so potent, a beautiful heat purled through her, making her dizzy. "Oh, you'd be surprised." His husky chuckle skimmed across her skin while he grazed her lips with his own. "But let's just say pretty much *everything*," he whispered, the warmth of his words melting into her mouth. "Just like you, Mrs. McClare, are to me."

34

*L*ogan couldn't stop smiling. "Good morning, Miss Peabody," he said with a grin, presenting her with a warm sweet roll from the bakery across the street. "Thank you for coming in early—I appreciate your help."

"Oh, my pleasure, Mr. McClare, and oh my, Danish? Thank you so much."

He gave her a wink before tossing his coat over the coatrack in the coffee room, along with his hat. He adjusted his sleeves and straightened his tie as he returned to the reception area. "Your favorite, I believe—peach, right?"

Her smile was almost as broad as his. "Oh, yes sir—thank you!"

"You've earned it, Miss Peabody, along with a hefty bonus that you'll find in your next check." He sailed past her desk and on down the empty hall, chuckling at the look of shock he'd seen on her face. By jove, the woman deserved it and more, coming in early, on Thanksgiving no less, to finish the paperwork for his partnership with Bram's father.

For the briefest of moments, he paused with his hand on the brass knob of his door, eyes slipping closed to relive for one glorious moment the sweet taste of Cait's lips. An almost holy reverence settled while his breath stilled in his chest, making him realize all over again that in a mere two days, his very best friend would become his very own wife and lover.

The grin returned, so wide he was certain his jaw would ache by the end of the day.

Thanksgiving Day, indeed!

By the time Miss Peabody delivered the final papers, he heard the buzz and hum of a busy office, laced with laughter and fun. Excitement was obviously high over the prospect of a rare three-day weekend. "Thank you, Miss Peabody," he said while he glanced over the papers. "Everything seems to be in order, so just escort Mr. and Mrs. Hughes in when they arrive." He paused. "Jamie and Blake are keeping Bram busy in his office with the door closed?"

Normally shy eyes held a glint of a twinkle. "Yes, sir, I believe Mr. MacKenna has challenged Mr. McClare and Mr. Hughes to a do-or-die game of darts—with the door closed, of course," she emphasized in a conspiratorial tone.

Logan flashed some teeth. "That's my boy."

Miss Peabody paused, head cocked as if to listen before consulting her watch. "In fact, I believe I hear Mr. and Mrs. Hughes right now."

She darted out the door, and Logan grinned again, spinning around to stare out the window. The thought of he and Cait presiding over her family together jolted him all over again.

One couple. One family. One flesh.

While a crooked mayor, political boss, and DA get their due without the McClare name ever being mentioned. Logan chuckled.

Except on the marriage license.

If possible, Logan's grin widened while deep laughter rolled off his tongue.

"Laughing over our devious plot, are you?"

Logan spun around. "Jeremiah, Martha!" He jumped up and

rounded his desk to offer Martha a hug and shake Jeremiah's hand before escorting them to the cordovan chairs. "I can't tell you how good it is to see you again. Once a year at Christmas is too far in between."

"Agreed," Jeremiah said with a glow in his face despite the vacant look in his nearly blind eyes. "But hopefully we can resolve that problem in the future, eh?"

Martha hooked Jeremiah's cane over the arm of the chair, the flush of her cheeks mirroring that of her husband's. "Oh, Logan, we've been as giddy as children since you called last week, and I can't thank you enough for telling us the truth."

Jeremiah issued a grunt. "Heaven knows that stubborn son of ours wasn't about to."

Martha offered Logan a dry smile. "Oh, and mercy me, wherever does he get it?"

Logan laughed, reminded of just how fond he was of Bram's parents. He glanced up at a knock on the door, smiling as Miss Peabody popped her head in. "Ready for Mr. Hughes, sir?"

"Ready as we'll ever be, Miss Peabody, thank you." She nodded and closed the door, giving Logan a few moments to go over his plan. "Jeremiah, I'll leave the explanations to you and Martha as to why you're here today, filling in a few minor details before excusing myself so you can talk to your son." His gaze sobered. "But let me say, just for the record, your son is—" Against his will, moisture burned in Logan's eyes, and he quickly cleared the gruffness from his throat. "—one of the finest human beings I have ever had the privilege to know, and a true example of strength and moral character in my own life as well. You should be very proud."

Martha nodded, her smile tremulous as she tugged a handkerchief from her reticule to dab at her eyes. "Oh, we are, Logan, more than we can say."

"And," he said with a wink, "if the angels are on our side, we should have a great deal more for which to be thankful by evening's end." Logan glanced up at a knock on the door. "Come in."

"Miss Peabody said you wanted to see me, sir?" Bram ducked his head in, blue eyes flaring in surprise when his parents turned around. "Mom? Pop? What are you doing here?"

"Come in, Bram, and take a seat," Logan said, nodding toward a third cordovan chair he'd placed there earlier.

Bram kissed his mother's cheek before gripping his father's shoulder in a firm hold, his smile more than curious. "So, to what do we owe the honor of Pop skipping out on work?"

Logan chuckled and shuffled Miss Peabody's documents into a neat pile. "Well, not exactly 'skipping out of work,' so to speak. More like finalizing business away from the docks."

A crease furrowed Bram's brow as he stared at Logan and then at his parents. "I don't understand, Pop—are you consulting Logan about your legal affairs?"

"Of course not, son, you're my counsel, you know that," Jeremiah said, "which is why Logan suggested you approve all documents before we sign."

"Sign?" Bram's gaze flicked back to Logan. "Sign what, sir?"

Logan nudged the papers toward Bram, leaning back with a fold of arms while Bram scanned the top page. The crease in his brow deepened. "You're partnering with my father?" He glanced at Jeremiah. "But why? And what about Darlington?"

The old man tsked, smile crooking while his enlarged blue eyes blinked behind glasses nearly a half inch thick. "Now, don't get in a huff about Henry, he's still part of the mix, just not the key investor anymore."

Bram dipped his head toward Logan. "You are, sir?" His gaze flicked to the first page of the contract, then back, confusion muddling the usually clear blue of his eyes. "Fifty-one percent? Majority shareholder?"

Logan gave a slight shrug of his shoulders, struggling to keep his grin in check. "I figure if you're going to invest in something, you may as well do it the right way."

"But, I don't understand—why?" Bram tossed the papers back on the desk and lowered into his chair. "No offense, sir, but you know almost nothing about the shipping business."

A chuckle broke through Logan's professional demeanor as he idly scratched the back of his neck. "No, but then I knew even less about city government when I was elected to the Board of Supervisors, but let's not spread that around." Propping elbows on the arms of his chair, he tented fingers to his chin, his manner suddenly sober. "The truth is, Bram, with the clean sweep the city is hoping to make in the Barbary Coast, the handwriting is on the wall for establishments I've invested in before. So . . . I decided to move my holdings to something far more reliable." He paused, his gaze piercing Bram's with deep affection and respect. "And far, far closer to home."

A muscle flickered in Bram's cheek. He nodded, gaze falling to the papers on the desk while a sheen of moisture reflected in his eyes. "Thank you, sir," he whispered.

"Which means, son," Jeremiah leaned forward, his voice low and fairly quivering with excitement, "you can take your life off the altar, Abraham Hughes—you're free to live as you choose." He paused, gripping his wife's hand when she slipped hers into his. "And more importantly, you're free to love whomever you choose."

———

Bram stared, unable to move or blink or breathe. His father's words circled slowly in his brain, as if trudging through quicksand, sinking in until he felt himself drowning in a sea of guilt.

Free. As if one could ever be free anchored to shame and regret. He swallowed hard, his gaze fixed to the papers on Logan's desk. "What about Amelia?" he asked quietly, unwilling to wound the young woman with whom he'd become good friends.

"Quite frankly, she was as relieved as we'd hoped you'd be," his father said, a thread of disappointment in his tone. "Her mother tells us she plans to return to Europe. Seems the young man she met over there is not the fraud her father led her to believe." He exhaled with a shake of his head. "Turns out Henry forged a letter supposedly from the boy so he could whisk Amelia home. So, once we explained *your* situation, Amelia was most gracious and understanding, wanting only the best for you."

He turned, mind in a fog over the sudden shift of plans. "My situation? What situation?"

His mother placed a gentle hand to his arm. "Why, the fact you've fallen in love with Meg, dear, and that she's in love with you."

Meg? His heart seized. *As if I deserve a miracle like her.* He forced a smile, squeezing his mother's hand. "Mother, I don't know where you've gotten a silly notion like that—"

"From Meg," Logan interrupted with a polite smile. "Or Cait heard it from Meg, rather, although we both know I heard it directly from you."

Bram bit back a frown, somewhat annoyed by the superior smirk on his superior's face. "That's all fine and good, sir, but you forget your niece is being courted by somebody else."

"Ah-ah-ah . . ." Logan wagged a finger. "Not anymore."

"Pardon me?" Bram tipped his head, his pulse taking a tumble.

Logan's smile twisted into a scowl. "I mean she gave Caldwell the boot when she discovered him last night in the arms of another woman."

Bram blinked, outrage playing tug-of-war with relief. Relief won—he grinned. "Good girl," he said with pride in his tone. "Wish I could boot the moron myself." His smile dissolved. "How is she, sir?"

"Miserable." Logan peered at him through narrow eyes, arms folded as if preparing for battle. "Heartbroken, depressed, thinks her life is over because she's lost the man she loves."

Logan's words stung, but not as much as Bram's fury at Caldwell for breaking Meg's heart. He bit back a few choice words. "So help me, I'd like to give that no-good—"

"I was talking about you, Bram," Logan said, his voice deadly calm. "And I'd like to know what you're going to do about it, because you have a choice here—you can marry my niece, or you can find a new job."

Bram's heart stopped. "Pardon me?"

"You heard me." Logan aimed a blunt finger. "Don't make me fire you, son, there's precious few men whose counsel I trust."

Throat tight with emotion, Bram gave him a quick nod, lips compressed in a tight smile to deflect the glaze of moisture in his eyes. "Thank you, sir, that means the world to me."

"And my niece means the world to me, Bram, as do you, so here's the plan. After you enjoy Thanksgiving dinner with your parents at the Darlingtons' tonight, you will duck out early and show up at Cait's for dessert at eight to close the deal—understood?"

Bram's heart and brain blinked before a slow smile eased across his lips that worked its way into a grin, euphoria traveling like adrenaline through his veins. "Yes, sir."

"Good." Logan rose and adjusted the sleeves of his jacket, piercing Bram with a firm look. "Then if you'll excuse me, I'll give you privacy while you disclose to your parents the true reason you were willing to marry Amelia Darlington despite being in love with my niece."

Bram stared, paralysis claiming his body.

"What's he talking about, son?" his father asked, brows beetled over blinking eyes.

Logan kneaded Bram's shoulder on his way to the door, his voice low with empathy. "It's time, son. I'll not have you bring burdensome regrets into a marriage with my niece."

Bram's eyes lumbered closed at the click of the door, remembering full well the exact moment he'd made the mistake of tipping his hand to Logan.

"You see, I owe my father a heavy debt, sir, one of which he's not even aware and one that I can certainly never repay."

His mother stroked his arm. "Bram . . . ?"

Moisture smarted beneath his eyelids, and he knew he had no choice. The moment he'd dreaded for over a third of his life had finally come. The moment when his parents would learn just what kind of son they had.

Angling to face them both, he hunched over the edge of his chair, head bowed as he knotted his hands. "I . . . have something I need to tell you. Something I've needed to confess for a long time now, but I was too afraid."

"Afraid?" his father bellowed. "What could you possibly fear from us, son, the two people who love you more than life itself?"

He squeezed his eyes shut, desperate to retain the hot tears that threatened to swell. "The . . . very loss of that love, I'm afraid," he whispered, his voice no more than a croak.

"Bram," his mother said softly, sweeping her hand the length of his bent back. "There is nothing you could say or do that could ever damage our love."

He shook his head, a heave jerking in his throat. "You don't know that, Mother. You haven't heard what I have to say."

Her hand stilled on his back. "Then tell us, son, so you can be free from this awful guilt."

392

Gaze fused to the floor, the maple hardwood swam before him in a watery blur of russet and golds while his voice sank to a drone, the painful words all but dragging across his parched tongue. "I was . . . responsible for . . . the robbery that night."

He waited for his mother's gasp, his father's growl, but neither came. The tick-tick-tick of Logan's clock might have been a death knell for all the raucous pounding that it made in a room as still as death.

"We know, son," his father said quietly.

Bram's gaze lashed up, shock expunging all air from his lungs. "You knew? All this time? B-but . . . how?"

"I found the crumpled paper," his mother whispered, the palm of her hand still warm against his back. "With the combination to Father's safe, the one hidden in the secret compartment of his drawer."

A low groan rose in his throat like bile, and slumping over in the chair, he put his head in his hands and wept, shoulders shuddering beneath his mother's tender touch.

"Bram," his father whispered, his gnarled hand stroking his head, "you were so young and angry, and those boys duped you. Let it go, son—it's in the past, over and done."

He slammed a fist to the arm of the chair. "No, it's not!" he shouted, his mind crazed. "I rebelled against you, Pop, and that very rebellion cost you your sight and your health. I stupidly gave them what they wanted, too drunk to even know what I'd done." Cheeks wet with grief, he gripped his father's hand, head bowed. "I never meant for that to happen, Pop, I swear."

"I know, son . . ." His father's gentle touch wracked more heaves from his chest. "But you were an angry boy still grieving the death of his sister, and I was an angry father who wrongly cast blame on that boy."

Face slick and swollen with tears, Bram stared, wild-eyed. "But I killed her!" he shouted. "And I almost killed you . . ." He clenched his fists, guilt smothering any flame of forgiveness his parents might hope to give. "How can you ever forgive that?" Staggered by shame, he sagged forward, his head in his hands while he wept, his painful lament the only sound in the room.

Until . . . another voice rose, halting and frail and yet so very strong. "How can I not, son, when my Father has forgiven me?" Bram felt his father's frail touch, and shock stilled his torment at the broken whisper of familiar words from a song he knew his father loved. "Amazing g-grace, how sweet the s-sound, that saved a wretch like m-me. I once was lost . . . but now am found, was blind, but now I see . . ."

Bram slowly raised his head, staring in awe at his father's upturned face. Streaked with tears, it was glowing with a holy sheen in vacant eyes whose vision was far greater than his son's. Falling to his knees before his father's chair, Bram clung to him in a crushing embrace. "Oh, Pop, forgive me, please—I never meant to hurt you."

"Ack, I forgave you long ago, son," his father whispered against his hair, "but I failed to ask you to forgive me."

Bram's head shot up, his voice a rasp of denial. "No! You need no forgiveness from me."

"Ah, but I do, my boy, because you see, I have a debt too." He cradled Bram's face with a withered hand, staring at him with a gloss of pain in his eyes. "It was my bitterness and rejection that pushed you away, Bram, at a time when you were drowning in grief and guilt, a burden I've borne as long as you have yours." Weathered lips curved in the faintest of smiles. "You were such a happy boy before your sister died, before my bitterness and blame turned you away." He strained his eyes as if he could see clearly, his fingers caressing every inch of Bram's face. "You know, I'd like to see that boy again, so I can love him and be there for him like I should've been then."

Bram clutched his father while joy coursed down both of their cheeks. "Oh, Pop—you don't need my forgiveness, but I'll gladly give it if it means we both can be free. God knows I love you more with every breath I take." He clung to the man for whom he would give his very life if he had to. Wonder welled in his eyes.

But he didn't have to.

Because of One who already did.

35

"That was the best Thanksgiving dinner I *ever* had." Logan gave Rosie a wink that quickly burnished her cheeks. "Cait—you need to give the woman a raise."

"Capital idea, Logan, as always," Caitlyn said with a broad smile, almost giddy over the bombshell they were about to drop on the children. She bit back a grin at the swag of Rosie's jaw, a wide gape that matched the whites of her eyes. "And Hadley too, of course," she continued, her own cheeks growing warm when Logan sent her a half-lidded grin that tumbled her stomach. She upended her water goblet to douse the fire inside, pretty certain it would be out of control in two days' time, once the vows were exchanged.

"I'll drink to that." Blake raised a toast. "Rosie is one of the finest cooks in the city." He grinned and filched an uneaten olive from Alli's plate, shooting a glance at the closed kitchen door after their housekeeper left. "And I'll even go out on a limb here and say Hadley's one of the finest to put up with her."

Laughter ensued before Alli slid him a wide-eyed smile, complete with a flutter of lashes. "Out on a limb?" she repeated with an impish grin, tapping on his head several times. "Oh, so *that's* what happened—you fell hard out of a tree onto your pointed and pretty little head?"

"A number of times, I think it's safe to say," Jamie said with a chuckle.

Blake flashed a dazzling smile, his confidence unscathed by his "fall from the tree" or from his family's grace. "Yep, and I've been falling hard ever since, for every beautiful woman I see."

Cassie grinned and rolled her eyes, aiming a pea at Blake's head.

"And for your information, Pretty Boy," Blake continued, tossing Jamie a smirk along with the nickname Cassie'd given him when they'd met. "The woman just called *me* 'pretty.'"

A dry chuckle rolled from Alli's lips. "Oh, you bet—pretty annoying, pretty pathetic . . ." She squinted, armed with another pea.

"What's 'pu-thet-ick' mean?" Maddie asked, following suit with a tiny handful of corn.

"Blake," everyone shouted in unison, causing Logan to grin at Cait.

"Madeline Marie McClare!" Cait said when corn flew over the table like confetti. "We do not throw food at the table!"

"Alli did," she said with an innocent scrunch of brows.

Nick tucked an arm to Alli's waist, reeling her in for a kiss to her cheek. "That's because your big sister is younger than you, squirt, and more of a brat."

Alli elbowed him in the side. "Ryan Nicholas Burke!"

Ping, ping, ping! Caitlyn quickly rose to tap her goblet with her spoon, capturing everyone's attention with a radiant smile. "Before there is more Thanksgiving dinner on our clothes than in our stomachs, I'd like to make an announcement." A lone vestige of silence and calm, Hadley removed Cait's dirty dishes to his tray. "Thank you, Hadley," she said, offering her dear butler an appreciative look. "And if you don't mind, I'd like you to fetch Rosie for a family announcement I need to make."

Hadley bowed. "No bother at all, miss, I'll be happy to feed the cake."

She clasped his arm before he could escape, pitching her volume. "We'll wait on dessert just yet, Hadley, but I do need you and Rosie for a family announcement."

"Very good, miss." With a short nod, he disappeared into the kitchen, and she shook her head and smiled, the noisy chatter of her children escalating all over again as Logan caught her eye. *I love you*, he mouthed, and her heart did a flip.

With a breezy swoosh of the kitchen door, Rosie and Hadley reappeared, and Caitlyn clinked her spoon once more. "Before Rosie and Hadley serve dessert, I thought this would be a good time to . . ." The moisture in her mouth suddenly evaporated. "Uh, well, tell you something very important."

"Is it about Andrew, Mama?" Maddie asked with an innocence that plucked at Cait's heart. "You know, being too sick for turkey?" Worry buckled her tiny little brows. "He doesn't have a tummy ache, does he?"

Caitlyn blinked. "Well . . . no, darling, not a tummy ache exactly, although it's true he might be sick to his stomach, I suppose . . ." She chewed on her lip, avoiding what she suspected might be a telltale smirk on Logan's face.

"Goodness, Mother, he *will* be well by the wedding, won't he?" Alli asked.

"Let's hope not," Jamie muttered under his breath, earning a swat from Cassie.

"Uh . . . well . . . about the wedding . . ." Throat parched, Caitlyn all but lunged for her water glass, alarmed to find it empty. Relief seeped from her lips when Meg quietly nudged her half-empty glass her way, the solemn look on her daughter's face soft with understanding. "Thank you, darling," Caitlyn whispered, gaze flicking to Logan before she inhaled Meg's water.

"Is Devin sick too?" Maddie wanted to know, now comfortably settled upon Blake's lap.

"Sweet thunderation, I hope so." Cassie's dry murmur brought a twitch of a smile to Meg's face, easing Caitlyn's nerves considerably.

Energized by the fact that Meg's heartbreak wasn't due to Devin, Caitlyn drew in a deep breath, further strengthened by the tender affection she saw in Logan's eyes. "As I was saying, about the wedding—there's been a slight change."

"Oh please—tell me you're not getting married, I hope?" Alli shrieked, her blatant joy prompting Nick to slide an arm over her shoulders, obviously reining her in.

"No, no . . . I'm still getting married . . ."

Cassie leaned in with elbows on the table. "So the wedding's still on, then, same time, same place, and the honeymoon too?"

Cait's cheeks burned at the mere mention of the honeymoon with Logan all of ten feet away, his low chuckle doing nothing for her composure. "Yes, of course the wedding is still on and I suppose the honeymoon too, although I'm not sure we'll be going abroad."

"Napa is lovely this time of year, Cait," Logan volunteered, his smile that of a little boy aching to misbehave. "The tail end of the fall colors, you know, and crisp nights just perfect for snuggling. You're certainly welcome to use my estate if you like."

"So, it's the honeymoon that's changed, not the wedding?" Blake asked.

Caitlyn absently picked at her nails. "No, no, I'm afraid there's a rather large change with the wedding too."

Alli's green eyes thinned to a blade of grass. "Just spit it out, Mother, what exactly has changed?"

"I think I can answer that." Logan rounded the table, his smile growing with every confident stride. Hands braced on the back of Cait's chair, he scanned the table, feigning that lovable scowl that always brought a smile to Cait's face. "I'm afraid Andrew won't be able to make it."

"What do you mean Andrew won't be able to make it?" Blake said with a frown. "Last time I checked, you need a groom to have a wedding."

"Excellent point," Logan said with his usual grace and aplomb, "so I have a proposal to make . . ." Reaching into his pocket with a wink, he produced an exquisite diamond ring. "Literally."

A collective gasp echoed in the room, and none louder than Cait's, as Logan dropped to one knee. "Caitlyn Stewart McClare," he whispered, "from the moment I laid eyes on you, you have been the desire of my heart and the love of my life. So with a heart of profound gratitude to the God who brought you into this family, I'm asking . . ." A shaky smile tilted his lips that almost made him look like a shy little boy. "And, admittedly, with more humility than I have ever possessed in my life . . ." A lump bobbed in his throat as a sweet sheen of love shimmered in gray eyes that shone like silver. "Will you marry me?"

No one moved or breathed, the silence as deafening as the pulse pounding in Cait's ears.

"Oh, for pity's sake, Mother, just say yes," Alli said with a groan. "At the very least, you won't have to change the initials on the towels!"

Nervous laughter tittered through the room before another hush settled, more taut than the last, every breath suspended when Caitlyn began to cry. And then with a sob that merged with joyful laughter, she flung herself into his arms, weeping unashamedly against his chest. "Oh, yes, Logan, yes—a thousand times yes!"

Wild whoops, shrieks, and laughter thundered the walls as everyone surged to their feet, surrounding Cait and Logan with laughter and love, weeping and wonder, over a true miracle in their midst. Caitlyn could do nothing but sob. *Oh, Lord, forgive me—I've been so blinded by fear.* Greatly humbled by the thought, she hugged her daughters, all of them with tears in their eyes except Maddie, who giggled and bounced in her arms.

"Merciful Providence, Mother—it's about time!" Alli said, cheeks flushed with both tears and excitement. "Everybody but you could see Uncle Logan is perfect for you, and I honestly couldn't understand why you were so blind."

Caitlyn chanced a peek Logan's way, cheeks flaming when he gave her a wink over Jamie's shoulder in the midst of a hug. "Yes, darling, well, fear is the greatest blinder of all, it seems."

"Is Uncle Logan going to be my new daddy?" Maddie shouted, and Logan's laughter all but boomed through the house.

"You bet, sweetheart!" He tugged Maddie from Cait's arms, promptly administering a snuggle-monster kiss which unleashed squeals that could have shattered the crystal chandelier. "Just call me Uncle Daddy."

Cait blinked, then chewed on her lip. "Logan, really, I don't think that's appropr—"

A sharp whistle silenced the room. "Hey, what's all the commotion?"

Caitlyn's heart leapt at the sight of their second Thanksgiving miracle, if her prayers held any sway. *Bram!* Her gaze darted to Meg, breath hitching when the blood immediately drained from her daughter's face. The poor darling had only seen Bram a handful of times over the last three months, and always later in the evening for pool tournaments with Blake and Jamie, never at dinner and *never* alone. Cait uttered a silent prayer, hoping the rest of the evening would go as planned. But all concern melted at the touch of Logan's palm engulfing hers, the tender brush of his lips to her cheek a heady reminder—*again*—that she needed to trust God, not fear.

Bram circled the table to pump Logan's hand with a wide flash of teeth, a twinkle in his blue eyes that Cait hadn't seen in a long, long while. "From one altar to the other, eh, sir? Congratulations to both of you, Mrs. McClare—I can't think of anything for which to be more grateful on this glorious Thanksgiving Day."

"Really?" Logan draped a leisurely arm over Bram's broad shoulders, his loaded chuckle braising Bram's cheeks with a ruddy color that matched the cranberry stains on Maddie's chin. "Need some help, Bram? Because I can."

"Hey, what are you doing here anyway, Padre?" Jamie quipped, slipping arms around Cassie's waist. "I thought you were having Thanksgiving at the Darlingtons'."

Bram grinned, his gaze searching out Meg to give her a wink. "I did, but I heard something about Bug's warm peach cobbler and Rosie's chocolate cake, so I couldn't resist."

———

Heat swarmed Meg's cheeks, Bram's fondness for her peach cobbler a well-known fact she'd exploited on more than one occasion. Dropping her gaze, she reached for her water, dismayed to discover Mother had already depleted it. She sighed. *Oh well, at least there's something he can't resist about me . . .*

"Sit here, Bram," Logan said, hands braced to Mother's shoulders. "You take Cait's chair, and I'll scout out another from the kitchen so she can sit next to me." Flashing a victorious grin, he took her hand to lead her to his seat at the end of the table. "I aim to keep her close until the vows are said. No sense in taking any chances."

"All right, everyone—name your poison," Rosie shouted as

she and Hadley pushed through the swinging doors with trays laden with pumpkin pie, peach cobbler, and chocolate cake. Meg couldn't help but smile when the crotchety housekeeper dared to give Logan a wink. "You first, Mr. Beware."

Uncle Logan grinned. "A piece of each, Mrs. O'Brien, if you don't mind."

"Don't mind a'tall," the crusty housekeeper said with more civility than Meg had ever seen with Logan before. She plopped a piece of each on his plate without ceremony, the edge of her lip tilting up. "As long as you make Miss Cait happy, that is." Dark eyes narrowed to spear him with a warning. "If not, you can name your poison anytime, sir, and I'll happily supply it."

"Rosie, really!" Mother said with a blush that matched the housekeeper's name.

Uncle Logan grinned while Rosie finished serving, nudging Mother's shoulder with his own. "I think she's warming up to me."

"It's good to see you again, Meg," Bram whispered, leaning so close, his breath feathered her ear. "You have no idea how much I've missed you."

She gulped before giving him a skittish smile, the clean smell of soap and the haunting scent of Bay Rum making her dizzy. *Good heavens, talk about warming up!*

"Sho, Brem, where's Melia?" Blake mumbled, peach cobbler rolling around in his mouth.

Gagging on her first bite of dessert, Meg slammed a napkin to her lips, more to hide the blaze of her cheeks than to cover her choking.

"Good heavens, Blake, we do not talk with our mouth full." Her mother was aghast, which mirrored Megan's feelings to a T. "One would think you were raised in a barn."

Jamie leaned close with a sniff. "I think that's a given."

Blake swallowed. "Sorry, Mother, just wondering why Padre didn't bring his fiancée."

Fiancée. A second piece of cobbler stuck in Meg's throat. The fact Bram had already given Amelia a ring didn't stunt her shock one whit. No napkin could prevent her coughing fit now, nor the fire in her cheeks that burned brighter than the tapers.

"Meg, dear, are you all right?" Her mother stared at her with concern along with everyone else, but she simply continued to hack, gulping the glass of water that Bram offered.

Which didn't help.

Meg shot to her feet, napkin to mouth. With a furious shake of her head, she flailed an arm at the door, signaling her wish to be excused for a moment.

For a moment? Her coughing now akin to the croup, she dashed from the room. *Try forever,* she silently moaned, locking herself in with the commode. One look at her red-rimmed eyes in the mirror, and her coughs heaved into sobs. She dabbed her napkin to her cheeks, blubbering like Maddie when she didn't want to go to bed. "Oh, Lord, it's bad enough Devin betrayed me," she whispered, wadding pieces of toilet paper to desniffle her nose, "but do you have to taunt me with Bram too?"

"Meg? Are you all right?" Bram's voice, as always, was deep with concern.

No, I'm not. She blew her nose. "Yes, just a coughing spell that's now under control."

Pause.

"And the crying spell—is that under control too?" His words held a tenderness that pooled more tears in her eyes.

"Go away, Bram," she said, her voice a weak moan as she leaned limp against the door. "You're not responsible for coddling me anymore."

"Sure I am, Bug . . . as much as I can through two inches of lumber."

She blew her nose again, louder this time, and could almost feel his smile through the door. He cleared his throat. "Can I come in?"

Memories flooded—hiding in closets when someone had injured her heart, weeping curled in a ball on her bed, locking herself in a bathroom to sob on the commode. Each and every time, Bram had found her, comforted her, held her until every tear had dried. Palm and profile pressed to the door, she closed her eyes, wishing more than anything she could hide in his arms like she did as a child. "I c-can't rely on y-you forever, Bram—I need t-to do this alone."

"No you don't, Bug—open the door." It was a gentle command, the kind he'd always given when he'd dusted her off and told her she could do whatever she thought she couldn't. A deep and silent authority that—then and now—always won her respect. Heaving a weary sigh, she put her hand to the knob.

"What's wrong?" he whispered when she opened the door. Taking her hand, he led her into the parlour. "Aren't you happy about your mother and Logan?"

"More than anything," she said quietly, perching on the edge of the sofa while he sat beside her. "It's just that—"

"You miss Devin . . . ," he said calmly, yet she detected a trace of hurt in his tone.

"No, not Devin." Her eyes trailed into a somber stare. "More the feeling of being loved and desired, I guess . . . scared that it may never happen for me."

"Meg." There was a wealth of tender emotion in the very utterance of her name, but she knew she had no right to it anymore, not with his ring on Amelia's hand.

"No, Bram," she said, shifting away to distance herself. "I'm a grown woman now, not a little sister you can pat on the head and soothe in your arms."

He reached for her hand. "Trust me, Bug—nobody knows that more than me." His thumb grazed her palm in lazy circles that quickened her pulse.

She shot to her feet. "Stop! You can't fix my heart anymore." Her cry constricted into a sob as she attempted to leave.

"Oh, I think I can," he whispered. Staying her with a gentle hold, he rose and gathered her close with a shuttered look that spiraled heat in her belly. "Because I love you, Meg, and I desire you too . . ." His words paralyzed her, but when those blue eyes sheathed closed and his mouth gently took hers, a shocked moan slipped from her lips. Fire surged at the press of his hands to the small of her back, possessive hands that drew her close when he deepened his kiss. "Meg," he said, a desperate ache in the very whisper of her name, "I love you—and want you—more than I ever dreamed possible." With an urgency that defied the calm and steady man that she loved, he skimmed her jaw with lips hungry to partake of a passion too long denied, coaxing another moan when his mouth found the soft flesh of her ear. "Marry me," he breathed, his chest heaving against hers, "and I will cherish and protect you forever."

She pushed him away with a harsh gasp of air. "But . . . but . . . Amelia!"

"Is in love with an Italian duke," he said firmly, his breathing as ragged as hers.

"But . . . but . . . your father . . . ?"

He chuckled, the love in his eyes weakening her knees. "Is far wiser than his son . . . and far more forgiving, thank God."

"So, y-you're . . . f-free?" she stuttered, her oxygen level painfully low. "To do whatever you want? With whomever you want . . . *whenever* you want?"

A boyish grin eased across his face. "Well, not exactly, Miss McClare." He shot a quick glance at the clock on the mantel. "You see, I'm told I'll be unemployed if a ring doesn't appear on your finger by the stroke of midnight."

She couldn't help it—she grinned. "Oh, glory be and God bless Uncle Logan!"

His eyelids lowered to half mast when his gaze flicked to her lips. "He already has," he whispered, swaying forward as if he were going to kiss her again. "Now it's my turn . . ."

Stifling a giggle, she held him at bay with two palms to his chest. "Excuse me, Mr. Hughes, but I believe there was mention of a ring?"

"Oh, right . . ." He jolted straight up while he fished a tiny box from his jacket, sporting a silly grin. Bending on one knee, he opened it to dazzle her with a diamond so bright, it surely glittered like the tears in her eyes. "Will you marry me, Meg?"

With a tiny squeal, she plucked the ring from the box and literally launched into his arms, bowling him over. "Oh, yes!"

Chuckling, he lumbered to his feet and then tugged her along. "Excuse me, Bug, but did you just knock me down?"

He took the ring from her hand and slid it on her finger, and she giggled, heart near to bursting. "Absolutely not, Mr. Hughes," she said with a sassy smirk, "you just fell head over heels in love." Giddy with joy, she held her hand up to admire the sparkle of her brand-new diamond ring. "You *do* realize this is going to alter our friendship, don't you?"

The smoky look in his eyes was back when he reeled her into his arms. "Count on it, Meg," he breathed in her ear, turning her limbs to jelly when his lips trailed off to explore.

"Hey, you two—you don't want your cobbler getting cold, do you?" Jamie's voice carried into the parlour.

"Cold?" The tease in Bram's eyes literally smoldered. "Better the cobbler," he said before his mouth descended for more.

"Wait!" Meg pulled back with a start, mischief brewing in her normally shy smile. "Does this mean I don't have to let you win at chess anymore? That I can just beat you outright?"

Bram's chuckle was husky and low, brimming with the quiet confidence the man always seemed to possess. "Or try."

"Mmm . . . I may have to lay some money on that."

"Awk, put your money where your mouth is, put your money where your mouth is." Eyes flashing, Miss B. two-stepped the bar right on cue.

Bram's grin grew as he leaned in to comply, melting her laughter with the warm breath of his kiss. "I've said it before and I'll say it again." His mouth nuzzled hers, tasting of peaches and cinnamon and the promise of love just as sweet. "That is one smart bird."

Acknowledgments

To my agent Natasha Kern and my editor Lonnie Hull Dupont—treasured gifts from a very wise God who knew exactly what I needed.

To the truly talented team at Revell—I am privileged to work with each and every one of you. Extra hugs to Michele Misiak for her kindness and patience, to Cheryl Van Andel and Brandon Hill for their remarkable talent and creativity, and to Barb Barnes, whose name *always* makes me smile when it pops up in email, and to her remarkably able assistant, Julie Davis. You guys ROCK!

To the Seekers—twelve of the finest women I have ever met—I am beyond blessed to claim you as dear friends, confidants, prayer partners, and therapists on call.

To Bonnie Roof—not only the top winner of my newsletter contest to have a character named after her in this book, but a dear, dear reader friend who has become so very much more. You are a true sister in Christ, an encourager extraordinaire, and a relentless prayer partner. I treasure your friendship more than I can say.

To Megan Joy Burdzy, Abbi Hart, Brittany McEuen, Sarah Baker, Beata Andrianova, Ann Miller, Linda Marie Finn, Wanda Barefoot, and Jennifer Fuchikami—all winners in both my newsletter and video contests to have a character named after them in this book. You are some of the kindest and dearest reader friends I've ever had the privilege to meet, and I thank God our paths have crossed.

To three ladies who cover me in prayer and without whom I'd be absolutely lost—my precious prayer partners, Joy Bollinger, Karen Chancellor, and Pat Stiehr—love you guys!

To my sisters, Dee Dee, Mary, Rosie, Susie, Ellie, and Katie, and to my sisters-in-law, Diana, Mary, and Lisa—thank you for your love, support, and prayers.

To my daughter Amy and my son-in-law Nate, my son Matt and daughter-in-law Katie, and to two of the most precious blessings in my life, Rory and Micah—I love you ALL to pieces.

To Keith Lessman—talk about "surprised by love"! God blew me away when He blessed me with you, babe, and you took over from there—blowing me away with a love that grows sweeter every day. I may be the romance writer, Keith Lessman, but *you* taught me what true romance really is.

And finally to the God of the universe—I am in total awe of who You are and the depth of Your love for me and each of us You call Your own. I pray the words that I write bring You both glory and praise all the days of my life.

Award-winning author of The Daughters of Boston and Winds of Change series, **Julie Lessman** was American Christian Fiction Writers 2009 Debut Author of the Year and voted #1 Romance Author of the year in *Family Fiction* magazine's 2012 and 2011 Readers Choice Awards. She has also garnered seventeen RWA and other awards and made *Booklist*'s 2010 Top 10 Inspirational Fiction. Her book *A Light in the Window* is an International Digital Awards winner, a 2013 Readers' Crown Award winner, and a 2013 Book Buyers Best Award winner. You can contact Julie and read excerpts from her books at www.julielessman.com.

Stay in Touch with

Julie Lessman

Visit **www.JulieLessman.com**

to learn more about Julie, sign up for her
newsletter, and read reviews and interviews.

Connect with her on

 Julie Lessman

 julielessman

Join your favorite romantic storyteller

as she moves to the hills of San Francisco for
more romance, passion, and surprising revelations.

"This is the most fun I've had reading a Julie Lessman book.
The McClare clan is wonderful and I loved all of them.
I can't wait to see what Julie does next!"
—**Mary Connealy,** author of
Over the Edge, In Too Deep, and *Out of Control*

"Guaranteed to satisfy the most romantic of hearts."

—TAMERA ALEXANDER, bestselling author

Full of passion, romance, rivalry, and betrayal,
The Daughters of Boston series will captivate you
from the first page.

> ## "Julie Lessman's passionate prose grabs your heart and doesn't let go!"
> —Laura Frantz, author of *Love's Reckoning*

Filled with intense passion and longing, deception and revelation, the Winds of Change series will leave you wanting to read all of them.